D0209219

THE ICE LOVERS

THE ICE LOVERS

Jean McNeil

McArthur & Company
Toronto

First published in Canada in 2009 by
McArthur & Company
322 King Street West, Suite 402
Toronto, Ontario
M5V 1J2
www.mcarthur-co.com

Copyright © 2009 Jean McNeil

All rights reserved.

The use of any part of this publication reproduced, transmitted in any form or by any means, electronic, mechanical, photocopying, recording or otherwise stored in a retrieval system, without the expressed written consent of the publisher, is an infringement of the copyright law.

Library and Archives Canada Cataloguing in Publication

McNeil, Jean, 1968-
The ice lovers / Jean McNeil.

ISBN 978-1-55278-802-8

I. Title.

PS8575.N433I24 2009 C813'.54 C2009

The Author gratefully acknowledges the support of the Arts Council of England in the writing of this book.

The publisher would like to acknowledge the financial support of the Government of Canada through the Book Publishing Industry Development Program (BPIDP) and the Canada Council for our publishing activities. The publisher further wishes to acknowledge the financial support of the Ontario Arts Council and the OMDC for our publishing program.

Design and composition by Tania Craan
Jacket photographs: landscape © Cliff Leight/Getty Images; glacier image © Veer; author image © Diego Ferrari
Text images: photo © Jean McNeil; map © British Antarctic Survey

Printed and bound in Canada by Webcom

10 9 8 7 6 5 4 3 2 1

Preserving our environment
McArthur & Company chose Legacy TB Natural 100% post-consumer recycled paper for the pages of this book printed by Webcom Inc.

FSC
© Mixed Sources
Product group from well-managed forests, controlled sources and recycled wood or fiber
www.fsc.org Cert no. SW-COC-002358
© 1996 Forest Stewardship Council
96%

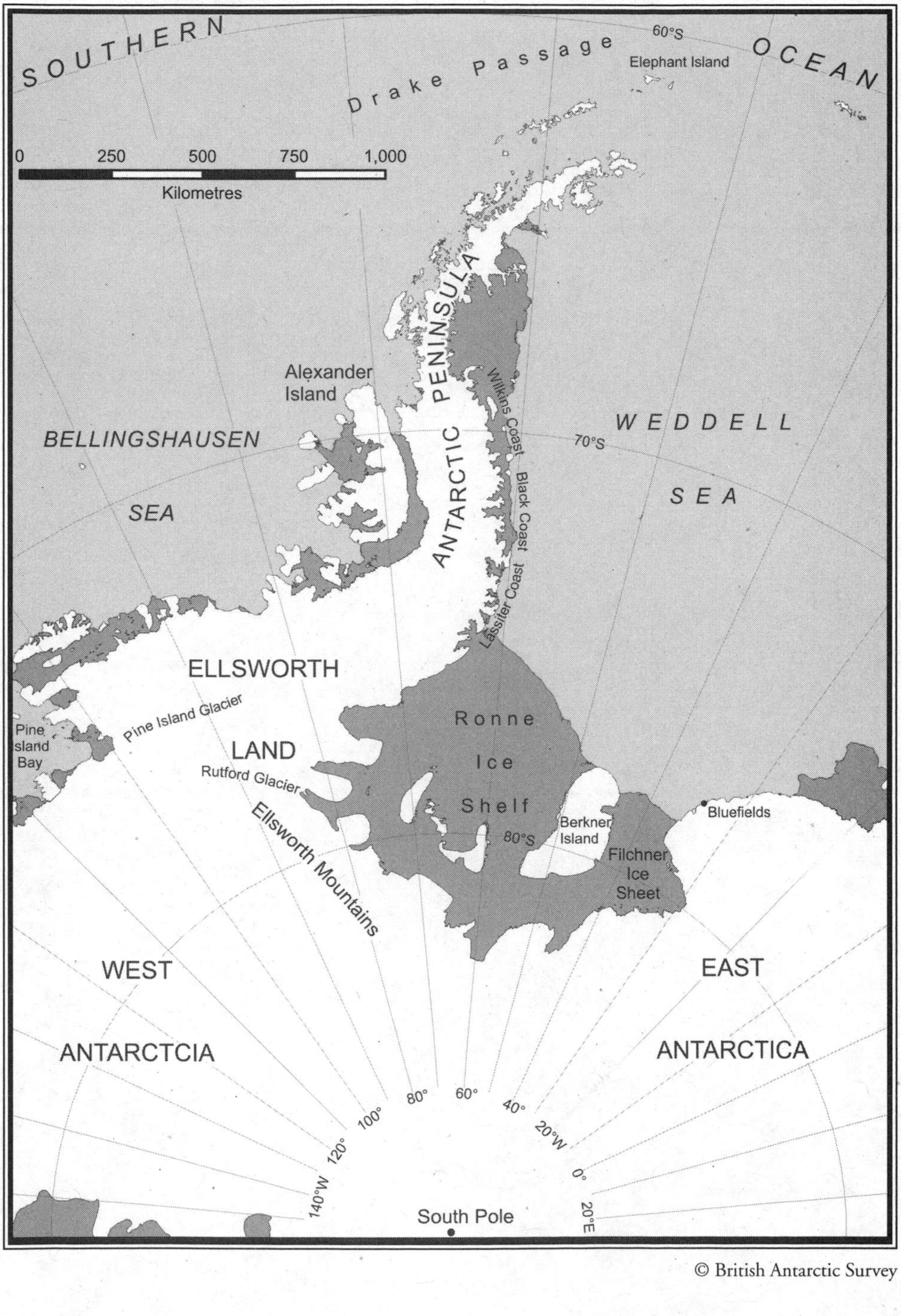

© British Antarctic Survey

Acknowledgements

The research for this novel was facilitated by a residency in the Antarctic, supported by the British Antarctic Survey (BAS) and the Arts Council of England's (ACE) International Fellowships programme. During the three and a half months I spent in the Antarctic in the austral summer of 2005–6 the fellowship allowed me access to BAS' Antarctic scientific programme, its personnel, ships, planes and remote field camps.

I remain deeply grateful to both BAS and the ACE for this unusual and life-changing experience, and for their programme, which has given many writers and artists access to a continent usually off-limits to all but scientists and officials. In particular I would like to thank David Walton and John Shears at BAS, John Hampson and Charles Beckett at the Arts Council of England's National and London offices respectively, and Natasha Messenger and Tim Eastop, formerly of the International Fellowships programme at the ACE. Thanks are also due to the Arts Council of England's Grants to Individuals fund for a follow-up grant to support the writing of this book.

I would also like to thank the Royal Literary Fund and Newnham College, Cambridge University, for their support. My fellowship at the University of Cambridge allowed me time and peace of mind during the final stages of working on *The Ice Lovers*. The Scott Polar Research Institute and the British Library were very helpful with research, as were the many scientists and Antarctic workers who shared their knowledge and experience of life South. Special thanks are due to Layla Curtis and Diego Ferrari for friendship during the research and writing of this book, to Kim McArthur for her unflagging support and to Maggie McKernan for her good counsel.

A note on place-names: Thanks to the Mapping and Geographic Information Centre at the British Antarctic Survey, who kindly produced the map of Antarctica in the front matter of this book. Those who know the Antarctic well, on reading this novel, may suspect me of spatial confusion with regard to some place-names. While set in the Antarctic, this book is a piece of imaginative literature. The novel refers to actual geographical place-names in the Antarctic (some of which are shown on the map), but also makes reference to places which either do not exist or are extant, but correspond to different geographical features than the ones indicated in the novel. Names for all ships and scientific bases, certain official bodies (such as The Polar Research Council) are fictional, as are all the characters in this novel.

The extracts that appear in this novel are credited as follows:

From *South: The* Endurance *Expedition* by Ernest Shackleton, originally published by William Heinemann, 1919, reprinted by Penguin Books (UK), © 2002. 'The Winter Night' by Fridtjof Nansen, reprinted in *The Arctic* by Elizabeth Kolbert (ed), published by Granta books, © 2007.

Bluefields

The ice shelf looms in the windscreen. Behind him, sea-smoke is rolling in. He loves its ermine swirl, even if it impedes his visibility. He fixes his approach. It is one of those albino days, the light bleached into a pigmentless colour; not white nor silver, but some new hue projected by the giant skeletal thrust of the ice sheet.

Underneath the plane the ice in the Weddell Sea is finally breaking up; from the air it looks like muslin – the thin, lacy frazil ice, ice flowers sprouting on the perimeter of meltwater.

It is an absolutely dingle day in December 2016. This is his favourite moment in the Antarctic calendar, early in the brief summer, watching the ice loosen its grip on the continent.

The sun is out so the contrast is good, he can see the sastrugi and the fractures drawn on the surface by crevasses. He will get it down on the deck without a bump. He has been doing this for twelve seasons now. As a pilot, he subsists on a volatile diet of experience and luck; these days it's the latter that preoccupies him, he goes over and over the chances he has taken and which so nearly went wrong: flying through too-narrow cols, brushing nunataks so that a geologist returning from the field can get some good photos of the strata. Once or twice in a season he has these 'moments' as he calls them; dips into air pockets, can't get the power he needs to climb, the stern grey face of the mountains loom in the windscreen and seem out to teach him a lesson. He likes to take risks, of course, he would be bored otherwise. He is counting on luck. But he has been doing this for so long now and he has a theory about luck: it runs out. Eventually.

His co-pilot is a nervy field assistant (what is his name? They are all called Andy or Mark; he's not particularly good at names, and keeps these two in reserve as guesses). Nervy Andy/Mark relaxes his shoulders. Little does he suspect how much worse it could have been, no vis, poor contrast, him deciding to land anyway on nerves, on instinct. Only inches above the deck thinking, *now*, *now*, *now* – he can feel it coming, sometimes, the land, he can feel it reaching up to grasp him.

He and the field assistant will spend two or three days flying aviation fuel from the ship further inland, replenishing stocks for the coming summer field season. The ship has just been in to relieve Midas IV, the new ice sheet station nearly five hundred miles to the east. He will fly there too, eventually, drop off the field assistant and take a shower, his first in a week. He will sit on the platform station, which hums all night with the vibration of the generator, watching the sun hover above the icefield. This time of year it never sets, only skirts the horizon, tantalizing it with the possibility of night.

First he has to blank down the aircraft. He clambers up onto the wings, releases the guy wires, and climbs down. It is just like tying a tent to the ground – he kicks the ice screws in, ties off the tension cord. The plane secured, he surveys the landscape: a white plain, unfiltered blue sky occupying equal vectors of his vision, the horizon smudged with seasmoke to the north, and feels a slight constriction in his heart. The emptiness fails to captivate him as it once did. Now he sees it as vortical and scrawny; immense, yes, awesome in its simplicity, but it does not grip and impassion him with that strange vacant frenzy, as it did in the beginning.

The diminishing of his enchantment had begun just before he met Nara, and he wondered now if this was not an accident; it had something to do with her, as if he had been waiting for someone to pass on the baton to. He never told her, but when they went to Berkner nearly four years ago, he had stood on the ice sheet with her and for the first time had seen the Antarctic for what it was, despite the tungsten light, the tangerine sunsets: a cold place.

Four years ago on their way to Berkner, he and Nara had taken off from this very white plain, blue-less and field-less, although the precise piece of ice they had used as a runway had long been dissolved into the sea. These days, parts of the Ronne Ice Shelf were only lightly soldered to the continent.

They had stood here together, four years before, unaware of what awaited them within hours, scouring the snowfields – fields of such deep, pulsating blankness they passed through an invisible colour barrier to become indigo, turquoise.

Since that day he had avoided coming here, he even avoided the name. Like so many places in the Antarctic, Bluefields was not even a place, just a fuel depot that moved with the shifting ice, marked by a line of bamboo flags. That the Antarctic had few place-names was one consequence of having the thinnest of histories. There were the Dead Men places: Charcot, Latady, Ross, d'Urville; the names derived from explorer mishap: Hope Bay, Cape Disappointment, Deception Island, and (his favourite) Exasperation Inlet; then the made-up names: Site 8, Base K, RABID camp – the kind of names they'd used when he was in the military, itinerant designations made to be folded into boxes when they'd outlived their purpose.

What had they talked about, that day? He could remember Nara telling him about the German artist whose name he could not remember. The artist had been a pilot in the Second World War. He'd been shot down in winter and saved by local people, who had transported him to the nearest village. What had saved him was their dual remedy against burns and cold: he'd been covered in lard and felt. For the rest of his life, Nara had told him, the artist had been obsessed by these two substances. Once he had covered himself in them and locked himself in a room full of wolves.

Together they had stared into the horizon, absorbed its barking, infinite light. The convection heat rays of the sun beat down with such intensity the snowfield wavered, as in a desert – which is precisely what this place is: the highest, coldest, driest desert on earth. In tandem they had dragged their hypnotised gaze away from the white plain, blinking into each other's eyes. Nara's were blue, he remembered – an uncommon dark blue, indigo or navy. Her black hair cut short, a small woman with a certain way of moving, something in her gait reminded him of a man. She was steely, she had absorbed many spiked tasks. Not unfeminine, but a dark horse. It was the Antarctic summer of 2012. In their minds they still called each other friend.

Now he will have to think of all this again, he will have to remember. Because back on base the ship is due in, with its cargo of new recruits for the Antarctic summer. This year the ship is carrying a journalist – or was it an historian? He can't remember the base commander's exact term, because what the base commander said next overtook his mind completely. The journalist was writing about the sea-ice incident. *She'll want to talk to you, I suppose,* the base commander said.

The plane blanked down, he and the field assistant walk toward the edge of the shelf, Mark/Andy probing for crevasses all the way. The ship sits fifty feet below them moored under the sheer cliffs, the crew on the lookout for ice falls. They will crane up the Wor Geordie, as the basket for moving people on and off is called, and he and the field assistant will clamber in. The plane will spend the night on the ice shelf above them, tied down so that the katabatic winds do not flip it over.

On the ship he will be too hot, too comfortable. He would

rather be bunked down in the back of the Otter – how he usually sleeps when he's out in deep field. He will be exhausted, but sleep will refuse to congeal inside him. Now that summer has arrived and there is twenty-four-hour daylight, he has trouble sleeping. That night he will lie awake in his bunk listening to the groaning of the ship as the swells nudge it against the ice shelf. He will think, is it possible to extinguish memories? That's the right word. They are fire. They are burning all the time.

On the ship he sits down on his cabin bunk, and drops his head into his hands. He is so tired, but also very, very awake. Lately he has been struggling with a feeling he calls 'unrealness' – even in waking life, it's as if he is in a dream of his own making, but cannot remember what the dream is supposed to be about, he cannot remember what he is supposed to do next. These days are like sea-smoke, he waits for them to be dissolved under the full albedo of the summer sun.

He hears the dank metal grind of the ship as it scrapes against the ice. No, this is definitely not a dream. It is just the beginning of another Antarctic season, ferrying fuel drums back and forth.

Somewhere around three in the morning, the floodlit daylight of midsummer streaming through his cabin window, he falls asleep.

PART I

The Crystal River

1

Before I came to the Antarctic I met a woman who told me the future is like a crystal river. She said that in all our futures some things are already decided. These events can be seen in advance, because they have already formed in the same way that crystals congeal, binding themselves to each other molecularly. It was these shapes the cards were reading; around them, the river kept flowing in narrow currents, eddies, outflows. This was the river of life. Here, some things were up for grabs, they had not yet been decided. Here, things could go either way.

That the future could be read at all astonished me. If you could read the future, then it meant someone or something wanted it, was willing it, to be so. I asked her what this something was and she said she didn't know. You must have some idea, I said, after all you make your living looking into this realm. She said she was not sure, and in any case she did not think there was an answer, or that the answer would be comprehensible to any of us, were we to know it.

I went to see her on an early winter afternoon: pale, worn skies. Windblown scraps of humanity in parkas, scarves, blown through the dank spidery avenues of Holland Park. Arriving on the doorstep of a smart terraced house, I nearly turned around and left, and perhaps it would have been better if I had.

The woman was elfin, almost necessarily androgynous. Her toenails were huge and ingrown (she did readings with her shoes off, so she could feel more connected to the earth). Her flat was crammed with amulets and statues. Isis, for example, stood sentinel by the window. Chunks of quartz and crystals studded every surface. There was one anomaly in this gypsy fairground picture – the woman's diction was that particular upper-class timbre, like a handful of diamonds falling on a glass table.

'But don't you wonder?' I asked her. 'Don't you want to understand?'

She gave me a blank look in return. I said that I believed everything was understandable. I said I believed in the human mind, but I did not believe in a will outside of human minds.

'Why come here, then,' she asked, 'if you don't believe?'

'Because I feel as if I'm dying.'

'And you want me to show you that isn't true.'

'I'm sick of the uncertainty. I just want to know what will happen.' I could have said, *and to hell with it.*

She showed me, then, what would happen. Or, as she put it, what *was wanting to happen*. I said, who wants this to happen? Who is this wanter? Someone else, it seemed, had designs for my existence.

That was when she told me that some things are written down already, and in the same way that the shapes in the crystal river have already cohered, these lines of text had also been decided upon.

'I am not a child,' I said. 'I will not have my future dictated to me by some outside force.'

'Your future is inside you. It has already happened. You know it, on some level, you know exactly what will happen, and you are only dreaming it into existence, and the cards are reading the dreams.'

'You mean I wanted my husband to die? That's why it happened.'

'Not consciously.'

The woman said *I see lots of travel*, and she showed me the card with two ravens. One looked straight at me with a single gleaming coal eye, the other had its head turned away, toward an unseen horizon. She told me that these two birds belonged to Odin; their names are Huginn, which means Thought, and Muninn, or Memory. Every day Thought and Memory fly around the world and report to Odin all they have seen. I thought, even the albatross, with its epic flights, cannot manage that. 'Nothing that is of any value is untouched by the eyes of these two birds,' she said. Together they had been to the Antarctic many times.

Perhaps, if the future had already happened it explained the dreams I had of the Antarctic before I ever went there, and which turned out to be true, in their own way – dreams of being stranded in a colony on a recently discovered continent, of red planes circling in a white sky, of not being able to leave.

Every time I tried to imagine being there, I could picture only a white plain, the gnaw of perpetual daylight. I could not see my feet on the surface of the snow, under which lay two kilometres of compressed ice crystals. I could not see my hands in that air. We have only a few ways of conceiving the world: personal knowledge, species knowledge, memory, imagination, and dreams. I could perhaps add books, reading. But none of these helped me imagine myself in that place.

Later, in the Antarctic, with winter closing in, I would only be able to remember a few of these cards: Odin and his two birds, a man and a woman in a clearing, surrounded by a forest embroidered by spring. And behind me, somewhere in the relatively recent past, Ragnarok – the end of the world.

And the final three cards the woman laid down. One was a wolf howling at the moon; in another a wolf wandered through an iron forest. The first wolf card meant that I would want something emotionally which I could not have. The second card meant fear. Last of all, she put down a card which showed a dark sky. In it, the moon was absorbed by a cloud.

'The nightmare card,' she said. 'I wonder what it is hiding.'

'What do you mean?'

'It's refusing to tell you something. Why you have to go there, perhaps. Or you have to go there to find out.'

I looked again at the cards on the table. My mind slipped off them, it seemed to need to reject the stark symbols they showed. I did not want to acknowledge that a nightmare awaited me. I had made a naïve calculation about how much shock and distress one would be handed at once, or how many episodes in succession, how much hatred and betrayal. I didn't know it then, but I had been living with a false sense of protection. I had assumed that from this juncture in my life I would flow through the crystal river, as if there were a quota of harm and corrosion dealt to us all, and I had exhausted mine.

Here, there is no sovereignty. In the Antarctic, everyone has to unite against the cold. We live in nobody's country.

Winter does not arrive, it congeals. The sea ice does the same; one day the sea is that blue-black of the Antarctic, the next day it is white.

The cryospheric cycle is one of lags, of flux and melt. It is about the way ice builds and binds. Over 10,000 years ago, at the beginning of the last ice age, the northern hemisphere summers cooled for an unknown reason, and the cool summers meant the ice did not melt. By the winter the ice was well established and it grew, advancing by inches each year, a many-fingered, cold hand reaching out from the poles, from the moutains, to the sea, to the plains of the grain-growing countries.

We we are living in an ice age, still. To a glaciologist an ice age means literally a period of glaciation and we are still in one because the ice sheets of Antarctica and Greenland still exist. Our current interglacial is called the Holocene; the present ice age began over 40 million years ago, with the growth of the Antarctic ice sheet. Since then, ice sheets have been advancing and retreating in 40,000- to 100,000-year cycles. The most recent intense glacial period ended about 10,000 years ago, just as Asiatic man was making his migration over the Bering Strait to populate the Americas. Predicted changes in the earth's orbital forcing, based on past records, show that the next ice age will begin in 50,000 years' time, regardless – possibly – of man-made global warming.

Or will this happen? Alexander's models of the ice sheets of the future were refusing to make ice. He and Nara sat together on base on those winter nights and he showed her how, when he input the data for current conditions and temperature rises, the ice sheets of the future would not form.

For years, the stories I wrote were all about endings. First, they were about war and destruction, the lives that had been abruptly and prematurely ended by history. Then, when I started to write about science, I discovered a new crop of endgames: glaciers which had accelerated far beyond their predicted velocity, local species extinctions, red algae blooms, the water poisoned by it, plankton and krill asphyxiated. *The species which will die out are those which are unable to adapt in time.* I wrote lines like that, passing sentence on entire categories of creatures, the end of certain species of temperate latitude fruits, a type of whale. The end, even, of winter.

People rapidly become accustomed to stories of ending, I found, until it is really the only story they will consent to hear. We need these narratives of termination in order to confirm our worst suspicions about ourselves, the fleetingness of our lives, the power of destruction we have, the harm we are capable of wreaking on all and anyone who strays too near.

This story of endings is the great story of our day – our present disintegration, our eventual extinction. The play has already been scripted, despite our rising mercury of emergency, and we are figures already exiting stage right, moving ghost-like, nudged by heat. I cast myself as the witness, valuable and futile at once, charged with documenting this slow Armageddon. How long these final days will last, was hard to say.

Then I discovered a different, although related, story. The sparseness and silence surrounding it intrigued me. Nara was part of a vast puzzle of researchers sent to discover clues to the future. She became convinced that the planet had a will, that it was adjusting its settings. This was the cause of her distress that winter, her uncertainty. But distress was fuelled by many things, not least that she heard voices in her head that she could not decipher.

I know very little about her; only a skeletal listing of impersonal facts. Born in London, educated there until her father, a university lecturer, took a position in Canada at a provincial though respected university. They lived there for six years before returning to the UK. She did a year as an undergraduate at an oceanographic institute in Canada, finishing her undergraduate degree at University College London, then a postgraduate degree at the University of East Anglia, in Environmental Science. She stayed there to do a postdoc. There were rumours on base that she'd had an affair with a married professor while there, and that this had ended unhappily. It was one of the reasons she came to the Antarctic, although she never said so directly.

Her parents refused to speak to me, either by telephone, email, or personal interview. I pressed my case, but only managed to press them into silence. So I would have to guess, or, to use a more intellectual term, to imagine. There is archival research of course, and photographs. But photographs are static tableaux, a false promise lurking within their fabric: that they will tell you something essential, definitive about the person depicted. But they are ciphers, ghosts in the machine. To know someone you must see them moving.

As for the man who is here with me, he is a surprise, and very much alive. I see all of them in him, their brokenhearted destiny – the dead men of this continent in their felt coats, woollen mittens, their pathetic provisions which stripped them of their strapping musculature as they hauled their sledges across its chrome surface. His great-grandfather was one of them. He has their physique – tall, well-proportioned, his intelligent brown eyes. A firm jaw, built for teeth gritted against the daily cyclone of the ice desert. The discerning, convince-me gaze he fixes me with, always, as if he is trying to decide whether I am friend or foe and changes his mind. *Now friend, now foe.*

We cannot avoid each other, even if we might want to. I find I can only feel desire when it is intertwined with sadness, or loss, or some dark valour that has nothing to do with any individual man. He is no hungry ghost, he is alive; sordid, beautiful, vague. Married. Not someone who inspires neutral feelings. Hostility or desire, yes; hatred, hostility and desire, a fiery helix of confusion. He is like the wood you find in stairwells of Oxford or Cambridge colleges. His very existence confirms that there is a submerged level in all of us, down several flights of stairs, through tunnels, dank labyrinths. There, nameless animals are alive and ravenous with anticipation of their next meal. These are our true selves, our vacuous battered souls. If I sit still I can feel them sometimes – a gnawing, a scavenger's footstep in my innards. Their fluttering little hearts, their sharp, insolent teeth.

2

After the meeting David walks – no, he stalks, he has been accused of this before, a long, swinging, laird-of-the-manor stride – the corridors. The Foreign and Commonwealth Office, despite its gleaming new exterior, is inside a relic. He swishes past the history, portraits of queens, kings, prime ministers, the corridor leading to the Middle East region, to southeast Asia, these sumptuous, well-funded sections with their terror analysts, their breakfast briefings with MI6.

This is where he had yearned to work, these hot regions of the world. For so long the polar regions office had been no more than an internal outpost. Although now of course they were very nearly the centre of a conflict, and he was suddenly deserving of his seigneurial stride: 'Polar Guy Comes in from the Cold,' his colleagues joked.

His release from professional exile had been so sudden his old habits still needed to be shaken off – long lunches, perusals of scientific journals close to his heart, conferences and symposia on glaciology, physics, marine biology. Science was a passion he could no longer indulge. Yes, now he was Arctic and Antarctic Man and they took him seriously, because the polar regions had caught up with the rest of the world. Polar Man was vaulted from the musty basement, where he had been hunkering with his reindeer skins, canvas jackets, his stories of icy sorrow and defeat, into the cauldron of politics.

Men like David had been running the country, if not the world, forever. He was not a dreamer. He remained uncaptivated by ideals. He thought in terms of manoeuvres and outcomes, like a military tactician.

Or rather this was the man he had tried to be, and failed. Because he was a dreamer; he was moved by ideas. He had never, not once, sat around a meeting table and not thought about some woman he had once kissed a long time ago, what his wife was doing at that precise moment, or dwelled on the challenges of manhauling across a glacier field, with its tumble of ice boulders. He had never been consistent, or certain, or acquisitive. He could no longer stand what and who he was, or loved and respected what and who he was. He could bear himself, but not what he did for a living. He accommodated these opposites within himself effortlessly, allowed them to rotate on a dais; perhaps he had inexhaustible incarnations up his sleeve. Who would he be tomorrow? Only someone he had not been today.

'Yes,' Edward his boss had said, as they were ranged around that long mahogany table. 'There's a journalist. No, an historian.' He looked down his nose at his notes. 'She's interested in that incident. I don't know why. She won't discover much, in any case. I'd like you to include chaperoning her in your annual visit, if that's all right by you.'

If that's all right by you. This was not all right by him, but what could he do? 'What do you think she knows?'

'Not much. She's talked to colleagues. The parents won't talk, of course.'

'Did she tell you that?'

'No, we got that from Cambridge.'

He will take coffee in his office next, he decides, while reading confidential briefings on Russian territorial expansion, on methane release from a thawing Siberia, on the mass extinction of krill blighting the Southern Ocean. Well, he thought, on the way there: three weeks there, another week travelling. Although he had never gone to the Antarctic and returned on his intended date. You simply couldn't schedule things as you could in the rest of the world, or any other situation.

A month away. That night, he would tell Kate.

David, alone of his immediate colleagues, takes public transport to and from work; he lives in the Thames Gateway, an area of regeneration, buoyed into existence by the Olympic Games. But the city ran out of money, for everything – gleaming antiseptic stadia, accommodation, transport infrastructure. At times his journey home frightens him. It is against his principles, but he is thinking, finally, of buying a car. The Olympic debacle had impoverished the capital, and he alone of his Chelsea-and-Fulham colleagues has to deal with the human rubble. He takes the Jubilee Line to Stratford, followed by an overground tram on which homeless men sit slumped, shuttling from one end of the line to the other, home to his gleaming showroom apartment overlooking an empty Thames. High up in his glassy water palace he thinks, how amazing, that eels once migrated here, that fishing boats once plied the wide estuary.

He receives a message from Kate. She will be out tonight, she is informing him, at one of her classes – Pilates, French, Yoga. He texts back, ok. Just the two letters. *A man of few texts*, as Kate says.

While waiting for the lift he thinks of the years he has spent attending conferences: Cold Facts of the Arctic, meetings of the Antarctic Place-Names Committee, of which he is chair, the Polar Symposia at the British library, meetings at the Geographical Society in Kensington. In the summer he goes to the Arctic, in the winter to the Antarctic. He rarely sees darkness; only London is dark, caught in a perpetual night, whereas the two axes of the earth shine in an inevitable white daylight. The Antarctic is his favourite of the two polar regions, although he feels guilty, on an intellectual level, for comparing them. It has something to do with the raw monumentalism of it, and its absurdity, which transmits itself so effortlessly to life there: in the Antarctic he becomes a child, the Fool, the spontaneous clandestine he really is.

But also he admires how Britain has managed to hold onto its claim to this remote part of the world, the opposite end of the Atlantic ocean. He loves the insanity of it, how on the way there he flies twelve thousand miles only to end up in Britain, or at least the version of Britain which is the Falkland Islands, or British Antarctic Territory, patrolled by Union Jacks and a faded Edwardian patriotism. He loves how everything is upside down: the seasons, the constellations. His release in this, his strange clattering euphoria.

He had wanted to be a scientist, and somehow that hadn't happened. Now he is surrounded by them and he is only the administration man, influential as he is, signing and dotting treaties, conference papers, government memorandums, laws, jurisdictions, while the scientists are searching for the key to the mystery.

Of the mystery itself, he is certain. The Antarctic is no accident – an iced continent does not form by fluke; no, it's meant to be there, this remnant of Gondwanaland, the ice cap at the bottom of the planet which drags its energy field down, so heavy that from space the earth appears not as a sphere, but more like a pear. If the Antarctic did not exist, the earth could not support life: the climate would be too irregular, the ocean circulation system would brew up a volatile, unfathomable world. He has met many, many people who thought: what's the point of the Antarctic? An empty ice wasteland, we can't even go there because the whole place has been ringfenced by sanctimonious scientists. What's the point of such a place? *Little do you know*, he thought. And, *maybe that's for the best*.

Of late, the world has become a place he is no longer certain he wants to live in. His glassy estuary palace, renewing his ID card, getting Iris scans for his new passport: he spends so much time complying with the surveillance superstructure yet feels a powerful urge to evade its gaze. But it is not so easy. Oyster cards have been twinned with identity cards, so that movements through the London transport system can be tracked on a live database. Purchases recorded on supermarket loyalty cards have been uploaded to the national database. Each email, the sparse text messages he sends, these too are logged. He is caught in a vast digital web. But who or what is the spider? He fantasises about ditching his Oyster/ID card hybrid and buying single tickets; it will cost him a fortune but at least he will be able to avoid 'them'. When he confides this thought to his brother, Ben gives him a steady look. 'But you're one of "them".'

Not in the Antarctic. No, there he was no one. No satellites are trained upon that empty slice of space (and if they were, he would be one of the very few people to know about them). He is alive in an age of monitoring, surveillance, profile-building, tracking; a wargames era with little hand-to-hand combat, only surgical strikes, tactical collateral damage. What would his great-grandfather have made of it? The man who, after narrowly failing to die on Elephant Island, had enlisted within two weeks of his return to England, then narrowly failed to die on the killing fields of northern Europe. In comparison David considers, he is living in a shadowy, cowardly time. One thing he is truly afraid of – disease, an epidemic, possibly one of the first real effects of the warming – stalks the land once more, for the second time in four years, a highly communicable strain of virus, as do strange environmental puzzles: Elm trees are losing their leaves from a mystery fungus, triggered by warming, the total collapse of honeybee populations causing a collapse in pollination, causing agricultural output to plummet 16 per cent from where it was in 2010. Storms scrape at Britain, more violent each year.

All this his brother had foreseen; Ben had told David and he hadn't believed him. At the time, Ben was an anomaly, a futurologist. Uncertain times sent people to soothsayers, although David had never expected to find himself living in such an era. And it was not individuals, but banks, governments, the corporate world, who went to visit Ben and his crystal ball. *Just another economist who can tell the future*, Ben had joked, at the beginning of his career. And then he found he could.

He turns the key to his front door. His flat is exquisite, he admires it himself, each time he enters. Ships glide up and down the Thames. In the distance, the cupolas of the Barrier. A soft estuary light.

Kate has left not even a coffee cup, not even the imprint of lipsticked lips, on the counter. She has washed and dried up so thoroughly that drops of water have been banished from the sink. On the sofa a book lies open, seemingly casually, but this is the copy of *Don Quixote* Kate has been trying to read for some months now. She is a woman who sets herself tasks, a self-improver.

He takes a quick look in the bedroom. What does he expect to find? Kate in bed with another man? Kate's belongings disappeared from her drawers, the clothes from the railing?

He makes himself a cup of tea, and the phrase comes to him unbidden – an old Antarctic saying, left over from the Edwardian explorers. It meant ordinary, everyday heroism, it meant the genteel comforts of English life transported to that blasted place. He misses the old days, when he went along in the Otters just for a ride, an extra pair of arms, an extra shovel. In the old days they would all pile in to go dig out a

Low Power Magnetometer, a sensitive temperature probe, near the Pole, shovelling down through four feet of snow. Then they'd climb into the Otter and fly back to base, all laughing – pilot, field assistants and useless officials like himself along for a jolly – saying, *home for tea and medals.*

3

Good ice year, bad ice year – this is what Antarctic veterans call them. A good ice year is when the ice forms to the thickness of three or four feet. A good ice year only comes one year in ten, now.

The sea-ice incident happened in a bad ice year, also the plague year, the summer thousands died from the virus. Because of the larger catastrophe, the incident was barely mentioned in the press. Helen caught only a glimpse of it buried on page seven or eight, classified as Home News, even though it had taken place twelve thousand miles away. At the time she hardly took notice of it, cloaked as she was in her own season of grief. Still, she had enough interest to clip it from the newspaper and save it in her haphazard scrapbook (scrapyard, she privately called it), increasingly a graveyard for never-to-be-written stories, articles, and books that would remain only phantoms.

Nearly three years later, she fished the yellowed piece of newsprint out of the scrapyard and did a bit of research on the internet. She found almost no mention of the sea-ice incident, only the story she had seen, archived on the newspaper website, and a Polar Research Council press release.

Her discovery of the article coincided with a larger shift: it was time, she decided, to get serious, to take her life of writing features journalism and her abandoned PhD in history and solder the two together. It was time to write a book, to see these places, meaning the polar regions; she would write about them just as she had written about child soldiers in the Lord's Army, about tribal politics in Afghanistan, or HIV infection rates in South Africa. She would find the untold story and she would write it.

Helen knew little about sea ice, or the continent itself. She learned that for a long time, before anyone had known for sure it existed, the indigenous peoples of Tierra del Fuego had called Antarctica 'the place where the wind is born'. The winds of the Antarctic were unlike anywhere else on earth, the katabatic winds driven neither by the earth's rotation nor by the Coriolis effect. These were the winds that made the frozen karst of the Antarctic plateau, fractured by fissures and sudden sinks called crevasses. These were the winds that, along with the ocean currents, made sea ice fractured and unstable, ramming it together with the violence of tectonic plates, piling mountain ridges of ice where they collide.

She never imagined that she would spend years thinking about the properties of ice, both physical and emotional; that she would see the light move along the 80th parallel, that low, sullen steely light. Hawk sky, black water. All this began as an idea, which was itself an escape, she understood – a detour, a distraction from a life which had become excessively real. For Helen, the Antarctic started as a single crystal which then grew, adding mass and complexity to itself, until it became a gigantic ice palace which would stalk her dreams for the rest of her life.

The crystal river woman had told Helen that the planet's life was changing. It was like a quickening, she said. 'Everything will happen faster and faster.' Helen listened, unusually patient with this kind of drivel – what, she thought, was *everything*?

'It's like the planet has a heart, and a mind, and they have just started to work faster. We will know who we are, soon,' the crystal river woman said, her voice unconcerned, bright with educated vowels, not at all baleful or spooky. 'We will finally understand.' The revelation would be about the reason why people were here at all, about the planet itself, although she couldn't say what, or when 'soon' was.

Helen was unimpressed by lazy apocalyptic pronouncements. This was one of the reasons she stopped going to see the crystal river woman – deciding she was over Eric, over death, over shock, over everything. From now on, she would bury herself in her research. She would give herself over to the facts, to the ice.

The Polar Research Council library has remained the same since the 1870s. In good Victorian style the bathrooms are always cold, the chairs straightbacked. Helen has joined the tribe of too-skinny men and young women with frizzed hair pursuing obscure PhDs who frequent it. They scribble their doctorate titles in the signing-in book: *cryospheric-meteorite interactions in the paleozoic shadows of the last glacial maximum*.

The ice scholars arrive, say hello to the librarians, put their belongings in metal lockers, turn the key, and keep the little number in their pocket. The lockers are not to stop belongings from being stolen, but to guard against people thieving books. There are many treasures in the library, thousands of volumes of explorer diaries, originals, photographs, the first cartographically correct maps of the Arctic and the Antarctic.

From time to time Helen takes breaks and goes to stand in front of a full-sized model of an explorer (Nansen, in this case, in Greenland) downstairs, inspects his moleskin trousers, reindeer jacket – its fur patches frayed, the white fur sallow, tattered deerskin mittens and disintegrating caribou sinews. Nansen was a poet as well as a man of the ice, Helen learns, he kept his sense of wonder fresh throughout his polar career. She reads *The Winter Night*, Nansen's account of a winter spent voluntarily iced in, his ship drifting with the Arctic pack ice:

> *Nothing more wonderfully beautiful can exist than the Arctic night. It is dreamland, painted in the imagination's most delicate tints; it is colour etherealised. One shade melts into the other, so that you cannot tell where one ends and the other begins, and yet they are all there. No forms – it is all faint, dreamy colour music … the sky is like an enormous cupola, blue at the zenith, shading down into green, and then into lilac and violet at the edges. Presently the aurora borealis shakes over the vault of heaven its veil of littering silver. Presently it shimmers in tongues of flame over the very zenith, and then again it shoots a bright ray right up from the horizon, until the whole melts away in the moonlight, and it is as though one heard the sigh of a departing spirit. And all the time this utter stillness.*

Before she took an interest in Nara's story, polar explorers seemed to Helen only rash self-abusers, dancing a dangerous pas de deux with death. But now she is transfixed by the mystery of why so many of these explorers were such superlative writers. In the library Helen reads everything she can about oceanography, marine biology in high latitudes, atmospheric science, meteorology, geophysics, glaciology and glacial chemistry.

Nara was a marine biologist, but she had trained as an oceanographer first. So Helen sets herself to read about the great ocean currents, the Antarctic Circumpolar current, an orbital highway of fast-flowing water, encircling the continent. She reads about Antarctic cyclones, how these can persist for days or even weeks – a week-long blizzard, the wind never abating from hurricane force. She reads about the properties of water: salinity, fronts and mixing, ice volume, temperature, alkalinity, carbonate cycle, CCD and Lysocline.

Everything, it turns out, even water, is much more complex than you would think.

Only slowly did Helen come to understand that in order to write her story – *if* there was any story to write – she needed to go there. Access to the Antarctic had become even more restricted since the Treaty had been violated, first by Russia, then by the United States, and tensions between Argentina and Britain were running at an all-time high since the Falklands War 35 years ago and it took her many months to get permission to travel there. In fact, in all her career, she'd never had to jump through as many hoops in pursuit of a story: permission was required from the Foreign Office, the National Science Council, the Antarctic Research Fund, the Polar Research Council, the Falkland Islands Government, and finally, the Royal Navy, via the Ministry of Defence. It took weeks of emails, telephone calls, even an old-fashioned letter or two to confirm her character, professional particulars. *I am an historian* – this is how she began her beseeching letters; historian sounded less slippery than journalist, she judged, and less of a threat. What has happened in the past is never as controversial as what is happening in the now.

Then national security clearance, criminal records checks, and a renewal of her passport so that it would be valid for two years from her date of departure. No one would give her a straight answer as to why, apart from saying that her passport had to be valid when she returned. 'But I'm only going for six weeks, not six years,' she'd said, when faced with the Foreign Office official (one of David's underlings – later she would realise, what if it had been him? What if they had met that way?).

In late November of that year Helen turned up at Heathrow and joined a group organised by the Polar Council.

They would fly to the Antarctic via Madrid, Santiago de Chile, and finally the Falklands, where they would join the supply ship. An old friend, a Spanish colleague, came to see her off. At the gate they said their goodbyes. Then, at the last moment, he turned to her and said, *el amor siempre es bueno entre seres humanos*. Much later that night, as she flew over the Brazilian Amazon, his phrase would reverberate in her mind: Love between people is always a good thing.

PART II

Land of Ice and Fire

1

In the austral summer of 2011 a Twin Otter flew through the lonely Antarctic skies. The plane's shadow flickered across the ice sheet below, projected by the white sun. The plane flew over muscles of ice driven by a vital current. The ice sheet undulated with these ice streams, high-velocity frozen rivers forced by friction melt from the ice cap into the sea.

Cloud Types for Observers, the cloud atlas Nara had brought along, lay open on her lap. On the way down she tried out the names: *lenticular, nimbostratus, altostratus, stratocumulus; nacreous, virga, corona*. On the intercom the pilot said, 'You see clouds down here like nowhere else on earth. Those are my favourite,' he pointed out the cockpit window, in the direction of a spaceship. Nara had seen one or two of these clouds over the mountains on base; they hovered, static, their edges whipped by wind into saucer-like rims. 'Lenticulars. You only ever see them near mountains. We try to avoid them, they have rotor systems that cause terrible turbulence.'

She stole a look at him then, from her position in the co-pilot's seat: a pleasant face, not handsome. A man in his fifties perhaps, his hair still dark. He must feel so capable, she thought. He can fly a machine across the world, he can fly it anywhere into this empty continent, armed only with a GPS coordinate. Now they were heading to such a place, only a collection of numbers on a still-unmapped part of the continent near Mount Vinson and Mount Gardner in the Ellsworth range, an area even now seen by few human eyes.

They had met for the first time that morning at the weather briefing on base. He was poring over satellite maps and weather charts. 'Looks like a dingle day,' he'd said. 'Dingle' was an authentic Antarctic word, it meant clear, and fine – much as it sounded, she supposed – a little bell ringing.

Then, as if he remembered she were there at all, the pilot looked at her and smiled. 'It's your first time out in the field?'

'Yes.'

'Well, you'll love it.' The pilot gathered up his charts. 'I'll see you in the hangar in half an hour.'

She realised, watching him walk away, that she hadn't asked his name. He would know hers, of course, at least her first name, and would have a vague idea of what she was doing in the Antarctic. *Nobody wants to know about us. We're just the bus drivers down here* – she had overheard another pilot say this in the bar one night soon after she arrived. She resolved that at the right moment she would ask the pilot about his life. She would ask him his name.

When they landed, the snowfield was a regal stunned sheet of white rising up to meet them. The skis touched down and a curtain of snow crystals flew up and covered the windscreen. The sky was an insolent, lordly blue.

Before Nara had a chance to register the cold, the wind, the stinging sun, she was out the door and helping the pilot shift boxes. They were there to set up camp and then fly back to the fuel depot. The scientists were being ferried down in the larger plane, along with the skidoos, the sledges, and the rest of the tents. All this had been decided in the same logistical haze she had barely become accustomed to. Everything in this new life was governed by the Field Operations Manager, or the weather, or a cunning hybrid of the two. Everything was beyond her control. She was expected to do as she was told. When did she join the Army, she wondered.

Amidst the dead weight of boxes, some far too heavy for her; squeak of snow; the zinc smell of Factor 60, its metallic taste hovering on the edge of her lips, she was overtaken suddenly by a powerful feeling she could not name. She could only say she felt forsaken, not by anyone she knew, any human being, but by a much larger entity that had suddenly appeared and expanded to fill the brass sky, the cold zeal of the air. Some brutal censor was looking at her, it had her snared in its gaze. She registered this with a thin, skating alarm. She was not religious, she had never had such thoughts in her life.

She looked up to see herself staring back at her – a reflection in the pilot's polarised sunglasses. These sunglasses, which were official issue, had the effect of thinning out people's faces and drawing up the corners of their mouths, making them look like a troupe of black-eyed aliens.

'We'd better get a move on,' he said. 'The Met said the weather could close in today. There's a low pressure system over the Bellingshausen. I reckon we should make tracks back to Ice Blue.'

They worked quickly, then, erecting pyramid tents in minutes, weighing them down with snow on the skirts, tying off valances. Then they rolled the skidoo from the back of the fuselage to where it would stay parked beside one of the tents, covered in a green tarpaulin.

She stole a moment to look at the landscape around her. The mountains were the colour of cinders. White cascades of ice streaked their flanks. The peaks were twenty miles away, but they towered right above, and she felt as if she could touch them. Then another fleeting impression, so strange she stopped in her tracks and stared: it was as if the mountains were moving, very slowly, toward them.

'We might be the first human beings to set foot here,' the pilot said. 'I'll plot the GPS and look at the data when we get back to base. Then we'll know for sure. How many people in the world can say: *I am the first human to ever stand on this spot.*'

The scientist within her said, 'Is it possible to know for sure?'

'Of course it is, this is the Antarctic. It's like nowhere on earth. In fact, we're not actually on earth, here, that's how I think about it. It's like outer space. A new planet, a new life.' His laugh then was strange and private. She could not see his eyes.

Seven hours later, the pilot was in the cockpit talking to base on the HF about a minor mechanical problem, discovered when he had revved the engines to fly them out. To the comms manager on base he spoke in a language she did not understand: *aft boost, oil press, carb heat, hung start, shutdown*. He still wore his sunglasses, so she had to look at his mouth for clues to the seriousness of their problem. The edges of his lips dipped, a slightly sour, masculine expression of disappointment.

The weather was closing in. The weather changed so quickly; she only had time to perceive a gleam of albedo before the sun was shuttered by cloud, then a gathering dark, unnaturally fast, as in an eclipse. This was the chrome edge of a blizzard bearing down on them from the mountains.

Her watch read 2, but it could have been 2am or 2pm; in the twenty-four-hour daylight they looked exactly the same.

Then the pilot was outside, sitting splay-legged on the wing of the plane, pliers in hand. She clambered out of the plane and looked up. Although the sun was behind a silver veil of cloud, still she had to shield her eyes.

'Is there anything I can do to help?'

'I don't think so, but thank you –' here he said her name and it emerged formal and slightly chastising, as if she were being told where to sit or put to bed. 'Maybe you could go and get some snow to melt for dinner. Not now, in an hour or so.'

Later, in the back of the Otter she put on her salopettes, her three fleeces, her thin summer windbreaker, not at all proper issue for this kind of weather, this far south. The pilot turned away discreetly as she put on more clothes, even though there was no flesh to be seen. Yes, he was old-fashioned, this man, he was courteous. She felt guilty for having judged him a sour man, perhaps disappointed, volatile, untrustworthy. She had been making a lot of these instant stinging judgements since coming to the Antarctic, and put it down a certain anxiety about being cooped up with strangers, about being at their mercy.

When she was about to step out of the plane she felt him clip something onto her back.

'What's that?'

'Your lifeline.'

'But I'm only going to get snow.'

'That's what they all say.'

One step beyond the fuselage's windbreak, she felt the wind. It drove snow into her face and stung, and her fingers were instantly cold. Bracing herself she picked her way, taking uneasy leaden steps in the fresh snow, testing the solidity of the ground beneath her. It was not uncommon for hidden crevasses to be prised open by the pressure of a plane landing.

She shovelled wedges of snow into a metal bucket. When she stood up a gauzy shield of white met her eyes. The plane had disappeared. She looked around, trying to find any sight line, any landmark, but the gauze was not only in her eyes, her ears, but in her mind. In the swirling snow she couldn't even see her own hand. She felt a sudden vertigo, then a slight but insistent nausea. She took ten steps in the direction of the plane. Stars gathered and dispersed in her eyes. She fumbled for the wire at her back. A frayed ribbon of shout on the wind – the pilot's voice saying, you all right? You still there?

Nara felt the tug at the small of her back, and then she was being pulled backwards. As she moved she thought: this is a new way of living, we are living each moment as a part of itself. And then, how powerful he is, the pilot; can we really be the only two humans for a thousand miles in any direction? Only he knows how to get us out of there. Otherwise, what are we? Corpses. Other people's guilt.

In twenty steps she was back at the plane.

'I don't know what happened.'

'You were heading off in the wrong direction. Good thing I had hold of you. How was your little expedition? We should call you Shackleton, or would you rather be Scott?'

'Don't joke about the dead. Not in these conditions.'

'What conditions would they be?'

She understood: he had seen so much worse.

The pilot smiled. 'It's dinnertime. Have you heard of that famous restaurant, The Twin Otter? They say it can be hard to find, but once you do, it's worth it.'

That night the storm intensified. They spread their P-bags on opposite sides of the fuselage. The pilot lit three Tilley Lamps and hung them from hooks in the cross-beams overhead. The lamps swayed with the plane when it was buffeted by gusts.

She took out her book.

'What's that you're reading?'

She turned the book toward him so that he could see the cover: *The Worst Journey in the World*.

He smiled. 'Ah yes, that Antarctic classic. Wait 'til you get to the part where they etherise the albatross to death on the deck of the *Terra Nova*.'

'Why did they do that?'

'They were killing it – either to eat or to take back as a scientific specimen, I can't remember. Now there's a sad, sad episode. All of them flapping behind the albatross, trying to pin it down. It never tried to escape because it didn't know not to trust humans. Albatrosses had no predators then. Sometimes, when I read that episode, I want to cry.'

She stared at him. He was physically similar to his colleagues, but he was so different from them, these lean weatherbeaten ex-bush and ex-Army men, hyperactive yet taciturn, perpetually in thrall to the next challenge. All the pilots she had met so far on base really did seem tuned to a higher frequency of life, so that they actually vibrated, like wires. In the cafeteria queue they clicked their fingers, rose up and down on the balls of their feet as if at any moment they might make a run for it. Luke was so different; well-spoken, thoughtful. Yet then he was not wholly unlike them, either. In the cockpit, on the way down, she had asked him why he became a pilot, and he had answered her, 'I like speed. I like machines. That's about all there is to it.' She thought yes, you could ruminate too much on the whys of something. *Why* could be a big waste of time.

'I'm not finding it that easy to read.' She paused. 'I've only managed the introduction. I think it's too close to what I'm actually experiencing.'

'You mean you could read it better on a hot summer day, lying in a park in London?'

Hot days. Parks. London. She registered that she had left that world – if not forever, then for a long time.

The pilot rolled over on his back. In the dim light she could only see the breath rising from his balaclava. 'I know,

I shouldn't talk about where we're not. It's like how you miss people down here. It's as if they've died. Or you've died and they're carrying on in a separate timeframe. You can't talk to them, nothing you say about this life makes sense to people who don't experience it, you can't touch them. That's what I think ghosts are like, you know – they're there, living right beside us, but there's this invisible curtain between us.'

A blow hit the plane. It swayed, then rocked.

'That'll be a katabatic gust, straight off the mountains,' he said.

'It felt like we were going to tip over.'

'We would, if we weren't blanked down. And this is midsummer. Imagine winter. Sometimes when I'm out here I think about what those men went through, the Scotts, the Shackletons.' He turned to face her again, propping himself up on his elbow. 'You know, though, what I think is the saddest story of all? Shackleton, when he went back to London. After surviving the wreckage of the *Endurance*, making his way to South Georgia, rescuing the men left behind on Elephant Island. It was 1918, the War was still on. He gave lectures to a half-filled Philharmonic Hall, twice a day. Imagine what the man had just done, how he had saved his men. And he had to stand up there and tell people how he had failed to cross the Antarctic, every day, twice a day. The hall should have been packed out but nobody cared. Because there was a war on. Because he had failed.' He paused. 'His secret was that he was able to get over disappointments quickly. He said "a man must shape himself to a new mark directly the old one goes to ground". I think about that a lot.'

This is the last thing she remembers hearing. From time to time the plane shudders in the wind. Otherwise, the silence is deafening; she can hear her own heart, even the blood humming in her veins.

Then she is in a different dimension. The storm, the plane, the pilot, they are all separate from her, they are all on the other side of the curtain.

She sees a man. He is talking to people, they sit row on row. Behind him, a film rolls, a modern video stream of ice floes. On them lie dark gleaming lozenges, like wet seals. But something is wrong, something is coming up, from the deep. When it reaches the surface, it will shatter this itinerant ice-floe world. The man tells the audience how the killer whales circled them, their horrible eye, big as a man's head, their black and yellow mouths. The fishy stench of their breath.

The man begins to cry. The film flickers against empty rosewood chairs. The few people left in the hall are all women. They sit primly under giant hats. The man's voice booms into the crevasses of empty rows until there are only two or three women left. Their faces lengthen and contort until they are all screeching like the figure in Edvard Munch's *The Scream*.

In the depths of the night which is not night, the pilot asks, *You ok*?

Is she talking in her sleep? It is so long since she has slept in the same space as anyone. On the ship she had her own cabin.

Someone else's words are in her head: the pilot's, the man on the podium's, the ghosts on the other side of the curtain. But it is sleep talk, fragmented, not unlike ice breaking up in summer – something about being proud of what you do, of having done your best, of being forsaken by God.

She was awakened by a sheer taffeta stream of sun on her face. The pilot was not in his sleeping bag. She dressed quickly and shuffled to the cockpit.

'Morning. At least I hope it's morning.'

He turned and gave her a quick, professional smile. He glanced at a chunky silver watch which had almost as many dials and sprockets as the Otter cockpit. 'Eight-fifteen.'

She sat in the co-pilot's seat. 'What time did you get up?'

'About seven. Same time I get up on base.'

She peered out the window. 'Weather's improving.'

'Hmmm.' He sounded unconvinced. 'I'll just call Adelaide on the HF and then let's have breakfast, what do you say?'

'Should I get some snow in?'

'That's all been taken care of. We pride ourselves on our customer service here in the Otter.'

Breakfast was porridge and instant coffee. 'You know,' the pilot volunteered while they were eating, 'you talk in your sleep.'

She laughed. 'What did I say?'

'Oh, you know sleep talk. From what I remember you said, "Nowhere to burn. Only wolves." Then a bunch of stuff I couldn't make out.'

'I never knew I talked in my sleep.'

'Well you might not normally. It might just be the situation we're in.' She stiffened at his use of the word. It was the first time he had acknowledged that it was that, a *situation*.

They spent that day and the next in the plane. The pilot made the first move, whenever anything needed to be done. He refused to have her put a lifeline on him, instead clipping it onto the side of the plane. She wondered why he had not done so with her; it would have at least freed him up to do other things while she was wandering around getting lost in blizzards.

She washed the dishes out with snow. It didn't quite clear the food off the plate; thin ribbons of beef Bourgogne froze onto the Melmac surface.

'Not a very good Antarctic dishwasher, are you?'

She couldn't tell whether he was teasing, or genuinely put out. 'Well, show me how to do it then.'

He retrieved a plastic scraper from the small compartment at the back of the plane, and began to scrape the plates.

'Can't we just rinse them with hot water?'

'First rule of Antarctic cuisine: don't waste your hot water. Hot water requires resources: dig, melt, meths, propane.'

'You know how to do everything.'

'Who's going to do it for you, here? That's what I like about this life; you have to be self-sufficient. There's no room for pride or status.' The pilot told her a story, then, about an artist he had taken down to the fuel depot one year, a wealthy and impatient man, who had left his bags on the ice runway next to the plane in order that someone should hoist them into the fuselage. The plane took off without his bags in it. 'That's what happens,' he said, 'if you expect someone else to look after you down here.'

She did not like going outside. It was not so much the weather, but the silence she encountered, away from the plane – the suffocated, chlorine silence of the Antarctic. She could hear the blood hurtle through her veins, she could hear her own heart pumping. The silence itself had no sound: it was not a whine, a ringing absence, but it was pristine, unarguable. Against the totality of the silence she found her mind began to manufacture sounds, so that the thin wires they used to blank down the plane zinged and the sun, hidden behind the low cloud, emitted a distant buzzing hum. Once, while walking back to the plane during those days she caught a muffled, distant sound, projected so that it was huge and clanging in her ears, a frozen carnival, but as she approached the plane she realised it was only the pilot's voice on the radio: *We're still hunkered down here. Weather window. Tomorrow or tonight.*

'Hey,' he said, when she appeared in the cockpit doorway, stamping snow from her boots on the footrail. She levered herself inside and closed the door, taking the co-pilot's seat. 'We could make it to Ice Blue. That's what I keep telling them, that as soon as the weather clears we can get airborne ok. As long as there's a mech at Ice Blue.'

'What do you think they'll do?'

'I don't know. The field ops man isn't known for his decisiveness.' His mouth turned into that sour pout, an oddly childish gesture on such an adult face.

They sat in the cockpit in silence, fully dressed. Outside the window the wind quickened. She had never seen a storm like this, how it gathered itself, over and over, into increasing waves of fury. The Otter snapped and groaned as the metal contracted with the cold.

That night they cooked another meal, then retired to their P-bags on either side of the fuselage.

'That's a one-metre drift today,' the pilot said. She looked up and saw him peering at his GPS screen. 'Strange, don't you think, that the ground is slipping away, right beneath us. That's why they call it an Ice Stream, I suppose.'

'But the ground is always moving,' she said. 'The continents are drifting apart, still. The planet is spinning at 1,600 kilometres an hour. We're always in motion, whether we realise it or not.'

The wind hurled snow at the fuselage. 'It sounds like sand, don't you think?' she said.

'You know, that's exactly what I was thinking. My exact thought.'

After that, she could not remember them speaking any more. They must have fallen asleep together, meaning at the same time.

*

The following day they fired up the engines; it was time, the pilot said, to see if they still worked. Without authorisation from base there was no question of them actually taking off, but there was the risk of the aircraft freezing to the ground. For the first time the pilot allowed her up on the wings to help him unblank the plane. At first she struggled with the tension on the wires, how cold they were to the touch, even through her gloves. In the end she had to take them off and blow hot air on the layer of rime ice that had formed overnight in the storm. The tips of her fingers burned, and she put them in her mouth.

'Let's just get her going,' he called out to her. 'Get in.'

She scrambled off the wing, down along the fuselage, and slipped through the co-pilot's door. He started the right engine first. The propeller whipped until it was a blur of black and white stripes against the white of the snow. He fired up the left engine and the plane began to shake.

He frowned.

'What is it?'

His voice came through the headphones. 'Generator.'

He radioed base. 'Hey – we've got a faulty generator down here.' His voice was tight with anger. 'I wish you guys would fix this once and for all. This is what – the third time this season? What about when BZ conked out over at Berkner? How long did it take you to get it back? A week?'

The reply was a rush of static. 'Sorry,' came the voice of the comms manager. It sounded more than distant, rather a voice sieved through space and time, from another planet. 'The ionosphere is acting up again.' He was referring to the electrically charged layer of the atmosphere that extends from eighty to four hundred kilometres above the earth's surface, and which absorbed much of the short wavelength radiation from the sun.

But that only happened at sunset, she thought, when a refraction of the rays of a setting or rising sun at certain angles caused havoc with radio communications. She checked the pilot's watch and was shocked to see it was 11:30 – at night, she assumed. Back on base, far to the north, there was no night, but the sun dipped toward the horizon around midnight, a hovering gold and mauve beacon. She hadn't seen the sun in two days, but behind the storm it was travelling round and round, above their heads, in an ellipsis.

The propellers slowed, then stopped. The pilot turned to her. 'Well,' he said, 'just like the old explorers, then.'

That night she dreams of him, and it is all so real, not like a dream or even a memory but a silhouette of experience unhappy to have been confined to the past, restless to be admitted to the present.

His skin. Like those rainforest woods: padouk, mahogany. His hair, much thicker than hers. To her he seems a more vital creature. Alive. Sudden flares of temper. All the glaciologists she has met are like this; flinty, obsessed. He is generous, hasty, like travel.

Her fingers trace the concave hollow between his belt – still a boy's belt, a piece of elastic, fabric, a cheap buckle – and his stomach. The quiver of a thin muscle, a glade of wiry hair. His smell there is not unfamiliar to her, nothing about him is unfamiliar, it is as if she has been poured into his bones, or he into hers.

In his body she sees not sensuality, vacant and common, but the edges of her dreams. This man is not an accident, but nor is he luck.

How quickly he has become necessary. He moves her. If this weren't the case she could take him or leave his barbed comments, his glossy eyes. He is inside her, somehow. He is her.

She woke up. The Otter was cold now, the Tilley Lamps long since burned down, the pilot asleep in the tungsten light of the polar night.

Tent days, the pilot called them, days when you were only waiting – waiting for rescue, for the weather to shift, waiting to be told what to do – days when time became an obstacle. Nara wondered how many days he had spent like this. She looked for signs of patience in his face. But his face, although thin, was not haggard with endurance. It struck her again that she was in the presence of a man with un-ordinary powers.

As for time, it was not the clammy indistinctness of the hours which unnerved her so much as the whiteness of their environment. Even under cloud the snow glared a hollow grey-white. On the rare occasions when they saw the sun, the white glint of the snowfield burned her irises. The whiteness seeped from the world around her, and entered her so that her thoughts were the white-yellow of raw silk, slippery, they followed one another without destination or will. If she ventured outside she was deprived of any perspective. She felt instantly seasick. The constant uncertainty of whether she was putting her foot in snow or air, the strain of guessing where the surface might be, waiting at any moment to feel herself pulled waist-deep into the snow, her shoulders hooking on a ledge of a crevasse, exhausted her. The pilot held her lifeline with one hand, with the other he cooked dinner, as was his habit. She was on the end of a fishing line and she was moving into whiteness. The blur in her mind grew and grew until it became an intense stinging buzz.

That night in the back of the Otter she asked him where his accent was from.

'Canada.'

'Which part?'

'I'm from a province next to the Atlantic Ocean. You won't have heard of it.'

'I lived in Canada for six years.'

'You did?'

'My father was a university professor. He got a job there, and we went with him.'

The pilot nodded, but did not say any more. Normally, she would have pressed him to talk about a country they suddenly had in common. But she detected a hesitancy, whether an instinct for privacy or a lack of interest in origins, his or hers, she couldn't tell. And here they were so exposed to each other; she did not want to annoy him.

They slept and ate and went outside to get snow, or to pee, or empty their bowels. They read and talked. They would take turns melting snow for water, transferring it to another pot, then dividing it in two; in the remaining pot they poured dehydrated mashed potatoes. Sometimes she couldn't finish hers, it was too heavy for her. Manfood – it was still called this, thirty years after the Antarctic had been evacuated of the last of the dogs and the dogfood and manfood boxes had been separately labelled – had a high caloric content, to help cope with the cold. They finished their meal with chunks of seven-year-old Bourneville chocolate ('quite fresh, in Antarctic terms,' the pilot said) then hung the Tilley Lamps from the metal loops in the fuselage, and read. She was only truly warm in her P-bag. Even then a fringe of damp, a buzzing cold needle of air, pressed at her edges. She began to dream of immersions, of being surrounded by warm water. A bath or a shower took on an almost supernatural appeal.

'I'd love a nice wood fire,' she said.

'Did you ever read that story "To Build a Fire" by Jack London?'

'I had to read it in school. I didn't like it very much.'

'Why not?'

'I think I was spooked by stories of hunger and luck.'

He laughed.

Suddenly, she felt desperate. 'You don't think it's serious? The situation we're in?'

'No, I don't. Not like in that story, anyway. But it wasn't just his luck, remember. He was warned by the old-timer not to do the journey alone.'

She nodded. 'Like Captain Scott. He was warned, too, wasn't he – and he still went ahead and trusted to luck.'

'Something similar, I suppose,' he said. 'They both thought luck was on their side.'

'What do you miss, down here?'

'Red wine, Syrah or Merlot preferably, grilled fish, something fresh and meaty. Monkfish. Dancing. A hot shower. Heat of any kind. Wood-panelled rooms, animals, music...it's easier if you don't think of things that are impossible.'

'But you think of them, still.'

'We're all perverse that way, don't you think?' he said. 'I only want things I can't have. When I find out I can have them, I don't want them anymore.'

She agreed. 'Almost everything I want, I can't have.'

'You wanted to come to the Antarctic, you must have. Nobody comes here without wanting it badly. And you got what you wanted. You're here.'

'Yes,' she said. 'We're definitely here. Wherever here is.'

A silence followed, long enough that she took the conversation to be over. But the pilot's voice interrupted her drift toward sleep.

'So what is it that you want so much and can't have?'

'A man.'

'So you ran away from love.'

'I ran toward something better. That's how I think about it. What about you? I mean, are you married?' For days she had been skirting round this question, trying to come at it from the correct angle.

'Me? Well, I got married when I was twenty-eight. We had three children, quite quickly I suppose. It's just what you were supposed to do, to get on with it.'

She wondered how long ago twenty-eight was. He might be twenty years her senior; it was hard to tell. He inhabited what was for Nara an indefinite age, too young to be her father, too old to plausibly be her lover. Although really, she supposed, there was no real limit on the latter.

The wind cuffed the plane once more and set it rocking. The pilot mumbled something then, some mild disbelief, or was it laughter? She asked him what he meant but heard nothing in return. In another moment she heard his breathing alter. He had fallen asleep.

What she will remember of those Otter days in the coming months: hunger and luck, the manfood too heavy for her to eat, the cold gnawing at her like a small, sharp-toothed animal. Their luck, if you could call it that, of a two-day field trip turned into ten. Awkwardnesses. Mad days connected to each other by a wire. *If I tugged, you would feel me.* Leaving the plane to relieve herself, trying to locate the pee flag in a whiteout, the lifeline on her back, the pilot discreetly turned away. Lemon stains on the snow now frozen to blocks of urine-ice. On the second day polar agoraphobia overtook her and she did not want to leave the fuselage; the pilot had to all but shove her out. Terrible constipation because she could not bring herself to defecate anywhere he might see her, the stalemate broken only by the blizzard that arrived on the third – or was it the fourth? – day and which offered her complete cover. Blinded by so much white as she squatted, vulnerability but also a strange power coursing through her. The thrill of their aloneness; who has ever been so alone? Pilots shot down in wartime, she imagines. The terrible story of Amelia Earhart and her navigator, crashed on a near-invisible Pacific atoll, only skeletons and one of the navigator's shoes left. Did they starve to death? Did they make love? Did they devour each other?

We're safe, he'd said, once, cooking dinner. *There's no need to worry.*

Don't worry, I'm not worried. And they'd laughed, and after dinner spent an hour trying to find synonyms for the word: preoccupation, anguish, concern, doubt, hand-wringing, brooding, getting worked up, anxious, tense, despair, dark night of the soul. *I always liked the sound of that*, she'd said, *but with a 'k', the man on the horse, you know, who comes to save you: all I want is a dark knight of the soul.*

Right away the pilot is there, floating around the dark fuselage of her dreams; in her dreams they are both suspended, gravity-less, as in a space capsule. His dark blue eyes framed by eyebrows of a certain, definite cast. His hands, surprisingly delicate and small. In her dreams he says, 'We're safe, don't worry.' Even within the dream she thinks how much of life is contained in this dispute between safety and danger: illness, family, dying, hope. *Life is not safe*, she remembers her mother saying, her voice hissing on the final word. Her beautiful, vengeful mother who had too much disappointment invested in such thoughts to risk optimism, like a dark day of rain that refuses to brook the light.

When she awoke the pilot was talking – at first she thought to her, or possibly to himself. Then she realised it was base on the radio.

'Well never mind…' A hiss of static. 'No we're ok down here.'

She went forward, her head bent in deference to the low ceiling of the fuselage, and slid into the co-pilot seat.

When he'd finished talking, she pointed ahead and asked, 'what's that?'

The pilot squinted at the windscreen. 'What?'

'There are people,' she said, simply. A haze had settled in her eye. But within it, very small, were the black shadows of people on the move, perhaps – a ring of people, dancing in the snow. They were towing what looked like a snowmobile.

'I don't think there's anything there.'

She closed her eyes, opened them. The figures were still there, black dots against a grainy canvas of white, round and shapeless, like peppercorns scattered on snow.

'It's a mirage. The air's so clear here, there's no pollution or haze. But also there's nothing to get a fix on in your visual field, and if one thing appears – a tent or a ridge or an island, your eye magnifies it. Isn't that interesting, how for us, emptiness is a magnifier? Everything looks a third closer than it really is. Even pilots misjudge the distances sometimes.'

She shook her head. She couldn't get the vision of the people towing the skidoo out of her mind.

'The less there is to see, your eye compensates by making things bigger, or manufacturing things to look at. That's why you have the hallucinations, the *fata morgana*, when sailors start to see towns and cities, or other ships, or icebergs. You usually see what you want to see most: a rescue ship, your mother,' – he hesitated, gave her a careful look – 'or other people, in your case. But there's nothing there. That's one of the things you watch out for, as a pilot,' he went on. 'In a whiteout, you start hallucinating horizons, then you ignore what your instruments are telling you, then you begin to tip the plane down. They call it the dead man's spiral. The eye sees what it wants to see, not what's there. You have to train yourself not to see what you hope for. It's strange, when you think of it, that hope can kill you.'

The following day the sun came out. Nara had not seen it for days and now its lordly beam seemed excessively intelligent, even malignant in its intentions.

She stepped out of the Otter and saw their world transformed. There was camp, more or less as they had left it, but with new snow cornices wrapped around the gear in sweeping parabolas, as in dreamy modernist architecture. The green tarp which covered the skidoo had disappeared beneath a drift. A line of green and red flags attached to an emaciated chorus of bamboo sticks led to the tents. Under the glare of the sun the snow burned the white-blue of phosphorous.

The spine of the Ellsworths soared above her; she had the impression the mountains were rising like loaves of bread, expanding, growing taller. The sun cast two black haloes above their peaks and she saw a black sky with white rings of powdered sunlight drawn in it. She had heard about these false suns, seen only in the highest latitudes of the polar regions. A single throbbing sun had parked itself over the tent, and to the right and the left, equidistant, two acolytes shimmered as if from behind a curtain of ice.

Later, back in the plane she told the pilot.

'We call them Sun Dogs. Ice crystals in the sky, they refract the light. At times I get so used to seeing two or three suns, when I see the single one I think, where have the others gone? Wouldn't it be wonderful, if we had multiple suns?'

'I think the planet would burn to a crisp, if we did,' she said.

'I suppose. But it would be so beautiful.'

'You see so much flying down here.'

'I see it, but I don't always understand it. I wish I had a better education, sometimes. Maybe if I didn't spend so much time with scientists – with you –' he said it hastily, an awkward gesture of inclusion, 'I'd be more content with the education I had.'

'I'm not sure we're so well-educated, just specialised, more and more in fact, until you can only look at your little corner of the universe. You've seen more with your own eyes in a month than many Antarctic scientists would see in their entire working lives.'

'I suppose,' he said. But this time the hesitant note had been evicted from his voice, and he sounded pleased, even vindicated.

The comms manager's voice stuttered into the cockpit on the radio. 'Bravo Bravo, this is Adelaide calling. You can expect company this afternoon. Over.'

The pilot went to the microphone. 'Roger that. Over.'

'Who will come?'

He shrugged. 'A mech, some scientists.' He no longer seemed to care whether they were rescued. And suddenly there it was, another plane, taxiing to a stop in front of them. They heard no buzz, no sounds of arrival. The other Otter opened its hatch and out spilled a mechanic, the spare part, some fuel drums, and two scientists.

The shock of other people made her euphorically friendly. She threw her arms around the pilot and the mechanic, although she had met them both only once on base. But she was also cagey, territorial about the Otter, the tent, the lifeline, their nightly talks about fear and survival. Only now, with the arrival of outsiders, did she realise how quickly had they built a universe between them, how complete it had been.

In an instant they tilted from a surfeit of time to a dangerous absence of it. Again her life became a haze of urgent actions: boxes; secure straps; blank down; valance; dig; snow. The mech was perched on the wing of the Otter, of *her* Otter, the pilot busy with dials. The other two scientists, whom she had never before met, would spend a month down in the camp she had painstakingly erected. They were geologists. *We heard you had to lay up*, they said. Back on base the field operations manager had been tearing his hair out – would have, had he any left, they said, and laughed.

Within an hour their plane was fixed. The pilot let her help unblank it. The plan was to get the plane going, fly to the fuel depot, then grab a couple of hours sleep and start back to Adelaide base. They would be flying all night, the pilot said. It would take them six hours, 'at least', he said, to get back home.

They accelerated, skis sliding down the ramp of pristine snow. The wind snagged the Otter's wings from above and threw them into the air in a violent, shuddering ascent. 'Thermals', the pilot said through the radio microphone, to reassure her.

The sun was a burnished white ellipsis in the sky. Fields of snow corrugated with sastrugi appeared beneath them, chromium in the glinting sun, raw mirrors from which they had to avert their eyes. As they rose, open meltpools appeared, then outlet glaciers, streaming toward the Bellingshausen Sea.

She looked back, over her shoulder, out the window.

'Don't look back.' The sharpness of his tone startled her. She hauled her gaze forward.

'Sorry, I didn't mean to startle you. But I never look back. It's a superstition, I guess,' he said.

The altimeter clicked, rolling its numbers higher and

higher: four, five, eight thousand feet. They cleared the mountains and levelled out, heading east, toward the fuel depot. For a while they flew straight, interrupted only by radio contact with Ice Blue, and base. Suddenly, the pilot said, *here*.

She understood immediately what he meant. She shook her head.

'Yes,' he said. 'You can do it. Just keep your eyes on the artificial horizon, then look out the window. Take your cue from the land. Try to feel you're flying steady, then look back to the instrument panel to check. Keep your altitude, don't vary more than a hundred metres. If I ask you to take it down, dip your wrists very slightly. Watch your trim. Here, I'll show you.'

She put her hands on the controls and the pilot removed his. In her wrists lay the heaviness of the aircraft. It vibrated. Like an animal, she thought – the trembling, the indecision, the willingness to respond. As when she had ridden horses and directed their tonne of flesh with a flick of her wrist.

She flew it under his watchful eye, for how long she didn't know – it might have been half an hour, or several hours. Time ceased to flow as it normally did, because everything she was doing was so new. She was coming into the world, all over again.

She flew until they were over the nunataks which ran in waves from the Ice Blue runway toward the interior. The pilot said, 'Here, I'll take her back.' They dropped altitude and she watched the arrow on the altimeter swing round and round: 9,000, 8,000, down to 500 and then suddenly they were on the ground and skiing to a stop.

The two field assistants in the melon hut gave them the same euphoric welcome she had given the stranger geologists. The pilot took a skidoo to do a radio check with base. She could imagine the field operations manager, the chief pilot, ordering him to stay the night rather than risk flying on no sleep and him saying, *I'll tell you what I'm not going to risk, I've got one generator down and an indicator, the aft fuel pump...*

At two in the morning they took off. When they had reached altitude he said *here* and again she took the plane in her hands. She had never concentrated so hard in her life. Her head throbbed with the effort.

The pilot might have noticed this because he said, 'Here, give her back to me. I'll take us down lower. You'll be able to see – can't sightsee much when you're learning to fly.'

He dropped low to the ground, well underneath the mountains of Alexander Island to the west, a hundred miles away, over sliding serpentines of turquoise, glacial meltpools, minor freshwater lakes forming temporarily at the foot of a glacier. Some had amoebic, formless shapes, others drew sharp calligraphy with sudden upright characters.

Then the plane whipped over the cold white river of an ice stream. There were long blank periods when they did not talk, only looked down at the icefields, so void-like that her mind – whether through fatigue or some ordinary hallucination – began to produce a prairie and she saw wheat, trees, a floor of flowers; faint things becoming visible, then melting back into the whiteness. She thought she saw wolves loping over the ice, but this was only the light, grey and feral, and the shadow of the Otter with the sun behind it.

She wanted to imprint all this on her memory: the sheets of sea ice beneath them, the cold gold light of the early morning sun on the snow, the pilot beside her, an exhausted vigilance in his eyes. But just as quickly as impressions formed, they slid from whatever had produced them, neurons or synapses, before she could capture them, and she understood that these moments were meant to be lived, not thought, not remembered or savoured. Any real joy and thrill contained within it this elusiveness, and she would have to learn to be still, to observe, not to grasp at these things, even as they slid away.

The evening light wanted to condense into dusk. Her body waited for it to happen, an unnameable force tugging from within her, at the strings of the universe, asking for night. But it remained stalled, just as the sun was anchored in the sky, low over the horizon but not set, emitting two flutes of violent mauve and gold. She had never seen a sky so phenomenal. It was like looking out to space from another planet, the heavens familiar but subtly rearranged.

Suddenly they were levelling out in front of a gravel airstrip. 'Keep your hands on the controls, but don't do anything,' he instructed. 'I want you to feel it.'

She felt the power then of what he could do. It was immense, it encircled her but was inside her, too, it emanated from the empty land below them and their aloneness and the clouds.

He powered the engines down and they opened the cockpit doors. The light that greeted them was of a perpetual dawn. The hangar doors were shut, base was quiet; only the Met man would be up at this hour. A gang of skuas circled lazily at the north end of the runway. The engines off, the only sounds were of the plane creaking from the effort of what it had been through, the hangar doors rattling in the wind, the distant hum of the generator, the skuas' raw squawk.

It was five o'clock in the morning on December 23rd, 2011.

'Well,' Luke turned to her, 'home for tea and medals.'

2

Time is circular. The sun goes round and round in the sky. There is no end to the light, and no beginning. Yesterday and tomorrow are as one, artificial delegations, unruled by daylight. Nara has had no shadow for weeks and finds that she does not need it, this ghostly chaperone which has accompanied her all her life one way or another, in all other places. In the Antarctic something is falling away, falling off her, this nameless weight she has been carrying around.

They go skiing on the glacier. There was snow overnight, not the usual snow of the Antarctic: fine, crystalline, bone-dry, no this snow was soft. Although not too soft; just the right snow, said the field assistants, neither powdery nor slushy. There were so many types of snow, she was learning: grainy, soft, slushy, hard crusts, the brutal sastrugi, useless for skis, the hard meniscus cracking through to loafy snow, like wading through wet Styrofoam.

Eleven pm, midnight, two in the morning, and they are skiing on the glacier. This was what you could do in the Antarctic: ski at four in the morning, lie down and make snow angels, like children. She is only too happy to participate, but it strikes her that there is only one kind of fun permitted in the Antarctic, an obligatory recklessness.

Only now, very late in the evening, could she look at the icefield without the protection of her polarising glasses. It seared a pain through the mind, which was not about colour or reflection but an overdose of blankness. There was no enchantment in the polar day, only a solar floodlit glare, ruthlessly simplified, dragging all energy into itself. The light fed and exhausted her at once.

She skis, breathless, down the V-shaped slope, rising stiffly against jagged exposed rock. The Bergschrund at the top, sagging where the rock and the icefield parted, a light turquoise congealed abyss. The moon is mute in the nightless sky, a gauzy white shadow.

Skiers hurtle down the ice sheet with the most gargantuan landscape they have ever encountered in front of them. The ordinary mountains of the pensinsula are as large as those of the Rockies, or the lesser Himalayas. Up and down they shuttle, skiing to the bottom, then hauled back to the top on the end of ropes by skidoos, the snow angels flapping in the snowfield – that was the original task of the angels, Nara remembers: they were messengers, transmitters from God to man.

She is a terrible skier. She is starving and her cheeks burn from the cold. The drynesss of the air sears her throat. Her mouth is bleeding at the corners. Two little open, messy wounds where spit accumulates, then dries, forming a thin milk crust. She is living so fast, here, everything refuses to stop and be understood. It feels like being out of breath.

At the same time she feels herself growing physically, her chest expanding, becoming man-sized, until she might explode. This intermittent feeling of power arrives accompanied by an indefinite hunger, she does not know for what: it passes through her with the force of one of those gravity-driven winds they called katabatic: not so much an explosion as a dream.

There must be somewhere beyond sentinel mountains, beyond the horizon. It seems too incredible that she is out of the world, she has escaped. She has been lifted out of her life and deposited on an Antarctic glacier by an unseen hand, among these people. Angels fallen to earth.

A week after her return from the Ellsworths Nara went for

her first dive in the bay to collect samples. She would place these creatures in her acquaria with their warming waters.

She slipped through a thin broken cover of sea ice, into the darkness guided only by her torch. Sea-sponges, gigantic, overfed on the cold nutrients of the water, sprouted on the seabed; she saw sea-squirts with their sodden turnip flesh, which attached themselves to the smooth basalt sides of an underwater cleft. Also sea-spiders, nematode worms, starfish the colours of bruises. The ice above her acted as a lid. No light, apart from a weak gleam, penetrated. On the surface the boatman awaited her signal.

Just as she was about to radio him, she spotted a sleek, mottled head, inches from her face. In a flash she saw the wraparound mouth, a slit almost to its ears, like a snake.

She refused to panic. She rose slowly to the surface, as she had been taught to do. But once her head was out of the water, fear flooded her lungs.

'Leopard seal,' she managed to say.

'Christ,' the boatman hauled her into the boat. 'We'd better tell base. No more solo diving here. Not for a while anyway, not with leps around. Are you ok?'

She nodded, although the truth was, she was having difficulty breathing. The leopard seal was the main danger for divers in Antarctic waters. The only seal that fed on other seals, if they mistook her for one they could easily drown her.

She put the net containing her specimens in the bottom of the RIB. The boatman looked mournfully at her collection of creatures.

'What's wrong?'

'They don't stand a chance, do they?' he shook his head.

'No,' she agreed. 'They'll die. They can't take more than a half-degree rise in temperature, as it turns out. Not much of a window for survival.'

'But if you already know the result, why carry on with your experiments?'

'Because I have to be sure. Some have a different upper temperature threshold than others,' she said. 'Some of them can hang on for longer.'

'But if the water around them is warming, what's the point?' he asked. 'You know they're all goners anyway.'

'We don't know for certain. That's why you need science,' she said. 'Until you have experimental data, it's all just conjecture.'

The boatman was a mature man – Luke's age, she guessed, perhaps even a bit older. He had worked in dive schools all around the world – Belize, Australia, Greece. She saw that he was unconvinced. To him, she knew, her experiments were just senseless killing of animals that would die anyway. Not that they would die straightaway: they might live for an indeterminate amount of time. But it was already proven that the oceans around base were warming so quickly, it might be only another twenty years before they were all gone.

Back in the lab, she removed the layers that kept her alive in the coldest waters in the world. She would not be able to swim for nearly two years. Although she would dive in the tar-black Antarctic waters, diving below the ice protected by layers of polyeurothane, rubber, steel; a choking rubber seal gripping her neck and hands, her prison suit of seams and zips and watertight seals. But she would not feel water slipping over her skin.

Lately she has been having dreams of swimming in lakes in Canada, where her father took them to live for six years when she was a child. There were so many lakes, no one had bothered to name some of them. In the city where here father teaches at university is a famous oceanography institute. She does her undergraduate degree there, returning to the UK with an accent she will struggle to shake off. She attends a concrete early 1970s university, an eminent if not elite institution where she does a graduate degree, then begins a PhD.

She has had to prod herself to be ambitious, to a degree, and acquire some specialist knowledge of the world which would guarantee herself a place in it. Her parents' professional background are influences, but also she is a woman of her generation in that she refuses to leave anything to chance, fate, biology, never mind a man. She studies marine biology and oceanography, struggling through the maths and physics courses but excelling in biology and chemistry. It is the diving she loves. There, beneath the surface, she is unburdened from the world above and its greasy mechanics, her father's long-term affair with a colleague – the real reason for their emigration to Canada, she will learn much later, was to follow his lover there – her mother's unhappiness.

In the Antarctic she dreams of the city they lived in for the first time in many years, its wide, eventless streets named after the billowing trees which cover them: Chestnut, Walnut, Larch, Tamarack. *The city of trees*, she called it, when they moved there. She asked her father why all the names in their new home were from animals, flowers, trees, and words in a language she had never known existed, with words that sounded like water running over stones in a brook. 'Because there's no history here,' her father had said – this from a history professor – 'because it's such a new country. There haven't been enough people. There hasn't been enough time.'

She dreams of the swarms of mayflies, strange locusts, mosquitoes, the pestering blackflies, the deerflies and horseflies that tormented her as she swam. She dreams of the roads the colour of faded denim. The giant boulders, slates of shale – she would learn the names for them in her geology class, *gneiss*, *schist*. The province was fissured with rocks, minerals, seams of coal. It was old, despite what her father said; the land was old, it had once been part of the Amazon basin.

She becomes a diver, partly because of her profession, partly through fascination with the sunken, mysterious world underneath the surface of the oceans. She is driven toward depths rather than heights. Mountains confine her, she has no fascination for them. Strange then, that her life will become intertwined with the Antarctic peninsula, with its grandiose peaks, its sea so cold that she would not survive even a ten-minute unprotected immersion in its waters.

In her dreams she is swimming in freshwater lakes, remnants of glaciers so recently passed, such is the startlingly intact trauma they have inflicted on the landscape: she can read the landscape like a map, its contours are the moraines, drumlins, the ragged thin snakes of topsoil raked away.

She swims too far out from shore, she risks becoming entangled in strange currents. In freshwater there are snapping turtles and leeches. The lake, the copper water, pine trees sentinel around it. Moose kneading the brackish water. Muskeg and moss.

She is young enough to believe that she will always be in the world. She has just learned about death, they did it in school: Week 4, Social Studies: Death. The shock still ripples through her as she swims. *But I thought I was here forever.* She is young enough to believe that all this is God's doing, infinite and complete. As if the earth has been broiled at the edges, then soldered until it is smooth, horizon and water one enamel plane, and she is moving through it, she is one with it. A lone silver swimmer, stroking silently through a copper summer morning. How far from the shore she is, is hard to say.

3

It was January and there was no night and the days seeped into each other, boundaryless, hungry to move through time. The light was white and savage and fell straight from the sky.

A solid wedge of indigo now marked the boundary of their white world, because the ice had broken up and was blown out to sea. Clear blue days took hold over the peninsula, and the intensity of its glare on the snow forced Nara's eyes shut, even behind her sunglasses. The blue and white world seized dominion of her mind and installed a spartan satisfaction there, as if she had never seen any other colours, and never needed to see them again.

The Antarctic calendar had its rituals, she learned; each season on base followed a pattern. Summer began in October with the arrival of the airplanes and the first fresh fruit and vegetables in seven months for the wintering population. November and December were frantic months, inputting scientific field parties; base barely stopped to observe Christmas and New Year's. By midsummer, in January, there was a pause long enough for the annual visit of the American oceanographic research ship, followed by the Russian tourist cruise ship, then the Navy's polar patrol vessel, followed by the annual Winter Olympics between the Navy ship and base staff: sledging, snowball throwing, snow-fort building, skiing, skidoo driving and snowboarding. Base celebrated Burns' Night even more raucously than New Year's, thanks to the always-strong Scottish contingent. On these nightless nights of high summer the bar always had to be cleared at two or three in the morning by the Saints, as the St Helena domestics who came to work on the base in the summer were called.

Nara had thought the Antarctic would be an isolation posting, but if anything there was too much activity, too much company. She felt the need to retreat; never before had she found such sanctuary in her thoughts. The Antarctic summer did not favour memories or tortured evaluations of one's life; it was too oxygen-rich, this environment of optimism powered by awe. For the first time in her life, she felt erased of her past, unburdened. Even if a darker current ran beneath this voluntary amnesia, one she could not grasp at all, although she heard its warning, a distant voice that said: *We are not meant to live in a continuous present tense.*

Outside the bar, silver crates of explosives were stacked, innocent as cases of beer. The geologists and the glaciologists were dynamiting that summer, in search of subglacial lakes kept liquid by thermal heat from the bedrock and by the tremendous weight of the ice sheets above. There were many lost lakes underneath the ice sheet, they told her – Lake Vostok, in the Russian sector, Lake Ellsworth in Ellsworth Land at the base of the peninsula were only two that radar had picked up; there might be many more hidden underneath the sarcophagi of ice. These lakes had been tropical swamps of Gondwanaland until they were slowly covered, the ice sheets crawling over them, sealing them in. If any organisms survived in that frigid black chamber they would be like deep-sea animals, she thought, adapted to live in total darkness: aquatic newts, diatoms, spectacular creatures that looked like fluorescent toothbrushes.

The sea-ice people had arrived too, to measure the extent of the summer ice. They told her that the Antarctic is a jellyfish, billowing, expanding and contracting on a sigh, casting skirts of ice toward the southern rims of the world, Hobart, Cape Town, Punta Arenas. Flourishing in the winter, dying in the summer, each year a little more. In winter, between March and September, the continent doubled in size and no ship could penetrate its ice shield. Planes could land, theoretically, but only in medical emergencies. Even then, flying into the Antarctic in winter, with its fuel-freezing temperatures and volatile visibility, was one of the most dangerous missions on the planet.

From her laboratory window she could see the low profile of Alexander Island. It was the size of Ireland but uninhabited; according to the map it was 150 miles away, but looked no more than 40 – Luke had told her about the landmarks that looked much closer than they actually were – another polar hallucination.

There was so much she did not know about this land. Everything Luke had said, she realised, had been a subtle instruction, so deft that she had been unaware at the time of how much she was learning.

She thought of the way Luke had done things, simple actions. How he had clambered, practised and agile, onto the plane's wing. His graciousness when faced with her uselessness in this new environment – anyone would have been a better co-pilot for him on this trip, than a newly arrived woman scientist – his hunger to know her thoughts. There was a soft, indulgent quality to him. Again she thought how different he was to the other pilots she had met on base, those brashly laconic types who snapped their fingers while waiting for food in the cafeteria queue, as if to test their reflexes. Though not unlike them at first glance, a lean figure in his orange boiler suit, walking toward her with his sunglasses on – not against the sun, for there had been almost none during those snowbound days in the Ellsworths, but as protection against the wind and the driving snow, and the glare which still emerged from it as if from a buried light, far below the earth's surface, slapping his gloves against his thigh to keep his fingers warm. He had a pilot's walk: jaunty, springing forward from the tips of his toes, bow-legged, too, his legs swinging wide around his hips. If she saw him from afar with a group of people, everyone dressed in their identikit Antarctic gear, she would know him from his gait alone.

Luke – she liked the name, near as it was to *luck*. He had told her his name, of course, before they even took off for the Ellsworths – she might even have known his name before that. But during their time in the Ellsworths she had avoided using or even thinking his name. She felt as if they were strangers hastily introduced only to tumble into an incontinent intimacy, and for some reason to use his name there would have been to breach a taboo. This man who now stood in the bar laughing with a glaciologist was the only living being she had seen for five days. She had never been so isolated and also so wedded to a single human and this – dependency, was the only word she could think of, although it was not quite correct – had left a faint imprint on her, indelible but definitely there. Why had she not found out more about him? She had missed an opportunity, she knew: not for love, or sex – on these levels she knew nothing about him – but for some kind of knowledge, as yet unidentified.

She saw him come toward her. There was a slight hesitancy in his expression.

'I'm going into the field for a week,' he said. 'Maybe two. A survey for MAGIC.' The map team were known by their acronym; Nara had seen it scrawled on the flight board at the end of the dining hall, and had looked it up on the intranet. It stood for Mapping and Geographic Information Centre.

'What does that entail?'

'Flying in straight lines, mostly.' Luke smiled. 'It's a challenge, believe me, to fly on the exact coordinates.'

'And you like a challenge.' As soon as she said it, Nara regretted the way it emerged: presumptuous, assuming too much familiarity.

'That's right,' Luke said. 'I do.'

There was a silence, during which he cast a slightly hunted glance around the room. 'Well, I just wanted you to know where I was going. People come and go down here. They just disappear and you're left wondering why they didn't say goodbye.'

Again, he seemed to have arrived at the end of what he wanted to say. But at the moment when she was expecting his body to angle away from hers he spoke. 'I was watching you the other night.'

'Watching me? When?'

'I don't mean it that way. I wasn't watching you deliberately. At dinner, I was sitting down the table from you. You looked so tired. You were sitting opposite – Yeah, well, I don't know his name. But it looked like he wouldn't speak to you.'

She felt her face grow hot. She propped her cheeks in her hands, to disguise it.

'And you looked so sad, and there was no one else for you to talk to.' He paused. 'It made me sad to see you so sad.'

She said nothing for a moment, then settled on a vague lie. 'I think I'm homesick.'

'Yeah, I know all about that. But don't waste too much time thinking of home. Because you'll find that when you're back, you'll miss it here.'

'How do you think about base, when you're home?'

'It's strange, you know. Every year, I come down here for four, six, ten weeks and I get bored, I miss my wife – my ex-wife, now. I miss the children. I used to have to stop myself from getting in the cockpit and flying the damn plane home. But no matter what happens, afterwards I always remember it fondly.' Luke gave her confused smile. 'I remember the good parts.'

She said, 'I'll miss you.'

'Miss me?'

'When you're away from base.'

'Oh, well, I'll be back soon enough.' There was a closed, satisfied quality to Luke's voice. She had given him something he had not quite earned, and he knew it. He was trying to brush off an innocent comment between friends, while actually hoarding secret pleasure in it. His reaction was all the worse for being nearly invisible, and because she had spoken the truth.

Luke left, slipping out of the bar without saying goodbye. He might have a rule against the word, like his don't-look-back dictum. She realised she had never heard him use it; he always said, *see you next week*, or *take care*. Perhaps pilots never said goodbye, she reasoned, in case it was for real.

4

Luke stood on the hangar apron, a windswept rectangle of gravel at the bottom of a grimy glacier. How many times had he stood there before, taking in this exact view, the ice in the bay, inert and frozen, or in spiralling motion, depending on the season? The ring of mountains in the distance. Skuas and blue-eyed shags coming in to land. Yes, this would be his last season. His heart soared at the thought. But also he felt that cunning sensation in his stomach, of the kind he only had when he was in real danger.

He catalogued the conditions: wind a good 25 knots or so, but not cold, maybe plus four or five. These days in January temperatures hardly dropped below freezing. In part it was due to the lack of night; twenty-four-hour solar energy prevented the temperature from falling. But then there was the warming: in the ten years he'd been flying, he had watched the ice retreat, stealthily at first, then with a consuming dissolution. All around them, the glaciers were pulling back, folding into themselves. Ten years before, the glacier above base still ran down to within a few feet of the runway and the average daytime temperature in summer was minus two. They had to look out for dewpoints, then, for icing in low cloud. These days the problem was fog. At times base became so cloaked in fog he had to lie up in the field for days, waiting for a weather window.

In the distance he saw a Gator approach, struggling down a pile of rubble driven by two red jackets in identical pairs of polarised sunglasses. The black and red and fluorescent orange everyone wore in the Antarctic was deliberate, of course – bright-coloured clothing could be more easily spotted in the white vortex of the ice sheet, should someone become lost, or need to be uplifted. And the sunglasses to keep the light at bay, which would otherwise corkscrew right through your corneas.

The scientists aboard, he took the plane swiftly into the air. The Otters were so eager to fly, they snagged on the thinnest of winds. He changed their heading for the far side of Porquoi Pas Island. Karol (or was it Karoly?, yes that was it, he was terrible with names) and Alexa (he remembered just in time) would photograph the shrinking glaciers there.

When the plane had reached a secure altitude, Luke allowed his mind to wander; he remembered his first sight of her, lugging a suitcase down the ship's gangplank and onto a Gator: a small, miserable-looking woman. In his experience, arriving in the Antarctic elicited either euphoria or a sinking dread, and for Nara it was the latter, he could tell straight away. And why not? She had left everything behind and flown across the world, only to arrive in this hardscrabble place, with its cold, repellent beauty.

By the end of the day this marine biologist woman would be installed in an impersonal pitroom, she would have had her mug shot taken by the base doctor in the surgery, assigned a little plastic rectangle with her surname on it for the tagging board, inducted into the procedure of signing in and out of the log book. She would wonder why she had imprisoned herself at the end of the world. She would know that eighteen months or two years – depending on which contract she had signed – of this life awaited her, living in a granite quarry on a peninsula in the Antarctic. Far, far away from anyone she had ever known or who had ever loved her, off the map, over the edge of the known world.

She had been good company on their trip, which had

turned out to be so much more eventful than he had bargained for. So many people turned into whining children when things did not go their way, stuck in an unpleasant situation by forces beyond their control. He took Nara's behaviour as a mark of maturity as well as grace. Threaded through her grace was a cord of tensile strength, slightly dark and virile, which he put down to a toughened grip of mind rather than body. Somewhere along the line, he thought, this woman had been tested.

Over the years he had observed a thing or two about the kind of people who came to The Ice. There were people who live by the truth versus those who can accommodate illusion, fantasy. They were so different, like the sun and the moon. To live under the beam of the sun is to have clarity and an upright, uncompromised splendour of the kind he knew in his life, before the divorce. Then there were those who came, far fewer in number, who were of a romantic disposition, people who slid from the darkness holding bunches of flowers in their minds. These were the people who said goodbye even if they were only going for a walk.

Nara was one of the flower-profferers, eager with gifts. Although he also recognised in her the coolness of the scientist. She would want to know the facts, the processes. She wanted to know *why*. But she did not give him the impression, as did so many women, of keeping herself locked away, a box inside a box inside another box; but what was actually in the box? He had to admit he was tired of the mystery of women. He wanted someone open, without secrets – if that were possible.

'Ok,' Karoly said, 'let's go do these lines.' He pointed to a map cross-sectioned with grids of varying colours. *Coal Nunatak, Moider Glacier, Dalgliesh Bay, Corner Ciffs, Nemo Cove, the Foyn Coast.*

Luke wished he could show Nara these – he would hardly

call them places; they were no more than formations, and small ones at that, marooned in a landscape of radical emptiness. Naming was a cartographic necessity, and as a pilot he needed these names; in an age of dependence on GPS, he often still flew by the landscape. But they also signified for him a touching if ultimately futile attempt to bestow meaning on a place which simply rejected it. This rebuff appealed to him: too many wars had been fought over place-names, rivers and valleys and industrial plains and mountain ranges. What a relief, he thought, to be somewhere there had never been a war, never had blood shed for it, apart from the accidental terrifying deaths the Antarctic exacted.

With a subtle sway of his wrist, they changed course. For the first time in a long time, Luke found he was seeing for two. He wanted to show Nara the bays, glaciers, nunataks – the peaks of near-invisible mountains buried in the ice sheet. He realised his mind had not only wandered on the thought of Nara, as it would wander when thinking of his children, his ex-wife, his friends back home, of sex, of food he wanted to try, of ways to invest the money he earned. It had snagged on her, a fish on a hook. Nara would be moved by all this, he knew. It was not that the scientists who now rumbled around the back of the Otter, checking laptops, outputs, line feeds, sensors, were not sufficiently awed; they were. But somehow their awe was incomplete and unearned. As he soared in and out of thermals, threading through brawny mountains, Luke found a feeling creeping upon him for these two harmless near-strangers, a feeling he suddenly had to fight hard to keep at bay: a watery intolerance, a commonplace derision, simply because they were not her.

'Look at that ice stream outflow!' Alexa pointed downward, about three o'clock, to where a glacier's gigantic white tongue lolled, falling into the sea.

'That's up on last year,' Karoly said. 'I estimate about 20 per cent.'

When he had first started working South, ten years ago now, the glaciologists had been cagey, predicting a thickening of the ice sheet in the middle, but a thinning at the edges. East Antarctica, they said, would increase its mass, while West Antarctica would begin an inexorable slide into the sea. He eavesdropped as the scientists recited a string of letters and numbers to each other. He would never have been a scientist, not because of his social station or education, or even his discovery that he was good at flying – no, he might have done anything. He could engage with the larger mysteries of science, the questions and the quests, and the increasing urgency to know what the future might hold. But the detail of it, the maths, the computer programmes, the numbers – they might as well be surgeons discussing a bypass operation.

He indicated to Karoly, then pointed out the cockpit window. 'That's the Shambles glacier; it used to reach halfway out to Pinero Island.'

Karoly smiled. 'You're right. Thanks.' He turned around as if to move back into the fuselage, then returned, put on his headphones. 'You don't say much,' he said. 'So when you do, we figure it's important.'

Luke smiled, then, because this was the exact impression he sought to convey. He kept to himself because he had nothing to prove. He had ten years behind him, ten Antarctic seasons, he had the authenticity of the adventures which had befallen him in the ordinary pursuit of his job. He enjoyed the respect that came with the job, how when he told people what he did for a living they were invariably amazed and impressed. He basked in this, although not the fatally inert basking of the seal, the animal which soaks up sun because it lives for so long in the cold dark. He was known on base as a daring pilot, someone who pushed the envelope; dextrous, a natural pilot, he had a feel in his hands for the dynamics of air and lift.

He flew them over what remained of the glacier, to more exclamations of dread from the scientists. Yes, it was too late to stop it now, the immense force of lubrication, of heat. The continent had been ignited from within. He longed to see this internal fire, lit by melt: oxygen-fed flames, red as Chinese silk, against the stark white of the ice sheet. He longed for it all to be burned up, consumed, ashes. Then he could finally go home.

He banked and flew them straight into the sun, into the calm brilliance of the day-long morning, gold fluting across snow-sheets, then sinking into hungry shadows.

That January base experienced a string of mild summer storms, and what would normally be snow fell as rain. On one of those stormed-in days Luke came by Nara's office.

'I just came by to see how you were doing.'

She smiled. 'I'm glad you came. I wanted to show you my animals.'

They donned their padded jackets; the aquarium was always kept dark and cold, to simulate undersea conditions. Inside, eight large tanks were illuminated. Nara stopped at each to insert her arm and extract one of the creatures inside. She presented him with starfish, sea-spiders, sea squirts, giant sponges. He took them in his hands, a little hesitantly. 'You never know what they might do,' he joked. The truth was, he found the marine animals in the Antarctic threatening; the giant sponges, giant sea-spiders, the carnivorous, snake-like leopard seals. He could not believe the small woman in front of him willingly dove among them, beneath the ice.

'Look – the sea-squirts have shrunk to half their normal

size.' She held one up for him. It looked like a soggy turnip, but shrivelled.

'What's wrong with them?'

'I'm killing them.'

'Why?'

'So that we can know the upper temperature threshold of survivability. We put more and more carbon dioxide into the water, and raise the water temperature to see how warm the water needs to get before they are adversely affected,' she said. 'We're trying to simulate the warming we expect to take place around the peninsula in the next fifty years or so.'

'So you get a sense of when they might become extinct.'

'Exactly.'

'But you can't do anything about it,' he said. 'I mean, to keep them alive. Long-term.'

She placed the sea-squirt back in the water. 'No.'

They moved on, Nara checking the sea urchins with their disintegrating limestone shells, the brachiopods, the latumula clams which looked like antique Dutch shoes poking from under brocade gowns. These clams lived in the mud of the seabed floor, she told him; the only way to bring them to the surface was by box-coring, a form of dredging, she explained. They came up, gold flecks in cement-grey Antarctic sea-mud. 'Fool's gold clams, they used to be called.'

The clams, he saw, were hooked to delicate monitors, like intensive care patients, tendrils of wire floating in the water like seaweed. 'What's that for?'

'To monitor their heartbeat and rate of respiration.'

'What does that tell you?'

'How distressed they become, as we raise the temperature. They all have a different threshold at which they will stop functioning. We think they'll be the first to become extinct.'

He shook his head. 'The thought of you spending the

winter here, in this cold aquarium, watching all these animals die.'

She looked at them, seeing them with Luke's eyes, suddenly: small things, trapped in incubators. Babies, ventilators, warm skin. Incubators give life, not take it away, as she is doing. Their nervous systems frayed like bad electrical wiring.

'In the Ellsworths you said you wanted to get away from someone,' Luke said.

She nodded. 'I didn't actually apply, you know. Or at least not intentionally. They rang me up because someone dropped out, and the interview panel knew my supervisor.'

It was late May when she went up to Cambridge to the Polar Research Council for her interview. She had sat in a hot train carriage full of mothers with flush-faced babies melting in pushchairs. The job had initially been offered to a woman who had become – suddenly and unexpectedly, Nara assumed – pregnant, and they re-advertised the post.

The panel fixed her with severe stares. Even now, twenty years after the first women wintered at Adelaide base, they said, the ratio of men to women was still three-quarters to one. 'This can be a difficult environment,' the chair of the panel – an eminent marine biologist – said. She would come under pressure to have a relationship, they told her, to pair off. How did she feel about that? She replied she didn't think she was a peer pressure type. If she got pregnant in the Antarctic, they said, she would be taken out immediately. 'The cost to the taxpayer for a winter medical evacuation is approximately three hundred and fifty thousand pounds,' said the physicist.

It was in her mind to say, *I won't get pregnant, no matter what*. Or, *If I do, I'll pay the taxpayer back*.

'Mistakes are expensive,' the biologist went on, 'and not very easy to rectify. If you find out that it is a mistake for you to be on the continent after early April, we can't fix it. If you pull out before, we won't have time to find a replacement, and the science that year will be lost.'

'These days people have such strange motives for going to the Antarctic,' said another man – a physicist, she thought, although she could not be sure. 'They want to get out of the world, get away from what's happening.'

'I'm not running away from the world. I'm going to the Antarctic.'

They left her to find her way out of the building. *Thank you, thank you. Nice to have met you. I'm sorry there's no one to show you out. That's fine, I remember the way.*

She did not remember the way. She wandered the wide, blue-carpeted halls, taking what she thought would be her last chance to examine a world she had briefly brushed up against, but which would never be part of her life.

The corridors were lined with large, lightbox-lit photographs of whales, penguins, ice-core drills, planes, ships, their hulls blood-bright against the ice. Down one particularly abandoned corridor she found the historic gallery – old expedition photos of men with beards and dogs, ice sculptures dripping from both noses. And her reflection, superimposed on penguins, on giant superstructures of bases-in-progress, or at least someone very much like her: a small woman, fine-featured, eyes two dark stones. She was judged pretty, she knew, by most men's standards, but an indefinite quality in her, a stillness like a dark bowl, would always keep men away.

The corridors were unusually wide; on each side were doors leading to offices or labs; each door had only a small slot window, like prison cells. She stayed there for some time, spying as white-coated scientists filtered seawater and slid trays in and out of mass spectrometers. When she finally found the reception area and the exit, it was by accident.

They were outside the aquarium now, taking off their jackets. Nara offered to make him a cup of tea, to warm up. 'So you see,' she said, 'I was second choice.'

Luke shook his head. 'I don't see it that way. You were meant to get the job, and the other woman wasn't.'

'I don't think anything is meant to be. I think things just happen.'

'Certain things could go either way, yes, but I think there are things which are supposed to happen, for one reason or another. The Antarctic is one of them.'

After Luke left she went back to reading the newspaper online: gun warfare on the streets of south London, ten people dead in a month. Migrants from Mauritania thrown to the sharks by their traffickers, a hijack attempt on an airliner in Russia by Muslim separatists. Two pages in the science/environment section were given to oil prospecting in the Arctic; since the summer sea ice had retreated sufficiently to allow exploration nearly ten years before, Russia had erected offshore platforms, just beyond the boundary of the ice. Seismic ships and temporary drilling platforms sucked oil from the Lemonsov ridge. In the International Court in the Hague, Russia, the United States and Canada were in dispute over territorial rights to the Northwest Passage: it was a new Cold War; the newspapers had dubbed it the Ice War.

The news seemed unreal. On base they called the rest of the world the *Real World*, or *Out There*. Out There, people were dying. In the summers they died of heat exhaustion, in the winter of influenza. Here, nothing would touch them. The world could combust in nuclear warfare, and the katabatic winds of the continent would protect them. Radiation would simply circle the earth thousands of miles above them, driven by the Coriolis effect, which had little influence on the winds of the extreme southern hemisphere. Southern

Patagonia and Antarctica would be unscathed. They would survive, for a while at least, until the food stocks ran out.

What they feared most in the Antarctic, it turned out, was not cold or disease, but fire. Fire could not be contained, it took hold in seconds, fuelled by the dryness of the air. If the buildings burnt down they would be left exposed. So they do fire drills, fire alarm tests, oil spill drills, fire-fighting exercises, donning smoke hoods, wielding fire extinguishers. The whoop of the alarm every Wednesday morning, all of them standing on the deck, shivering.

In the Antarctic, the change of the seasons is abrupt. Suddenly the dynamic brightness of summer is gone, like a giant klieg light switched off. There is no enchantment in the polar day, she realises, only these solar floodlights, ruthlessly simplified, dragging all energy into reverse; the sun was so full of light it turned black. It lacks vigour, somehow, this blizzard of white, an overdose of blankness. It feeds and exhausts her at once. She is thirsty, always. Her skin is puckered with need for moisture. Her throat is parched.

The eternal whiteness of the savage day. Outside her window, the glacier burns, consumed by its lack of pigment. This place, is it one of possibilities, or impossibilities? Soon it would reveal itself. She has no memory now – of the lakes, of swimming, years spent trying to untangle herself from her family. Here she is safe, but also futureless. Here, seeing means nothing. This place has been unwitnessed for so long, it repels the human eye effortlessly. These early winter nights before she falls asleep a voice springs up inside her head – it is not her voice, perhaps it is not even human. It is coming through her, travelling from a long way away. It asks her a hunted question: *Will the world end in ice, or fire, or will it simply wear away?*

PART III

Running Out of Night

1

He does not know her yet, but she sits ten rows behind him on the Dreamliner, Boeing's long-range, low-emissions aircraft which had come into service a few years before. He declines to travel business class, even if the FCO would pay. He doesn't believe in privilege. *You burn up the same carbon whether you sit in first or steerage* is Kate's response, whose use of 'steerage' makes him wince; it strikes him as vulgar and elitist. Outside his porthole is the dark night, the Brazilian rainforest beneath him.

He rarely reads on flights these days, or watches films. He finds enough to entertain him in watching the flight map: the skycam, the tailcam, the plane silver and spookily artificial, like a holograph, clouds scudding beneath it, the temperature screen (–63°C), the kilometres to destination (4,603). At the bottom of the flight map is a blue-white landmass. The map gives it identifying place-names, but not its one true name: Antarctica.

He silently recites the names of its explorers: Drake, Darwin, Cook, Weddell, Palmer, Biscoe, Bellingshausen, Ross, who as captain of the ships HMS *Erebus* and HMS *Terror* was an early oceanographer, undertaking comprehensive studies of the ocean. It was he who first saw the great volcano, which he named after the *Erebus*. Then D'urville, Drygalski, the Scot Bruce, Charcot, whose expedition was named Porquoi Pas. Why not, indeed? Why not go to the Antarctic, why not perform mapping, geology, glaciology, botany, tidal observations?

His great-grandfather had been part of this world; a naturalist, he signed on to Shackleton's *Endurance* expedition in

1913 and spent 1915–16 trapped in ice, fighting for his life. His great-grandfather had been a great naturalist, but ended up being remembered for a feat of survival. He ought to have followed his ancestor's example, chosen a life of a frenzy of cataloguing, acquiring knowledge of the earth, doing inventories; the simplicity and reassurance of measurements, of inquiry. Instead he had waded into the slew of politics.

Ten rows behind him she is unknown, even if he has caught a glimpse of her while standing in the queue at Heathrow, the sort of glimpse that is so instantly forgotten it turns up later in dreams, and he wonders, *how did I dream that stranger's face into being? I am sure I have never seen that face before*. But he has, of course, in the queue at Heathrow. On the Dreamliner Helen might be a dream, she might not exist at all, she might be someone he invents in a future reverie. We dream ourselves into being as much as anything that could be said to lead to a more solid existence: David firmly believed that much of life was illusory. This was a great secret, especially in the circles he moved in, of facts and decisions and legal measures and instruments. He thinks. *We glow, we are blind arrows in the night.*

At the instant the thought blooms in David's mind, two fishermen in one of the countless tributaries of the Amazon River near the town of Santarém look up into the sky and see thin lights, far away: a slim fish, high above them, streaking through the night.

Later, Helen would not be able to remember the first thing they said to each other. It must have been in Chile, at their Santiago hotel. A comment about the weather, the sudden rush of heat and light of the southern hemisphere summer. It was late November and they had left behind a watery, mild autumn. The sun shone in her eyes.

'I can't find my sunglasses,' she said, and squinted unhappily.

She wanted no man to see her wrinkled brow, the two lines which had appeared, seemingly overnight, beneath her eyes only a year ago and had spent the past twelve months entrenching themselves. Until recently she could have been taken for a very young woman. Now she saw people sizing her up, trying to date her. She might be very young or surprisingly old.

For all she knew, this was what he was thinking, this tall man in front of her, obscured by a stab of sunlight. His face wanted to be stern, she could see, but it had a sensitive cast, with large brown eyes.

'Is this your first time South?'

Antarctic people referred to the continent with this shorthand – 'South' – as if nothing else southerly existed. Before she'd had a chance to challenge this man's geographic arrogance, his mobile phone rang. 'Sorry,' he said – unusual enough, these days, to apologise before taking a call on a mobile – and he'd walked off, beyond hearing distance. She watched him for a second or two, his expression concentrated, unsmiling. A checking-in, I'm-here-yes, expression. *Wife*, she thought.

Around them, a group of Chileans circulated. A corporate meeting, she guessed, the men in suits, the women in skirts of dusty pink or orange, far more colourful than you would see in England at such a function. She wondered what they made of the motley Antarctic crew who had stumbled off the plane only two hours ago milling about restlessly, pale from a distant winter.

David was still talking on the phone. She considered leaving, but their hotel rooms were still being prepared. She sat down on a lounger next to the pool, underneath an unfamiliar tree with blood-red leaves. From that position she studied him. He had made another call on his phone; now his expression was alert, despite his obvious fatigue: work call. Helen had the impression she knew him. It was not impossible; their paths might have crossed at some function or other, some seminar on future climactic doom. But when they had been talking she'd had a flash, a visual picture, of a glassy flat, a silver river rimmed by marshlands. It had come and gone in a second.

And then perhaps they exchanged a word or two in the airport the next day, before boarding the plane that took them on their hopscotch flight to Puerto Montt, then Punta Arenas, then finally to the Falkland Islands, which the LAN-Chile crew rigorously called Malvinas/Falklands, although with a scurrying pronunciation – 'Vaklan' – as if they did not want to say the word at all.

Then the terrifying landing at the military airport on East Falkland, the plane sheared sideways by the most forceful crosswind she had ever felt in twenty years of white-knuckled landings in terrible places, skirting mustard-coloured hills streaked by rivers of grey stone. Then the shock of the military nature of the airport – jeeps driven at breakneck speed by men in fatigues, planes with no distinguishing markers, which reminded her of the renditions flights she had seen sitting on the tarmac in Kandahar, the squat Chinook helicopters on the apron, also familiar, their bellies slit open to reveal troops in combat fatigues. Inside there was a separate queue for civilians and personnel. Alert Code BIKINI, read a sign above the luggage carousel. Was that good or bad? she wondered. Beside it, a sign informed them that THE ENEMY IS LISTENING. Yet another instructed people in Spanish to prepare their passports for inspection, and listed items which could not be brought into the islands, among them guns and fruit.

They milled about outside the airport. She was unused to milling, to waiting for other people. They were a manifest, a sequence of names to be herded onto the rickety bus that would carry them from the military airport into the capital, where she will be billeted, two or more to a room, with other women. She wanted to turn to someone and say, 'I don't remember enlisting in the Army.'

On the trip into Stanley she looked out the window and saw dingy sheep, the road lined with Danger! Land mines! signs, little black skulls on them. The sun came out and she had to close her eyes. How strange the light of the Falklands was, she thought, like staring into white bones.

By the time they pulled up in Stanley the day had darkened. The town centre consisted of a few government buildings, a supermarket, a church, and their hotel. Helen was just old enough to remember the grainy images of the War on television, the crippled destroyers listing in the water, their hulls ripped open by Exocet missiles. Even though she had done her share of war reporting, she had never expected to find herself in the landscape of those photographs and faded videos. The place looked just the same: windswept and jerry-built, the mustard hills, the mottled khaki grass.

At their hotel, the reception desk was empty. Eventually a man with a Midlands accent wearing a kitchen apron and carrying a meat cleaver showed up, opened an envelope, and out spilled their keys. 'Sorry,' he said. 'Have to go back to making dinner.' She exchanged looks with the tall man she'd spoken to in Santiago.

'It could have been worse,' she said. 'He could have gone for us with the meat cleaver.'

'Welcome to the Goose,' he said; in his voice a hint of *You'll see.*

The hotel was perhaps an intentional simulacra of a Scottish hotel of a hundred years before, with musty carpets of blue and pink thistles, matching floral sofas and floral wallpaper. Their meals were paid for, but drink was not. Cash only, no cards accepted. The Islands were in a twenty-year-old time-warp of their own, Helen judged, marooned somewhere around 1995. The islanders looked like they'd stepped out of a BBC newsreel, with their too-big spectacles, their amphibious Barbour gear. They had a ruddy-windswept complexion, but also wrinkled and haggard – victims perhaps of the low ozone cover over the Islands.

Helen caught sight of the tall man again at dinner. He wasn't eating with the rest of the conscripts in the dining room, that was clear; he wore a dinner jacket and a tie. He looked hurried, and distracted, as if there was anywhere one could hurry to, in such a place.

After dinner she went for a walk in a stinging, bitter wind. Wavelets lapped against the shores of the narrow harbour. The few streetlights cast a smudged light onto the pavements, and jeeps tore up and down the main road. She walked facing the wind and the sleet. And this was summer!

She arrived back at the hotel in time to see the tall man leave the front door, his dinner jacket covered by a windbreaker, walking head down up the road, into the wind.

David's visits to the Islands follow a pattern: there is the meeting with the governor at Government House, followed by a reception for the local councillors and the MP, if she is in the Islands. During the summer season when the HMS *Resolute* is in town, he has a briefing with the Navy commander.

The governor's house is stocked with antiques that had taken a battering on their journey down the length of the Atlantic. Chipped edges. A cloudy mirror. Sherry (they still served it!) was doled out before dinner. *Is that so? I would have thought Falklands House and the FCO might have joined forces on that one.* Conversations with the governor, the chief of police, the commander of Mount Pleasant base.

Tonight he was on automatic. He liked the Islands, he cared about their fate. Why then could he not concentrate? His eye was drawn out the window, where pale lupines blew in the wind. Something the woman had said, in Santiago, the historian/journalist. About always having been fascinated by the stories of the explorers' trials, but feeling locked out, because she was a woman.

He'd said, it's not like that anymore. You can trek across the continent, if you want to. Plenty of women have done it.

Not plenty, she'd corrected him. In fact, only five or six. And then listed their names. Oh, he had said. Point taken. And felt foolish, then. As if he were in a meeting in a cabinet room, arguing over the nuances of fishing rights. He could have said something witty, encouraging. *Point taken.*

'David? How long do you think The Hague will take to rule on the Weddell Sea claim?'

'Not as long as they took to rule on the Scotia Sea, let's hope.'

The exploration operation for seabed oil was run out of the Falklands. Seismic ships were anchored in Stanley Sound. He would make many, many more trips to the islands to sort through the thorny matter of resource exploration, natural gas sinks, the inevitable outrage of the Argentines.

'What do you think, David – will the Treaty hold?'

'That's what I spend most of my time on now. It's not easy. The Russians are riding high on their oil finds in the Arctic. People are desperate to find new supplies.'

He had not answered the question. This was his special and relatively recently acquired skill, to dodge giving a truthful answer. The FCO had sent him on a flock of courses: Media Management, Public Speaking, Techniques of Information Disclosure. So he did not say: *I think the Antarctic Treaty's days are numbered.* Soon it will no longer be a continent set aside for science, free of land grabs, of pollution and exploitation. The world had given up on the ice caps; all the science pointed to their inevitable disappearance. *Let the ice melt, then, if there's nothing we can do about it, and get on with mitigating the damage.* These were sentiments uttered in cabinet briefings, in phone conversations between world leaders that David was suddenly privy to, as Polar Man.

In the meantime the ice sheets could be mined, for data, yes, for clues as to how they were all going to survive a sudden five-degree temperature rise, because this had happened in the past. The ice cores proved it. But the last time the temperature had jumped five degrees there had been no humans on the planet, or very few.

Their ship was delayed somewhere around South Georgia; the governor informed David, but in fact he'd already heard the news from the FIPASS chief, who'd got the news on HF radio. News travelled fast in the Falklands. This was another reason he liked the Islands – the chain of command just did not exist. You found out vital pieces of information in the queue at the West Store supermarket.

Eventually, someone said, as they always did, *Did you know David's great-grandfather was*... And pointed to the picture hanging above the mantelpiece. David was required to turn his face and pay homage to his ancestor.

'He was one of the men plucked off Elephant Island by Shackleton,' the governor explained to his guests. 'Just as they teetered on the edge of starvation.' *And, some said, insanity*, David added, mentally.

His great-grandfather was another reason why David was Polar Man: he had the pedigree, and even while he fought against privilege, against inheritance, he realised it had shaped his life. He turned to face his ancestor, who stood with his comrades, four men in fishermen's jumpers, their skin blackened with soot from the blubber stoves they cooked on, underneath the upturned lifeboat which was their only shelter. His mother used to tell him he was a carbon copy, with his tall frame and large brown eyes, a face with the skin pulled tightly to the skull. David wasn't sure. His great-grandfather looked tense, handsome, transfixed by a remote awareness, one that was made available to very few human beings. His was a learned face, not in any way indulged but not corroded either, by lassitude or self-satisfaction or by any other flaccid, difficult-to-spot vice. Perhaps he had been burnt by other, more delicate terrors – luck, randomness, will. Life was random, unearned and undeserved – of this David was sure, and he hadn't had to spend three months marooned and left for nearly dead on a sub-Antarctic island to find this out. The most deserving suffer, the spiteful prosper. This is not God's will. These are just the things that happen. *That's life!*

'Yes, yes,' David said, a little impatiently, he realised. 'That was my great-grandfather.' And now, exactly one hundred years later, a toast went up to him, and all the men who had survived the disaster of their expedition.

Dinner was over. People were looking to turn in; the Falklands kept farmers' hours, still. And then he was free – out into the night, free to think his own thoughts, to craft renegade opinions. Should anyone have observed him at that moment they would have seen a man walking alone down a deserted street, dressed in a dinner suit and windbreaker, grinning.

At the hotel he finds the group sitting in the bar. Although his official intention is to go to bed, he decides at the last minute to take the only empty chair, next to the journalist – *historian*! He has her labelled as a journalist, and somehow he knows this will annoy her. Helen, that's her name.

'How are you getting your bearings?' he asks.

'I have no idea where I am,' she says. Her smile is wide and unstable. 'We've all been drinking since dinner. I'm shattered. I have no idea where I am. Oh, sorry, I've already said that. Where have you been all night then?'

He tells her about the Government House reception.

'It's good to know Maggie's memory is alive and well –' she points to a portrait of the ex-prime minister, hanging triumphant on the hotel wall.

David thinks, this woman will be Labour or Lib Dem, so he refrains from saying, *actually I quite admire some of the things she did when in office. I think history will absolve her.* Instead he talks about the Antarctic. 'It's completely insane, the appeal of the place. You'll see. When you're there, you miss home, the people you love. You think, get me out of here! As soon as you're out you start scheming to get back. That's all you want to do, all you can think: get me back to the Antarctic.'

David so loves this chapter of the experience: unless you were flying in and stuck in the Falklands due to weather, the days before leaving for the Antarctic always harboured expectation, the pull of an enigma. Even if they would eventually pull up to a stark wharf ringed by green outbuildings situated among piles of loose shale, like a granite quarry, and they would all be shocked at the isolation, at the simplicity.

She laughs, and he can see this delights her, too, this paradox and wonder. They are going to a place where there is nothing, and they are so excited, like children. Look at him, he has been to the Antarctic eight times now, and he still loves it.

'Even here, in the Islands,' she begins, 'I can feel the pull of something, just over the horizon. It feels like we're about to go to a colony, or another planet. I feel like I'm leaving the world.'

'You are,' he said. 'Travelling to the Antarctic is like going nowhere else, except maybe outer space. It's the last place in the world without money or cars. And home to no one. It's nobody's country.'

'Do you think about the Antarctic,' she asks, 'when you are home?'

'Yes,' he says. Then, ' No.' He pauses. 'I mean, yes and no.'

She laughs and again he sees her wide, spontaneous laugh, how alive to the contradictions of life she is. And also something else… she has been set free, although he is not sure from what. Not from drinks parties, official duties, the burden of serving Her Majesty's Government. No, her release is more mysterious.

'Yes,' he clarifies, once and for all. 'I think about the Antarctic all the time. I miss it, even when I'm there.'

'Why?'

'I think it's because I'm always aware of leaving. That it will soon be time to leave, or other people are leaving, or that no one can ever stay there. The Antarctic forces you to live for the moment. You want to stay there forever, and you know you can't, and are simultaneously relieved that you will eventually have to go.'

He finds she is staring at him with a sobered expression.

'But don't quote me on any of this,' he smiles.

'Don't worry. I probably won't quote you on anything.'

He looks at her, momentarily shocked, then sees she is joking. 'Good,' he says, and laughs. 'I'd be really put out if you didn't quote me on something.'

Their group roars with ragged, disapproving laugher, some shared and ribald joke that David and Helen have missed due to their private conversation, and they all order another round.

He stays up far too late and drinks far too much. On his way to bed that night, climbing the uncertain stairs up to the second floor and no longer in Helen's company, David has a familiar feeling; it is very like what he feels for the Antarctic when he is away from it, or has been prevented from returning to it – an indefinite, treacherous growl of separation.

The next morning Helen walked out into a bleached, punishing sun. She had been warned to wear sunscreen in the Islands, no matter the weather. The ozone 'hole' may have partially knit itself together, but ozone cover was still very thin in the Southern Ocean.

She had read that the Islands lay at the same latitude south as London occupied north, more or less, 51.15 degrees, but the light was entirely different. There was a harried, beacon quality to it, as if it were eager to move on once it had identified what lived under its spotlight. The light did not disperse itself through the sky, but fell in shards, like glass or metal. Then there was the wind, which arrived in bucking sheets from the west. The weather changed several times a day – sun, cloud, hail, sleet, then sun again, within hours. But always there was the wind. It never seemed to calm.

David was walking down the road on the other side in the other direction. She watched as he crossed the road, first looking out for hurtling Land Rovers.

'Did you hear about the ship?'

'Yes, I saw.' A scrawled piece of paper had gone up on the hotel notice board that morning to say that their ship would be three days late coming into port.

He stuck his hands in his pockets and straightened. A blast of wind hit him in the back, and he lurched toward her, stopping just shy of her body. 'Sorry,' he said. 'It's not unusual, but it means we'll be late getting away. There's a lot of cargo to be loaded I hear.'

'I'm actually relieved,' she said. 'I wanted to spend a few more days here.'

He raised his eyebrows. 'A few more days to get blown down by the wind and shop for stuffed penguins?'

'I sort of like it here.' She threw her gaze out to Ross Road, taking in the brightly painted houses and picket fences, the Araucaria trees, the gift shops that catered to cruise ship tourists which lined the harbour. 'It's surreal, flying all this way only to end up in the UK.'

'But it's not the UK at all. It just looks like it is; actually the Islands are becoming more and more South American.'

'Do you come here often?'

'Once a year, usually. Some years delegates come from the Islands and we meet in London. I always feel relieved not to have to come all the way here – carbon guilt and all that – but I find that if I miss a year, I miss the Islands. It's strange.' He frowned, obscurely. 'So, are you going to the Curry Night tonight?' The hotel's weekly menu stated that Wednesday was curry night, Thursday pizza night, Fridays was an *asado* – a barbecue. 'I guess that's the one Argentine word the islanders let pass,' Helen said.

'No, there's quite a few, actually,' David said, with enthusiasm. 'All the words for horses' tack, and for sheep-shearing, are from Patagonia. They call each other "Che", too, which is as Argentine as you get. Although you have to be a real Falkland Islander, born and bred, to earn the right to be called that.'

There was the faintest tinge of politeness in Helen's expression. 'Sorry,' he said. 'I have a tendency to lecture.'

'That's all right. I have a lot to learn.'

They went their separate ways, then, Helen into the wind, and David down the street, blown along by ragged gusts.

The following day the wind dropped; in the summer, Helen had been told, windless days in the Falklands were rare. On David's suggestion they went for a walk to Gypsy Cove – he usually did this walk when he had what he called 'downtime' in the Islands.

They set out along a footpath which skirted the harbour and FIPASS, the floating dock facility where they would board their ship in two days' time. A fisheries patrol vessel was moored next to the *Resolute*.

'That's where I'll be tonight,' David said, pointing at the destroyer. 'Officially, it's a drinks party. But I have to sneak away and discuss something with the commander.'

'*Something*,' she smiled. 'I see.'

'Well, you're a journalist, aren't you? I can't exactly spill the beans.'

'I used to be a journalist. I'm more of an historian, now.'

'But you're writing about something that happened four years ago. That's journalism, not history.'

'I don't think there's any rule about how much time has to pass before something is considered history.'

They walked on, picking their way through the dense scrub of the shoreline. Clumps of spiny moss, like shrunken shrubs, threatened to trip her up. 'That's Diddle-dee,' David said. 'It's actually a shrub, although it's so small you'd never think it. There's an amazing biodiversity on the Islands, considering how barren they are. There's even a native strawberry. You'd never think anything so delicate would survive here.'

'You know a lot about the Islands.'

'I've picked up a few things over the years. Interminable UK Overseas Territories Conservation conferences, that sort of thing.'

She had the impression that the rueful tone was somehow for her benefit, and that David actually enjoyed these conferences. She might think him a jobsworth civil servant, someone towing Her Majesty's line – sherry parties, House of Commons lunches. And he might be right, she might have made these judgements, had they been anywhere other than in the suspended animation of the Falkland Islands, walking together past rusting hulks of abandoned ships to look at penguins.

'Why don't they get rid of these things? That's the fourth wreck I've seen in the harbour.'

'There are ten in all, maybe eleven. They're part of the history of the place. Who would do it, anyway? They've got no value as salvage.' This might be the voice David used in meetings – impatient, clipped, enamoured of the facts. 'So what is it that interests you about the sea-ice incident?'

She had been waiting for this question. That it came now, between gusts of wind as they walked up the powdery track to Gypsy Cove, was merely a matter of timing. He'd been wanting to ask it, she had sensed, since they had met.

'I met someone who knew her, a friend of hers. She showed me some of the emails she sent from base that winter. And –' here she paused as a sheet of wind tore the words from her mouth. 'I was intrigued. She wrote very beautifully –'

'About what?'

'About being in the Antarctic, about what she was feeling, what she was experiencing.'

'There were rumours that she lost it, basically.'

She ground to a halt. 'You mean, lost composure?'

'I mean lost sanity. But I didn't want to say that.'

'I don't think she was insane at all.'

He studied her. She could imagine him thinking, I've hit a nerve, there. Or perhaps, that's what women always say, defending insanity out of some suite of emotional hurts.

'Most people think it was suicide.'

She had heard this, too. Beside her, he was waiting for her reaction – how she would weigh in on the issue.

'I don't know. I never write my story before I write my story.'

'The Antarctic can be a very bad experience, or it can be very, very good,' David observed. 'It's hardly ever anything between.'

'Thanks for that,' she said.

'You know, I didn't ask to be your chaperone. I don't work for the PR department. I work for the Foreign Office.'

'I didn't ask for a chaperone. The only reason I have one is that you have something to hide.'

'I have something to hide?'

'Not you personally. But, I mean –' here she flung her hands down in frustration. 'Someone *died* here. Did you really think there would be no interest in this? That no one would care?'

'We let you come down, didn't we? If there were anything to hide, that wouldn't have happened. Why are you interested in it? Is it some indirect vengeance of yours?'

He was smarter than she thought, this man. She did not answer, or tell him the reason for her interest, because she did not know herself. For the first time in her adult life, she had decided to allow a mystery to overtake her. She could not explain her motivations.

Depending on how well she got to know this man standing beside her now, dressed in a blue windbreaker and a boyish knit hat, she might tell him why, as far as she understood it. She might tell him everything. Nothing about him invited her confidences; perhaps that was why she wanted to give them to him.

David was walking ahead of her now, making his way down to the beach, threading through the Danger! Land Mines! signs. She hadn't seen these since Afghanistan, ten years ago. Although the mines lining the Falklands shores were much older. They had been left deliberately, as a live memorial to the war. Occasionally sheep wandered into a minefield and were blown up.

Ahead of her on the path down to the beach, David turned. His body had a 'aren't you coming?' inflection. He was stiff, she decided, it was there in the way he walked – a tall, upright man, a militaristic bearing, but also somehow the posture of someone who had missed his calling. This was a subtle, vaporous impression, but it was there.

'The clouds –' she pointed to where grey clouds spiralled in the distant sky, like a tornado.

'Oh, we'll get a bit wet. Don't worry.'

'As long as we don't get blown up.'

'That I can't promise.'

She followed David down the path to the beach. As she descended, she noticed little hillocks on either side of the path, framed by an aperture, perfectly round. These were the burrows of Magellanic penguins. The penguins themselves had gone for a swim. She watched as they emerged one by one or in pairs from the sea, shaking themselves dry at the edge of the breakers. Magellanics were small, dinner-suited creatures. The penguins waddled up the beach and right past them, as if the two humans did not exist at all.

2

It was late afternoon when Luke left Bluefields. His co-pilot, the nervous field assistant, was so exhausted from their days of shifting fuel drums that he'd fallen asleep on takeoff.

In any case, whether Andy/Mark was awake or not, he was flying alone. Not that the younger man didn't talk, rather Luke was struck by how little this new generation listened, a deficiency he was convinced was linked to their inability to live in the moment, preferring to take photographs out the window before turning the camera on themselves to take a self-portrait, already basking in their audience's amazement. They were too busy recording the moment to live it.

Nara had been different. She was quiet, thoughtful. She had listened to his stories of the years he spent flying in Alaska, the Yukon, the landscape made ragged through successive waves of grandeur, glaciers, the rigid permafrost, hurtling seasons of melt. He had seen some wondrous things beneath him, he had told her: the mighty Mackenzie River, snaking all the way up to the rim of the continent, herds of caribou gathering and dispersing across the tundra like clouds, floating ice sheets fermenting with heat, nudged by Russian and Canadian icebreakers. Blankets of wildflowers; from the air, they throbbed, dark, lurid mauves, pulsating in waves of undulating colours, or sharp dandelion yellows.

After those years of adventures, he had gotten married and taken a job down South. If he had ever been Canadian, he had discarded that identity years ago, shuttling as he did between South Africa, his wife's country, the UK, and the Antarctic. A British passport had bought him a spell in the Army, when he had been deployed to Kuwait in the first Gulf War.

After he left the forces there was a stint as a commercial pilot flying 737s out of Edinburgh and Glasgow. He truly felt like a bus driver then; the job had been less about flying – the planes did it all for you these days anyway – and more about signing off manifests, calculating fuel payloads, paying his union dues and licences, cardiograms, eyesight tests, programming the airliner to pick itself up and put itself down, flying with a co-pilot whose name he often did not know and promptly forgot, to his embarassment, to Brussels, Amsterdam, Copenhagen, Oslo, Bergen; this was his route, the dark channel of the North Sea, studded with increasinlgy twitchy oil rigs, siphoning the last of the North Sea oil from the seabed floor.

To all this, Nara had listened. He had felt the force of this young woman focussing on his life, and was flattered. Had he been so mistaken to think that listening of that calibre and intensity might itself be a kind of love?

That summer on the ferry flight to Canada he wrote to her all the way; every time they put the plane down he raced to find a computer, such had been his feeling of separation. She was down there – that was how he saw her, beneath him, underneath all of them, holding up the planet with her thin, girlish shoulders – trapped behind a wall called winter. Even while he was fending off mosquitoes and having ungainly conversations with his children about how school was going, as he refreshed his flying skills in a simulator at the aircraft manufacturer's headquarters, the sun blaring outside, bears lumbering through the forest, berries thickening, he would think of her in that barren place, the sky lacquered with cold stars, the steel dusk, and feel afraid for her.

For the first time in a long time, since his children were small, perhaps, he was afraid on behalf of someone else, afraid that he might never see her again, that some accident, some unforeseen occurrence (his licence not being renewed because of a bad result on his ECG, you never knew) would prevent him from returning to her. And he had felt another apprehension, far more difficult to define: that she would suffer in a way not of her own making, in a way she would not be able to escape from.

The black strip of the runway was in his sights now. He retracted the skis. It was near midnight but the sun glared, silver-orange, his constant beacon. How sweet it was, that he never saw winter, only migrated from the steepest curve of the northern hemisphere summer to the southern equivalent every season. What was that word? *Heliotropic*. It meant an animal or a flower that follows the sun. He was tuned to the earth's magnetic field to guide him up and down the planet, and like an Arctic tern he barely saw darkness. He had become, without meaning to, a creature of the light.

3

On the ship I decided to keep a diary, but found I could only write about the weather:

December 5th, 2016. We have been at sea now for three days. Lead sky polished by sunbeams. Tobacco undersides of icebergs, stained with brown algae. Toothpaste mints; greens, blues. Sallow oyster sky on overcast days. Sky and sea, sky and sea, and the ice a mirror between them.

On our journey to the Antarctic, every day everything changed: the light, the sea, the birds who accompanied the ship, ecstatic to be given a free supper from the krill churned in our wake.

The forgetting started there, on the ship. The mind intent on avoiding pain is shy, elusive; one of those small slinking animals. Anything might set it off – the sight of a plum, a candle, skin of the same hue. A cold finger on my wrist, where my husband used to touch me, to get my attention. Not a loving gesture, more a controlling one – I never realised that at the time. Perhaps these memories wait for us, until we are in some careless endgame stage, and we can plunge into them again and again, as into a warm swimming pool, in the time before we die.

What is the direction of the flow of memory? From the heart to the mind, or the other way around? The ice rivers here flow in a one-way system: from the interior plateau to the sea, downward, funnelled between rocks, called 'runs'. It is these ice rivers that are pumping out the majority of icebergs excreted by the Antarctic and Greenland.

Psychologists say that memory is born only when an experience is definitively past. But it might work differently in the Antarctic; the lack of new input, the isolation and the unchanging society combine to create the impression of stalled time. Because time never ends, nothing is ever past, and memories do not form. They have to be constructed afterwards through a laborious process of isolating pieces of time. To remember is like visiting a ruin. Jungle palaces, strangled by vines; there we are only tourists in our pasts.

On the ship I realised I no longer thought of the way Eric walked, the flowers he liked, the spot on my throat where he used to kiss me. Other memories, more delicate and dangerous, which my mind avoided as if they had suddenly been furnished with spikes, also vanished.

If memories begin when experience is definitively over, then when does the forgetting start? Only when we are dead, I suspect. I had died there in London, with Eric, and so there was no more memory or thinking or forgetting to do. For years, I felt like a stone. I thought: I can take anything they (I didn't know who I thought these 'they' were) throw at me, now, because I am no longer human, I am only part of the landscape. Of the money problems, the weather, what was happening in the world I thought – but this is ordinary unhappiness, we're built to take this. This isn't really a country to be happy in, anyway. When has England ever been a place to be happy?

I had choices in those years: I could have become austere, I could have been thwarted. Bitterness would gouge my edges like rust. I waited for a choice which did not taste like cold steel in my mouth. Life became an anteroom, somewhere I hung out after the fact, because I had allowed myself to be betrayed, and stupid people worthy of betrayal belonged in waiting lounges, while others flew to throbbing foreign cities. Then, when I was firmly ensconced in this blue room I would argue the other side: everybody's been betrayed. So what? People are completely unreliable, every story you've ever done, every war you've ever covered, has been about that. Did you think you were above ordinary sexual betrayal?

For a long time, maybe a year, I had difficulty sleeping, difficulty letting go. Partly because these silent arguments between myself and myself, this civil war between two internal factions I hadn't known existed, refused to be silenced. Partly I couldn't sleep because it mimicked death, consciousness closing down, the slipping away, followed by a blow, monumental and instant, then a darkness.

I remember turning off the old analogue televisions. Now, with digital, they just snap on and off. Before, the screen never extinguished itself instantly, but remained for a moment, burning – a small white light, nearly invisible, in the middle of the screen. A reluctance, a last look back, a longing.

4

Those first days of the voyage David spent on the bridge. It hummed and blipped with capability – radar, satellite pictures, GPS screens, neon diagrams of the ship's engine and hydraulics systems, depth soundings of the ocean floor. On the radar icebergs showed as untidy yellow wedges. The icefield lay far in the distance still, the officers said, inside the Antarctic Convergence.

He could feel the continent long before it arrived. Soon he would taste that flint air again. The dryness scratching at his throat.

The day before they crossed the Antarctic Convergence icebergs began to appear. David thought of the iceberg as an environment of collapse, a puzzle. It had detached itself from its home, and was now only intent on melt. Glaciofluvial processes had choked it out, until there was nowhere for it to go. *Lacustrine formations. Ogives. Eolian processes. Geliflluction* – he loved the language of melt.

Change was not a simple manoeuvre, performed by temperature rises, flux, ablation, water from ice and ice to water. In human lives, change required crisis which in Greek, as he had never forgot, since doing a single Classics option outside of his social sciences Tripos at Cambridge, means *decision.* The *krisis* is the moment when you walk down one path and forsake the other.

There had been few such moments in his life. For as long as he could remember, David's life had been mapped out, as if an advance cartographic team had been sent into the territory of the future.

His father was Vicar at Great Tew, one of those Cotswold villages on the itineraries of American bus tours in search of the *Brideshead Revisited* version of England. His younger brother Ben had loved growing up there among the stone cottages, the fields with their furtive sheep, secretive forests of ancient pines, rumoured to be undisturbed since Arthur's time. But for David it had been a velvet coffin, a place so comfortable you didn't notice you were actually dead. Of course many heroic men had come from similar places; the moist hedgerows and hydrangeas of England had spawned an entire generation of the horizon-obsessed, men who flung their lives into deserts hot and cold. David could understand why; the only way to neutralise the excess of gentility of such places, their killing reassurances, was to fling yourself at anything wild in a desperate attempt to feel alive. Not being born into an age of exploration, David put his energies into science, then government, but for him these were only tickets to the wild places where he would either find or lose his soul.

Ben had gone to Oxford, and he to Cambridge. This had formalised the rivalry between them. He could see the logic in it: Ben was the more outwardly ambitious and his ambition had a brute muscularity to it. Cambridge, the slightly more effete and intellectual institution of the two, suited David's wayward, questioning nature. They both came out with Firsts, but no one in the family congratulated them. Such a performance was simply expected.

Wood-panelled rooms, candlelit dinners where the ritual decreed no electric lighting could be used, a medieval re-enactment of monkish scholarly solidarity, more men than women – he remembered his education in fragments, visual puzzles. A certain terror of being a 'failure', although in truth failure was a disaster zone he might visit, briefly, as a tourist.

He learned his capacity for self-questioning later, and self-doubt came only in his late twenties. I must have been insufferable, he thought. Only a character like Kate, with her angular confidence, her lack of interest in being understood, could have found him attractive. She was unusual among women in that she did not want anything particularly emotional from their marriage. Outwardly graceful, with a powerful public charm, inwardly she recoiled from love; it was not repression, only her nature – she had been born that way, with the sinuous arrogance of a young prince. He had liked that about her. She would never cling, never make him feel the claustrophobia he felt in the company of many women, who seemed only to want him for the transformation he could enact, in the form of children. He saw this as a game of cold strategy dressed up as family. Or maybe he had simply met the wrong women.

Day two, day three. They were doing oceanography on the way down. Every year they did CTDs of the transport in the Drake Passage. From his perch on the bridge he watched the instrument go down, he watched it come up.

A thought dangled in his mind, an ugly puppet. *I would like to love someone, but I love someone already. Why then this yearning?* And then, *I don't want to give up. Is that the only reason?* This interior judge, a stranger until recently, interrogates him. *Is that all you can come up with?* He tried to keep these thoughts under control by imagining himself wringing their necks. He took each thought in his hands as if it were a delicate animal, and squeezed until he heard it rasp and choke.

He lurched; the ship hit one of the rolling breakers the Drake Passage threw up, and he was thrown sideways.

Yes, he was happy, because he was going to the continent-sized paradox again, the giant mirror at the bottom of the world where the purity of the ice is equivalent to water that has been distilled three times. What he feels for the place is unmistakeable; that is what love feels like, to him, always: a narrowing in the heart, a constriction. As if he will have a heart attack. As if he will die.

He has not made love in a long time, or been made love to. He wonders if this is something you could forget how to do.

He came to look for her, knocking on her cabin door. This alone surprised her, that he should seek out her company.

'We're about to pass Elephant Island. You should take a look. It's not often the ship takes this route…'

'Just give me a minute to get dressed.'

Once on the deck, the wind tore at their throats. They had only been outside for a few minutes, but already she was cold.

'Do you want to go in?'

'No,' she shouted over the wind. 'I just need a few minutes to get used to it.'

Elephant and Clarence Islands were visible on the horizon; a pair of black crags half-covered in cloud, steep rock clad with ice.

'There,' David pointed to a miserable beach of scrappy rock covered in penguin guano. 'That's where my great-grandfather survived.'

David reached in his pocket and brought out a small bottle. 'Family tradition,' David said, unscrewing the cap. 'As soon as we see Elephant Island, we both have to take a drink. I didn't think to bring an extra glass. Sorry. You don't mind, do you?'

'No,' Helen said. 'I don't mind.'

The ship steamed toward the island. It was half shrouded in cloud. On the one side, dark rock streaked by ice. The island sheared the cloud open with its sharp rock.

'On the lee side that's Gnomon Rock. Terrible-looking place, isn't it? They say it has the worst weather in the world.'

'What exactly happened to your great-grandfather here?'

He told her the story, in snatched, breathless phrases, severed by rushes of wind.

'They thought this place was their salvation, but I think the first night they spent on the island was their worst, in their entire journey. Even the ice floes were an improvement.'

Wet, cold, hungry, they had not slept for days. The winds tore down their tents. *We thought for sure we would die*, his great-grandfather had told him. *No one admitted to it later, but yes, we were prepared to die in that place, that night.*

Now here he was, sailing past it in comfort, on a modern ice-strengthened ship. A four-course meal in the salon, jackets and ties, gin and tonics in the bar. What separated him from a starving man, exposed, frozen, lost on that narrow shore, was only time.

'One day part of the glacier across the bay broke off and caused a tsunami, a thirty-foot-high wave, to rush across the bay at them,' David went on. 'The men were completely exposed on this tiny strip of shore. They watched it coming. They were – transfixed, I think. They couldn't move, they could only wait to die, because there was no higher ground – the rocks were covered with ice, the glacier above them unscaleable. But loose ice in the bay broke its crest and the wave swept under them.'

Each day presented some new challenge to the men's survival. They had no real hope of rescue, only faith. They went ashore in April, and Shackleton and three of his men left for South Georgia. May, June, July passed. From August 1st, each day they would rise in the morning and pack up their belongings. Each day they would say, *Today maybe the Boss will come for us.* They had no way of knowing that Shackleton and his men had survived the journey from Elephant Island to South Georgia in the lifeboat called the *James Caird*, shunted across 640 miles of the wildest sea in the world in a leaking wooden dinghy with a makeshift sail and no shelter. By rights Shackleton should have been dead, and his men abandoned to madness or cannibalism or both on Elephant Island.

But the Boss did come, just in time. Two men were 'on the point of losing their reason', as Shackleton later wrote. It took the Boss three attempts to get to them, each time he tried to ram through the ice to them, increasingly desperate. Only five miles of ice separated Shackleton from his men. Once he was close enough to fire a gun, but it sounded too much like a glacier calving and the men did not heed.

For much of his life, David had been thinking about who Shackleton was. He read biographies, he met his relatives, and learned of his charm, his pathological optimism. He was not sure if such characters existed anymore. What had driven them from the world?

If his great-grandfather had not been rescued, finally, on Elephant Island, he would not exist.

But did he possess those men's steely core? He has seen it, in so many members of his family, and in other people descended from the explorers. They are a clan: vast, dispersed, one of those sprawling families who can't remember exactly how they are related. Like the famous actress he met once, a descendent of Scott on her mother's side. He can't get her face out of his mind: a classical face, completely unforgiving. She had the unusually prominent vein running from the skull and transversing the forehead, a feature he remembered from his great-grandfather's stories of her ancestor, the great explorer. 'You could tell when he was angry,' his great-grandfather had said, 'because this vein stood out on his forehead, throbbing like a live wire about to explode.' The actress had a doer's face. David had inherited the face of a thinker. They separated like that in his family: on the one side the doers, the engineers, Army Majors, the explorers. On the other side the scientists, historians. There was no one 'artistic' in his family. Yes, the actress had something of his great-grand-father's self-containedness as well as her own ancestor's heroic profile. Although she herself was small and fine-boned, like a sleek little horse, but with the inner core of molten ice. At a drinks party her eyes had rested on him, and he found himself captivated by their icy grip. She was one of them; he wondered if she knew it.

David passed the bottle to Helen. She tipped it up, took a draught. 'Thank you for surviving on that lonely shore, against all odds, to come back into the world and to give us David, who joins us here on earth now, because of your perseverance, your optimism, your faith. Thank you.' She handed the bottle back to him. 'Sorry, I'm a cheap drunk. No. Cheap speech-maker.'

'I'm in government, I've heard plenty of cheap speeches. Yours isn't so bad. To my forebear, and to Elephant Island, for failing to kill him.'

The Island came and went. There was no trace of those nights spent under the upturned boats, the raging wind, the men blinded by blubber soot, wet to the skin.

They stayed on Monkey Island far longer than either of them meant to, until they finished the bottle of Scotch.

I am being given a chance for a new life, with this trip.

How rare, to discover a portal back into life, through this frozen world. Alive-yet-dead; dead-yet-alive. Would she ever again feel herself to be truly part of life? She is haunted by the thought that she is just a dreaming ghost. On waking, she will discover she is not alive at all, as when ghosts rattle around a beloved house until they can be convinced they are dead.

We do not own our bodies, we do not own our fates. As it

ages, Helen's body is becoming her mother's body. Her fate is not her own, either, but has been decided by something else.

David, too, has been disowned of something he thought his. His great-grandfather's experience has seeped into him. He has been abandoned on a blasted shore. This knowledge is lodged in every cell. In his cells, reindeer wander through the snow. Seals loll in brown pools of blood and urine, the shores slippery with penguin and albatross guano. When the men lay down in their tent that first night on Elephant Island, their body heat melted the guano underneath them. They awoke to find their tent lifted from them by the katabatics sliding down the steep ramparts of the glacier. The stench was unbearable. Their place of salvation was no more than a fresh hell.

David returns to this place every year, under the guise of a professional migration. But the truth is that his body is not his own, his fate is not his own. At times he wonders if he even owns his memories. The tough pale grass which looks like no other grass he has seen in his life, the stern stone covered with a mustard-coloured lichen, hard and ruptured, like barnacles. All this is embedded within him because he felt so at home, the first time he came to this rim of the world, the distant Southern Ocean. *So this is where I belong*, he thought, amazed. He was right, he had been unburdened from a dangerous misperception. He did not own his memories. He did not own his past. These had been bequeathed to him by a force he could not name, and he was merely their caretaker. In the end he would have to hand them back.

They sit in the bar. David is a bit drunk and drink makes him strident.

'What do you expect to get out of this?'

'Get out of it? You mean like resource extraction? Oil? Natural gas?'

'I meant, for your career.'

'I know what you meant.'

A silence. He is bewildered, rather than offended. He tries a different tack. 'How did you become a writer?'

'By accident.'

Why should she tell him that by thirty-five she'd put two abandoned careers behind her: a PhD in history, then journalism. Why should she tell him she is a person who leaves things unfinished, fundamentally a wayward character, fascinated by contradictions, accidents, ironies, bad luck, bad faith.

To the casual acquaintance, Helen would seem a high-spirited character, good company, able to roll with the punches. But in reality she is a Russian doll; several selves collected within this outer carapace, each of them smaller, denser with loss. This was the heaviness, like a shadow in her eye. David was aware of it and like most people he shied away. He was unused to corroded characters, and so fascinated by them, too.

The more time he spends with Helen, the more he is aware of having to keep a complicity at bay. He hopes they will not sour to each other, as often happens – and so quickly – in these environments. Helen is the only person here who is on his level; he sees something of a comrade in her, a true adventurer overtaken by a papery existence, fighting her own destruction. He wonders if she feels the same about him. He knows he is not an easy person to like, remote as he is, detached, given to rituals of austerity. He is a runner, then sits in the sauna, he watches his cholesterol. He rarely drinks. No, he has never been one of those people others flock to, there has never been any admiring throng in his life, only his brother, a few close friends, his parents, his wife.

And Helen, perhaps. Romantic, penitent. Doing time for what sins, he doesn't know.

It is this thought which prompts him to try again. 'There's

nothing there,' he says. 'That's the conundrum of the Antarctic. People love it, they are fascinated with it, but there's nothing there.'

Helen rallies to the thought. 'It's like loving a ghost, then? Or a dead person?'

'I suppose. Most people don't see the point of giving yourself with little expectation of getting anything in return. These people have no business setting foot in the Antarctic.'

'You think it's misguided to ask for something back?'

'People who think they should get something back, that you are somehow owed something in return for having given your heart – yes, I think that's misguided. Or childish, at least.'

'Look at what happened to Scott. He loved the Antarctic, so he expected it to be on his side, and it killed him.'

'He killed himself, more like it, I think,' David says. 'It's a risk; if you love someone or something enough, you can die.'

The ship saws to the side, pitching her into David's shoulder.

'I'm sorry,' he apologises. 'This is all a bit heavy. Seeing Elephant Island always has this effect on me.'

'That's all right.' She pauses. 'I think it would be a sobering sight even if you weren't related to one of the survivors. I always thought, they must have been so relieved to have solid ground underneath their feet. Do you know that when they abandoned ship and formed what they called Ocean Camp, the ice-floe camp, Shackleton was so worried that the ice would give way at night, he ordered the dogs to sleep in their harnesses. He wrote down instructions on a piece of paper for what to do in case the ice broke up, and pinned it on every tent.'

'No,' he says. 'I didn't know that.'

'I saw the notes,' Helen says. 'In the Shackleton Institute.

They have the originals.' The ink had faded to the colour of thin coffee, but she had been able to read them: *muster point at the Boss' tent; leave everything; save dogs, socks, provisions. The cook goes into the boat first.*

David realises this woman knows far, far more than she lets on – about the Antarctic, its history, even his ancestor's expedition, he supposes. She is an historian, after all, why wouldn't she? And yet she has listened to him, never saying, I know that already.

They say goodnight, unsteadily. As they make their way to their cabins the ship lurches underneath them, the stairs rushing up to greet them, then rushing away, so they are sliding down the handrails more than walking They crash into the walls on either sides of the corridor. A groaning sound fills the ship as the hull scrapes against ice.

Helen woke, four hours later, in the middle of the night.

A foggy light filtered through the porthole – she had forgotten to close the nightshade. Now that there was no more night she would need to draw it down in order to sleep. Her throat burned, and she regretted the whisky. The ship's air was very dry.

A chill shot through her. Helen said it aloud, then. *What?* An energy, very powerful, passed through her. As if she had been handed someone else's rage.

In the dusk light as she dressed, she saw – or thought she saw – shadows in the mirror. A pair of eyes that were not her eyes. Hair, longer, darker than her own. There was something about a camera, a flash – someone was taking photographs of herself in the mirror. But when? It wasn't happening now. And then a folding away, as if she had nudged open the edge of an envelope, only enough to see an outline of its contents, before it sealed itself again.

She was so shaken she had to sit down on the edge of her bunk. There was a shadow inside her, but it did not belong to her. It was a mocking, white, scalded rage. As if once released, it had never found anywhere to settle. All this time it had been looking for someone who was open to receiving it. She had never felt anything like it.

That night she spent on the bridge in the company of the Second Officer, who did not question her appearance on the darkened platform high above the ocean in the middle of the night. They sat together in an easy silence, watching the searchlights probe the dusk ahead of them for growlers, those near-invisible lumps of ice substantial enough to sink a ship, and which lurked just beneath the surface.

5

Nara and Alexander met across a dinner table at their hotel in the Falkland Islands, the same musty relic where Helen and David would stay one day in the shadowy rim of time we call the future.

She noticed him, not only for his looks, but because he stared at her. His stares were not searching, or teeming with interest, or even ordinarily judgemental. There was a dull, brutal quality to them, as if he were trying to decide what kind of treatment he would mete out. She stared right back, until he seemed to become aware of it, and averted his eyes.

The ship was delayed coming into port, and their group had several days to kill in the Falklands. They were all dazzled by the light, by daffodils in November, the seasons turned on their head, their sudden release from the encroaching northern hemisphere winter, at being tipped out at the bottom of the world into wafting clouds of yellow gorse.

The stern magic of the Islands astonished her. The capital, Stanley, had a Toytown charm with its white picket fences, its bright-coloured houses of painted corrugated iron. The sharpness of the white in the light, as if giant searchlights had been turned on overhead, setting up a pulsating beaming, ribbons of clouds in the sky, harried, windswept clouds – all this seemed familiar and exotic at once.

Nara and Alexander walked together out to the little airport where red Britten-Norman Islanders came and went, servicing outlying communities. There they found in the departure lounge a giant-scale map of the island. They looked at the jagged coastline, frayed and gouged with coves and fingers and islands brewing with sea lions.

They walked and talked, and she fell in with his long elliptical stride. There was something instantly familiar about his presence and spirit – it was even in his walk, the way his bones moved next to hers.

He talked easily about himself, without self-interest but with a willing spirit. She liked his lack of ceremony, and the bright alertness of his mind.

He told her he was from Devon. He had grown up in a large but not ostentatious house, *an Aga in the kitchen*, he said, with a fond irony – for his mother's predilections, or his class, or the conventionality of it all, she didn't know. He told her his father had been in the Army and that he was dead, killed in a mountain-climbing accident, and that the house was full of photographs of him. Every wall and every corner, he said, his voice wary and wry, like a shrine. Outside the shrine was a rose garden, not decorative but wild.

He was a glaciologist, travelling to the Antarctic on a postdoctoral fellowship. He would spend the winter of 2011–12 there to consolidate his research. Nara asked him what he might do, after the Antarctic, and he replied that he might want to take a job abroad, in Switzerland, or in the US; these were the two world leaders in glaciology. He said all this with a breezy complete optimism, so powerful that he began to take on a golden glow. There were people in the world like this, she knew – doors simply opened, as if on an electronic signal. These people would never know what it was like to scrape and scrape at brick walls until your fingers bled.

Alexander pointed into the sky. 'Look, you can see Venus and Mars tonight.' Mars hung low in the sky, to the southwest, a reddish, ceramic hue. Venus shimmered bright, it threw many times the light of any other star.

There was no light to blur the stars, there was no other land, for thousands of miles. For a moment she thought the lights moving across the sky were planes. But it was only the beam of satellites, and drifting clouds of stars. This was an empty quarter of the planet. Punta Arenas and the tip of Argentina and Chile to the west, and to the east, only random specs: South Georgia, Tristan da Cunha, St Helena, until Cape Town. Planes from Chile to Australia crossed the Pacific. South Africa was thousands of miles to the east. No one flew over the Antarctic because there was nowhere to land, in an emergency.

'I miss seeing the lights of planes in the sky. Here there's only the flight from Ascension,' she said.

'Don't forget the military planes,' Alexander added. Every day, a dank roar ripped through the skies, so loud Nara felt her ears were being torn open. The sound travelled through her; she could even feel its tear in her heart.

They walked through clouds of perfumed gorse, past banks of lupines, past the church with its sculpture of the four giant ribs of whales. The night glowed with a strange undertone, like the dark red of overripe strawberries.

They had done no more than walk under rough skies harried by rigid southerly winds, like tearsheets of corrugated iron. They counted ten shipwrecks in the harbour, rusting in the peaty waters. They read the plaques that spelled out the stories of individual disaster. Ships run aground, or abandoned, long interludes of war, of isolation. The copper water lapped against their sides, rusted to the hue of ceramics. DEFENDER and ENDURANCE were spelled out in white stones across the harbour on dull hills. These were the names of ships which came to rescue and protect the islands in a time of war.

'Well, that's one way to show your gratitude,' Alexander said. He towered above her, wind running through his hair, fastened down with a knitted hat of some Scandinavian design, his windbreaker rustling, his mouth, normally a disdainful cast, erupting into a sudden smile.

They had walked on, sunglasses lowered against the glare of the sea, and the smell always present, fishy, peat, copper, the glitter of the southern Atlantic. Strange birds appeared in the undergrowth, lush geese with velvet heads. She saw brilliance in the dun, savaged hills, in the minefields, in the dirty, half-feral sheep that scrabbled away from the bankside on stick legs, crashing against the stark stone that littered the islands. This was no bitter landscape, but lush with flowers, and gorse, a reversed spring, penguins marching in their huddled armies on deserted white beaches and in tourmaline bays.

They had done all this together, and his presence was familiar and exciting at once. Only a week after meeting him, she felt that if he were to disappear from her side a cold rift would open up inside her.

'Goodnight' he said, and left her at her doorstep.

She opened the door to her temporary home, exhausted by the light, the ground they had covered, and by the knowledge that she was not alone at the end of the world.

The ship was called the *Astrolabe*, named for an instrument used by early astronomers to measure the altitude of stars and planets. Night disappeared somewhere at the bottom of the Drake Passage, after Elephant Island and the tabular icebergs, the exact stretch of ocean where Helen and David would one day salute his ancestor, darkness thinning to a solemn dusk between two and four in the morning. Nara slept only lightly. Every morning she rushed awake, rising buoyant up and up, as if from a depth chamber, harried by a strange zeal.

Everything about the icebergs astounded her. They easily dwarfed the ship. Some filled the horizon and she could not see where they began or ended. As the ship picked its way through them, she saw that their cobalt hems did not look like ice, but some harder substance: steel, or quartz. Depending on how the light fell, in the dusk of night the icebergs were not white at all but a rose pink or cement grey.

Nara and Alexander watched the ice citadels from their perch in the high deck engineers' chairs in the lab at the rear of the ship. From here they had a nearly 360-degree view of the ocean, low enough to be eye to eye with the cape petrel and sooty albatross, the ship's vigilant chaperones, with their hawkish unblinking eyes.

He was a keen climber, he told her, even though his father had died on a mountain. Sometimes he could taste the rock, he told her; through his sweat, or when he inadvertently licked it. His explanations were, like he himself, largely physical.

He told her about the equations which bound mass and gravity, driven deep into ice by parameters, by hypothetical elasticities. He was interested in thresholds, moments of poise which continue for centuries. The ice sheets flow, or hang back, strung on filaments of forever. They are too grandiose and slow, these processes, to be understood by humans.

The beginning of an ice age was like that of a hurricane, Alexander told her, only much, much slower. What he wanted to model was the moment before the forces gather, when the Caribbean Sea is ruffled by wavelets, and flying fish still ripple through silvered air. The moment before the storm attracts the attention of the fates, with all their rage and scores to settle and lives to erase.

It occurred to her that might be this, too: the moment before the storm. With one half of her being, she thought: *I must avoid him.* With the other half she thought: *I love him.* Or it was beyond thought, it was simply a reaction, much as the hydrogen and liquid react in the ice that scrapes against the hull of the ship to create something solid, if not particularly durable.

On the ship, when Alexander walked into her cabin, Nara

had the sensation of the room being flooded with sun. When he left, the sun was extinguished and a cool light took up residence: this was the light of her soul, her being. It was the only light she could emit, a timid blue hue. But like the sun he was unstable. The light he threw gave the impression of constancy, but it was born of flarings, firestorms, dark ruptures. Not the kind of light that warms the soul, or promises understanding. Even as she understood this, she wanted that dark flare for herself.

The following day, they encountered pack ice for the first time. For a while, the ship was able to make headway. But eventually the floes nudged closer, then locked around the ship. One engine was kept running, as in port, and it hummed vague and distant. The only other sounds were the crack and sway of ice and the distant cries of birds.

Nara went to the bridge, where officers scanned the horizon for signs of dark water sky. Their charts show reefs, rocky underwater islands. In order to get to base they must thread their way between these reefs and the mainland. But the pack stood in their way. They were *icebound* – this was the term the officers use: *stopped*, or *icebound*. Never *stuck*.

The captain revved the engines, took the ship back, then rammed it forward. She heard a whine of hydraulics, then a rent – the sound of steel groaning – followed by a dull crash. She watched as the floe yielded a fracture, then another, moving aside sluggishly. But the ice stiffened in front of them, and the engines did not have enough horsepower to break through.

The captain ordered the ship stopped, so he could fill the steam compressors on either side. The ship listed to the right, then to the left. *Sallying*, the engineer yelled at her, above the roar of steam. They were sallying from side to side, nudging the ice open. Still the ice stayed fast, locked around them.

They were far south and night was already a relic of a past

life. Now they lived only in the light. To look out onto the icefield from the bridge, even with its tinted windows, sent a searing pain into her corneas. Everyone had to wear their polarised glasses now, to avoid ice-blindness.

Nara and Alexander sat in her cabin and stared at the icefield at midnight, one, two in the morning, as if keeping vigil. The cape petrels and albatross had disappeared. The ship felt abandoned without the birds, without the sound of water lapping against its hull. Seals, sleeping or drowsing in the midnight sun, were scattered like gleaming slugs across the icefield. They took no notice of the red and white monolith which had installed itself in their world.

The sun slunk along the surface of the floes. To the east they could see the unmistakeable tower and continuity of an ice sheet rising from the sea, and beyond it, mountains. The base where they were headed nestled on the other side of these mountains in a sheltered bay. It was only some forty kilometres away as the crow flies, but it might as well have been four hundred.

In her cabin, Alexander said, 'I wonder how we're going to get out of this.' She had to manufacture the right note of alarm, in order to give him the impression that she, too, cared whether they escaped. She had found a stalled paradise on this ship, with Alexander, stuck in a white world which will not let them go.

In their stopped world, some of the officers became landsick; a version of seasickness, because they were on a ship and not moving. Some were so nauseous they couldn't eat. Everyone fell asleep at odd times, and stayed up all night. All Nara's dreams became convoluted parables.

The captain informed them that if the ice did not shift and they were still stopped the following day, then he would back out of the track they had cut in the ice, and head north.

Their voyage will come to an end. They might be split up to be flown in from the Chilean base on the north of the peninsula, or they might have to return to the Falklands and try again later in the season.

That night, she made a decision. She will make love to him in the icefield. She wanted time itself to stop, and circle upon itself, like the polar sun which traced ellipses in the sky.

They talked until three, four in the morning and a chromium light singed her cabin. A solemn thrill took hold as she squared herself to her risk. Her attraction for him had been growing by the day until it was a black vein in all this whiteness, a lethal sun. Until she needed it to take up its place in the world, in the whorls of fingers, in hair, in mouths and ripped flesh. Until she needed it to exist, to be an ice-devil creature: red, black, magma, oxide, volcanic. Until she needed to split this white world apart.

PART IV

The Known World

1

'I've never seen a summer this warm,' Bobby, one of three domestics from St Helena, declared. On base they were called the Saints. Luke had the impression that the Saints saw and heard everything that went on, a silent, knowing chorus protected by their apartness, their lack of investment in the gossip, power struggles, the cliques and allegiances they saw fracturing like summer sea ice all around them.

In late January the MAGIC team's work finished, and Luke was detailed to the ice-coring team. He would spend the rest of the summer flying to and from the ice dome on Berkner Island – an island in name, although it didn't look like one from the air. Its contours could only be seen with radar; the island itself was iced in, trapped in the vastness of the Ronne Ice Shelf.

The physical hardship aside, Luke looked forward to being at Berkner. Gregory, the ice-core driller, was a good host. The season before, he had shown Luke his handiwork, taking him down to the underground chamber where they worked in refrigerated temperatures even colder than at the surface. Luke had marvelled at the long tubes of ice, so perfectly shaped and formed, brought up from the depths by a giant machine which reminded Luke of those cigarette makers they had when he was a child. *This is history, Luke, more than you'll see in any museum.* Gregory was always making these eager pronouncements, as if he were being interviewed by a television crew (and indeed Gregory did sometimes appear on the news, in his parka and polarised sunglasses, standing on an icefield). Luke had the sense that Gregory tried them out on him, to gauge their effect, before deploying them in the classroom or in front of politicians.

In the tent, where they retired for tea, Gregory powered up his laptop to the solar panels and took him to a website called *The Physics of Glaciers*. He spoke to Luke about ablation, velocity, visible and invisible stress, about the mathematical relationship between friction and melt. He did not simplify or condescend. Then, in the ice-coring chamber, an underground cathedral of cold, Gregory shaved off slices of this core, no more than slivers of ice dotted with what looked like hundreds of tiny bubbles. Each was a chapter in the story of the earth, Gregory informed him, that unwritten saga whose ending was still being considered, through ghostly murmurs, unknowable contracts, cement factories and coal-burning plants and the fossilised future remains of humanity, possibly. This was how Gregory saw things, he confided to Luke, during those long tent days they spent together, laid up on Berkner: that the future of the planet would be determined by a shadowy conspiracy between known and unknown forces, human and inhuman. Not a very scientific approach, is it? Gregory asked, with the resignation of a man carrying a deathly burden.

For his part, Luke wondered how bubbles could divulge so much – past cataclysms were contained within their tiny gaseous membranes, extinctions of entire species, volcanic eruptions, nuclear fallout, gigantic forest fires. As it turned out, Gregory told him, the history of the planet was only carbon, nitrogen, sulphur. That was all there was to the planet, and to human beings, 'basic elements, collusions and explosions – with a little water thrown in.' At one time, Gregory told him, the earth's atmosphere had been suffused with carbon in a cycle of gigantic volcanic eruptions, one after the other. Tonnes of carbon dioxide caused the earth's temperature to rise by ten degrees. But the planet had managed to absorb all that carbon, sinking it into its oceans, chlorophyll, the trees, until it became fossilised in the form of sea-bed crustaceans, their shells almost pure carbon, or in coal.

'And now we're digging up all that fossilised carbon and burning it,' Gregory said. 'You see, the planet managed to absorb the carbon, but it took several million years. We're putting all that carbon back into the atmosphere in the space of a hundred years.'

Luke nodded at the portent of what the glaciologist was telling him. He had heard similar estimations over the years, in different forms, but all pointing to the same conclusion: that it was not the damage itself, but the speed at which it was being done. And the question underlying all this clamour was, how quickly can our species adapt? How finely balanced is our survivability? Very finely balanced indeed, Luke thought, if their civilisation could be so disrupted by even a two-degree change in the earth's temperature.

For a long time, he had not wanted to think about it all: his children, their future in a terrifying world of decay, conflict, hunger. *Did you know it would be like this?* they would ask him, later. And he would have to say, yes. *What did you do about it?* He was an observer, he would say. He was only a pilot who had found more than his ration of happiness in his job, and in the white continent. He flew above the ice nearly every day, six months at a time, for twelve austral summers, he would say. He watched it happen.

Alexander stood in the door of her laboratory. Nara had to sit back very slightly into her chair. It was like having a live spark, a vital machine, in the room with her.

He had gone to the bootroom, put on boots and jacket, walked down the hill, just to see her. With him, these everyday volitions were a kind of miracle. He never went looking – for her, for anyone or anything. Mostly he waited for people and situations to arrive at his doorstep, and he did not have to wait long.

'We wondered,' he began, 'what it was like, being stuck in the Ellsworths.'

'It was like – like being out of the world.'

'We tried to imagine what you talked about, you and the pilot.'

'We talked about everything.'

His mouth twisted into an odd shape. He did not wait for an answer. 'I'll come back later. Will you still be here?'

She nodded. She stayed late in her office that night, telling herself she had to stay anyway to analyse her samples, then input the data, then correlate it. With one half of her being, she knew he would not return. With another half, hope thrived so sharp she was afraid.

It was one in the morning when she left. She was shocked to open the door and find a kind of darkness on the other side of it – it was too translucent to be called night, exactly, but neither was it the floodlit day-in-night she had become used to. She had completely forgotten night existed. She put out her hand to feel it, tentatively, as if she were touching velvet or the pelt of a dark animal.

With the return of night the weather changed. Night meant colder temperatures, the land freed from its twenty-four-hour solar oven. In mid-February the sun narrowed its expansive ellipsis in the sky and Nara found she had a shadow, suddenly, after months of walking alone.

Luke invited her for a drink in the shed that doubled as his office. It was a wooden survivor from the eighties, a type of Portakabin hoisted above the ground on wooden pallets beside the hangar. Here the pilots made their tea and the mechanics kept inventories of parts.

'I dragged out the old maps for you,' he said. 'Back in a sec.' He stepped outside and returned with a bottle of Bailey's. 'I keep it outside, in the shadows between the hut and the hangar. I like it better chilled. If I let the sun get at it, it would boil.'

'It's colder now,' she said. 'Even though it's still summer.'

'This time of year the weather starts to go a bit changeable. It's always the way: once the Otters start twitching to get away, the weather closes in. I see it year after year.'

'How much longer will you stay?'

'Oh, we'll take the Dash back around the 8th or the 10th, depending on weather. So I've got a good ten days left, at least.'

'Do you know the route you'll take back yet?'

'We knew the ferry flight routes about a month ago. They can change, of course. Anything down here can change, any time.'

He poured her a glass. She slid the thick cream around her mouth. The chill cut through the cloying sweetness.

'I like your office,' she said. 'It feels like being in a caravan, like we're on holiday.'

'It does. I used to sleep here, in the old days.' He told her of the days when people used to sleep all around the base, because the pitrooms were full or when the new accommodation wing was being built, and regulations were not adhered to as strictly. 'People would bed down in P-bags in the sledge store sewing loft, they would sleep on the floor in the wooden container we're sitting in now – anywhere with some heating,' he said. 'There was a certain –' he paused, '– *intimacy* to base then. It's become rules-and-regulation-health-and-safety. It was more like home in those days. As much as a place like this can ever be home.'

He extracted books of maps and flight manuals from the shelf. Something was missing from the picture. Everything else spoke of time passing and disuse, but there were no mites streaming in the light, no dust particles, no fluffballs or spiderwebs, no signs of the lives of small creatures, of parasites and scavengers, because no insects could survive in the Antarctic, and the cold flint of the air kept paper, wood, or steel pristine.

'I look at this often,' he handed her a book. She read the spine: *Historical Maps of the Antarctic*.

'It's amazing to think that Aristotle imagined the Antarctic, before anyone knew for certain even the Arctic existed.'

'When was that?' she asked.

'Around 330 BC, or so the book says.' Luke sat down opposite her. 'And that was a time when the known world was the Mediterranean.'

Nara found the first map drawn of the continent. In its corners lurked sea monsters, half dragon, half whale. She read the explanation:

> *Aristotle speculated in* Meteorology *that the earth was a sphere, divided into northern and southern zones, each identical, but opposite. Even before Aristotle, ancient geographers suspected that the world was a globe which spun on axes, that the fiery realms to the middle of the earth at the equator were countermanded by frigid realms at the axles of the spinning globe. These were wastelands to Aristotle, and for hundreds of years afterward, peripheral and uninhabitable, they remained frozen possible apocalypses, unmapped and feared.*

'This is another handy one.' Luke handed her *Antarctic Maps and Place-Names Gazeteer 2007*.

'But isn't this out of date now? It's nearly five years old.'

'Not really. The ice might move, but not much else changes. It takes years to even assign a new place-name. There's a committee that regulates naming in the Antarctic, did you know that? But they haven't got much to work with. Everything's still Ross this, Shackleton that. At least in the British Antarctic. There's so little human history.'

'I think it's a relief, sometimes, to be in a place where there's hardly anything of human civilisation.'

'I don't know,' he said, a wistful look in his eyes. 'As time passes I miss museums. I miss human comforts. Maybe I've just been coming here too long.'

'But there's a thrill in being able to survive somewhere you're not supposed to be at all,' she said. Every day they were reminded that the Antarctic isn't habitable, that only five industrial food freezers and VSAT dishes and a generator and a desalination plant and regular shipments by sea and air made life at all viable, even for a small number of people. 'Sometimes I think we're not supposed to be anywhere at all, on the planet. And it's only in coming to the Antarctic that you realise it.' She paused. 'I feel closer to the planet, here. To how it works. Sometimes I even think it's speaking to me.' She laughed, to show she was not completely serious.

She did not tell him that lately she had begun to hear a voice. It was not inside her head, rather it came to her from a long way away. Like a train heard in the distance, at first very faint, building and building. Some force was gathering on the horizon. Also, there was something else – the voice told her that whatever was coming had been programmed – whether into the species or into the holographic game most of humanity took for reality – and that this something had to do with payback for something long, long before humanity even existed.

He gestured out the window of the Portakabin. 'I know,

it's this landscape, it does some strange things to your mind. I used to be obsessed with it. Maybe I still am. Every year, I try to get away, I think of taking a job flying helicopters for search and rescue in Scotland, or bush planes in the Northwest Territories. And every year, I come back South.'

'It's a magnet,' she said.

'It is that,' he said, nodding solemnly.

They were quiet then and their silence was like in the Ellsworths. She had never felt such ease in silence with a person she hardly knew at all.

'You know,' he said, 'you remind me of a character in a novel.'

'What kind of novel?'

'I don't know. Even your name. *Nara*.' The use of her name sounded wrong. Something in the way he said it emerged as old-fashioned, or foreign or both. 'I mean old novels. I'm sorry, I haven't read much, but I do know what I'm talking about. A woman – not quite modern, I guess. Those serious, adoring women.'

'They were too easily destroyed, the women in those novels, by some philanderer, by bad luck, by life not living up to their ideals. I don't want my life to end like that.' Her voice was unhappy.

'Well, nobody says you're going to.' He pursed his lips – a sign, she knew by now, of annoyance. 'I just think you're special, that's all. There's something different about you. You're not a run-of-the-mill person.'

She looked at the man opposite, who she might yet call friend. He would leave soon. He would fly one of the planes that now sit in the hangar up through the world, passing from snow to ice to the rough late summer of the Falklands to the subtropics, the tropics, the wet Caribbean, through springtime Texas, landing in the tail end of the Canadian winter. He is allowed to leave, and even if he weren't, he could still escape. *I have the keys to the airplane.* She has heard him say this, more than once, when he was fed up with the place.

'Well,' he said, 'it's two-thirty in the morning.'

She said, 'I never know what time it is on base.'

'Time doesn't matter here.'

They walked back to the main building together. The emergency lights of the base lit their way with a thin, yellow light.

Their names hung together, alone, on the tagging board; everyone else was signed in.

'Goodnight,' she said, and for the first time since she arrived on base two and a half months ago there was night to bid welcome to.

'Goodnight.'

In the middle of February, the field operations manager decreed that Nara and Alexander should help shut down King George Base, five hundred miles down the peninsula, for the winter.

She did not see him until they were both in the hangar, waiting for the pilot. They would fly down with another pilot, not Luke; this man, George was his name, was younger and less experienced than Luke and needed to clock up hours at the end of the season.

As usual, on its takeoff run the Otter barely needs to get going before it is airborne. They were off the ground before she could register the surprise of an escape from base one last time before winter.

Without the possibility of flying the plane, the whole venture lost much of its thrill. Her hands literally itched to take the controls. She dared not ask George, although he was friendly enough, masculine and jovial without being crude.

Nara and Alexander watch landscape slide by below. Water

channels snaked into the sea at the base of glaciers, loose pancakes of ice dot the open sound. Three years previously, the King George Sound had opened completely for the first time in known history. For perhaps for many thousands of millennia the sea ice had formed fast on its waters. Around ten years before, cracks had started to appear along the perimeter of ice cliffs, widening with each summer until channels of open water snaked through the sound.

The pilot banked right. 'There's the hut.'

She pressed her face to the cabin window and saw a red dot on a white sheet and felt a pang of familiar betrayal. She thought they were going to a place, somewhere, but actually they were just going to a hut.

The genny mech and the carpenter were there to greet them. It was an hour's journey from the skiway to the hut; they would take the skidoos for twenty minutes, then leave them where the snow ran out and walk the rest of the way. The Eros glacier which had once spilled down from above the field station was retreating half a mile a year. 'They say that as late as the 1990s you could taxi right up to the door,' the pilot said.

She helped the pilot blank down the plane. Three much taller and stronger men stood below her while she clambered onto the wings and hooked the ropes into the apertures as the pilot hammered ice screws into the snow. When she finished she jumped down, launching herself from the footring outside the cockpit door.

'I assume you learned to do that down in the Ellsworths,' Alexander said.

'The pilot taught me.'

'What else did he teach you?'

'How to wash dishes.'

'Ok, enough chatting,' the pilot said. 'Let's get going.

We've got the all clear from the Met but you never know. We don't want to be stuck here for weeks, do we?'

The trail to the hut followed the perimeter of King George Sound; on their right was a black mountain of scree; to the left the thawing sound stretched in front, across to the mainland, thin snakes of blue water backed by sloping glaciers.

It was not very cold, but already the sun had lost its sting, its ability to bore a hole through the chill of the air, its solar furore. Now the air was simply limp and cold. A blue shimmer to the sky, the reflection of the open water revealed by leads in the sea ice, embroidered the white-sheet blankness of the ice cap. Stranger, though, were the black mountains. Darker than basalt, and much less grainy, they shimmered. When the sun caught their flanks, they glowed as if lit from within. Inside these, hills of dark, soil fossils were trapped. They were so easy to uncover, Nara had heard, that you could go for a walk anywhere, at any time, and brush your hand against the scree and a shape would emerge. Trilobytes, small lizards, birds and even small dinosaurs, all etched into the rock.

They each carried a backpack; in it was alpine rope, a change of clothes, sunscreen, water, an overnight bag in case they had to lay up. For each stride the men took, she had to take two. Alexander looked over his shoulder to see if she was all right. Nara knew he did this because he was well-brought-up, taught to be gentlemanly. None of the other men looked out for her, and she struggled not to notice this, then not to be angered by it, then not to be grateful when Alexander gave her his automatic, frowning look of non-concern – but somehow he was concerned. It was the emotional indifference that hurt her. He was as concerned for her as he would be for any woman.

They turned a corner and the hut came into view, a red dot at the bottom of a mountain of more black scree. Inside, the station was a polar country cottage: coffee thermoses lined up on the wooden counter, yellow plastic washing-up basin, washing-up liquid, bright orange bottles of sunscreen everywhere. A stuffed owl twirled above the desk where the radio equipment sat – a laptop, a VHF, ancient box files from the 1960s, the 1970s. On the table sat an empty gin bottle surrounded by little yellow cans of Schweppes soda water. A frying pan with 'Pilot Repellent' scrawled on its base in white-out liquid hung above the squat Rayburn stove.

They all had a list of end-of-season tasks to do. As these were read out, Nara caught sight of a newspaper on the floor. She picked it up. Three front pages were taken up with pandemic stories: the dead, the survivors. Epidemiology. Maps with red, blue, hot pink, green zones. Hospital staff in full biological-alert protective clothing, yellow and orange suits, white masks, police, grounded airliners. Weeds growing between the cracks on tarmac. She felt a flurry of panic. When had the nightmare returned? It was a few moments before she saw the date: the newspaper was nearly a year old. She hadn't noticed because newsprint did not oxidise in the Antarctic.

'Ok, time to go to work.'

She was given a girl's job – to close up the food store (dubbed 'Tesco's'), and to shut up the caboose, which functioned as overflow accommodation. At least they didn't suggest she do the dishes.

The pilot sat down to talk to the Met back at Adelaide on the VHF. When she returned after doing the Tesco's inventory ('stacking the shelves', as the genny mech had put it) he was still sitting there, wearing a similar expression to the one she had seen so often on her pilot's – for this is how she thought of him, to distinguish them – face during those days in the Ellsworths.

'What's wrong?'

'We're not going back tonight.'

'Oh,' she nodded. 'What's the word on the weather.'

'Horace says it's going to mank out. I still don't trust a computer model. Even if they're right most of the time.'

'What does the Met say?'

'He toes the Horace line. They all do, these days. I remember when a Met man was capable of making a prediction based on weather obs and feel. But we'll get out of here tomorrow. So says Horace, anyway.'

Dinner was spaghetti Bolognese with dried onion. They ate together at the tiny wooden table, next to the bunk beds. A motley group, one unlikely to be found sharing the same living space anywhere other than in the Antarctic – the carpenter, an old winterer (this was what they were called, those who had spent the previous winter on base, by this point in the season; she was 'a winterer' now), red-faced, quite young, probably, who had spent two years doing voluntary work teaching carpentry in Indonesia. This was all she knew about him. About the generator mechanic, also an old winterer, she knew even less – from his accent she deduced he was a Yorkshireman. And them.

'I haven't seen a child in a year and a half,' the genny mech said.

'Nor a cat.'

'Nor a flower. A real one. Not that plastic stuff they put on the dining tables on Saturday night.'

'Car. Truck. Random motorised vehicle.'

'Oh,' the generator mechanic's expression was cryptic. 'A *car*.'

'Bathtub.'

'Dog.'

'We did animals already.'

After dinner, they all went for a walk. The sunset was good, the genny mech told them, if viewed from a higher point, because it set more to the west now, rather than to the south, and threw very pretty colours onto the half-melted ice sheet of the sound.

They started out for Benemnite Valley just after 7pm. At first they walked as a group, all stopping at the same point to shuffle away dirt and gravel, hunting for fossils.

Again she fell to the back of the group. She wanted to give the impression that she desired to be alone. She did not know why. Perhaps it would impress Alexander, her composure, how much she did not need him, now.

At one point he stopped on the path. She caught up with him. There they were, in the largest and most empty wilderness on the planet, and she could not avoid him.

They fell into step together easily. He kept his head high, alert, scanning the landscape. The others moved on. They wanted to climb Pyramid, the 2,500-foot peak behind the hut. Surely he would want to climb it too. She wanted to say, you go ahead with the others. I'll be fine. But he stayed with her. He did not seem to mind her silence. After a few minutes she heard it again, that nameless sound she had first noticed in the Falklands. A low hum emanated from inside her, a contented, reassuring silence skirting the edge of sound.

'Look –' he pointed to a strata in the rock. 'Pre-cambrian. I wonder what we'll find here.' He scraped away at the rock. Fossil-hunting in this manner was technically outlawed – regulations, again – but everyone did it.

He looked up the sheer side of the rockface, frowning. 'This looks do-able, on a traverse, at least.'

'You mean rock climbing?'

'Yes. It's ice-free. It's not frost-shattered the way a lot of rock down here is. You think you could climb this?'

'If I'd brought my gear, yes. Why don't you climb the mountain with the others? It'll be dark soon. I'll stay here.'

'Because I don't feel like climbing right now.'

She nearly said, but you'll never get here again. Take the chance. In the Antarctic, you need to seize the moment, or the moment disappears.

The instant stinging happiness she felt in Alexander's company returned, all at once. She noticed again the subtle physical characteristics that others missed; how delicate he was in his extremities: hands, feet, ears, how this delicacy sat so uneasily with the emotional flint of him. He had the gift of never looking the same twice. There was always some change, some almost unnoticed difference in his hair, his skin, the marks and scratches and scars of him.

They returned to the hut in near darkness. Clouds of breath-vapour condensed before them.

'This is the first time I've seen my breath,' she said.

'Can you smell the seawater?' Alexander asked.

'I haven't smelled anything in months.'

Nara and Alexander slept in the caboose that night, in bunks, side by side, listening to the hum of silence.

'Think about it,' he said, 'we're here in a caboose, sleeping in bunk beds, and there's no one between us and the South Pole.'

'I'm glad I'm not here alone.' What she meant was, I am so happy you are here with me.

He did not answer, and in another second she heard his breathing alter. He had fallen asleep.

2

The Antarctic has no autumn. The planet tilts and suddenly it is winter, which comes with a volatility and a darkness unknown anywhere else on the planet, including the Arctic. In the previous week they have lost three hours of light. With the darkness comes an internal emergency. She registers it first as panic in her stomach, it feels heavy and palatial, as if she has eaten too much food.

As their days together on base diminished, Luke talked to her more and more of his marriage. He seemed hungry for her perspective. She had no experience of anything as grave and durable as marriage, and was flattered that this older experienced man would be hungry for her opinion. Once received he was avid and possessive with it, although he stopped short of being possessive of her, personally, a restraint which impressed her. Perhaps he really did think she could explain what had happened to him, and why. Perhaps that was all he wanted.

They arrived at the Cross. They stood side by side, surveying the bay. In the evening the cold lustre of the water shimmered unevenly, like a drawer of knives caught in a dull sun.

'When did you get divorced?'

'Last year. No, eighteen months ago, now. Time flies when you're miserable as well as happy, it seems.'

'What happened?'

'She met someone else. At least that's the end result.'

She had been prepared to probe further, carefully. But the bitter stab in his voice stopped her in her tracks.

After a while he spoke again. 'Every time I asked her, she would deny it. The closest she ever came to saying something was when she said, *but you weren't here.*' His eyes were dark and clouded – an altogether different expression from the annoyed, stubborn glint she had seen in situations where circumstances, mechanics, wind patterns were against him.

'Where were you?'

'Who the hell knows where I was? On the ice cap, in a tent, cooking dinner on the Primus with a couple of scientists. Or here, where we're standing now.' He shook his head. 'It's not like I thought I was the only man on the planet. But we were married. I thought we had a good marriage. I thought that meant something.' There was another long pause. 'Every time, I thought, I believe her. She denied it and I believed her. I don't understand how we can know and not know something at the same time.'

'Knowing and believing are two different things,' she said.

A shadow passed across his face. 'I don't feel like that anymore. Thank God. I'm just waiting, I think, for the pain to go away. People say a year and a half isn't very long. But I wonder, this kind of pain might be like a disease, one that's never really cured. It just comes and goes and I'm waiting for it to go into remission.'

'But you had many good years, which is so much more than a lot of people get from the experience. I think with marriage, the fact that it ends overshadows everything that went before, everything that was good.' Even as she said this she thought, what could she know of his ex-wife, of Luke's life away from the Antarctic? She would never meet his ex-wife, or see his family home in Scotland. Life down South was like that – you knew only the Antarctic version of the person, you never saw their other life.

The sky was grey and leaden now. Standing there, looking

out to sea with Luke, Nara felt an obscure yet powerful impulse to know this place, to feel it hers. It was impossible, when faced with the landscape's indifference – impossible not to want to depend on him, not for survival, but for something even greater, although as yet obscure.

She looked at Luke and remembered that he knew how to take an aircraft into the air, knew how to land it on an ice sheet. There were not twenty men in the world who could do what he did. She struggled now to see him as just another man, a pilot, someone she had been thrown together with by circumstance. He had become something so much more; the embodiment of a dream she did not even know she had – to fly, to be freed from the grasp of gravity.

The following day she did not see Luke, nor the day after. He must have been busy in the hangar, coming over to base only to eat his meals late, after everyone had gone to bed. The next day she heard that the pilots would have to fly up to Stanley and return in the same day because the weather would close in. They had only one day's window to fly the last crew of non-essential personnel north, pick up some sup plies, and return.

She was still in bed when she heard the plane take off early in the morning. Later that day, five or six in the afternoon, the Point of No Return siren sounded over the runway. He would be back within two hours.

Luke came to find her in the lab office that night. He sat down, wearily, perching on the edge of the chair.

'You look tired.'

'I am. I can't stay long. I've got to hit the sack.'

'Did the flights go all right?'

'Oh yes, everything went smoothly.' He paused. 'But I didn't get a lot of sleep last night.'

'What were you doing?'

'Oh, some of us had a party in the sledge store. After the Saints called time in the bar we got a bottle and went to sit in the sleeping bags in the sewing loft. We talked 'til four in the morning.'

'Why didn't you come to get me? I would have come.'

'I thought about it,' he said. 'But I thought you were already asleep, probably.'

As his girlfriend, official or unofficial, she would have had a certain status on base. She would have been privy to these private impromptu parties; most importantly, she would have had his company, which she loved. She wondered if he were demonstrating to her, subtly, the things she was forfeiting, or might yet forfeit, in the future.

Luke rubbed his forehead, now very freckled from the sun, with his hand. Nara had seen him do this before, in the Ellsworths. It seemed to be a gesture of fatigue, but it had within it a note of despair.

They're loners, these pilots. A scientist had said this at dinner one night and the judgement had lodged itself in Nara's mind. Perhaps they had turned him into a loner, those cold hours in the cockpit. All the years he had been married, he had told her, an internal compass had guided him, pointing in the direction of his house, his children, his wife. Now that it was all over, his compass swung round and round in wild speculative loops, now north, now south, just as in the days before GPS, when he had to find his way based on the earth's magnetism, and the extreme pull of the geomagnetic pole had distorted his compass.

'I'm sorry,' he said. 'I was hoping to get back in time to have a drink with you, but the truth is I'm just bushed.'

Sentences were being constructed inside her, then just as quickly dismantling themselves: *Don't go, I need you. Please take me with you when you go.*

She would do whatever he wanted, she would learn to love him, or come to love him, because that invisible turning point had not yet been reached, she would still have his love, she would still live in the real world, with its diminishing oil stocks, its failed wheat harvests, its rumours of an epidemic illness that would kill millions, its swollen seas, drunk on melting ice. She wanted the real world in all its mortal glamour, and not this snowbound antiseptic colony.

Luke's eyes glistened with fatigue. Soon he would be gone, for good – or for seven months, and how these months stretched in front of her, an endurance test, white and cold with silence. His imminent departure had become a doppelganger – something that looked exactly like Luke, but wasn't. She saluted this creature in the corridors, dreamt about it at night, ate her meals with it by day.

'Well,' he said, 'goodnight.'

She flips on the dim light of the aquarium. Her sponges, sea-spiders, worms, sea-sponges, glow in the semi-darkness. They had gone into winter mode now and were slumbering. They hibernate by a genetic mutation which stops ice crystals from forming inside their cells as the temperature drops and they descend into a cryogenic sleep. This natural antifreeze is what keeps their blood liquid in subzero waters, through the three-month-long Antarctic night.

But she is waking them up, warming the water in the aquariums very slightly, turning the lights higher to simulate increased UV exposure. The monitors attached to their hearts blip louder, and faster, as in hospital wards when patients go into cardiac arrest, she half expects them to start blaring at her in a single pitched howl.

This is what the voice tells her: that the pace of the world is quickening, heating up, ice shelves moving toward the ocean with a new purpose, toward some disastrous deliverance, an astounding regeneration. Even if she did not hear the voice, the SHALIB Ice and Snow Database at the University of Colorado would tell her so. It shows graph upon graph ascending, always, never turning down. The upward swing is sudden and unstoppable. Carbon dioxide did not change much in the first eight hundred years of the last millennium, but it has shot up 30 per cent in the past two hundred years, the graphs show. The temperature cycle graphs illustrate the warming and cooling of the planet, long troughs, followed by sudden spikes, like a cardiograph.

Here in the soundless Antarctic, she is certain she can hear it: the planet's racing heart, beating with a new frantic purpose.

As they rounded the Point a rotten-egg smell came on the wind: sulphur from the ionised seawater in the sewage treatment plant.

Nara said, 'You won't be missing that smell, I suppose.'

'I always find it a relief, to smell anything,' Luke replied. 'The minute I step out of the plane in the Falklands, the smell of the grass – it just hits you, as soon as you open the door. I never knew grass smelled so wonderful.'

She stopped to smell the wind; now she could only smell the familiar empty flint of the Antarctic. 'Why do you think there are so few smells here?'

'It's a pretty antiseptic environment. Nothing grows. But you don't even smell the seals when they calve, the blood, or the salt in the sea.' He stopped beside her, squinting into the sun. 'Let's have a seat,' he said. The day was brilliant. The shoreless sea around the Point sizzled with melt. Dark granite rocks absorbed the sun until they were warm enough to sit on. Icebergs lolled in the bay, eroded by a summer of melt into fragments. Soon they would be frozen in by sea ice.

As soon as they had sat down they were startled by the sound of the explosion. A small iceberg only a few feet away popped and turned over, displacing a group of blue-eyed shags, which bolted into flight at the sound. With her eyes she followed their confident strokes, their long, thin necks straining.

'I love to watch them fly,' he said. 'They're so committed.'

'Will they head north now?'

'Yes, they'll be gone for the winter, to the islands north of the peninsula.'

'You must be looking forward to seeing your family,' she said.

'I am, yes.'

They looked out toward Pinero Island, the sun painfully sharp on the water. The tide of ice rose and fell on the gyre, ice scraping against the rocks, then clinking its withdrawal.

'You know,' he said, 'I think the most exciting thing in life is discovering that someone else is attracted to you. I think that's by far the most exciting thing that can happen to you, don't you?'

'More exciting than flying?'

'Oh – so much more.'

He waited for her to say something, and she knew he was waiting.

They sat reclining among the rocks, hands clasped behind their necks for support, Weddell seals basking around them, their torpid, cinder-coloured bodies, listening to the wash of the bay, a distant breathy sigh of wind, the crack as icebergs expanded with the heat of the day, on this unnaturally warm and clear day, so late in the season.

The peninsula was warming twice as fast as anywhere else on the planet, apart from swathes of Greenland, and the boreal forests of Canada and Siberia. This had been known for ten years, now. For Nara, this knowledge had always been with her, through school, university, her doctorate. She was too young to remember a time when the earth had been in a perfect equilibrium, the ice sheets stalled immensities, when Greenlandic hunters did not go hungry.

She said so to Luke.

'I've been to Greenland,' he replied. 'I flew a season there once, in the summer. I remember I met an old Inuit hunter who I uplifted from a place up north. He'd gotten stuck on the sea ice, for the first time in his life. It was too thin and it had caught him unawares. When he asked me my name – he didn't speak much English – he misheard me and went around calling me "Luck". I said, that's a good name, maybe I'll keep it.'

She laughed. But Luke looked pensive. 'The old man told me that there is no such thing – he said, what you white people call luck is actually the secret arrangements of the spirits. His nephew had been killed in a helicopter accident, he told me, the year before. His body and the helicopter were both entombed in a frozen fjord. He said that was the doing of the spirits. They decided everything, including whether a winter would see starvation or plenty.' He turned to look at her. 'It's quite a thought, don't you think? That the spirits are at this very moment listening to our conversation, coming to their shadowy decisions about our futures?'

He didn't give her time to answer. He stood, pointing to his watch. 'We'd better get back, special dinner tonight and all.'

They rose and headed back to base.

That night a farewell dinner was held for the pilots who would fly the Otters out the following day. For dessert they had ice cream with fresh mango – a first on base. The base chef had requested a crate of mangoes and Luke had flown them in from the Falklands himself. They had come from the rainforests of Brazil, via Montevideo, then to the Islands, then down to their lonely base at the bottom of the peninsula.

The taste – sweet, thick, with an undertone of bitter wood – when had he last tasted that? He remembers sharing a mango with his wife in Arniston. They went to that windswept village one Christmas, its Cape Dutch cottages, bone-white in the bleached sun of the southern ocean. She peeled the quadrants, offered them to him, her fingers dripping with juice. He remembers the months they spent on that lonely cape, shuttling between Cape Town, Hermanus, Struisbaai, Arniston, Mossel Bay, one white compound to another. His wife had grown up in post-Apartheid South Africa, in a family made wealthy by mining. Every few weeks they would move; she had the bored discontent of rich people everywhere, looking for opportunity, always, business opportunities, romantic opportunities (although he did not know that then), for the next thing that would vault her into pleasure and intrigue. When their marriage ended, his shock was total, because he had never seriously considered another woman, and yet he was the one who ended up alone. Why did life do that – reward the sinners? He had never thought in those terms before: saints, sinners. He was uninterested in guilt, retribution, judgement.

They should have stayed in South Africa, that is what he thinks now. He could have earned his living flying tourists up to the safari camps of Limpopo, Kruger, even Botswana, Namibia – those other deserts of Gondwanaland. He would have been at home more, he could have kept an eye on things. Year after year he had gone back, spending five months away from his family, keeping in touch by email, by Iridium phone. He could not shake it from his mind, his dreams. He had been dazzled by the continent, sucked in by its white-cold eye.

*

That night the voice woke her.

What?

It was calling her, although not by name, from a long way away. The voice erupted from a cloud of static, as if she'd left a radio on in the room on an unoccupied frequency and someone had begun broadcasting.

She was moving through a wood-panelled room, somewhere hot. The voices were there. She was with two other women, strangers, and she said: can you hear them? No, said the other women – girls, she saw, on closer inspection. They might not be more than twelve years old.

Who are they?

The voice said, *They're dead. But don't be afraid.*

Yes, it was a dream, then. She was not awake, after all. She strained, listening for more. Then she heard a thumping sound, like a heartbeat.

The next morning she went to the Communications Officer in the control tower.

'I've heard the atmosphere makes noises,' she said. 'Can I hear them?'

'Sure.' He was an eager type, this man. He clapped a pair of headphones onto her ears. 'Listen to this, I recorded it last night. The sun is low enough in the sky to hear the ionosphere now.'

He turned the dial on the digital recorder, and she heard the familiar hiss of the HF radio. She heard static, but also a pattern of blips and bleeps that were unmistakeably electrical. After a while the static began to pulse, like a heartbeat. She listened to this empty fuzz, hoping to hear the voice she had heard in the middle of the night leap from it, until a voice burst in, an Argentine Ham radio operator. Nara listened to the rough Spanish for a while, then translated for the communications manager. 'He's saying, "First you take the B-road, the 109, then you turn right at Comodoro Rivadavia and drive for twenty kilometres? Got it?"'

It was gone, the heartbeat in the wilderness.

The next day Luke flies up to Stanley and returns in the same day. No mangoes in the cargo this time, just a few drums of avtur and the last delivery of fresh fruit and vegetables the winterers will see until October, seven months away.

The last Point of No Return of the season is a milestone to be marked, and is called over the tannoy. They troop, as one, to watch the plane make a rare night landing, which is also the last time they will see the Dash land for eight months. So much of life on base is about this, now – the rituals of leaving and ending, and looming abstinences: the last banana, the last cucumber. It feels as if they are all about to walk the plank. And they are, in a way; in the Antarctic, winter is a door which, once closed, cannot be prised open.

The plane appears first as two sparks under a black sky, the four overwing lights piercing the darkness. Behind it, snow-capped mountains, mute with solitude. The runway lights are lit for the last time in the season; in two days' time they will be covered with old oil drums. Drifts will accumulate around them during the winter, in windscoops, cornices.

The charcoal runway gravel, the striped sky, the steel mountains, the sudden appearance of the four wing lights, like four powerful stars, the plane framed against Adélie Island coming in heavy and slow, the methodical workhorse plane it is – suddenly she knows she has loved it here, at times, that this is her life: now, and here, and there can be no other.

She watches the plane land against a sunset of mauve, purple, scarlet. The feeling, watching the plane buzz to a stop, is indescribable. The rush of thrill, the pride she feels as it lands, knowing Luke is flying.

She sees Luke emerge from the fuselage. The return of a friend is not the same as the return of a lover. Still, his return feels like salvation; it feels like he has been gone forever.

They cleared sight of base, turning the corner at the north end of the Point, and stopped to admire the view. It was a moody, dark evening, a sky of brushed steel.

Only a week before they had sunned themselves on the rocks. It was cold now, from the lack of sun, and from night, which was claiming more and more time, a dark stain seeping over the peninsula. The cold had changed from being merely cold – a dry, invigorating chilliness – to a biting, wanton substance.

'Now that it's here, winter, I'm not sure how I feel about staying,' she ventured.

'You just have to get through it. You have to enjoy every moment of it, if possible. Think about it, how many people get to do what you are doing? In the future, you'll look back on this year and it will seem like the most intense and exciting time in your life. No matter what happens, you'll only remember the good parts.'

'I remember you saying that, at the beginning of the season. That somehow you remember only the good.'

'It's true, you'll see.' The smile he gave her was different; embedded in it was a new note of reassurance.

'Are you glad to be getting away?'

Luke answered with a small, subdued laugh. 'I never know how I feel, leaving base at the end of the season. Every year I wonder what it would be like to leave for good.'

'What else would you do?'

He shrugged. 'Fly for someone else.' He looked at the ground, knocked one Rigger boot against the other. When he looked up again, his face had a new expression, hard and unswerving, staring down the horizon. 'Every year I feel I'm tempting fate by doing another season. That there is only so long you can go before something gives way, either luck or judgement or both.'

He walked on ahead, slipping from time to time on the rime that covered the loose shale of the shoreline. He had the absent, distracted air of someone who was leaving soon. He was slowly fading out, like a still frame at the end of a film. They might email, she supposed, if he were the writing type. They might talk on the phone once in a while, so she could tell him how the winter was going – sporadic, friendly contact. Not sustaining, not electric.

They came to a stand on a small rocky promontory. She had never seen cloud come so close to the land. At times there was only a stripe of blue, or luminous white, a thin ribbon between its grey overhang and the sea.

She shivered, involuntarily. 'I can't believe how the weather has changed.'

They finished their walk in an uncertain silence. They arrived at the tagging board, and moved their tags from 'Around the Point' to 'On Base'. He moved their tags for both of them while she signed them in on the computerised logbook.

'There's something I want to show you. Wait just a sec, I'll be back.' When he returned he was carrying his laptop and a bottle of Spanish red wine, a little plastic bull dangling from its neck.

They sat in the Air Unit office. He opened his computer and started to click through folders. Images paraded past: ice, snow, plane, mountain, ice, snow, plane, mountain, and came to rest on a single photo – a helicopter, mangled in the snow.

'What's this?'

'The helicopter off the *Resolute*. They had an accident last year, near Bluefields. They were flying and lost their vis, two Navy pilots. Easy enough to happen.'

'Have you ever lost visibility in the planes?'

'A few times. Helicopters are more unstable than planes, though. They're more manoeuvrable, but you've got less control.'

'You fly them too?'

'Used to. I loved them. They're like toys, you can make them do almost anything.' The photo gallery froze on an image of Luke next to a Twin Otter. Behind him was a grey-white murk.

'Weather looks terrible,' she said.

'It was. I flew one of the Otters over, picked them up, and flew them to Midas. The doctor stabilised their condition. Then I flew them here, and out to Punta on the big plane.'

The photos slid into each other: more flat grey snowfields, evidence of poor contrast, eventually presented to the Ministry of Defence, the two pilots in their uniforms, bandaged and on stretchers, one with a broken leg, their arrival at Midas, the medevac flight from a stormy base, the Araucaria trees and dingy sheds of Punta Arenas.

'They had a lucky escape. The planes were still on base, but only just. We were due to fly out for the winter in a week's time.'

For a moment Nara wondered why he was showing her all this – to impress her, to confer upon her an understanding, in advance of her first Antarctic winter, how she had entered into a stark terrain of life and death, where anything was possible.

A figure appeared outside the window. In the darkness, she could just make out the profile. Alexander was looking at something – the moon perhaps, just risen. He would have been unaware of the light coming from the office behind him. He stood fixedly, as if at attention. She knew this stare of his, rivetted, unnatural. It was one of the first things she noticed about him in the Islands. She envied him his self-sufficiency. She had been too much alone and she craved the company of people. On the ship, when they were both on the observation deck, she went over to the railing, where he stood in his contemplative posture staring into the ice, and asked him to read the ice for her. He did, but after a few minutes he went away, saying he would be back, but he did not return. She tried to copy his invincibility but after a while she became self-conscious. She looked too much like a woman waiting for a man who would not return.

'His heart is locked away.'

She was not sure she had heard Luke correctly.

'You won't get it,' he said. 'No one will, probably. I'm a man. I know,' he said.

'You know what?'

'I know. I just know – men like that.'

'Because you're just like him? You set someone up, then punch them in the face. Because you have no heart?'

'I don't know. I don't think so. I hope not.' Luke pursed his lips. 'Sometimes it just doesn't work out. You don't know why the other person doesn't respond, or wants to take another path. In any case there is no why. You just have to accept it and move on.' He paused. 'I don't know, he seems –'

'I know what he seems.'

They sat in silence, then, swilling wine in their glasses, not looking at each other.

'I just can't stand to see you– waste yourself.'

Nara flinched at the word. 'What do you mean, *waste*?'

'Yes, as in go to waste: your kindness, your experience, your love. Your body.'

Something in the way it emerged from his mouth –

fatherly, disinterested, yet with a trill of the sexual underlying it – caused a faint disgust to flicker through her.

Luke put down his wineglass. She watched him stand: lean frame, dark hair, although greying now at the edges. A serious, intelligent face, angular, moody and changeable. She had seen this man every day for four months, with his trousers of many pockets, capable shoes, a trainer/hiking boot hybrid all the pilots seemed to wear and which squeaked in the waxed corridors of the base, his forearms muscled and weathered from the sun, the platinum watch on his wrist.

She had never known anyone like Luke before, she might never know his like again. But she had not given him what he wanted. Perhaps it would not have been so much to yield.

'Keep this.' He handed her the plastic bull with the little flag of Cataluña tied round its neck, yellow with thin red stripes. 'For luck.'

She told him that she would miss him.

In return he said, 'Goodnight.'

The Air Unit office was his domain, not hers. But she sat there anyway, long after his departure, turning the plastic bull over and over in her hands.

It is winter now. All around the continent the ice tightens its grip. Beneath the surface, winter water is collecting in thermodynamic colums of vertical mixing; threaded through them is a deep layer of very cold surface water.

As water cools, it gels on the surface. Hydrostatic pressures are higher on the floating ice shelves, and this lowers the freezing temperature of the water, and the ocean below the ice shelf deepens its frost. Deep in the ocean, far beneath the continent, Antarctic bottom water churns, dense, depthless, blind with blackness. The Antarctic icefield is a self-reinforcing system: land, water, air – they all depend on the ice. Ice makes more of itself, becomes more itself. In becoming, its being is strengthened. The pack forms.

Water is slow: the Antarctic circumpolar waters circulate the world oceans every one thousand years, creating velocities of cold, eddies, thermal columns which govern the great currents of the oceans – the Gulf Stream, the Humboldt – and which affect the planet's climate. In this process, the sea ice is key; it acquires structure through sinews of ice crystals, it melds, binds into a static ice scuplture garden.

Less is known about the continent, its processes, its intents, than anywhere else in the world, apart from the deep oceans. It is a cold terrestrial moon, another planet, this cold node of the known world.

The day of the plane's departure was overcast and cold. Nara walked over to the plane alone along the gravel path leading past the accommodation block and across the runway.

She found Luke in the hangar, supervising the payload, calculating fuel. She watched as they loaded the plane. She said goodbye to the summer base commander, to the Met man, who had left his five-day forecast behind for the winterers, pinned to the flight map. After that they would have to predict the weather for themselves.

Luke emerged from the fuselage. He was wearing his orange ventile jacket, the one he had worn in their days in the Ellsworths. He had told her how this jacket had been invented during the Second World War, how it had saved the lives of Allied pilots who crashed in Greenland, in Iceland. 'That's its genius: the wind passes through you, but you don't feel it.'

Now he said, 'I almost want to say, if you need anything, let me know.'

'I know, but you can't help me, here.'

'No, I can't.'

The chief pilot was calling him from within. Luke turned to her. His expression was difficult to read: ecstatic, but grave; a grain of regret, but also the happiness of release.

He said, 'I'll see you in October.'

She nearly said *goodbye*, but at the last minute caught herself.

The door is closed with a groan more human than mechanical, and the plane's propellers start to chop at the air slowly at first, in fits and starts, then building to a smooth rotation. The plane remains on the apron, all four propellers spinning, the plane trembling while the pilots run through their checklist and speak to Stanley on the HF for the latest weather. Then the plane begins to move, tentatively at first, as if it has not yet decided to leave. It taxis to the southern edge of the runway where it executes a deft, balletic turn, and lines up at the end of the airstrip, where it stands, its trembling now a shudder. A roar, and gravel spews as it charges. It is already flying when it passes the hangar apron. When the plane has cleared the icebergs in the cove it climbs sharp, then banks right to turn around the peninsula where it disappears, hidden by the hill back of base. When it reappears it is flying low for the traditional fly-by past the comms tower. At the height of the laboratory roof it comes back over the runway, the propellers whipping the dust. Behind her the cook says, *holy fuck*. Just at the moment when the plane's position seems untenable, when gravity is about to reach up to snatch it, the pilots climb and the plane soars over their heads. She sees the pale underbelly of the fuselage, hears the roar of the propellers as they chew the air above her. A single shaft of silver sun breaks through the clouds and flashes off the fuselage. The silver slash stays with it as the plane journeys upward and begins to be consumed by cloud. She watches as these points of silver light congeal in her mind, absorbing their negative radiance, the grey of clouds, lead and pewter dispersing, until she is only looking at a place in the sky where the plane had been.

PART V

Wintering

1

Life began in burning ice and biting flame. In the south, Muspell was fiery. The fire shone all day and all night. Only those who are born to it can endure the heat. Niflheim is in the north. It is an icy realm, swept by vast currents of snow, gelid rivers, frozen lightning.

Between these two realms lies Midgard. Here it is mild, warm, a perpetual summer's evening. In Norse myth, these tepid latitudes were where most people lived, and were built for – neither in fire nor ice but a pleasant if undramatic realm between. But Midgard is sickening, becoming violent in its moods, driven by erratic currents.

The first sign was the rubbish. It accumulated, fermented and stank. Initially I thought: it's no worse than a strike, a protest over working hours. So we have to live with house arrest, it might last a month, two months. But viruses could, theoretically, travel on air. Or anyone who came to visit your house, any friend or official bearing advice. And so we had to seal ourselves in with tape, and commit to not opening a door until we were told it was safe.

I watched the plants on my balcony wither, yellow, droop, then die. I stood so many times, water bottle in hand, my hand on the sliding balcony door. Only the vision of myself in a hospital bed, or worse, at home in my own bed, putrid, bloated and decomposing, stopped me from opening it.

The dog owners had a dilemma. I saw them, sometimes, in the wedge of gritty green that passes for a park in front of my flat. They wore little white masks and looked around them, constantly, as if they could spot it coming. The dog owners, once so willing to share tips and observations, to let their dogs sniff each other, became tense when another approached. They backed themselves up against trees and looked the other way.

After a few weeks the dog owners stopped coming to the park and this stiff choreography ceased. Perhaps, all over London, dogs were spontaneously combusting, unable to hold in anymore the shit and piss and energy which drove them to tear back and forth across playgrounds and parks.

Plague Ground – a sub-editor's triumph. Next to the headline was a photograph of a deserted swingset. Playgrounds had become incubators of disease. The parents, sitting on a park bench, watching their children scramble through jungle gyms, slide down the metal sliding board. Everyone smiling and laughing as the sun glints off the slide, silver and sure, more throb than light.

A virus has a brain, an engine, a black heart. As for its DNA, the normal rules of sickness and sickening, tried and tested on so many vulnerable bodies, plashy and defenceless as the fens that were at the same time being inundated by the rising sea, did not apply. The backwards logic of this particular sickness meant that if you were young and healthy you were more likely to die, the middle-aged and even the elderly sometimes survived, because the virus overwhelmed the young body more quickly, spurred on by the vitality of youth. The body was so eager to pass it on, eager to be an accomplice in its own destruction.

Airports shut, the wispy contrails disappeared from the sky, as did the familiar whine of aeroplanes powering down over London as they took their place in the landing queue for Heathrow. I missed that sound, of hydraulics, the groan as the plane's bellies slit open and landing gear dropped down, more than I ever would have believed.

The signs of the unravelling came in November 2012; they were small and at first indirect: a sudden lack of fresh milk in the supermarkets, then the almost instant disappearance of UHT milk. Mothers with young children had official priority at supermarket queues, which began to be staffed by police, or, in some cases, Territorial Army reservists. At the beginning I would walk into a supermarket and see it invigilated by people in combat fatigues and camouflage patiently helping an old woman with her shopping trolley, and reassure myself that this was a good sign, this was quite normal, considering.

The first defections came from the ambulance crews and the paramedics. Even though they had received doses of retrovirals, and had priority for preventative and curative treatments, they got sick, and died, one by one. The virulence of the virus' communicability was plain. Next were the front-line medical staff, the immigration officers, the police. Once they saw their colleagues sicken and die within a matter of days they too thought twice about turning up for work, Hippocratic oath or no. Calls for volunteers were put out; those who answered them were deemed suicidal. Their families deserted them, they were shunned by friends. They too – over 70 per cent of them, the official figure – died.

It won't happen to me. It will happen to someone else. As it turns out, we are simply not very good at imagining our own deaths, we refuse to believe in them. We kept going to work; there we were on the Tube, ineffectual white masks over our noses and mouths, like an army of surgeons heading for the operating theatre, incubating viruses in canisters. Seven to ten days later, over half the occupants of a carriage where a carrier had been standing, would all be on respirators, 'fighting for their lives', as the free rags with their steady diet of celebrity and threat would later put it.

The fight was silent and almost invisible. They were

unconscious while the virus wended its way through their bodies, attacking organs systematically: liver, lungs, kidneys. Then the hospital staff stayed away, there were no more respirators, and people too ill to walk crawled to hospitals only to lie down in cold corridors and die.

In more organised and stalwart countries, things were better. The scenes of chaos and cowardice were not as common in Germany or France, with their relatively dispersed populations, their better-ordered systems of authority. Where had the fighting spirit of the British people gone? What about we shall fight on the beaches? Commentators wrung their hands; we had become a mercenary nation, in thrall to profit and fear. Then began the large-scale desertions of those who were employed to save lives, the looting, the random attacks, the failure of public transport and other essential services.

We were confined to my flat, Eric and I, secure in our cocoon of automated systems – internet, telephone, television, heating, electricity – feeding off the stockpile of food and water which I had dutifully created after the first warnings of the coming epidemic.

I busied myself with ordering my boarding passes alphabetically by country, so that I could see all the places I had travelled to over the previous years, places I might never see again. I put all the books on my bookshelves in alphabetical order and straightened them on the shelves, tugging their spines into a neat procession as I had been taught to do the summer I worked in a bookshop as a student. I invented a game for myself in which I would plunk my finger on a place-name in the back of my world atlas, and then identify its latitude and longitude.

Eric was restless. He would say to me, 'I have to go out.'

'Go where?' In the plague world there were no buses, no tubes, no planes, no cars.

One morning I woke up and Eric wasn't at home. The door was unlocked. He left a note: *out for a walk*.

I panicked, but there was nothing I could do, no one I could call. He'd left his mobile behind. He will just go for a walk, I reasoned, and then he will come home. He will not pick up the virus floating on the air, it doesn't work like that. You have to be in close contact with someone, in order to contract it. He will go for a walk and then he will come home.

We are supposed to reckon with our lives in these moments of fear and terror, to swear change, to take oaths, enter into elaborate pacts with deities that may or may not exist.

But I found I just wanted to go on living, as I had before the sickness. This was all I wanted. I wanted Eric home, his sweetness, the deep pleasure of his smell. As if my genes and cells could rest, next to him. But Eric did not come home.

We arrived on base four weeks ago, just before Christmas. My stay here should be over by now, my original departure date was to be tomorrow.

The news came from Cambridge, but within minutes we could have read it on the internet. The base commander called an emergency Sit Rep. The borders are closed, he said. No one can get in or out, anywhere. A spike in infections, most of them contracted on long-haul flights. There are fears that another pandemic will build again, three years after the initial scourge, but this time in spring and summer, when it will be harder to control, harder for people to stomach the necessary house arrest, holidays ruined, children driven mad by enclosure, rubbish accumulation. These fears cause every Western industrialised country to take drastic action.

The night we hear this, we are hushed at dinner in our cafeteria. We know what we have escaped: mob scenes in airports, panic. Although there are no cases in the Falkland

Islands or southern Chile, the authorities there have also suspended entrances and departures. No one can get in and out. So we have to stay in the Antarctic, we are told, until someone figures out what to do with us.

I've had so much less time than I thought I would have for writing, for research. Because I've unwittingly joined the Army, I was required to do three days of field training, followed by a co-pilot trip down to King George Base, followed by a mystery stomach bug – there are no viral infections here, the air is too dry, the population too endogenous. I thought I would conduct interviews, but there is no one on base who knew her, apart from Luke, the pilot, and he has been flying off base during the weeks I have been here. Now this surprise of our enforced confinement and I can't think. I am stunned by this turn of events. The claustrophobia is back, as if it has only been in remission these past three years.

After the base commander's announcement I try to talk to David, but he has to make phone calls. I imagine he has some hotline to the prime minister's office, and that he can press a button and eject us all out of here. I see little of David. I suspect he keeps himself apart from me, out of expediency. I'm not popular, or rather my motives aren't, so why would he want to be seen as my confessor, my accomplice. Who knows what this writer will dig up? Who knows what confidences she will betray? She is a spy in a place where she does not know the rules, where she does not belong.

It is early February, and winter is just around the corner. 'Winter comes fast in Antarctica,' the base commander tells me. 'Soon we'll see night again.'

I don't say, I can't stay here, and list the reasons why: my flat, my plants, my friends, my mortgage. I don't say, a winter in the Antarctic will ruin me. There's no point saying any of this, because we are all in the same boat. The planes can't leave, the ship which brought us here, the *Astrolabe*, is in dock in the Falklands, and is forbidden to leave. The British and Argentine navies are patrolling the waters, escorting cruise ships back to Punta Arenas or Stanley, where the ships and their inhabitants will sit in quarantine.

At dinner that night the plumber jokes, 'Well, at least if we're stuck here for the winter you can write your book.' The panic in my stomach is so sudden, and so severe, I feel I will throw up.

I go to speak to the base commander. Gerry is given to reading poetry and philosophy. I see Stendhal on his reading shelf, next to Rilke. He sees me spying his books. 'Lots of time to read down here, over the winter. I'm working my way through the classics.' A steady, sensible type, Gerry is from Fort William in Scotland; a climbing-outdoorsy-kayaking sort of town, he tells me. He works the summers up there in an outdoor sporting centre and does the winters down here. He never sees winter, only summer in the north, followed by summer in the south. But this year he will spend winter in the Antarctic. Fort William is so warm now, he tells me, that the winter sports scene has all but shut down. No snow on the mountains means no challenge for the ice climbers, who now go to New Zealand, where the climate has been remarkably untouched by the global pattern of change.

I ask Gerry what he thinks will happen to us.

'To tell you the truth, I don't know. I talk to Cambridge about it every day, who talk to the FCO, who talk to the Falkland Islands Government, who say they want to maintain a shutdown. They could send the ship and put us all on it, but where would we dock? The ship can only carry food enough for all of us for thirty days. It's a risk.'

'And the planes?'

'The planes are grounded. They are only certified to fly in Antarctica now, or to the Falklands.'

'But if we all got on a plane and went to the Falklands, what would happen?'

'Well, first of all, only sixteen of us can get on that plane at any one time. They might scramble a fighter plane from the military base, and force us to turn back. Although we'd probably have to land, by that point, there wouldn't be enough fuel. The Chileans wouldn't allow us to land at Marsh, that's for sure. They've been very accommodating, considering the political situation, but with a global influenza alert I don't think they'd let us in.'

'So you think the military would let us die, ditch in the ocean, before they'd let us land in the Falklands.'

'No, I suppose not. They'd probably let us land, and then put us in quarantine.' He pauses. 'But tell me, would you rather be here, free to move about, to eat what you want, and safe from the virus, or would you rather be locked in a shed in a military base in the Falkland Islands?'

I don't answer, because I am not sure what I feel or think. 'And if we stay here?'

'We have food here enough for a hundred people to last the winter.'

'But we're only fifty-six people.'

'That's right. That's what I mean – contingency. We have enough food for twice our number, and it will get us through the winter, and then into next spring, when they could get a ship in.'

'So you think that's what they'll do, then? Leave us here.'

'I'm asking for your discretion. Don't go broadcasting this around base. And it's not as if I'm in the know, either – go and ask the FCO man. He likely knows more about what's really going on than all of us combined. But yes, I think it's their best option, and cheapest, too, by the way: to keep us here until things settle down.'

'What about our civil rights? We're being kept here against our will.'

'I think you'll find that civil rights have been suspended everywhere, and the human rights of people in the Antarctic is the last thing on anyone's mind.' He pauses. 'It's the safest place to be, in the world right now. Imagine that, we're the envy of everyone, down here. We can go skiing, we have enough food at our fingertips. We're our own little society, we generate our own solar power, we desalinate our water, we have our own sewage plant. And no one who is diseased is going to get here, to get at us. We're safe.'

I tell the comms manager I need access to Nara's files. I say there are some research facts I need to check.

'I don't know where they are,' he says. 'But you're free to rummage around on the old drives. She would only have put her public files there, but you can try.' He gives me a quizzical look. 'You're not doing this as a make-work project, are you. I mean, given the news.'

'I meant to do it all along. I just didn't think I would have time.'

I file through the old drives, the archived music, field assistants' reports, winter trip reports, inventories of equipment in the sledge store, lab reports, drafts of projects. Then, buried within a file unhelpfully titled 'Science', a directory with her name. The folders inside are all about experiments: CO_2 uptake, carbon uptake, CTDs, Sea-Squirts, Chemical Analyses, Mass Spectrometer and Experiment Design. In a folder labelled 'home' I find a file. I try to open it, but it is password-protected. I ask the comms manager. 'Nothing I can do,' he says. 'Unless you know the password, that is.' I try various passwords, but none of them work. Why should they? I know so little about her – not her mother's maiden name, the name of her first lover. Nothing which might unlock the key to her existence, never mind any random combination of numbers and letters she might have used. Then I think of something, out of the blue, and try the word: polargirl2012. The file blossoms into life.

It is called *Wintering*.

2

At the lookout point over Charcot Bay three plain crosses marked the deaths that had happened on base. Two were for a Canadian-crewed Twin Otter which took off too heavy and failed to clear an iceberg in North Cove. The third cross marked the sea-ice incident. There were no bodies underneath, buried in Antarctic shale. The bodies were long gone, flown back to their home countries, or never found.

Helen and David stood looking out into the bay. A beam of sun sunk under the horizon, tracing the edges of the glacier with a cold yellow.

'She died somewhere out there.' He pointed to the southwest, past Adélie Island. 'The plane came down on the sea ice, which was breaking up at the time. The island is only fifteen miles away, but that's fifteen miles over disintegrating sea ice. They took the RIBs, but by the time they got there it was too late. They couldn't even find the body, although they dove for it.' He paused. 'I flew with her down to Ice Blue that summer, it must have been about six months before she was killed. We just happened to be on the plane together. She was going to input fuel, and I was on my way to see Mount Vinson for the first time. She was so – so *thrilled*. She was so enthusiastic, like a child. It reminded me of what I'd felt, my first few seasons down here.'

'You don't love it here anymore?'

He looked away, as if stung by her question.

'It's the simplicity of life here I like,' David said, finally. 'Deal with the cold, survive, do the job at hand.' He paused. 'Once you've known this life, you never forget it. It – it holds you, in some way. It's like a marker you measure the rest of your life by.'

They turned their eyes back into the sun and Helen felt the pull of the horizon: thinking, now the sun will sink, *now, now, now*. But the sun remained in the sky, stalled just above the horizon, hovering over a sea greasy with congealed ice. Mountain, ice, water, sky; and those unnameable colours: lava, tangerine, mauve and another colour, nameless, between rotting plums and black – the black-purple of dog's gums, or embers in the middle of fires, when they have burnt low.

The sun will be extinguished. Only animals, burrowers, hibernators, will survive. Raptors – hawk-eyed animals: eagles, owls, lions. They tell me this. At night they appear on the dark screen of my eyelids. The world will be only glittering snow and cold, ice. Cold stars in the sky, their dazzling silver light, like swords. Dark horses graze into a starved future.

This is what the planet was saying, Nara wrote. The voices she heard only very rarely spoke in words, but when they did she transcribed their message in the Wintering file.

David appeared in the doorway of the unoccupied laboratory Helen had taken as her office. He found her staring at the computer. When she saw him, she changed the screen.

'They'll pull us out of here before winter. Don't worry.'

'You sound worried,' she said. 'That's what worries me most of all.'

'What are you writing?'

'Oh just – just notes.'

'I won't try to read it.'

'You could read anything here, if you wanted to.'

He gave her a steady look. 'Maybe, but I don't want to.'

'I found a file,' she said. 'Nara's file. A sort of diary,

although interspersed with work notes, with experiment observations, weather observations.'

'And what are you getting out of it?' He didn't say: *of your spying*. That's how he classed reading other people's diaries, even if they were dead. And he knew a thing or two about spying.

'Did you know she heard voices?'

'Whose voices?'

'Not people's. The planet – she believed the planet was speaking to her.'

He nodded, but said nothing.

'Maybe she really heard them,' Helen pressed on. 'Perhaps it was real.'

'It can't be.'

'Why not?'

'Because the planet doesn't speak.'

'How do you know?'

'Do you know how many people suffer from depression and anxiety in an Antarctic winter? Over half. If they all said the planet was speaking to them, would you believe them?' David shook his head – slowly, again a gesture more of regret than disbelief. 'It just isn't possible.'

'Do you always need to be certain in order to believe?'

'Believing in something is serious, you know. It's a serious matter. If you get it wrong, you can lose everything. Even your mind. Look at what happened to…' he stopped. 'To her.'

She thought he would leave, then. But he didn't – he stayed in the door, a lean, tall figure in moleskins, regulation fleece, woollen socks fraying around the edges. He flinched.

'What's the matter?'

'Electric shock. I'm getting tired of zapping myself.'

'I know, I've never had so many electric shocks in my life – here, on the ship. I notice I hesitate before touching metal now.'

'The charge builds up,' he said. 'There's hardly any moisture in the air, there's nowhere for it to go.'

'Doesn't it bother you, this – ' she threw her arms open, 'this *confinement*?'

'Yes it bothers me. Meanwhile everyone else out there in the world, that's all they want, safety, at any cost. People will give up almost anything in order to be safe.'

'I don't want safety at all costs.'

She found he was looking at her. There was something of the intellectual in his gaze, the cold thrust of fact. He was like a doctor, or a psychiatrist, this man. One of those men who was evaluating you, always one beady eye tuned toward your flaws. He had the arrogance of knowledge. He expected to be consulted, to be deferred to, he expected to dispense reassurance but it would be of the barbed-with-truth variety, it would never be fully reassuring because he was too avid for the facts, for the *point*. She wanted to say, don't you know that all emotion and thought – anything that was worthwhile about human life – lives between these points. Life took place between peaks of facts. Life took place in troughs, in hollows.

An hour later David sits in one of the old pitrooms which serve as telephone booths. The room's only decoration is an ice axe hanging by a single nail on the wall. He thinks, well, if I can't take it anymore there's always the ice axe.

In front of him, the telephone twitches. He finds he can't pick it up.

He is not thrilled about being kept here, but neither is he anxious, devastated, desperate to leave. He is beginning to suspect he may have been handed a piece of luck.

Although what is *luck*? There wasn't much of it in the annals of polar exploration; at best it was an elusive substance. In normal life, away from the flare of the great icefields, it was like a clock; it ticked along, soundlessly. Once every while it chimed a floating hour, and life became an aqueduct of dreams. But he distrusted this – that happiness seemed only a substance to be hoarded, then savoured when it was withdrawn. Life was very rarely graced with happiness, David believed; apart from that, happiness was exactly like luck: it had very bad timing, present at the precise moment when you are least likely to be aware of it and absent when it is most needed. These gruesome emotional mathematics held him in their spell, because he was a descendent of his great-grandfather's luck, a disciple of his survival.

He tells his wife about his week, she tells him about hers. They speak about events, not thoughts or feelings. Kate never asks David about the people he was stuck with – that was how she put it, *stuck with* – and he never mentions anyone directly by name. Instead he refers to them by their job titles: the base commander, the boatman, the historian.

Kate has never been jealous. They were of the same tribe, that of the effortlessly confident, who knew that their existence was approved of by the universe. If something were to rupture this fantasy, their anger and disappointment would be as huge and neverending as the wind. He is afraid of his wife. Yes, he fears her, because she is him. They are the same creature.

There's more than one way to starve. Helen had said this, on the ship, months ago now, when they were talking of Elephant Island. And it struck him so bluntly at the time that he promptly forgot about it, until this moment.

He is certain now that Helen has had to overcome something enormous, she has had to cut herself off from joy. A small woman, possessed of a certain vigour, the body of a twenty-five-year-old even in her early forties. This is where David placed her – late thirties, early forties, a tumbledown age when the weeds are starting to gather but have not quite invaded the flower patch. She might yet have a second blooming, and turn her face toward the sun.

What else has he noticed about her? She wears dramatic bracelets more like armour than decoration, chunky rings that if properly employed would be like a set of brass knuckles. Her voice has a Scottish tinge, and indeed she comes from Edinburgh, originally, although she told David she had lost her accent, or toned it down to the extent that it was only a lilt snagging on certain vowels.

All this she'd told him on the ship. They'd spoken little since coming to base. Ships were good for trading confidences, but somehow being on land deterred them. On the ship Helen had told him she came from a bad-luck family. They had lost all their property, they were squanderers, she told David, biting on the word. They were stupid and unlucky and she feared she had inherited this trait, much as you would inherit a gene.

He had been on the edge of asking her if she would like to have a drink in his cabin. He imagined removing her jewellery, as if divesting her of the arguments she might use against him, running his hands along her fragile ribs.

But then he had gathered himself, fortified by both the memory and idea of Kate, and by his discomfort with lies and secrets. He is not a man for mysteries, for secrets. He would never find himself under someone's influence, or live a clandestine life. He would never have affairs. Women picked this up, as if hearing a homing signal, and immediately understood its value. Some woman or other had always wanted him.

Yes, if he had to lie to his wife, it would be akin to being seasick, for years to come. If he were going to sleep with Helen, he would have to first call his wife and tell her their marriage was over. That was the only way he would be able to do it, this thing people called betrayal.

His boss did not ring him that day, nor the next. On the rare days when the satellite dome was not covered in sticky snow, David tried to call himself, but no one picked up the private, unlisted emergency number he dialled. David knew this meant they had gone into crisis mode. Millions of British citizens, stranded around the world. It would be like living at the epicentre of an explosion – crisis lines, the internet gone down, people hysterical, ringing all the units, apart from the polar unit – or perhaps they were, and his deputy at this moment was taking Valium.

During the last pandemic he had slept at his office, they had been under lockdown. For three months he did not see Kate. His heart had been taut with anxiety, just as it was now. He yearned to be anchored again in that galaxy of wrath and privilege and proximity to knowledge and power, the sun from which he took his bearings. But most of all he wanted the world to stop spinning with death and distress. Skirmishes in airports, train stations. People hot with desperation, their saliva zinging between mouth and nose, microbes flourishing.

They were trying to contain something that was uncontainable. In those days David had often wished he had been stuck aboard a ship in the Arctic or in the Antarctic. But he'd been in London, preparing for the Arctic summer season, for VIPs, 'melt tourism' for ministers, flying over Greenlandic ice streams, over Svalbard's glaciers, so that they could see the devastation of melt with their own eyes.

He missed the stilted, inadequate everyday life to which he had become accustomed and attached: his lukewarm marriage, his hair-shirt daily commute, lunches with his brother to hear what the future held, holding the painful knowledge at bay, that he was different from his family. He knew he lacked their supernatural fortitude. But why? It was something to do with the wild brazen hope that had sustained his great-grandfather, his ability to blinker fear and panic. Might not this hope, though diluted, run through David's veins?

Here he is, trapped under the narrowing ellipsis of a winter sun, forced to spend the winter on a well-provisioned Antarctic base, hot water in the showers, three hot meals on the table every day, a warm bed to sleep in. His great-grandfather spent his nights on Elephant Island under an upturned rowboat with the stench from the penguin guano warmed by their bodies, and his only sustenance for months was barely cooked penguin steaks, their greasy flesh.

His great-grandfather would have felt his future dissolving in front of him. He would have had that day, and maybe the next. And after that, who knew? His future was only a dark, glistening animal, like the Orcas which had terrified them when they were stranded on the ice floes. Shackleton and his men felt the thud as they lay in hastily erected tents, trying to sleep on the unstable sea ice. The killer whales were trying to break the ice, so they could devour the men, whom they mistook for seals.

There were two ways to be in this world, David knew: you could be submissive, or you could be devouring. You could accept your fate or you could fight it every step of the way. You had to stand up to life as if to a bully; it was much more powerful than you, and your conviction and defiance were the only weapons you had. He intuited that Helen understood this, and possibly had always known it even before he did, protected as he had been by his vicarage upbringing, by the sanguine and durable marriage of his parents. How was it that he alone of all of his family, with all its Army majors, politicians, explorers, understood that fundamental truth of existence: that life was not what you lived, but the force that tried to kill you. It had to be faced down like a tiger on a dark jungle path.

She found David in the dining hall, making himself a cup of tea.

'You're not going to ask me what's really happening, are you? Because I don't know.'

'No,' she said. Although in fact, she had been about to ask him just this question.

A silence followed, the only sound his spoon banging against the cup.

'Have you told – people at home, yet?' he asked.

'Yes. But – they're busy looking after themselves. I don't think they've even noticed I'm gone.'

'You're not married?' This question had taken him six weeks to utter, although he had wondered many times. She wore no ring, but then many people didn't, these days.

'I was married.'

'You're divorced?'

'Widowed.'

'I'm so sorry.' David wore an expression she had not seen before – sympathy, perhaps, or concern. It sat, lopsided and slightly uncomfortable, on his face.

'He died during the pandemic.'

'Oh, God. But you didn't get it?'

'No, I didn't.'

'That's lucky.'

'Yes,' she said. 'Although I didn't see it that way at the time.'

'What did you do – afterward?'

'Well, I had to be tested, although I wasn't with him the last week of his life.'

'You weren't?'

'No, he was – elsewhere. So.'

'And then what happened?'

'And then three years passed. I thought time had stopped, but actually it had kept going, all along, with me in it.'

Of those years, there was so much she would not say. They were too recently the past and not quite over. She could have asked David the question that those years had taken her to pose, although never answer: we know how to live, or we think we do, but do we know how to die? We only find out in the doing of it.

In the past three years death had become part of her life, and the possibility of it was suddenly everywhere. She had to step back from Tube trains, she found, lest the urge to hurl herself onto the tracks overcame her. Lorries hurtled by her as she crossed the road, and she had to force her step faster to avoid them. Death was so available, sometimes she had the impression it sat down with her to dinner.

She saw he was looking at her intently. 'What did you do?' he asked. 'I mean, for work?'

'I decided to write another book,' she said. 'I began to look around for a subject that would take me as far away a possible – off the earth, preferably. I wanted to write about something extreme. Man-eating saltwater crocodiles in Australian estuaries, suicide bombers, jihadi training camps. You name it.'

'And your extremity of choice was the Antarctic?'

She had expected David to say something just like this, remote, rigid with irony, rejecting the emotion she had revealed to him. Their shipbound intimacies had evaporated in the cold light of base life. She missed them. Now she felt uneasy with him; she always did with these privileged, go-for-the-jugular types, their ruthless dedication to the truth honed on some notion of their own superiority. Perhaps it was the vulnerability of their situation, perhaps she felt bested by him. He was married, and she could no longer hide behind the grandeur that marriage conferred. She would be just another person he met in the road. He had met plenty before, she presumed: ambitious women, scientists, intellectuals, and he would meet plenty after.

He turned his gaze away, to the window, a black square of

implacable polar darkness. 'You feel let down by life,' he said. 'But it can't be about our individual expectations any longer,' he shrugged. 'They're just not important enough, given what will happen to the planet. What is happening now.'

The anger she felt was like a silver, igniting light.

'What do you know about my life?' she found herself saying, before she had even thought the words. 'With your illustrious ancestor, your public school, your Oxbridge university, your career in the foreign office, for Christ's sake. What do you know about *life*?'

She nearly said, *your wife is alive*.

David pulled out his chair, scraping against the linoleum, and left.

Helen sat with her hands wrapped around her cup of tea, to gather warmth, but it had gone cold. She stared out the window at the glacier. It was covered in a thin glaze of ice, which glittered in the night.

3

Each day light is subtracted from our sky. The dark water sky is hardening to the white enamel of iceblink. Frazil ice glues floe to floe in the night, when the cold is most intense. The pack ice has gelled the ocean currents. They are forced under the surface, wending through the submarine alleys and tunnels of ice. On the surface, the departure of waves and tides has deepened our silence. The sea has frozen around us, a fist of noiselessness.

It will be two months before the ice is thick enough for us to walk on. Only ten years ago, Gerry the base commander told me, the sea ice froze to a thickness the length of the human body. Now it might only be inches thick and instead of locking themselves into ice, icebergs loll in slushy moats. We wait to see what the winter will do, whether it will be a good ice year.

I am reading one of the diaries kept by the early explorers, an Australian. He wrote that when summer came to the continent, 'the days passed fleeting and swift, as in cities.' But now, in winter, the day is night, we are living through a three-month-long polar night, and the days last forever.

According to the calendar it is May. In England there is a drought. The bluebells and apple blossoms have already come and gone; on average spring comes three weeks earlier than it did fifty years ago. May is summer now, although the month is plagued by violent storms which threaten to drop rain, but mysteriously never do. These tantalisations infuriate farmers. In May the grass is already parched and cucumbers and strawberries ruined.

I can't look at photographs of growing things. I can't look at the news, the internet, photographs well-meaning friends email in an attempt to keep me supplied with greenery, because my body says it is May and this should mean a lightening of body and spirit, a growth of hair and nails and a surge of melatonin, but instead my body is shutting down. My skin is dry, my hair limp. I feel no yearnings of any kind, not even hunger.

David has apologised, after a silence, an awkard choreography of avoidings. But we can't avoid each other here, and we all seem to understand that disputes have to be settled, as in families, before greater damage is done.

'I shouldn't have left like that,' he said.

'We're in a stressful situation. I shouldn't have said what I said.'

'I'm sorry, for what happened – to you. What you told me about.'

'I'm sorry, too,' I said.

Last night David showed me his great-grandfather's journal, a photocopy of it. 'I keep this with me, not the whole thing, but a few pages of it, always.'

'Always?' I am thinking of him on the Tube from his flat, winding underneath the sandy shale beds of the Thames, on his way to work in the corridors of power.

'Yes. You think that's a fetish, don't you?'

'Well, it is a little extreme, maybe.'

We read it together. At first I have trouble making out the spindly, fading hand:

It is 1915, or 1916; we are not certain. We have to keep moving. A blizzard can last two weeks, and snow builds up against anything stationery.

I wonder, what are we doing here? We were mappers, explorers. All gone now, our only purpose here is to survive.

Some nights it is too cold to sleep and we poke our heads out of the tent to count the stars. We travel over the sea ice. Last week one of our horses disappeared. After that we gave up talking.

Now we walk and walk over the slush and I can think of nothing. I used to recite the names of cities to myself, silently. Marrakesh, Antannarivo, Rangoon. Only later did I realise they were all hot, tropical cities. Places I might never see. I would spell them and re-spell them, try to remember their coordinates, the latitude and longitude, in my head on the slog, often in darkness, against only the moonlight. Moonlight as it turns out is excellent for spotting crevasses.

We feel like sinking boats taking on water. There is no respite, it seems, and no end, to our suffering. The dogs starved, one by one, or we shot them, because we couldn't take them with us on our journey toward the northern islands. There wasn't room in the boats, you see. Boris, the big husky, chewing on a penguin's wing, just as the Boss crept up to him with his rifle. The dog didn't even look up as the Boss aimed – that was how much those dogs trusted him.

Hope was with us, then. Rotten men are everywhere on this earth, but there are none among us; we know each other's strengths, our weaknesses too. We don't know if we are mad or very, very sane.

Our satellite dome becomes covered with what the comms manager terms the wrong kind of snow. It sticks in glutinous pancakes, then freezes overnight. The signal is obstructed by these patches, and the phone and internet is hazy with static. For two days not even the Iridium phone works. I immediately imagine a national crisis. One possibility is that our satellite connection is fine, the snowstorm a smokescreen for Cambridge, who are cagey about what is happening in the outside world. In communications blackouts we all feel our vulnerability and our aloneness more. We look at each other with expressions of hounded friendliness.

To reassure us, base commander Gerry tells us about the old days when there was no email, no internet, no Iridium phone over the winter, and the base commander would send a maximum of two hundred words per month off by satellite fax to Cambridge. A month's life, recorded in two hundred words. These missives are collected in binders stored in one of the disused pitrooms in the old building. No one looks at them anymore, but one night I turn the handle and walk into a cold room, its walls lined with coffee-coloured carpet.

The room is lined with ring binders stuffed with legal-sized carbon copies of the original typewritten accounts of sledge parties. They all date from the early 1970s through to the end of the eighties.

I take them to my office and read. They talk of men returned safely, of sun up and sun down, of the health of all on base. *A long sledge journey over sea ice to Porquoi Pas, out and back in three days. All men and dogs well and fighting fit.*

I read about the sea-ice accident when four men died sledging back from Stonington, a base long defunct, some twenty miles down the coast of the peninsula. The men thought the ice had frozen fast, but a blizzard brewed up and the sea ice blew out, taking the men with it. Two dogs made it back to base. Around their necks were remnants of their ropes, which had been cut. The men had cut the dogs free because they wanted to give them a chance. It took the dogs two months to find their way home to base. They had probably survived on penguin. The men were never seen again.

The reports are titled *good ice year, bad ice year*. Occasionally, about one in eight years now, it will freeze solid enough for sledging parties to make it to the coast of the mainland peninsula. If we had a good ice year, we could travel further off base, across the bay to the mountains which remain out of reach to us, even down to San Martin, the Argentine base. I learn that the ice is not a prison, but a highway out of here. Only when it fails to form are we truly trapped.

I find the report about the exploding dogs. This is a famous incident, part of the lore of our narrow culture. At Stonington a team of wintering men had to abandon the base ahead of schedule; the ship could not get in to take them out, because – this was in the 1970s – there was too much sea ice. A plane was sent down to get them out before winter closed in. But the plane developed a mechanical problem and it would only be able to make one journey to evacuate the men. All equipment, including the dogs, would have to be left behind.

The dogs would starve in an Antarctic winter. The men could not bear the thought of the dogs, increasingly feral and desperate, living on the occasional penguin or seal they managed to rip apart, devouring each other, or freezing to death without their kennels. No animal, even the Arctic husky, could survive the Antarctic winter unsheltered.

In those days large stocks of explosives were kept for geological survey work, to blast away rock. The men took the dynamite, strapped it to the dogs, and constructed a remote timer. When they were in the plane, out of sight of the base, they pushed the button.

For a long time I thought about the exploding dogs of Stonington. One particular vision haunted me: a dog, sticks of dynamite, un-detonated, attached to his increasingly skeletal body, wandering through the darkness of the Antarctic wasteland, far from home.

David and I sit in the bar together, long after everyone has left, with cups of tea or hot chocolate. Here, where alcohol is freely available, we rarely drink. I have the feeling we are keeping ourselves under wraps.

He says we are eccentrics, ice priests, or ice disciples. (His use of 'we' means I have been admitted to the Antarctic fraternity.) He says we drill down through time; ice coring is about depth, he says, but depth equals time. The further down you go, the further back you go. We are doing this to scry into the planet's future; he says we have all become obsessed with the future, but our methods are about the past. Some of us have written obscure books, some of us are on telly every night, on the ten o'clock news. Melt prophets, hired apocalypticians. That's what we have become. All of us transfixed by events that took place 200, 400 million years ago.

I say, the Antarctic, is it really a place, or a giant outdoor laboratory? I feel sorry for it sometimes. Us crawling all over it with our theorems of exploration, elaborate computer models, me with my story of death, those dead bodies of explorers grinding through the ice even as we speak. We could disappear into it. This place could swallow us whole.

I don't tell David that at times here I feel as if I have been filled with lead. I feel I ought to pray – me, the atheist. I have never felt this before, not in the most violent deserts. Pray for what, to what? For absolution, for protection from the cold-eyed God who sits suspended in this upside-down sky.

That winter Nara wrote: *There are the dead, and the living, and what between them? Dusk. A collusion. There is no dusk here, and that is why life seems unreal. There are no inbetween states, there are no ghosts. So we haunt ourselves, having no one else to do the haunting for us.*

I see him here, in his lab, in front of his computer screen. A conqueror's profile, like his namesake, Alexander the Great. His body was like this, too: he belonged on a Greek urn. He was sweet, sly, vicious. Nara did not like uncomplicated people. He was forty people in one. A stark, arresting presence, not one of these flaccid characters our modern age throws up, self-obsessed, languorously narcissistic, go-with-the-flow types to whose hands the future of the planet has been unfortunately bequeathed.

He was a hot sandstone palace. He was one of those people you either took against, and violently, or fell in love with. Most people on sensing this slunk away, taking their discomfort with them. But Nara had lived in discomfort, she had conquered her own challenges, and knew about both: that was why she had returned the look he had given her in their first, light-dazzled days in the Falklands; returned it to him intact, and perhaps even more steely with challenge. Our fates are decided in such moments.

He is only someone she never should have considered. But she was here, trapped in the ice desert. Anthropologists study such situations, of siege and nearness, of sex and attraction in a limited population. You look for sexual partners in your immediate environment, because there is no other environment. And suddenly the impossible becomes the only possibility.

She was marooned in the Antarctic winter with the one person she loved, who was also the one person she should have most avoided. It ought to have been a stalled paradise. She hated him, I realise now, for refusing her, there – here. He was not passing her over for someone else, which would have had its own pain, but for an idea: the idea of the woman he would one day love. She admired this self-control, this honesty. She loved him all the more for it, and carried this appalled fascination around with her that entire Antarctic year, heavy chalices slurping with the poison of disillusion. But she had her own honesty, too. She did not console herself with a lesser love, for Luke. Like Alexander, she was holding out for the real thing.

When it was light all the time I had no difficulty sleeping. Now that it is dark I wake up every three hours. I miss the noises of the city at night: the fox rummaging in the garden, the traffic streaking down the road. Here trying to sleep means empty, sandblasted hours, the sound of snow spitting against the window, blown down here on the back of katabatics of the Weddell Gyre.

I give up and get dressed. At two, three, five in the morning I go outside and watch satellites careen through the night sky. At first they look like shooting stars or planes, but they have a too rigid trajectory, they are travelling too fast. Who is up there? NASA, Google Earth. Iran, the newly resurgent Iraq? North Korea? China, probably; China is spying on everyone, along with the Russians. I wonder if they can zero in on a lone woman in the Antarctic night, wearing three hats against the cold, staring into the sky.

The moon looks closer, here, and far more real. I stare at its dusky seas, the surface pockmarked with craters, so etched and alive, reciting to myself the names I learned from the planet atlas in the physics lab: *Mare Imbrium*, Sea of Showers; *Mare Tranquillitatus*, Sea of Tanquillity; *Oceanus Procellarum*, Ocean of Storms.

PART VI
Glimmer

1

In the month after he left base that March, Luke wrote to Nara nearly every day. It couldn't have been easy for him to find the time on the ferry flight; he would land the plane, he told her, do the customs formalities, then look for the nearest computer. Each email had as its subject line the name of his current stop on the way back to Canada: Montevideo, Santa Caterina, Rio de Janeiro, Recife, Bélem, Manaus, Curaçao, Mérida, Houston:

If you ever come to Belém with me, this is where we shall stay. The Selva Hotel is the exact opposite to base. It is where you belong. The building is full of tropical plants and is painted in warm colours. I can just imagine going on a relaxed tour around the interesting-shaped rooms and hallways listening to your impressions. Yes – that's a nice thought to go to bed with I think.

Usually she opened his messages straight away and read them with real interest, but within a few lines they became directionless, claustrophobic, even vaguely accusing, when she did not answer him quickly enough. Once she did not answer for several days; she had a scientific paper to finish for a tight deadline. Messages began to accumulate in her inbox, each one a crescendoing plea for news of her safety. *Did you fall down a crevasse?*

She logged off her email and went for a walk around the Point. There was only a narrow window of light now. In the midday twilight she walked through slush, over rocks, through brown stains on the snow – seal blood – through tufts of moulted penguin feathers, watching as the sky changed from the colour of sallow bruises to teal, then lead, then indigo, finally a solid night in which the silence and darkness become moulded into a hard transparent substance, like black resin.

She saw that the skua chicks were fully grown, at the beginning of winter. These were the survivors: two chicks were born to each pair but the parents or the sibling routinely killed the weaker chick, so only one survived. Very few fur seals remained but they growled and barked at her as always, like sullen sentries to some fabulous ice kingdom.

She took a shortcut past the Cross and headed back to base. She had to grab a few hours' sleep before starting her night shift. In summer the Saints took turns to be on nights, but in the winter it fell to the winterers to devise a rota. Twenty years before, the base laboratory had burnt to the ground because the night watchman had failed to spot a rubbed wire, which sparked in the friction of a door, which ignited the tinder-dry wood. The entire laboratory burnt to the ground within the hour.

At night, base had the aspect of an abandoned ship locked in a belt of ice, static and humming, exactly like their icebound ship on the journey to the Antarctic. On this terrestrial ship Nara did her rounds: lab, kitchen, offices, genny shed, incinerator, carpentry workshop, flicking on lights, flicking them off. The carpentry workshop required the most careful investigation – an entire shed full of wood, twitching for spark.

When she could no longer keep her eyes open she went outside in her shirtsleeves – the temperature was minus twenty – to jolt herself awake. She craned her head and looked into the sky. The stars were mute and cold. The night sky in the Antarctic was blacker than any sky she had ever seen, full of dark voids which suggested collapsed galaxies, black holes, bursts of entropic energy.

The light was on in one of the labs. She went to turn it off and found Alexander there, sitting slumped over a piece of paper.

'What are you doing up?'

He put a pen down on the table with a clack. 'Can't sleep.' He ran his long, lean fingers through his hair. 'Have a seat.'

On his desk an atlas lay open to a double-page spread of Finland and Sweden. The computer screen was open to a coding programme, and pieces of paper criss-crossed by graphs and plots were scattered on his desk. On the pages were curving precise lines, like an architect's first sketches for a building.

'I'm working on hypsometry. I'm looking at paleo-scenarios and it helps me to draft them out by hand first,' he explained. 'Here, I'll show you.' He opened the coding screen. His ice sheets were not real but a series of equations and calculations fed into a computer model. He worked with two models coupled together, he explained to her, an ice sheet model called FAMOUS. The 3-D ice sheet model was called GLIMMER.

She stared at the hieroglyphic train of symbols and numbers. He watched her watching. He seemed to observe her every move, as if she were a private experiment of his. 'I feed in observations, which are then correlated to equations.' He switched screens to the 3-D function. 'A few years ago this didn't exist. You couldn't see the model, it had no existence other than as a string of coding.'

Behind the coding screen ice sheets started to form, hardening first from a grid, then the bottom layers of ice, then the top crust. Colour poured in – white, threaded with thin striations of grey grit. The ice sheets undulated, covering a computer-generated landscape like sheets of frozen meringue.

The landscape looked familiar – was that not the glacier

opposite the accommodation block? 'That's the end of the last glacial maximum, here on base,' she said.

'You recognise it.'

'But I thought you were modelling the future.'

'To know the future you have to look at the past. I'm modelling the last stage of the last ice age in order to try to figure out what's going to happen in the next few decades.' He opened another file, a computerised version of his architectural sketch. It showed vectors, alignments, depths and surfaces. 'If I put today's observations and measurements in, with the model set for twenty years from now, it refuses to produce ice.'

'What do you mean, *refuses*?'

'It should be creating ice through the coming hundred years. But according to the model it's gone in twenty. All the ice around base.'

'But that's impossible,' she said.

He switched the screen to the 3-D model of the ice sheet and pointed to its edge, to the hollow of ice where the glacier from the centre of their island flowed into the sea. 'This is the outlet glacier. That's where it starts to pull back. I can't run the whole time-sequence for you here, the server doesn't have the capacity. But once I get back home to the supercomputer, that's what it will show – a receding edge, taking everything with it, until even the centre is gone. Even if we add the precipitation to the model, the ice still thins.'

Nara understood: The ice was thinning at the edges faster than it could thicken in the centre. 'You add precipitation, snow crystals, and you should have more ice. But you don't.'

He nodded. 'Because it's too warm.'

The sheets were restructured by heat, by melt, Alexander explained. For melt, there were two processes, mechanical and thermal. Thermal melting began the process of disintegration, but then the top melting percolated through to the next layer and created firn. The waves carved holes, scalloping and weathering its edges – these were the mechanical processes. 'Ice melts from within, but also from the outside. When these two processes happen together it's the end of the line for the ice. That's what's so interesting,' he said, 'its life cycle is just like ours, birth and decay, although over inhumane timescales.'

When they were on the ship Alexander had told her, 'That's why I'm here. To see for myself what an ice age would have been like.' He wanted to witness the stately process of being frozen in for the winter, of watching ice accumulate, advance. He wanted to know the grandiose, slow, invisible dawn of the ice age. Even if in the Antarctic it happened quickly, over the course of a winter, with grindings, the explosions as icebergs capsized in the water, the mortar fire crack of two grounded bergs colliding.

He gathered up his papers. He had beautiful hands, fine and delicate, but strong. Those hands could trigger her happiness, like a spark.

'Look, the sky is clear, for a change.'

They put on their parkas, went outside and walked beyond the verandah, beyond the reach of the emergency lighting. There in darkness they could see the stars better.

The world was spinning so fast, Alexander told her, 1,600 kilometres an hour at the equator, and they didn't even feel it. But on their latitude, 69 degrees South, the earth spun much slower, so that if they turned round fast enough, they would keep pace with the earth's rotation. At the South Pole, Alexander said, the planet spun only a centimetre every minute.

'Do you think time is slower, here, because we're not moving?' She asked. 'Time and space are linked, after all.'

'No, our perception of it might change, very slightly, but not in any way we would notice.'

'I can't believe we're spinning, all the time, and we don't feel it.'

They put their arms out and began to turn, faster and faster, heads craned, eyes fixed on the sky, alone in the Antarctic night on a deserted continent, invisible apart from satellites streaking through the sky on their hasty missions.

She slipped and Alexander put his hand on the small of her back, to steady her. She felt again the strange electricity of his touch, and with it a fleeting ghost of the happiness she had felt with him those days in the Falklands, when they were waiting to be transported to their white world.

That dark morning she fell asleep in her pitroom, nearly happy for the first time in months, listening to the thin, stinging sound of snow flung against her window.

The winter days turned to night. The sea became unnaturally calm before it froze, because the ice floes muffled the ocean swells. Nara watched as the ice changed from gruel to porridge, then a hardening, so that the only sound is the clink-clink of ice floes welding together, not a delicate glassy sound, but metallic and rupturing, like steel girders grinding together.

The short journey from the sledge store to the accommodation block became an ordeal. Wind whipping around the corners of the buildings now smothered in seracs of snow caught her unawares. Snow bit at their skin, like a thousand tiny insects. The skin on their lips chapped until it fell off into the soup and floated there, like flakes of salt.

Winter is a door, Nara wrote. Once shut, the Antarctic winter was a door which could not be opened. It had to be passed through, like a ghost.

2

Cirrostratus, Cirrocumulus, Altostratus, Altocumulus, Nimbostratus, Stratocumulus, Cumulonimbus. *You see clouds in the Antarctic like nowhere else on earth.* The echo of these words surprised him – he did not have a good memory, normally, either for names or for conversations. But yes, he remembered now that Nara had sat beside him on the way down to the Ellsworths, the cloud atlas open on her knees, and he had instructed her in clouds.

He flew through layers of cloud. A pilot had to be able to read the sky, especially in the Antarctic, where the weather changed on a dime. Luke knew that clouds are made of tiny water droplets, ice crystals or both. The frigid temperatures of Antarctica's interior meant little or no water vapour was held in the air, which could inhibit cloud formation; at the South Pole, for example, there were hardly ever clouds. But along the coast there were many, because of the influence of the sea, the circumpolar current and the powerful storms that congregated along it.

He usually looked forward to arriving back on base, to having a shower, a drink. This time, though, some kind of reckoning awaited him. Would he tell this writer woman how Nara had inserted herself effortlessly, almost clandestinely, in his thoughts, three – no, four now – years ago, on what had begun as a routine trip to the Ellsworths. For those few months she had filled the space between moments, thoughts, the spasms of necessary concentration while flying, wondering about her intimacies, those secret things she could never tell anyone, wrapped in cloaks of shame and need, the principles she had violated, the people she had been unkind to. He considered that you could say you were in love with someone only when you were more interested in their failures, in their sadnesses, than in their triumphs.

Then, when he thought of her, it was preceded by a feelng in his heart: not a comfortable feeling, but a small convulsion, like a sickness. He remembered a TV programme he had seen just before he had come South for the season, a documentary that proved that the heart had a nervous system, that the heart had cells that 'thought' for themselves. These cells sent messages to the brain, not vice-versa. That must be where the old saying came from, *let your head look after your heart*. Or, *that's the heart thinking, not the head*. But how incredible that it was true, that the heart could think for itself!

Before his divorce, he'd paid little attention to the workings of the heart. There would be only two chapters, rough-cut, in his emotional life: Married Life, and After Divorce. The end of his marriage was receding now, so that it felt like something lived through in another era, such was its connection to a previous version of Luke. Yes, he had been a different person, when he was married. Complacent, happy. Far kinder.

He had tried to remain that person. He made sure he and his wife went to counselling, first to a bearded man in a glassy Cape Town apartment, then when they were in Britain to a clinic specialising in couple therapy in one of those airless suburbs where people lived and died in the mausoleums of their Victorian houses. But the counselling only stiffened his wife's resolve.

Then began a time of learning. He learned, oh, so many things he had never wanted to know: about bitterness, the snare of love, the black tar taste of hate on his tongue. The casual damage people inflict on each other. Patience and treachery, the quiet growl of time. He had no doubt that he was becoming more humane. Although at what cost? He was moving closer to death than to life, and all this tarnished knowledge was taking him there. He was on the downward slope of experience: overaware, no more desire in his brain or body, a refusal to believe in almost everything, bruised from days and nights spent on Antarctic bases between flights, waiting to be given orders.

Into this desert walked Nara. He was so unalert he didn't even notice her until she was sitting there in the cockpit, beside him.

He banked and turned northwest over the Lassiter Coast; he was only an hour from base now. Beneath him he saw the wreckage of ice sheets. It was not a melt, but a slivering. When an ice sheet breaks up into the water it looks as if someone has tipped over a vat of needles. The water hovers at the freezing point, perhaps one degree above, and the needles melt. Now the coastal water was nearly always two degrees above zero in the summer, and the ice sheets dissolved like icing sugar.

Another season was nearly over, another season of flying glaciologists, aerial mappers, surveyors, ice-core drillers, into the scene of their destruction. He loved working with scientists, even if he lamented the destruction that drew their interest. Science was a refuge, he considered, the only asylum from the vulgar scrum of politics. Scientists were wise for the simple fact that they were disinterested. He always liked those ice corers, geologists, glaciologists he worked with and for; less so the VIPs, the ministers, the royal family members on fly-by-night visits to the Antarctic to raise their environmental credibility. They sat in his plane, flying over the most amazing landscape on earth, and did paperwork or fell asleep. And he would sit in the cockpit and shake his head, the sour expression Nara would notice in the Ellsworths playing with his lips.

She would not be there. She hadn't been there for years, now. No one knew where she had gone, just as no one knew why desire came to an end, or what to do when it did. But he had no doubt Nara had been one of them, the lovers of ice. To be enchanted by ice takes a particular kind of soul, he considered; most people saw death in the frozen continent, they saw lack. It took a strange nature, a person somehow divorced from themselves, from their interests, their destiny, to appreciate its pale fire.

The woman found him quickly, the next morning in fact. She was about forty, he guessed, possibly younger. She was slim, not tall, not short – an indefinite person, the sort who wouldn't stand out in a group. She'd obviously been on base long enough to pick up the garb. She was dressed in the full Antarctic uniform: fleece, Polar Research Council T-shirt underneath, moleskins, standard issue woollen socks.

She held out her hand. 'I'm Helen. You've probably heard of me.'

'I have,' he said. 'Listen, I'm a bit tired. Why don't we talk tomorrow. Or maybe the day after. From what I hear, we've got plenty of time to talk.'

'Sure. Whenever is good for you. Just let me know.'

She would have to find him, to lure him. Both understood this perfectly well.

The following night he gave a talk and a slideshow on the salvage work on Midas III. Everyone came – fifty-six people ranged around tables in the dining hall, the evening gathering outside.

He explained that Midas IV, the new base, would have to be moved inland from its present position. That was what the director of the Polar Research Council had determined on his visit to the base, a thousand miles to the east. They had radared the ice shelf and it was ready to fracture somewhere around the position of the present base. As for Midas III, Luke explained, the ice shelf had broken off a year previously, taking the old base, by then only three miles from the edge of the shelf, with it. Midas III set sail, now buried in a twenty-mile-long iceberg. The Polar Research Council had to find a way to get onto the iceberg and dismantle the base, Luke explained. He was asked to provide air support, although most of the dismantling had to be done by ship.

'It was a delicate operation,' he explained. 'They had to pull the ship up next to the iceberg, and anchor it, even though they are mooring and it's moving. My job was to fly there, landing on it as if it were still part of the landmass. I could still see where the old skiway used to be. But icebergs are more prone to crevassing. Because their bottom, however deep, is in contact with the ocean, they split and fracture. At worst, you could lose a plane down a crevasse.'

Helen stared at the photographs projected on the screen: the *Mercury*, the *Astrolabe*'s sister ship, moored alongside the iceberg, men driving small tractors to the edge of an ice cliff, lowering down beams, drums, canisters, containers with gigantic cranes. Luke landing on the iceberg, coming in for one run to strafe the ground with his skis, to see if any crevasses opened up.

When Luke finished his talk there was a question and answer session. 'Why don't they just leave the base there?' Helen asked.

'They can't. International regulations require us to dismantle it.' Eventually, he explained, the ice shelf would melt and disappear beneath the waves. The base would become sea junk, excreting toxins.

'But surely it would be no worse than any shipwreck,' Helen said.

'You never know what's in those chemical containers in the laboratories,' Luke shook his head. 'You just don't know.'

After the talk David caught her arm.'It's incredible, isn't it?' he says. 'What they can do, here.'

She agreed. 'Who would have thought they could dismantle an old base on a moving iceberg.'

'The pilots here, there are only ten or twelve men in the world who can do what they can do.'

Luke turned his head slightly, as if he had overheard them. Helen watched as he turned off the projector and the photographs of tractors, cranes, the ship dwarfed by the ice cliff, all dissolved into a dark screen.

Luke was just as Nara described him; in four years he had not changed – perhaps a deeper line etched here, a loosening of skin there, but he was still that dark-haired man, a well-made if not handsome face, grey-blue eyes, in good shape, a man who, at twenty-five, must have been startlingly vital. His Army training had kept him in condition well beyond the years when it ended – Helen had seen this, too, with other men of a similar age in their late forties or fifties, in Afghanistan. These men never lost their military bearing, however much they might have wanted out of the military. That life put its stamp on them.

She approached him. He glanced in her direction, then away. Eventually he said, 'What is it you're writing again? A book?'

'Yes, a book.'

'On what?'

'On death. Death in the Antarctic, specifically.'

'Oh, well.' Luke laughed. 'You've got plenty of material, then.'

She said, 'You must see her everywhere, here.'

He stared at her for a moment. 'Memories fade, don't they, with time?'

She shook her head. 'I don't think they do.' She paused. 'What did you think of Alexander?'

'He was – ' he stopped. 'Am I being interviewed here, I mean, formally?'

'I'm not the police. I don't conduct formal interviews. We're just talking.'

'I don't think talking with you people is ever just talking.'

She wanted to say, *us people*? What category have you assigned me to? Lawyers, insurance salesmen? Spies?

'I sat for years with her, just here – ' he flung out his arm toward one of the cafeteria tables.

He said no more and turned away, possibly so that she could not see his face. Helen had the impression that everything within him had curled up into a protective posture, a question mark of silence.

'I've got to pack up here,' he said, gesturing toward the projector, the laptop.

For a second Helen wondered if she should tell him about the Wintering file, then decided against it. She nodded, then walked away.

I can hear…what it is saying.

He and Nara sit in the Air Unit office. Between her fingers she is twirling the little plastic bull of the bottle of Sangre de Toro he had given her as an end-of-summer present.

It is the night he'd flown into base for the medical evacuation, and he is so tired. He and Chris are on four-hour shifts; every four hours they fight their way through the wind and snow over to the hangar to check that the heaters are preventing the aircraft from freezing to the spot. He is so tired from the effort of rescue, from flying five hours worrying about icing, about knottage and windspeed and fuel and power, and yet he cannot sleep.

He needs to talk to her. It will be another two months before he sees her again. This is still in a time when two months away from her feels like a sentence, a miserable longing.

Who is talking?

Not who. What. It has a voice. It tells me – it comes from the earth. It's not human.

But if you can't hear what it is saying, how do you know it's speaking to you then?

I don't. It's just a – a feeling. Or a signal. It's more like a signal I'm picking up, from a long way away. I'm trying to understand what it's saying.

He is thinking: she is sensitive. Perhaps too sensitive for this place.

It says God doesn't exist.

He snaps back to attention. *Does it?*

It says that it is God, or rather that God is in it, that it is His embodiment.

That's not so outlandish, he thinks. I've heard that before. Perhaps it isn't so serious. Perhaps she will be okay, yet.

Now, four years later, he sits in his pitroom, the storms of early winter howling outside. He has never been on base in the winter, apart from the medevac he did that year in early August. He has no experience of this live animal called winter which paws at his door as if desperate to come inside.

When has he last thought about God? Not since that night, possibly – the last night he drove the road to Digby Neck.

He would see it so clearly from the air in the planes he would fly years later, gliding over the narrow, gouged province of his birth on his way to more worldly places.

Digby Neck is unique; he doubts there is anywhere like it in the world – a long, thin ribbon of land, bordered on one side by a gigantic bay raked by the highest tides in the world.

On the lee side, dunes, hair grass, a smaller narrow bay. The large bay drains twice daily, refilling, driven by the most powerful tidal gyre in the world. Here the difference between high and low tide is fifteen feet. On the mudflats, sand pipers, clams, Junebugs, sand worms, quahogs, mussels, barnacles are exposed, their skins glistening in the sun. Overhead crows, hawks, bald eagles, and seagulls wait to spot the glint of the sun on flesh.

The tide does not arrive, it storms. You can see it on a silver wave, coming. On the other side of the neck is a thin bay, much more static. For some reason the tide does not penetrate here.

He has to make a decision: whether to leave, or to stay.

Every night that week he drives the Neck, with its narrowing road. At the end, toward the open mouth of the bay, the spit of land fragments into three narrow islands. Here ferries must be used to cross the water, tiny four-car ferries, engineless, pulled across the sand banks on a chain.

He secures the jeep, looks at his murky headlights clouded by the corpses of wasps, bees, mayflies. The road narrows toward the end, were there is only one lane. Hair grass on one side, sand dunes. The hair grass thin, resinous, like violin strings.

He has lived in this narrow province all his life. This is where he grew up, learned to fly at the local glider club, before going to Florida to train, then to the UK, then South Africa, then the Army, then Scotland, then the Falklands, and finally the Antarctic. Punta Arenas, Santiago, Cape Town, the Falklands, those Southern Hemisphere rim-named places he frequented and their turbulent, empty seas: he would develop a fascination with the southern hemisphere, because it was so empty of land and people in comparison to the northern half of the world, but also for its difference – the stars, the sky, plants, birds, the wind. The Antarctic he will think of as the place where the wind is born. He is a pilot, and he lives by the wind.

He is twenty-four and his girlfriend of four years is pregnant. That October, she will have their child. He knows what he should do: marry her, settle down here, give up dreams. Drive from Zellers to Canadian Tire, along hushed wooded highways, misted vaulting valleys. And one day, if he can stand it for long enough, he will bring his daughter here to Digby Neck, to watch the tide fill the Bay of Fundy, then retreat.

Driving the road to Digby Neck that night for the last time he knows nothing of his future, nothing at all of the woman he will marry and divorce, the lonely flat roads he will drive with her at the bottom of the world, Cape Agulhas, Struisbaai, Arniston, sand dunes there too, an emerald empty ocean beyond them. Why is it that we can't see ahead? He will never accept how life is so gauged against our survival; if only we could see around corners, he thinks, we could protect ourselves from our futures, from our fates.

After Luke's talk, Helen retreated to the laboratory which had become her office. On the walls were maps: a geophysical map of the Antarctic, showing the four south poles – geographical, magnetic, relative inaccessibility and 'true', and an Ice Extent map, which showed how the Antarctic doubled in size due to the growth of winter sea ice. What was she doing in this place? She yearned to see a painting, or antiquities, to see green, to meet strangers.

On her computer screen was Nara's Wintering file. On this precise date, March 5th, four years earlier Nara had written, *In the Antarctic time feels like something to be got through, rather than lived. The present is only about endurance. Here, the only things that exist are the past and winter.*

2012, 2013, 14, 15: these are the numbers of Helen's recent past, numbers filled with trips, assignments; November 2012 in her diary of that year read: *November 6: Baghdad*

Airport, where she went to do a story on the newly reopened airport; *November 21: Kandahar*, where she would research a story about the aftermath of the British Army's pullout from Afghanistan, the instant clandestine economies which sprung up to fill the void, the private armies, the reversal to warlord practices. The past was only vacuums and eddies quickly filled by more time, so that within months it was impossible to say what had really happened in a particular place. Time cauterised events like wounds closing in on themselves.

She had always felt a compulsion to shoulder other people's tragedies. This was a more selfish instinct than was immediately obvious; it allowed her to draw her own boundaries, to see how much she could take. She would absorb displacement, rape, murder, starvation, all that while harbouring an underhand assumption that by putting herself in their path, on behalf of others, she would be granted a celestial immunity from their effects in her own life.

All that changed in late 2012. She stopped travelling, because no travel was allowed. Her diary was empty of places and tasks. Instead it read: *Feb 15: Someone has cloned my debit card and bought £800 worth of kitchen tiling. Feb 20: Can't get up in the morning.*

Helen realised many things in that year: how she refused to believe in the wholesale destruction of the planet, even while she worked on stories about war, environmental collapse, climate change. How angry she was: she wanted to erase nations, for the harm they had done. She wanted to erase the easy cynicism she saw in her own country, which had become nothing more than a money-obsessed dissolute old victor, a serial adulterer who held values of loyalty and truth in open contempt.

From the sick pride of nations, the bad faith, the Antarctic would save her. Because she would be in a continent owned by no one. She would go, for the first time in her life, to nobody's country.

Luke slid open the doors to the aircraft hangar. Inside, three Twin Otters huddled. He walked around them, running his hands along their fuselages, over the rivulets, the embossed penguins-and-propellers emblem. He knew each of their quirks – the fickle generator on BZ, the sticky trim on BC, the bounce of BB, how it flew into the sky more eagerly than the other planes, thrilled to snag the updraft. The Twin Otter was the world's greatest bush plane, and for him it was a creature, a living thing.

He stopped beside BB, the plane he had flown down to the Ellsworths that year. That trip was the beginning of everything. For years, he hadn't felt that way about anyone – not on base, in Stanley, in Calgary, where he spent his summers. While he was married there had been one or two women he had found attractive, yes, but he was married and that was that. Then after his marriage had ended, he'd felt…nothing; this solid nothing, cold and hard, coagulated within him. He would call it an iciness, but he knew now how many names there were for ice, how many properties it had, and that it was a more complicated substance than most people suspected.

He leant against the cool fuselage of the Otter. He should speak to this woman writer about Berkner, he should tell her what happened. Then he would finally be free.

For the first time in years, he wished he could talk to Nara. The desire was so powerful he thought he might cry. Everything they had done together, everything they had exchanged, had ended in the appearance of this woman four years later, picking over the bones of those moments. As for the woman, Helen, he might like her personally, in different circumstances, but he distrusted what she represented. He thought Helen misguided in her entire project. Nara was dead, that much was true. And while the truth could perhaps be pieced together after the fact, it would never be whole again; the fissures and fractures are too deep. And what would such an archive yield anyway? A record of desire, or thoughts, or deeds. But nothing to match the splendour of life, those days they had flown together in the empty Antarctic skies, or sat in silence as fog blanketed the base. He wanted to tell Helen: don't you know that the truth can only be lived? If you go looking for it after the moment is over all you will find are ashes, cinders.

He found himself walking to the laboratory that had been Nara's office, now occupied by another marine biologist, hoping to find her there. He stood in the doorway and addressed Nara's empty chair. *Why aren't you here? Where are you?* As much as he wanted to speak to her he wanted to grasp the sense of having loved her, or at least the memory of it. Since Nara what had there been? Encounters. Squall people who formed and dispersed on his horizon.

There would be a war, soon, he thought. It would be fought over oil and ice, in the form of water, in the form of its potential. No one cared much about the ice itself; to them it was just an obstacle. Wars would happen, yes, they were part of the unending bloodsport in which the human race engaged, and he would continue to fly over the ice sheets, as long as they existed. Because in order to exist, he believed that you need a witness – someone who is consumed by you, concerned for your survival. Otherwise what were we? A mirage: half-human, half-smoke. A ghost.

3

Nara's visions started around the time the sun went away. If she closed her eyes, they were there; she had the impression they were looking at her always, but were invisible. Only on the dark screen of her eyelids did they make themselves known.

The creatures had long white faces and slit eyes. Their expression was difficult to describe; it was not indifferent, nor benign, nor threatening; rather it was a flat evaluating look. They were making decisions, she felt, coming to their own conclusions about her, trying to decide what they wanted from her.

She began to feel the will of a presence – a disembodied thing, not a person, but not an object, either – looking at her. On those winter nights when sleep refused to overtake her she lay with her eyes closed and the white faces foamed out of the darkness of her mind. It was as if they had taken a cold interest in her. They had been there all along (they existed, she was certain), but she had attracted their attention only now, for some reason. When she opened her eyes, they dispersed. But the impression of something threatening in the landscape, a rigid intelligence which cared nothing at all for her, for them, for anyone, remained.

She became afraid to sleep. What was happening to her? She was a scientist, well-educated, rational, schooled in materialism, empiricism, the process of hypothesis and evidence, she was an agnostic, and an entirely ordinary person with ordinary powers and capacities – the last sort of person to see ghosts, or spirits, or to lose her grip on reality.

She was prepared to accept that the polar night offered an uncanny clarity, that people and spirits might intermingle in its dark pane. Many of the old explorers had experienced hallucinations, even temporary madness, which had been dispersed by the return of the sun. But still, there was something real about these apparitions, with their canny children's eyes, their cut-out faces. On one of those nights she asked them, *what do you want with me*? They did not answer but remained on the inside of her eyelid for longer than usual, forming and reforming, as if from smoke.

Over the winter her visions sharpen in focus, the Viking-Aliens, and sometimes wolves who give her a disapproving but not exactly menacing stare. At times she has a powerful sense of a great consciousness passing through her hands, her lungs, possibly her mind. Mostly this happens while she is diving, when she is far underwater, away from the realm of man. Here among her giant sea-sponges, the starfish and sea-spiders, she felt a living, breathing thing that slipped through her fingers, like a multitude of fish. It was sleek and ungraspable, on its way to another destination.

How amazing, that knowing and believing are not after all the same thing: she knows these things are real – the intergalactic Vikings, the world-spirit in the ocean – but yet she does not believe in them. At the same time, she believes in them, but she cannot know them; there is no experiment she can devise to confirm their existence.

She tells no one about these grandiose, spooky fantasies, or her feeling that the pulse of the world was quickening, that somewhere a giant heart was beating, louder, faster.

That winter Alexander teaches her about ice. There are the icebergs: glacier bergs, ice islands, tabular bergs, growlers, bergy bits, brash ice, blue ice, dirty ice. The sea ice: the pack, ice floes, hummocks, ridges, pancake ice, stalactites, undersea ice, frazil ice, ice flowers, rotten ice. The coastal ices: shore ice, piedmonts, glimmer ice, ice cakes, fringes, grounded ice, anchored ice, ice shelves, ice lobes, streams, rime ice. The mountain ices: cirque glaciers, piedmont glaciers, valley glaciers, pinnacles.

She knows that Alexander undertakes lone missions around the Point, to catalogue the ice. He contravenes all the rules by not tagging out on the tagging board. He will not talk to her about his motives, but she understands: this is his fleeting rebellion against the rules that their whereabouts be known at all times, against the tagging board – the base equivalent of CCTV, which will be introduced within a year, after Alexander's accident – his attempt to carve a crucible of privacy, however small, in this secretless place.

Midwinter Dinner is followed by a ceilidh. The cook plays fiddle, the vehicle mechanic has been practising his accordion. June 21st, midsummer in the northern hemisphere, is the Antarctic Christmas.

In the outside world the summer has turned volatile: thunderstorms, flash floods, savage weeks of kiln-like heat which turned the fields of the Mediterranean into ceramic. In the Pacific a red tide of algae wiped out krill stocks. Grey whales are dying in unprecedented numbers, their corpses clogging currents just as horses abandoned by the conquistadors once bloated the horse latitudes. Seven small islands in the Pacific were evacuated due to King Tides; on the internet Nara saw photographs of flooded homes, schools drowning in brackish water, the children's desks full of suctioning molluscs. In the North, light rains down on the planet, caused by bursts of solar fires which are now accepted to be adding to the catastrophic droughts in Australia, in Kenya. On the internet the news is full of picnics, sunscreen – everyone wears factor 75 now; too thick to be absorbed, it covers the skin in a thin layer of white zinc, and photographs show armies of pasty-faced sunbathers, like extras in a film set in the Elizabethan era.

But in the Antarctic they are safe. There is turkey, presents, a Christmas tree, the windows are dark squares onto a moonlit snowfield. There is even mistletoe.

They eat and drink and dance reels. At some point in the party, Nara finds she is being forced near Alexander. He, too, is being driven toward her. The fiddle and accordion blare in her ears.

They have all been kissing under the mistletoe. Not chaste pecks on cheeks, but full-on kisses. It is some kind of midwinter dare.

Someone says, 'the only two people who haven't kissed.'

Nara looks at the mouth she has kissed before, although not recently. A cruel, casual, deeply sexual mouth.

They both manage to break free from their captors. The desperation in their limbs gives them away. They are both ready to fight, just to not have to touch.

Everyone backs away, against the wall. They dissolve into the shadows, they go to get a beer. The winter won't be the same, from now on, knowing that among their number are two people who despise each other.

On July 22nd the sun came back. The winterers knew the date in advance – the sun returned to the peninsula either on the 21st or the 22nd of July each year, depending on the weather and subtle changes in the rotation of the planet.

At 11am the winterers assembled at the south end of the runway, facing southwest, looking into the still-dark sky. The moon was a wolf, a loping shadow creature inside a white mist of stars.

They stared, in silence, into the darkness. At first the light was only a movement deep inside the sky. But then an invisible shift inside the light revealed a sudden garnet glow. The first ray of sun to fall on their land in months came so fast, and the light so searing, that many had to close their eyes against it. Nara was one of the few who defied the urge to blink and was rewarded by a rush of black, as if it were being thrust from the sky by a giant hand, come roaring across the half-frozen bay. Then the stab of green, as sudden and unexpected as an explosion. Then the dark receded from the green energy, draining back over the sea. Flutes of light spread, then, refracted between the mountaintops and narrowed into spires. Emerald light leaked from the sky's indigo hem, and on the outskirts of the light, where the sky faded back into darkness, stars glittered.

A group of twenty-one people, dressed in parkas, in hats and mukluks, stood there in their line at the bottom end of the runway, their torsos and legs in darkness, their faces slowly tilting, like flowers, to face the sun. No one spoke. The wind threaded its way between and through them. For twenty minutes they watched as sunlight shared the sky with the moon: one half yellow, that watery yellow of winter Mediterranean cornfields, the other a brittle silver. Then another shift in the light, an imperceptible nudging, and the spires dismantled themselves. And then, with another glimmer of movement behind the horizon, far away and inside the light, the sun sunk away.

A blizzard paws at the windows. The wind is from the south – the coldest, most driven of the Antarctic winds. In the skies, high above them, temperatures of –190°Fahrenheit help to form nacreous clouds, those clouds of raw pearl created only by extreme cold temperatures, the clouds Luke promised she would see in winter.

Inside, a group of five people sit at the cafeteria tables, playing Twenty-One. It is Nara's turn to be the croupier. She slaps the cards down on the table.

Alexander leans back, extends his arms and shoulders over the chairs around him, widening his scope, also creating a shield.

She comes to him. 'Stick or twist?'

She waits. He stares at her, shrugs his shoulders.

'What do you want me to do, read your mind?'

'Isn't that what you are, a mind reader?'

That night, she sits alone in her pitroom. The blizzard is still going strong.

I love

I love –

Words shred themselves in her mind until it is full of their tattered silks, like the flags they fly on base and which are ripped to shreds, after only one winter, by the wind.

She finds him in his room. She walks straight in and sits on his bed. He perches, wary of her proximity, on the chair.

'I thought being here would help me get over my fear.'

'Fear of what?'

'I don't know.' She puts her hands to her face. There is a constant buzzing in her ears, like a swarm of bees. 'I'm more afraid than I've ever been.'

She looks at him then, grave and tempted, as if she is constantly keeping a confession under wraps. His mouth is like a statue's, a disappointed Inca, a cruel ruler. She would want him for his mouth alone.

It was his coldness, and his unresponsiveness, that had won him her heart. He knew this and fully intended to abuse it, but stopped short. This was how Alexander discovered the existence and limits of his compassion, through her. He was not a scrupulous soul. He saw what he wanted to see, and moved on. To love without wanting something in return was foreign to his nature. To him her distress was almost comic, but also a marvel, that he could move her to such an intensity, merely by performing a number of acts which to him were instinctual.

Before she knows it, she is upon him, her nails are dragging themselves down his cheek, little tracks of skin and red and exposure.

He is much stronger than her, he throws her against the wall easily. He blocks her exit with an arm over the door.

'Let me out!'

He takes both her hands, at the wrists, and holds them above her head. The wood of the door bites into her back.

Her gaze fixes on his fingers, the whorls of his fingertips. To think they had been already formed when he was barely a thought inside his mother's head. When he was a spark, flashing out of the darkness of the universe...

He says, 'I don't love you.' He drags her to the bed. She sees his expression shift, in one moment, from indifference to the trauma of lust.

When his fingers curl around her neck, her legs, they are not vicious fingers. In his normal, everyday persona, he is incapable of violence, but as a sexual being he is someone else. He treats her roughly, an instinct which has its home in a kind of automatic, depthless passion Nara will never understand.

Later, he falls asleep, but she stays awake, staring at the ceiling. A thin knife of winter air, minus thirty-five, slices through a crack in the window, near her head. She dares not move; Alexander sleeps carefully, with the unconscious concern given to a stranger in his bed. Before he had fallen asleep he had taken her and squeezed her so tightly she wondered if he meant to strangle her. Very carefully, she puts her ear to his back and hears the bass sound of a heart twice the size of her own.

In the days that follow, they avoid each other, as much as is possible on an Antarctic base. In these days the howl in her mind becomes louder, now that it has a shape – the shape of his body, which she cannot touch. She is an open wound of loneliness.

In another week she can no longer eat. Like parents monitoring a food-shuffling anorexic, the winterers close around her in a protective posse. They feed her soup. The doctor insists upon taking samples for her stomach problem.

She caves in. 'It's not that I can't eat, I don't want to eat.'

'Why not?'

'My stomach doesn't feel like mine.'

The narrowed, suspicious eyes again. 'Who's is it?'

'I don't know.' She has enough self-preservation not to say: *If I feed my stomach I am only feeding the animal that lives there.*

New visions have replaced the wolves. Flowers, black, canopy-like – miniature umbrellas – blooming in fields fertilised by flesh. Fungi flowers feeding on the rancid cadaver of hope.

She closes and opens her eyes, willing the flowers away.

The blue hour. This was their light, now: three hours of lilac light in the afternoon. In the sky, pale planets. Venus and Mars throb uncertainly on the western horizon.

She drives herself outside, into the storm. She doesn't have enough clothes on to weather the cold. The snows of winter on her eyelashes, just like those years in Canada, where she alternately froze and broiled through successive continental summers and winters. They were doing it *for his career*, her mother said. Those winters had not melted. They were still turning over, savage and frozen, inside her. Snowflakes becoming heavier and heavier until they weigh her eyes shut. She closes her eyes against the storm, hoping to obliterate all traces of the world.

What would it take? She would only need to sit down, or

lie down, and it would be over. She hadn't tagged out. No one would know where to find her, or even that she was gone.

She is freezing. Her core body temperature has dropped, but not significantly. The little burning core of her hums along, intent on survival.

One of the mountaineers finds her there and gently guides her back. The touch on her elbow, firm and frightened, is not Alexander's. She is not even sure he would save her, if he had the chance.

Two days pass. She does not leave her pitroom, she refuses to eat. Screeches tear through her ears and she only belatedly recognises them as her own. Then she remembers: the doctor, an injection, hands on her shouders.

Where am I?

You're in Antarctica.

The base doctor is a young woman Nara's age. Her face comes into focus. The doctor's expression – professional, poised with instruction, even clinical – tells her that she is a normal, intelligent, accomplished young woman. She could never let this happen to her.

She says, *I love to swim in the sea. It purifies me.*

In the darkness behind her eyes they are back, the cold-eyed animals. Raptors, predators all of them – eagles, lions, tigers. The wolf. When she closes her eyes they peer at her with a bold stare. They have journeyed all this way from their planet to tell her that she is in the wrong place. She is not favoured; yet she belongs to them. It leans on her, despite her defiance, the throbbing intelligence behind them. It turns its attention to her with the same energy death has, a langurous, almost willowy swishing of its cloaks, a giant eye suddenly discovering that she is there. It focuses on her, briefly. It is much, much bigger than her. She is frightened, yet defiant. She tells it, *go back to the future*. She says, *it's not me you want. Go away.*

She can no longer tell when she is asleep and when she is awake. Outside the surgery Nara thinks she can see the old maps tacked to the walls. The peninsula, the Dead Men Islands, the detailed maps produced by the MAGIC team. Giant-scale maps of places with place-names, but there are no cities, towns, villages. There is no reason to go there. There is nothing there.

Then the figures, rising from the ice plateau, through the air. She will not see these men again until that day on the ice floe. They have come to tell her that she is starving, there is a famine. The sun has been extinguished, all the food has been eaten. She and Alexander are alone on base. Everyone else has left, taken off on the ship. They have been left together in the Antarctic, in a kind of penance. These men's faces are stern with unconcern, they are fixated on their mission. She knows who they are: they are the explorers, famous men who had to die to attain their fame, in love with the horizon, so much so that night after night they march, their only witnesses the stars, dissolved in a nightless sky. Heroes, giants of the plateau, marching across its empty expanse, their hearts exploding.

4

May 25th, 2016. As winter takes hold it sets a scattered geometry in motion: trapezoids, polygons of ice, the open leads snaking between the floes; on the ship I learned these are called polynyas. A sky smudged with grey. Granite ice, diamond ice, cloud ice. The light is bleached bone. The sea is black; against its dark canvas the sea ice flickers, glowing dully, or suddenly iridescent, caught in a beam of sun.

Out in the real world, an estimated 8 million people are dead, nine weeks after an international lockdown has been imposed. Airlines are bankrupt, the food supply in major cities is precarious.

The Ministry of Defence has decided our fate. They have rung Gerry on the satellite phone and told him that all non-essential personnel can leave, if the Polar Research Council can arrange our evacuation. But go where? We can only get as far as the Falkland Islands. We are told that if we elect to stay the winter, the MOD will pay our costs and fly in or take us out by ship in spring. *You could do worse than overwinter in the Antarctic*, Gerry says. There is enough food to see us clear through until next year. They have counted and recounted the stocks.

Luke will go – by pulling strings, contacts in the RAF, he has managed to get his ex-wife and three children down to the Falklands on the MOD flight from Brize Norton. It was there they weathered the previous pandemic, tucked away on a desolate shore of West Falkland.

At night we talk – hushed, uncertain conversations, overshadowed by the choice we have to make. Everyone else has gone to bed; the Saints have mopped the floor, tipped the chairs up on the tables. It feels just like a university cafeteria after closing time, and here we are, the FCO man and the writer, two overgrown students whose final exams are long over.

David tells me about a trip he took to China, back in 2005, to meet their polar people. He tells me of fog-cloaked cities. Small pine trees, their torn roots. A grandmother sitting in a doorway smoking a pipe, her grandson next to her, holding a bowl of tea. He had stopped and talked to them. Through his interpreter he understood that their house, which was made of wood and dated from the eighteenth century, was soon to be demolished. They would be re-housed in a concrete block. He stood in queues for everything – apples, train tickets. He refused to be the official, whisked here and there in dark cars.

So many people – he was thinking then only with his climate change brain, which was at war with his humanitarian brain. For many years, he was anti-people; he saw more dignity in those small pine trees with their dying roots, in the silk blue nights of the wilderness. In people (he tried to include himself) he perceived only failures, knives, a dim future of pitiless sun, swelling oceans. It seemed now that he and Kate went to more funerals than weddings, and they were only thirty-seven, for Christ's sake!

In China, the boy in the doorway asked: is there war in your country?

Yes, he found himself saying. There is a war against the sky, against the land. But most of all against the ice.

But that is an indirect war (the boy couldn't have been more than fourteen!).

Yes, David said. Exactly. There are two types of war: direct and indirect.

He tells me he had hoped he could do something good for the world. Make a contribution.

He tells me of the things he misses: twilight, for example. Here, at this time of year, the coming of morning and night are like having the lights turned off, then turned on. He meanwhile is a man for in-between places, for departure lounges, hiatuses. We set about finding synonyms. He is good with words and retorts quickly: limbo, longueur, purgatory, halfway house, transition, pause. He says that now, in our present situation, he has met his match: this will be a hiatus to end all hiatuses.

I read aloud to him from Shackleton's book about his great-grandfather's expedition:

> *We laid a course roughly for Hope Bay, and the boats moved on again. I gave Worsley a line for a berg ahead and told him, if possible, to make fast before darkness set in. This was about three o'clock in the afternoon. We had set sail, and as the* Stancomb Wills *could not keep up with the other two boats I took her in tow, not being anxious to repeat the experience of the day we left the reeling berg. The* Dudley Docker *went ahead, but came beating down towards us at dusk. Worsley had been close to the berg, and he reported that it was unapproachable. It was rolling in the swell and displaying an ugly ice foot. The news was bad.*

Words and phrases suddenly leapt out: *grievous disappointment; northwesterly gale off Cape Horn; retrograde movement.*

'My great-grandfather was in the *Dudley Docker*,' he said.

'Ice beset them from all sides,' I say, astonished at their vulnerability. 'They had to try to fend it off with poles.'

'Read more. I like the way you read.'

> *The temperature was down to 4 degrees below zero, and a film of ice formed on the surface of the sea. When we were not on watch we lay in each other's arms for warmth. Our frozen*

> *suits thawed where our bodies met, and as the slightest movement exposed these comparatively warm spots to the biting air, we clung motionless, whispering each to his companion our hopes and thoughts.*

I think of those men, tough men, explorers, ex- or future soldiers, clinging to each other in the bottom of rickety boats, their arms wrapped around one another, whispering. A rough intimacy, moral, imperilled. Bargaining with fate, desire and memory, that shadowy trio of destiny. Did they beseech each other: *Stay in the moment. Don't leave me. Remember your mother's bread pudding!*

Then we troop downstairs together to the bootroom, put on mukluks, fleece, jacket, gloves, hat. We walk to the tagging board. I take our little plastic disks, our surnames emblazoned on them, military-style. I put mine in room 14, and move David's to room 6. My hand lingers there, perhaps only a second too long.

I look at him. Suddenly he is not a tall thin Englishman. There is a rawness to his physique I have missed before, he is more rugged than I thought. It is as if he is expanding, growing in his dimensions, beside me.

Outside a blast of cold wind, like having gravel chucked in your face.

'Well,' David says against the wind, before we ever reach the accommodation block.

'Goodnight,' he says.

'Goodnight.'

We are losing over an hour of light every day, half in the morning, half in the afternoon. In the mornings we shuffle into the bootroom, shed our clothes and footwear and put on our indoor sandals and slippers, avoiding the meltpools on the floor. Upstairs in the dining hall sunlight-simulating bulbs greet us with an artificial stare. Even with the bulbs we look terrible; bags and grey circles under our eyes, our skin is oily and flaccid despite our daily showers and our circuit-training regimes. Yesterday I found another patch of grey hairs on the top of my head. I pulled them out.

David comes to the office I have been assigned, Lab 7, and catches me looking at photos of the winter of 2011–12 on the archived drive.

'This must be good for your research,' he says, his tone formal, also arch, simultaneously conniving and inviting. At times he speaks to me as if I were an acquaintance, someone he has only recently met.

'I try to work in order not to panic,' I say.

David sits down, he does not answer immediately. I realise he is having difficulty speaking. When he does, his lower lip trembles, very slightly. 'I've spoken with my wife. She said that because she can't fly down to the Falklands, and I can't fly home, I may as well stay here.' He drops his gaze. 'What will you do?'

'I have nothing to go back to,' I say. 'Apart from a few dead plants. A ransacked flat, maybe. That's if I could get to London. I have friends in Brazil and Argentina, but their borders are still closed.'

I look out the window to where the glacier was growing, daily, coated with fresh snow, and beyond it the fortress ramparts of Adélie Island. 'I don't much want to stay here, either. I'm afraid of feeling trapped.'

'I know,' David says. 'That's a reason in itself for spending a winter in the Falklands. At least you can move around there, however much the military have the place under lockdown.'

'You must be given special–' I can't think of the word I want here, *dispensation? Freedom?* 'Clearance?'

'Yes and no. I'm not really sure where I would be allowed.'

'What does your work want to do?'

'They advise us to stay wherever we are, all of us. In fact I think I'm the only person in the whole FCO who can move right now, if I want to. Even if it's only to the Falklands.' He pauses. 'Once you're here for the winter, you're here. The sea ice is already beginning to form, I doubt a ship could get in to pick us up in a month's time. So it's now or never.'

'Well, not quite never, hopefully.'

'No,' he says. But he looks as if he has not heard me.

The next day we learn that the summer base commander, the field operations manager, the meteorologist and a handful of summering scientists will leave on the last flight. Luke will fly the plane to the Falklands. We have not spoken for weeks, now, apart from an exchange of pleasantries in the bar. I can't blame him for avoiding me. He knows that in my mind she is not dead, and that everything that happened is still happening, over and over again, as if on a revolving wheel.

David joins me in the dining room to say goodbye to the departing personnel. We all shake hands, even Luke and I. The others ask me if this was a difficult decision and I say yes, that it is one of those decisions taken negatively, not positively, without any desire or volition but because I can't see what else to do. In that sense it is the easiest and also the most difficult decision I have ever taken.

Luke comes over to me, already dressed in his fleece, his hiking boots. He is the capable pilot, the man striding toward you in a bar or a hotel and you think yes, this is a real man, he will be a hunting guide, a major in the Army, an engineer.

'I think it will help your book, staying here.'

'In what way?'

'Few people in the world have lived through an Antarctic winter. It will bring you closer to her.'

And then he is gone, striding away, to calculate fuel and payload, to fly his plane out of this antiseptic colony and back into the real world.

From the dining-hall windows I watch the plane take off. It is a dusky, overcast day. At the last moment, as it stands lined up on the runway I realise I should be on that plane. I have made the wrong decision. I feel trapped, despite the internet, the newspapers, the satellite link. When the plane is gone I go to my pitroom and lie down on my bunk and stare at the bottom of the bed above me, the slats of the wood, the pink and purple mattress, the frayed edge of the sheet which covers it.

The nightmare card, the crystal river woman lays down a card for my future, in a position that represents about six months ahead. It shows a black sky, the moon hidden by a cloud. She looks up at me, her elfin face dwarfed by zebra-striped glasses. *I wonder what it is hiding?*

At three o'clock in the afternoon it is pitch dark outside. Nara is bent over her microscope in the room they call 'the freezer', kept at minus 80. A hunched figure, swaddled in layers of clothing.

I know from her diary that during many of those winter days, when she ought to have been attending to the creatures she was slowly cooking in the aquarium, she was actually looking at snow crystals under the electron microscope in the walk-in specimen freezer kept at a temperature of –80 degrees. She wore mukluks, two parkas, three hats.

Here she was conducting a private, sacred experiment. She was photographing snowflakes before they melted, taking meticulous notes about each of them: '0.08mm diameter, classic snowflake shape, spikes like the North Arm of Newfoundland. 12-sided, a flower in the middle. Branches gutted.' Others she labelled as 'waterlilies' or 'diatoms'.

Later she would learn via the internet that these shapes had scientific names: the boxy crystal star was a *stellar dendrite*; those with a transparent circle in the middle were *stellar plates*; there were also snowflakes called *fern*, *rimmed crystal*; *sectored plate*. It really was true that no two snowflakes were exactly alike. What they had in common was that they had all taken hours to fall to earth, their journeys were perilous, and they had been changed en route. Nara noted all this in her methodical scientist's hand. But these observations were a feint. She was trying to see through the crystal, into the future. She believed that if she looked at them correctly, swivelling them this way and that, like a prism they would divulge a shape greater than themselves, and which pointed to a grand design, like a divine intelligence. She was not the first person to believe this; far from it, for centuries people had been scrying into the future, using crystals. She did not know how, exactly, but she believed these crystals were a blueprint for the future, that most dangerous of countries.

5

It is three in the morning. Helen cannot keep from falling asleep, her head lolling on the cafeteria table. She walks outside in her shirtsleeves into minus 25 to jolt herself awake. Outside the air is so cold that her skin cracks, the lines around her eyes etch themselves deeper. She is losing weight. She is becoming an outline of herself.

She enters rooms, turning on and off lights, switches, shining torches in dark corners, looking for spark. She collects adjectives in her mind as she goes about her rounds, chippy shop, genny shed, lab, boatshed, MiracleSpan shed, Accommodation Block 1, Accommodation Block 2; blunt, overbearing, cutting, opinionated, unfeeling. An instinctive BBC impartiality urge prods her to add: honest, astute, witty, forthright, experienced. Stubborn, restless, pessimistic, grinding. Secretive – yes, that's what he is, fundamentally. He's a government employee, very likely a spook.

When did you become so suspicious? Who was it, who had asked her this? A friend, somewhere along the way, and recently. I'm a journalist, or at least I was one. I was trained to be suspicious. *No, not like that.* Like what then? How many levels could there be? There was suspicion and there was suspicion. No, she was not paranoid, only wary, wary of self-deprecation, of people with natures steeped in dreams, wary of social backgrounds and childhoods and explanations, wary of pleasure and values and scandal. Also of suspicion itself, and seduction, of dull brutes, of immaturity. Wary most of all of the incestuous love she had felt for her husband, at the end, as if he had been her brother or father and not her lover. When he died, it had been a year since they had made love.

And now men are a distant country. She is susceptible to the constant harassment that she be thin, beautiful, young, but she is no longer sure why, or she has forgotten: oh, she slaps her forehead, mentally – *so that I can attract men*! That is how remote it seems, to her life, the whole game. No more impossible positions, no more sick contortions called love, sex, passion. Passion kills people. It is only the most effective murderer; she would call it euthanasia, if it were not so violent. Eric's just another wasted death, his head spiked on passion's gate.

She guards her locked vault of sparse secrets: catastrophic crushes, usually in war zones, when her safety was under the command of some Major or other, as if she had been programmed for this, to fall in love with the man who protects her. *Caveman instinct.* The wedding ring on their fingers, always. Outside the situation they were in, at Kandahar, at Camp Bastion, where Helen had been 'embedded', they would not have a word to say to each other.

All this took place after her husband's death. Only then did she understand the true corrosive nature of experiences: there were some things that could happen to you, on this planet and in this life, which, while bad enough, were survivable in themselves. But the really insidious thing about life, the clever trick that lived at its black heart, was that just as you were congratulating yourself for having survived them, you realised a fugitive was harbouring itself in your gut, your mind, your heart – a succubus. And this fugitive had handed you a baton of sorts, setting in motion a process of invisible destruction: *Over to you now*. But the trick was, the weapon would be wielded by yourself. *Ingenious! Life does not have to do the killing after all. We do it for ourselves.*

Not that she tried, or not openly. But these missions – to Afghanistan, in the dying days of the war, when it had become very dangerous to be a journalist there, to Somalia, Chad, Eritrea, desert countries rippling with unstable militias – had in fact become covert missions of self-destruction. At least she would die on the job. At least she would die moving. In the end, that was all she needed, as far as death was concerned – to die while moving.

At six in the morning, an hour away from the end of her shift, she finds David making a cup of tea in the dining room.

'Would you like a cup of tea?' he proffers. 'You must be tired.'

She says yes, she is tired. She does not answer directly about the cup of tea. David must take this as an affirmative, because he sets another cup on the counter.

'I'm impressed, you putting yourself down for nights. You're getting into the life here. You've made yourself one of the team.'

'Why are you up?' Next to David's careful constructions, Helen's question hangs plain-clothesed, awkward. A scarecrow next to a human being.

'Because I can't sleep.'

They sit down, scraping out their chairs on opposite sides of the table.

'How is your wife coping with all this?'

'Not very well. I've had to stay away before, but not like this.' He runs his hands through his hair. Several strands stay between his fingers. They dangle there, like Christmas tinsel. 'Is this happening to you? I'm losing my hair. I feel like I'm going into hibernation. You know, no one has had an enforced overwinter in the Antarctic in thirty years, not on this base.'

She nods, even though she didn't know that. 'I have problems with claustrophobia,' she admits. 'This is my way of dealing with it, I suppose, by keeping busy.'

He nods. 'While the planes are here, it doesn't bother me. But as soon as the planes are gone and the ship is the only way out, I feel – ' he puts his arms around himself, hugging them to his chest '…It's like a prison. A pleasant prison, but it's not as if we can leave. Then again, we only have the impression of freedom in everyday life. We can't necessarily walk away, or go anywhere, either.'

'What did you do in the pandemic?'

'Stayed in the office. We were ordered to.' He pauses. 'How about you?'

'House arrest.'

'My wife did that, although not at our flat. She stayed with friends, she couldn't bear to be on her own, so she left while she could. We didn't see each other for two months.'

Helen is preparing to give him a sympathetic look when he says, 'It was good for us, I think. To have that time apart.'

She reins in her look and considers her options. She finds she cannot ask, why do you say that? She wonders, does she fear an answer negative or positive? Does she fear finding out that he is, after all, separated?

'How did you manage?' he asks. 'I mean, during that time.'

'I try not to think about it much.'

'I'm sorry.'

'No, it's all right. It's just – ' she cannot finish the sentence.

'Do you have anyone – at home? I mean, you said your husband was dead – ' He falters.

'No, I have no one.' She pauses. 'After my husband died, I wasn't able to – well, I was able, but I had no luck.'

After Eric's death, she had been hopeful. She expected things to improve. She expected to be granted happiness, and not any happiness, either, but of an exceptional kind in direct compensation for what had happened to her.

'No luck?'

She gives David a direct look. 'My husband had been having an affair, for a long time. I'm not sure how long. That's why he died, because he was desperate to see her, and he left our flat. She was already sick. He caught it, and died. They died together.'

We're going to have to test you, I'm afraid. We don't know how long he had been there. She didn't know either. She didn't know how long he had been seeing another woman, from whom he had contracted the virus. She didn't know if he had passed it to her.

She lost weight instantly, while listening to what the policeman had to say on the telephone. Her trousers slacked around her waist, her hair lost its sheen. She was dying, anyway. Her stomach turned to stone. Her fingernails split, her skin hung flabby and sallow. She aged. Her first grey hairs sprouted from her head. All this happened that day, and those that followed the telephone call.

She learned that her name was Claire, a name she had never much liked, its lightness, airiness, transparency. How they had met, she would never know. After Eric died she found some photographs of her on his computer, but erased them.

At night, and for the following month, Helen took diazepam to sleep and woke feeling sick. Her smell changed – for the first time in her life, she could smell herself. The scent was old, disused, the scent of a body which would not make love or be made love to in a very long time. She slept and sweated in sour sheets, which she did not bother to change.

With the Antarctic, this sinister requiem finally came to an end. Or so she had hoped.

When she finishes speaking, she finds David is staring at her openly. Spurred on by some reckless instinct, she tells him about going to see the crystal river woman. She knows he is likely to mock her. But then she is not sure she has ever had his respect, so perhaps there is not much to lose.

He listens without interrupting. When he finally speaks, his voice has changed. The challenge so often nailed across it has been removed and a new note, barren and raw, rings through.

'Do you really believe that we can know the future?'

'Some things you can know, yes. Other things have not yet been decided.'

'Decided by whom?'

'I think it's by what,' she says. 'Not who.'

'By what, then?'

'I don't know. That's the mystery.'

David sits back in his chair 'I'm less interested in the future than a lot of people.'

'I'm not sure I think much of it myself.'

She means, she doesn't like the lack of clarity in her – in anyone's – relationship with the future. With the past she has an intimate bond. There was a time when the ice sheets were intact, when Greenlandic hunters had enough to eat, when caribou did not starve. In her own lifetime, she can remember this: that there was a moment, finite, identifiable, when everything was in perfect balance. And now this moment is gone, never to return.

David frowns. 'I'm not sure I'm as interested in the future as most people are. Or not in telling it; and anyway, I don't think that's possible.'

He shakes his head. 'The way I see it, the only real threat to our existence is ourselves, and other people. I don't think there's anything else…out there.'

'I know. I can't prove that things are this way.'

'Yes, all you have is an unproveable hypothesis. But worse,

you're using this story as a kind of proof, in order to confirm your darkest suspicions about life.'

Helen stares at him. She has never encountered someone so sceptical of her existence, her motives, her very soul, so prepared to deflate and question and consign her to the wounded category where all unviable things live. She has the impression that David views her, her beliefs, suspicions, fears, as only a particularly vexing logistical problem.

'You want to go back and change what happened,' he says.

'Isn't there anything you've wanted to go back and change?'

He does not answer immediately. His expression has become cloudy and dense. She expects him to get up, to scrape out his chair and leave, as he did before. But he doesn't.

'Did you know about what happened at Berkner Island?' she asks.

'You mean the accident, on the way back?'

'No. I mean what happened between Nara and the pilot.'

'No. Why didn't you ask him?'

'I know already, I know from what she wrote.'

'So you are on her side, then?'

'I don't take sides,' she says, firmly.

'But doesn't this happen with writers, that you take on the life of your subject?'

'Not usually. If you take someone's part you lose any objectivity you might have. But I'm here, aren't I? I'm in the same space, I use the same office she used, I read her diary, I'm stuck here for the winter.' She pauses. 'I think sometimes, existences can overlap.'

'Is that what your crystal river woman said?'

'No. Yes. She said sometimes we are unaware that we are sent on missions in this life, on behalf of other people, to right certain wrongs, to bring things full circle.'

'Were you glad, when he died?'

She stares at him. She wonders if she has heard David correctly. 'Who?'

'Your husband.'

'Why would I be glad?'

'He'd betrayed you. Did you think he'd gotten what he deserved?'

Her answer came to Helen from somewhere else, as if it were being dictated to her. She says, 'People who live through a time of death are not the same as other people.' She means, living through a time of death taught her that retaliation was not her right. In the end, life takes its own revenge.

PART VII

Vanishing Point

1

Mean temperature 38°Fahrenheit or 3°Celsius. Wind 25 knots, gusting to 30/35 Northeast, Dew Point 4°C.

It was raining, of course. What did it do in the Falklands but rain? It drove against them as they walked down Ross Road, past the West Store, the Capstan Gift Shop, the Upland Goose Hotel.

Takeoff would be worst; they would be lucky to get 2k vis on liftoff, but once above the cloud mantle this would stretch to 6k. Luke studied the forecasts just in from the military base, deciphering their numbers and codes. In another ten minutes they would radio base and see what Horace was saying. Trust a computer model to get it right, and the forecasters be wrong. It had happened before.

Nautical Twilight 6:12 AM FKT and 5:48 PM FKT. Astronomical Twilight 5:32 AM FKT and 6:28 PM FKT. Length Of Visible Light: 10h 15m. Once in the Antarctic, the visible light would be about half that, he calculated: a five-hour window of dusky semi-darkness.

Clouds were the thing to worry about; high cloud and the icing would affect the propellers; low cloud and they might have to land on visuals in dusk without a runway beacon. You couldn't win. Overnight, they would refuel, then start back the following day.

Luke looked again at the report: high cloud at 8858 feet. Weather charts, little flags of wind speed and direction harried, clumping, showed a forecast of a 70-knot tailwind the following day. 'With that kind of wind in your tail you hardly need fuel,' he said. Chris looked ruefully at the charts. He knew Chris would prefer to go in and come out on the same day. If they risked staying overnight they might be there for days, possibly weeks, if the weather closed in.

Years ago they would not have even contemplated flying in the four-prop plane at this time of year. Then the only way in would have been with the Otters, which were built for polar environments and could take almost anything the weather threw at them. But now it was warm enough that severe icing was, while still a possibility, a remote one. Now the runway could be cleared for a wheeled rather than a ski-fit aircraft, although it took an effort to shift the snow from its kilometre-long stretch. Down on base they had begun clearing it two days previously with the snowblowers, working in two shifts, day and night.

It had taken five days to fly the aircraft back down from Canada to the Falklands, leapfrogging from Houston to Merida to Curaçao to Manaus; then a giant leap of faith which pushed the aircraft to the limit of its range to Rio de Janeiro, then, after the first good night's sleep in a week, to Florianopolis, Montevideo, Stanley. He had been hiking in the woods with two of his children when his phone vibrated. On its screen a Cambridge number appeared. His summer holiday had ended, there and then.

He had never done a winter medevac before, in all his years flying. Very few people had ever done it; all they could do was try. He and Chris had calculated the Point of No Return, with Marsh as their divert. If Marsh was fogged in they could get to Punta Arenas, provided they turned back in time. Past their PNR, if the weather closed in, either they lost visibility on the ground or they encountered icing in low cloud, they would have to get to base, no matter what.

'Ok,' Chris said, 'we're going in.'

A shiver ruffled up and down Luke's spine. There was nothing he liked more than a challenge.

They donned the survival gear which had hardly changed

in one hundred years, layer by layer: silk underwear, moleskins, fleece, padded boiler suit, parkas, boots. Once they were airborne they would peel these off, one by one, unless they had to climb above the aircraft's official ceiling, where the air would be cool and thin. Luke had done this many times before – gone high to save on power and fuel; in this way he increased his range. Even in the Otters he never suffered from altitude sickness. It was officially forbidden; if they went above altitude neither he nor Chris would log it in the flight book.

They went through the takeoff checklist: Number 1 engine, then number 2, 3, and 4. Fuel pumps, auxiliary fuel pumps. Chris was captain, but Luke would do the flying. He recited the flight plan: once airborne, steady climb to 5,000 feet, reduce power, set autopilot course for the Drake Passage, shortest transect possible. Once they reach 12,000 feet, radio Marsh. How, and where, and at what altitude they would turn the aircraft around and head back. Normally these rehearsals of plans B and C were routine and speculative, but on this day they might actually have to use them.

Then the landing: arriving in darkness was, while a possibility, something to be avoided. He and Chris knew the descent to base better than anyone, they had the most hours racked up on the aircraft. If anyone could bring it down safely in poor vis, in weather, in wind or snow, they could.

In the back of the plane sat the mechanic and the medevac doctor, strapped into passenger seats shoved hastily amongst the cargo. The medevac was also a chance to get essentials onto base – ten boxes of fresh fruit and vegetables, and eight drums of Avtur to be deployed on the Pine Island glacier the following year.

The doctor, an improbably young woman flown down from Cambridge on short notice, looked pale. She had seemed fine until she saw she would be sitting on top of aviation fuel. Luke was about to tell her, *The wings are full of fuel anyway. Even without the drums, we're a flying bomb* but at the last moment he opted for gentlemanliness, and assured her it would all be fine. The mechanic did not look particu larly confident, either. He more than anyone knew what they were up against. If anything went wrong with the aircraft he would be on his own, with the prospect of being stuck for months if he could not fix the problem.

The first moments of a flight into or out of the Antarctic were the hardest. Luke knew from experience how difficult the transition could be; sometimes he had had to pit himself against it mentally. For years, flying into the Antarctic had meant saying goodbye to the people he loved for months at a time, and it had acquired a heavy air of regret, of absence, of resolve to find a job that would keep him closer to home.

After takeoff he felt immediately how different it was to flying in summer. Night lapped at their edges from all directions, like a dark tide. Below, the sea foamed with whitecaps. 'It's a wild old day down there,' he said and Chris nodded in agreement. The most stable ship would struggle in these seas. These waves were borne by a relentless dynamic, unbroken in their journey from Australia through the southern Pacific, driven by the most powerful winds on earth through the botteneck of the Drake Passage, their loping kinetic force squeezed and torqued until they rose up and folded back on their own power, yearning for something to smash apart.

The moment Nara awoke in the surgery, she knew she had been sedated. A chemical burn lingered in her mouth, and there was a fogginess in her thoughts which refused to disperse.

She looked up into a wall of boxes of medicines, stacked in a perspex cabinet. Many of the boxes were empty; these belonged to the coveted drugs – antidepressants, the painkillers, the codeine and morphine, which were kept under lock and key.

She walked, uncertainly at first, then with more confidence, through the cafeteria, the bar, the hallways, prepared to meet eyes which refused to focus upon her. But base was empty. She went to the comms tower. There she found Alistair, the comms manager. Before he could look away she asked, 'Where is everyone?'

'Skiing.' His pursed lips. Evaded eyes. Yes, this was how it would be for some time, for months to come.

That night she did not eat dinner with the others. At midnight she crept into the kitchen and made herself some soup. At breakfast, she did the same – waited until everyone had eaten, then slunk into the cafeteria to make her own.

Alexander was tagged in on the tagging board. The doctor walked by; her eyes swivelled away.

She was seized by a feeling that something was wrong. It grew from the pit of her stomach, rose through her heart, then finally reached her brain.

'What day is it?'

'Thursday.' The doctor's voice said: *Does it matter?*

No path existed around the Point now, only snow-covered boulders and a hazy fissure of snow and ice where the fragile shore ice began.

Underneath her feet the snow squeaked. This meant it was minus fifteen, or colder.

There was no moon to guide her, only a pale glow on the horizon. The days were lengthening rapidly, now that Midwinter was past. Three hours of perpetual dusk had become, within only four days, an hour of visible light in the sky. Still the light was sealed off, as if contained on one side of a vast glass wall. Nacreous clouds glimmered in the sky. At times she stumbled. She stopped, stood still, listening to the lordly, unaccommodating silence. It thudded through her. After a minute she realised it was her own heart, beating.

The moment is one of balance. Of poise between safety, between a humdrum ice observation mission, back to base for a cup of coffee, back to his computer screen, and disaster.

Some part of him chooses disaster.

Alexander did not want to slip, he did not want to lean into gravity, but his body chose this for him. A mind not entirely in control, an instinct, a spiral. Before coming South he had had it – they all had – drummed into him that in the Antarctic, accidents never have one causal factor. For things to go wrong, one mistake had to lead to another, then another, until the situation becomes desperate.

His unravelling began with a footfall which sunk into snow to his thigh. Then a tipping, as his long body leaned downslope into the unexpected sinking. After that, a handbrake which failed to arrest his topple, then, with his right leg, a slip. Very quickly he was sliding down the sharp drop underneath the cliff, to the sea.

He carries no ice axe. It is just a walk around the Point, the Antarctic equivalent of a stroll around the park.

The fall and scrape of ice against his young, hard body created immediate drag, but not sufficient to arrest his fall. He can feel the bruises forming, their heat and swell. Baggy capilliaries, flush with blood and hurt.

With a relaxing of the angle of the slope, the drag on his body increases, and he slides to a stop just short of the shoreline. He tries to stand, but cannot. Adrenalin is masking the pain of a fractured tibia; the break occurred, unnoticed by him, two seconds previously when he had put out his leg in an attempt to arrest his slide. The shiver of pain he receives if he tries to put his left leg to work means he would not be able to walk, or swim, he cannot climb back up the glacier. In another, colder, year – cold enough for the sea ice to form – he would have been able to drag himself across the sea ice, around to the wharf, and home.

He is only four hundred metres from the base's door, close enough for rescue, but his name is tagged in on the tagging board. He never tagged out, for his missions around the Point. He is not a man to be known or controlled.

He knew that everyone assumed he was lying low, after what happened, that he was avoiding her. It might be another day before anyone thinks something is wrong, and knocks on his door.

Before he can form a response – whether regret, rueful laughter, or grim determination – he is flooded by a fear so powerful he stops breathing. The fear is spiked with panic and pain and in its heart lives a dark, worming purpose. It invades him from all directions, enters every pore, a stampede of snakes.

He has just realised that the overhang of the slope means no one can see him. The way he has fallen, he is out of sight.

Three hours into the flight they called PNR. On base, the siren whooped over the runway for the first time in months. Base radioed them. It was Alistair, the comms manager. 'The cloud mantle has dropped.' Chris' reply was immediate. 'How much?' 'From 5,000 to 1,000 and dropping.' Why didn't you tell us half an hour ago?'A crackle of static, before the answer. 'Because half an hour ago it was at 5,000.''That's impossible.''No, it's not. It's a different place here in winter, Chris.''What's the coverage?''Eight octas.''We're past PNR, you know that?'Another static pause. 'Roger. We've sounded the siren. The runway is clear.' 'We're going to need some help to land this thing,' Chris said. The bite in his words: *this thing* – that was new to Luke. 'We'll have to get them out there with flares, just in case.' Luke nodded. It was the only way.

Luke never thought: if we ditched, that would be it. He always considered that he could get the aircraft down, no matter what – get it down in some form. Landing was for him a moment of grace, of suspension, power and accomplishment. He could not imagine it ending in disarray, in explosion and charred skin and kerosene. He didn't know if this were optimism or recklessness, only that for him landing was the fullest expression of his competence as a pilot. In those moments when he set an aircraft on the ground he felt a surge of power, and he knew he would never have consented to live a life in which that feeling of mastery and control was not possible. He dreaded the murk and hedge of most people's existences: squabbles with the boss, jockeying for position on the commuter train home. He was free from all that, and secure in his power. Only ten or twelve men in the world could do what he was doing now, and one of them sat beside him. If they couldn't do it, nobody could.

Nara was short, so she was assigned the position in the middle of the runway. As a short person she ran less of a risk of being injured or killed by the plane's landing gear and wheels. Tall men were positioned at the edges of the runway – their flares were the crucial signals, they would keep the pilots from landing on the edge, or worse, off the runway entirely.

Fifteen years previously a man had been up on a mast doing some rigging at Midas base when the wheels of a departing Twin Otter severed his head from his body. The pilot hadn't seen him. Nara had never given the Midas incident much thought. Now, she considered it: a headless body in the snow, his bloodied orange boiler suit. The same plane would have had to return to fly the body out. She wondered what had happened to the pilot. She wondered if Luke knew him.

They lined themselves up, backs to the runway, facing Adélie Island. Dressed in red padded boiler suits, hard hats, any reflective gear they could find, one line at the south end of the runway, one line to signal the turn onto the hangar apron. They could not even see Adélie Island; it was lost in the blanket of fog and low cloud that had smothered base, and so quickly.

They waited for the shear: they would feel the plane before they heard it. The strange sound dynamics of the Antarctic meant that sounds did not creep up from a distance as they usually did, but burst from a vortex.

There was nothing more to be done than to hold these flares aloft in the dark, waiting for the roar of the plane to come upon them.

At 11am blue and gold soaked the southern horizon. The light lasted for only ten minutes, but it was enough to show Nara Alexander's tracks, where they stopped, close to the edge. She inched her way out to the overhang and looked down. Little whirlwinds of panic in her mind, lashing her to the moment, to a sudden gripping inertia.

The sound of her voice was alien to her. The silence consumed her shout as if she had never made a sound at all.

She did a quick calculation: fifteen minutes to get back to base – no, twenty, from the precarious position she occupied. Fifteen minutes to get geared up, to get the field assistants on search and rescue duty out here. Fifteen more minutes to pull him up.

He was not moving. She could see that from where she stood.

She had rope, two snowstakes, a sling, her harness, jumars, karabiners. In fifteen minutes, she could get down to him herself. She could put a sling on him. If he were conscious, he could jumar up. If not, she would leave him down there with the sling, and go and get the field assistants.

She pounded in the snowstakes, fashioned a triangular sling to equalise the distribution of her weight, and roped up. She had no crampons, only her winter boots.

She lowered herself over the ice cliff, her crampon-less boots sliding uselessly on the iceface. On the way down she was so dehydrated she could barely swallow. She was breathing heavily, so that her breath condensed in globules of frost, which stuck to her eyelashes.

They would take the southeast approach. Descend to 9,000 feet, bank right. Every summer they did this two, three times a week. Their wide-angled approach to base was high enough to clear the peaks which jut all around them. They would fly in from the south, into a stiff, capricious wind.

As they levelled out, base and the shoreline were obscured by cloud. Peaks of mountains they were used to seeing in summer, bared, their chocolate-hued basalt providing markers for their approach, were now covered in snow. Ahead was only a white definitionless land; inside the emptiness were mountains, lethal granite towers. At last they saw a familiar landmark: the island's peaks prodded the tops of the cloud. If it weren't for Adélie Island, they would not have been able to even find the base.

Then, puncturing the cloud, a small throb of red light – the human runway beacon. It went against all their training to have people in the way of the landing track of an aircraft. But then you couldn't really train for what the Antarctic threw at you.

'We're too high. We're going to have to drop out of the sky. What about bergs?'

'Comms man says there are none on the path in. Let's hope he's right.'

The pilots took their last look at the steel mountains, wide-hipped, inevitable, overlain with sheets of fresh snow. Then ailerons curled down over the wings, and the plane descended into cloud.

The roar did not come upon her from the outside; the machine came from inside her body. She dove to the ground, the flare still in her hand. The fuselage sleeked above her, its underbelly congealing out of the air. She lifted her head from the runway in time to watch it touch down, then to be covered with a spray of gravel and snow. She lay on her back on the runway, the expired flare held aloft in her hand.

The winter base commander stood above her. He extended a hand, which she grasped. She thought he was going to joke, to laugh at her, splay-limbed on the runway. Usually, he was the joking kind.

'Christ,' he said, pulling her to her feet. 'That was close.'

She took off her glove and reached her fingers toward Alexander. When they encountered his throat they felt no warmth, but there was a throb, muted, insistent. His lips were blue, and his extremities were cold. But the overnight temperature had not been very low, for the Antarctic winter, so he had survived.

She could not see a way to get him out of there on her own; she wouldn't be able to jumar them both up, his weight was too much for her. If he had been conscious, she would have been able to convince him to climb out. She didn't yet know about the fractured tibia.

She would have to leave him, and go for help. She stood up. The familiar dark pewter mantle of cloud hung over the point.

Again, she felt its presence: the grinding, like a wheel, a mechanism, gigantic and diffuse. Whatever it was, it was older than them, better than them, and so much more powerful. This skulking force brooded around him like a scavenger looking for a way into a house. She recognised it as the same giant eye that looked at her so casually at night in her bunk, when she couldn't sleep and the visions refused to disperse. But she was fierce, now, she was in life and at the height of her powers. She bared her teeth against it and felt the hairs bristle at the bottom of her neck. Her growl sounded like one of the fur seals, there was nothing human about it. With this growl she fended this presence off, because Alexander was not able to. The presence mooched about, disappointed, then slunk away.

His dark skin was so pale, his lips the lightest blue. He looked like a religious statue.

She spoke to him. 'I have to go and get help. Can you hear me?'

She saw an eyelash flutter.

'I'll be back in half an hour. Don't stop breathing. Don't fall asleep.'

Another flutter of an eyelash. His mouth opened, very slightly.

She turned her back on him and began to climb.

The propellers kept spinning while the pilots went through the post-flight checklist. If they were going to leave right away they would keep the number one engine running in case of generator trouble. But taking off today was a remote possibility, now that there was fog. The takeoff track would take them over icebergs, and they needed visibility.

She glimpsed Luke through the cockpit window. From the back of the aircraft two figures, stiff with fear, strangers, emerged – the doctor and the air mechanic, a Canadian who had never been to the Antarctic before, pressed into leaving the summer behind by an offer of a substantial bonus and a vacation in Hawaii.

Luke appeared last and walked down the stairs. He took off his gloves – a summer habit. Soon he would put them back on.

'Good news,' Luke said. 'We're staying for dinner.'

The smile which emerged from Nara then came from her deepest being. He had come back.

Dinner that night was lavish: Uruguyan beef with parsnips, fresh carrots from the Falklands, candles on the tables, plastic flowers in tiny vases.

After dinner Nara went down to the surgery. Alexander was hooked up to a saline drip which had been slowly warming the core temperature of his body over the past several days. He was conscious now, although he refused to speak to her, refused to even look at her. But he could not stop her from sitting beside him.

'We had salad. With avocado. They brought a crate of pears from Uruguay.'

He turned his face away.

She said, 'You're leaving tomorrow.'

Finally, he looked at her, a strange look of barren triumph. 'You must be glad I'm going.'

'I'm glad you're alive, that's all.'

His face was still drawn and bloodless from cold. 'I don't understand,' he said.

'You mean you wouldn't have done the same for me. You mean you think I saved you because I am in love with you.'

He stared at her for a while. In his mind, she knew, doors were opening and shutting themselves; these were his thoughts, his decisions, no more anchored in the world than hers were, but so much more vital and buoyant, because he did not think, he only felt, and this was the source of her fascination for him. She had so wanted to be true and wild, like him. She had so wanted to be free.

Luke was tanned; that was the first thing she noticed. But he was transformed in some other way, also physical. He looked much more vigorous than the Antarctic version Nara had said goodbye to five months before. This place takes its toll on people, she thought, and considered her own extreme paleness, how thin she had become.

This shimmering envoy from the northern hemisphere summer sat down opposite her but kept his hands planted on his thighs, as if he might use them as a lever at any second, and get up and go.

'I can't believe you came back.'

'Don't take this the wrong way, but I didn't have much choice.'

'You look exhausted.'

'Well, flying down here in winter, you never know…' he gestured obscurely toward the window. She follwed his gaze there and saw a black square of night; in it, their reflections.

'That's an amazing thing you did, out there,' he said. 'He was tagged in, I hear. There was no reason for anyone to worry.' When she said nothing, he prodded. 'So why did you?'

'Just instinct, that something was wrong, and that he was involved.'

How could she tell him how the universe had taken a darkling cast that morning, a subtle change in the albedo exchange between the ice and the sun, the closing of an eye of the wolf. Something small and unnoticable. Mothers probably had such instincts about their children being in danger.

Luke's look then was penetrating, restrained, judicious. She flinched slightly underneath it. He might not believe her, on some level.

He said, 'It was a good hunch.'

She had so wanted to hear that note of warmth, of appreciation, in his voice. It had always been there; some times too much, and she had heard the honeyed tone of desire. She reminded herself now how only a few months before she had felt confined, even trapped, by his admiration.

'I never thought I'd see you again before October.'

He laughed, a little brightly, for him. 'No. Well. Never say never. I never thought I'd be doing this job as long as I have been.' He paused. 'You know, in winter this place gets to everyone. Even the steadiest characters.'

'I'm not insane, if that's what you're implying. They say I had a nervous breakdown, but I don't know.'

'Look – I know how intelligent you are, and all. I think you're the most intelligent person I've ever met.'

'And how do you think that helps me, my intelligence?'

'I think sometimes, you can think too much, take things too seriously – '

'What things? You don't think the Antarctic winter is serious?'

'I'm not talking about that.' He paused. 'I think you have to accept to live life as it is, on the terms we are given. You know, stuff happens. That's life. Maybe the point is to just live. Not to think too much about things that don't work out.'

When she had not spoken he said, 'Did you ever once give a thought for me, for my feelings?'

'Yes, I did. As a friend.'

'You're my friend, are you? In what way?'

'I want you to be happy.'

'And you don't see any connection between my happiness, and you?'

She felt regret, or remorse, accompanied by a residual note of hope – hope that she could yet have had a friend like him, an Antarctic pilot eighteen years her senior. It was his friendship, uncomplicated, freely given, that she missed. What luck she'd had, of having found so unlikely a friend. Why could they not love each other in that way? Like family.

She looked away. This array of thoughts and feelings percolated through her within a single second. And, rising from them, stronger and pointed, something new in her relationship with Luke: a wish to please.

'No, well,' Luke said. 'I thought so.'

She said, 'You must hate me.' And waited for his denial.

'Sometimes I can't tell the difference between love and hate.' He did not look directly at her.

Luke might have saved her simply by asking, 'What's wrong? What went so wrong for you here, in only four months?' But he had done enough saving for one day.

He rose, then, deploying those capable hands of his like the landing gear which had come down upon her from the sky, only that day, but how long ago it seemed. She was certain they had both just lived through the longest day of their lives.

He left her office. He did not say goodbye, he did not look back.

From the end of the corridor she heard the tiny clack of his plastic tag being hung on the nail above his room number. The tag with Luke's surname had sat on the tagging board all winter with the other pilots and mechs in the 'Flying Off Base' section. Many, many times during the winter Nara had stood in front of the tagging board, scanning it for where Alexander might be, avoiding Luke's name hanging there, avoiding missing him.

*

The following day the plane left, with Alexander on board. Nara did not go over to the runway to say goodbye. She watched it take off from the dining room.

In the bay, the sea ice was breaking up, far too early. The week before Alexander's accident, the wind had come up and blown the ice out, then blown it back in. But by then the ice was ruined and unstable, and for the rest of the winter it would not cohere.

2

The Otters arrived first, bringing summer in the form of pilots, fresh fruit and vegetables, the summer base commander, the field operations manager, all on the first Dash from the Falklands.

It was late October, the beginning of the austral summer of 2012. Spring that year was the purest relief Nara had ever tasted. It was as if one of the cloud mantles that hovered inches above the peninsula had suddenly lifted. The arrival of summer brought the return of the Antarctic Nara loved: volatile, surreal, high-spirited, the delirious cameraderie, the air overstuffed with oxygen.

Luke flew the first passenger flight into base. The first she saw of him was on the veranda of the main complex. He mounted the stairs, P-bag slung over his shoulder. She thought: he looks changed. But she could not say how.

'Hello there,' he said.

'Welcome back.'

She waited for the moment when he would drop the bag from his shoulder, and come toward her, the moment when they would give each other a hug or a kiss on the cheek, as they used to do.

He shifted from one foot to the other.

'How was the flight down?'

'Totally routine, thanks. No problems at all, compared to the last time we came this way.'

His Canadian accent had solidified in the two months since she had seen him; he had spent those months in Canada, she knew, driving his children through the Rocky

Mountains. She felt a satisfaction – this was what had changed, why he looked different.

'Well, got to unload the plane, check in with the field ops man.'

She nodded, a moment, fleet and sparing, of happiness dashing through her. 'Summer's back,' she said, and smiled.

'I guess so.'

Two days later she learned that Luke was on the roster to fly the ice-coring equipment out to Berkner; the base carpenter would go along for the ride as his co-pilot.

'How long do you think you'll be gone?' she asked.

'Could be back tomorrow, could be next month. They'll likely base me at Midas, and I'll fly back and forth. Berkner's a brutal place. You should see it. If I get back to base I'll try to get you out there. Deal?'

'Deal,' she said, and smiled.

He was gone for six weeks. They managed several email exchanges during his time at Midas. He sent her photographs; the base looked like Space Station Earth. It was constructed of several pods of blue plastic cladding and porthole windows, and sat five metres above the ice sheet, raised there on hydraulic legs. As the snow accumulated, the base could be jacked up by only two people. *They call it an architectural wonder*, Luke wrote. The summer sun never approached the horizon at Midas, because it sat four hundred kilometres nearer to the Pole than Adelaide base. *It's a special place. Bleak, but beautiful. Folks here are taking very good care of me.* Luke's emails from Midas arrived with transmission times of three-thirty or four in the morning. *We've had some late nights, or early mornings You really never know what time it is here.* At Midas, Luke told her, he instinctively looked toward the sea fifteen kilometres away, and closing fast. The edge of the Brunt ice shelf was creeping ever closer with melt, which ate away at the towering ice cliffs. He saw iceblink: the clouds reflected the ice, so that the sky was white and the sea ice dark. He saw the *fata morgana* – mirages caused by refractions in the curvature of the earth, and the lack of any visual markers in his field. He had hallucinations – of towering icebergs which did not exist, of fabulous cities gathering and dispersing in the ether. *I wish I could show you all this*, he wrote.

December came, the supply ship came and went, and still Luke remained flying out of Midas to the Ronne ice shelf, working with the ice-core drillers. Once he flew a mission to take the Midas plumber eight hundred miles east to the German base to fix their solar water heater. He wrote to Nara of the abrupt needling peaks of a practically unknown mountain range in Queen Maud Land, the gigantic and endless ice shelf he saw beneath him, and the fracture which spelt its imminent calving. Soon this shelf, even larger than the Larsen B which had broken free from the continent ten years previously in 2002, would begin its journey toward disintegration in the southern ocean.

Nara had her second Christmas on base. The chef baked a giant mince pie; on it, miniature marzipan penguins played hockey, in deference to the team of Canadian air mechs among them. After dinner everyone went skiing wearing Santa costumes and jester hats with tassles topped with bells. Everyone had bright, tanned faces. Everyone felt an exhilaration which Nara registered but which somehow passed through her and out of her, on to an unknown destination.

On the 27th of December Luke returned with the ice-coring team. She saw them walk up from the runway together, the men haggard versions of the characters she had seen six weeks previously, unshaven, their faces pinched by constant exposure to cold and the mean winds which raked the island.

As for Luke, he had changed again: his face was thinner,

tanned to the mahogany hue of the Antarctic, where the skin was bombarded with more UV rays in two days than it would absorb in an entire northern hemisphere summer. She looked at him and saw the same man – although subtly different, as if he had been subject to a mysterious reversal – she had met almost a year before to the day, when they were stuck in the Ellsworths together.

They met that night over a cup of tea.

'I'm thinking of moving on,' he said.

'What do you mean?'

'I mean it's time to do something else, or do the same thing somewhere else. I might go to Africa, for a while. I used to live there you know.'

'You're tired of the Antarctic.'

'I am, yes.' He gave her a hunted look as he said it.

The idea that Luke might no longer love the Antarctic life affected her deeply. She realised that her love for the continent, for her life there – if love is what it was – was linked to him, somehow.

'I don't think I'd want to be here anymore,' she said, 'if you weren't here, flying.'

His surprise was visible. And underneath it, in those prism eyes of his, a sheen of hope. She could say nothing to disperse it, because she herself did not know if it was love which caused her to say this or a raw survival instinct, a cheap form of self-preservation, a pact with herself Luke knew nothing about. She had an obscure instinct to say *I'm sorry*.

'I thought I belonged here.' Nara put it in the past tense, because her belonging was over, somehow. 'And then – what happened to me last winter…'

'I know.' In his voice she heard a glimmer of their old understanding. 'Listen, it's been a long day. I don't think I've slept well in six weeks and I'm bushed.'

She could hear his footsteps retreating, his hiking books squeaking on the linoleum the Saints kept pristine with daily applications of bleach, down the corridor lined with fire extinguishers, with photographs of the old Antarctic, its Nansen sledges and long-dead dogs.

Nara remained sitting at the desk, the little plastic bull from the bottle of Sangre de Toro in front of her, its foreleg stretched out in anticipation of the coming fight. She had never wanted to see a bullfight. It was an abattoir turned to sport, a spectacle for savages, the matadors only dainty, arrogant little brutes.

She threw the bull across the room. It rebounded off the far wall, leaving a tiny, nearly invisible mark beside the picture of the Welsh coastline, then fell to the floor.

The bull will lie there, unnoticed, dustless, until the scrub-out the day after the ship leaves at the beginning of the following winter, when someone will put their broom aside, pick it up, twirl it between their fingers exactly as Nara had done on so many occasions, before throwing it in the bin.

3

The propeller spun, a black insect slicing at the air. The Otter projected itself beneath them onto the ice sheet and this replica trailed them, a faithful shadow. Out the cockpit window was a blue-white horizon so wide and commanding it curved in at its edges, like a convex mirror.

Over the Bowman Coast Luke pointed out jagged edges of ice. 'Cliffs down there must be a couple of hundred feet high, at least.' These were the remnants of the Larsen ice shelf. Luke banked south, then, heading over the Wilkins, Black, and Lassiter Coasts, the mountains beneath them rolling into blue ice glaciers, then a pale turquoise hem of meltwater where they met the salt sea.

At 75 degrees south they saw a long seam of white spread across the curved horizon – the edge of the Ronne Ice Shelf. Beneath them the ice in the Weddell Sea was breaking up: pale blue rivers of fresh water snaked through wedges of white ice. Ice pans fragmented into rectangles, trapezoids, rhomboids. From the air it was impossible to tell how large they might be. Between these intervals of ice were sheets of transparent lacy ice, like muslin, seamed at the edges where two floating sheets of icy lace overlap. 'Like a wedding dress someone'd taken a knife to,' Luke said. Nara looked down and saw the ice slashed, torn at its seams into thin sheets of fabric. Within days, this would all melt.

Then they passed over a field of unbroken white. 'That's the Ronne. The edges of the shelf are actually afloat. See there?' Nara could see thin tracings on the snow, geometric, like the perforations between pieces of a jigsaw puzzle. They appeared as narrow veins of the lightest grey on a field of white.

'What are those?'

'Grounding lines. They show where the ice starts to float.'

Luke had been true to his word. He organised it for her to be a co-pilot, so that she could see this landscape. The ice-core team were uplifted a week before, they were already back in the UK. Nara and Luke would collect equipment left behind; they would stay at Berkner for three or four hours and then fly back to base.

Luke banked the plane and swung them out to sea so that she could see the sea-smoke and the frazil ice. Then he levelled out the aircraft to approach the ice shelf with their nose to the south.

They touched down with a jolt. The now-familiar flurry of ice crystals flew up and coated the windscreen. They bumped to a stop, and he cut the engines. They climbed out into a silence so profound it had a sound, like bells ringing all around them. It was New Year's Day.

For a while Nara stands completely still on the ice sheet, forearm thrown across her brow to shield her eyes. Here even her sunglasses are not enough to cut the glare. Unlike in the Ellsworths, there are no mountains to puncture the skyline at Berkner. There is no visual field, only mist, veils, languid sheets of white muslin. They hang in the air until dispersed by wind. The light and energy mass balance do not change throughout the day at this time of year. The snow is different from the snow on the peninsula. Here it is hard white meringue, sliced by sastrugi.

She can see the plane's ski tracks from where Luke has come and gone before, when the ice-coring team were there. Then he had also landed into the south, making his final approach over the ocean. He'd had no windsock to guide him, only the Met Man's predictions over at the base, whatever Horace the computer model was saying about wind direction over the Weddell, and his intuition.

They look toward the sea. The edge of the ice cliffs is twelve kilometres away, but it looks more like a few hundred metres. A gigantic iceberg is adrift, not more than a kilometre from the coast. But this might be an illusion, the mirage they call the *fata morgana*.

Nara walks toward the camp, mounting and descending each of the sharp sastrugi wavelets, the wind tossing miniature clouds of snow crystals upward. A smoky, dry ice place, vapourless. An intense dryness burns the back of her throat. Parked on the ice sheet, the plane looks enormous, much larger than usual – another optical illusion.

The surface of the snow shines, hardened gelatin under an enamel sky.

They put on their full padded thermal boiler suits and went to work. First they fired up a skidoo and harnessed a sledge to tow the boxes into the plane. But first the Avtur fuel barrels would have to be placed in the underground ice-chamber used for this purpose. If time allowed, they would fire up the plane's Primus stove and have a cup of tea. Then they would load up the plane and leave.

Luke laid two planks out of the back of the Otter as a ramp for rolling the fuel drums out. Once the heavy drums had thundered down their makeshift slide, they lashed them to the sled. Nara towed them to the fuel depot on the skidoo while Luke manoeuvred the remaining drums into position at the top of the ramp. They input ten drums this way, in preparation for next season's drilling.

It was time to pick up the ice-coring equipment. The A-frame aluminium hut that covered the ice-coring chamber was blown in with snow. They each grabbed a shovel and dug. All this they did in silence, without stopping to comment.

Then they broke for tea. She went to collect snow while Luke fired up the Primus. They did this without any discussion or negotiation over who would do what. They decided to have their tea outside, in the sun. There they sat, backs to the corrugated wall of the weather haven, while the sun beat down on them. Between the exertion, the heat of the sun and the tea, they were finally warm.

They rose from their tea break in silence. The rest of the equipment was stored in a weather haven fifty feet away from the A-frame entrance. She went to fetch it. Inside the weather haven, it was cold. She put back on her layers, readjusted her salopettes, put on her fleece.

The door opened. She turned around to see Luke standing there. Behind him, the flimsy door slammed shut in the wind. Suddenly it was dark inside.

He advanced toward her. She did not feel fear – she had never been afraid of him – but her heart pounded painfully, driven by a giddy recklessness, a bizarre expectation. She told herself, whatever happens, I won't care. I will survive it.

His face was drawn; little hooks tugged at the edges of his mouth. His blue-grey eyes were darker than she remembered, the terse, brooding look within them denser. She had seen this before, this was nothing new. But in the past she was able to brush it away as tiredness. Eyes so tired from looking at empty sky.

'Luke?' How strange it sounded. She used his name so rarely. It was not an idle or self-protective use. It was not a shield.

He stayed there, in front of her.

She had a powerful feeling of things gathered, or gathering in front of her. Spies or sentries had forewarned them that she would take this path, and they had been waiting for her.

Luke came closer, his body blocking the light from behind him. The weather haven became darker, as if a cloud had passed over. But there were no clouds in their sky.

She stared at his mouth, watching it become larger and larger, until his mouth was the world. She felt his mouth on hers. The kiss was soft, not insistent. She kissed him back. There was no word for the loneliness that overtook her then. It moved through her and inside her, like a gust of wind searching for an exit.

He turned away. The weather haven was suddenly an empty chamber of cold. Outside it, the white plain unpleated its skirts. Apart from a few emperor penguins, the seals, the Orcas and leopard seals that patrolled the waters of the Weddell, they were the only two things alive for at least a thousand miles in all directions.

She wanted to say, *I'm so sorry*. She wanted to say, *You are my family*. But she could not open her mouth, she could not form the words. She had an urge to sit down and let events overtake her. After a while – later she would be unable to recall how long – she walked out of the weather haven to see the plane taxiing along the snow.

She stood still, she could not move; it was as if she had suddenly put down roots into the ice. She watched the Otter slide away from her. When it lifted off, she half-cheered it into the air, out of habit.

At first she took an interest in her abandonment. She thought: *How strange*. She imagined him returning, imagined herself climbing, sullen, miserable, unresponsive, into the cockpit. *What are you going to do next? Crash the plane?*

She watched as the plane rose into the sky, knowing in some chamber of her being that her life depended upon it, yet curiously detached, thinking: now the plane will turn. *Now, now, now.*

As he flew away he drank in the bitter chromium glint, the sun, the blinding blankness of the ice sheet. He no longer loved this landscape, he no longer even liked it, he realised, although he could tolerate the landscape around base, the mountains with their bruised glamour.

Almost as soon as he was in the air the camp – weather havens, bamboo flags, the aluminium A-frame which covered the entrance to the ice-coring chamber, the skidoos covered with tarpaulins – vanished into the ice sheet. He concentrated on his instrument readings, on the empty sky in front of him, on the distance he had to go, until Midas.

Watch, altimeter, speed, fuel gauge, watch, altimeter, speed, fuel gauge.

He banked left and flew over the ice shelf. It was thinning rapidly at the edges into a thin parchment of frazil ice. He saw vast sheets of ice flowers, rime, glare ice, ice pans. Yes, this was his favourite time of year, the time of the high summer sea ice. In a week perhaps the tetrahedrons would fragment into smaller and smaller floes, and the Weddell would open, if only for a month.

It was in this sea, just to the north of his present position, where Shackleton's *Endurance* had become trapped in pack. Over a hundred years later they were still all but unnavigable, these waters; apart from heavy, powerful icebreakers no ship could get in. Years ago he had spent a week in a ship in these waters, moored off an ice shelf, flying fuel from the ship into the Bluefields depot. He remembered only the cold, grit ice crystals in his face, as if it were a sandstorm.

Yes, he wanted to live by the facts of experience, and not by abstract ideas. Occurrence is mysterious. He liked its dark energy: the positive, the negative. Both were present in all the things he had seen in his life – the black snows of Marble Hills in the silver Antarctic sun, so platinum it looked like moonlight, or the abyss of the crevasse, the white body of the albatross as it rode the endless thermals.

He does not know what he will say – to Midas, to field ops. But he will think of something. He has an hour and forty minutes to fly yet.

The plane flew away, higher and higher and still she expected it to come back for her. Something must have gone terribly wrong; Luke had lost his rudder, his hydraulics, and he could only fly in a straight line.

She was hit by blowing snow in the face, because she had taken off her sunglasses to strain for the plane. It stung; the snow was thin and grainy, like sand. The white was too sharp, too intense. She risked burning her corneas. She put the glasses back on.

The wind caught her unawares, from the back. She knew that Berkner was one of the most windy, exposed places in the western Antarctic, much more so than the peninsula. If the wind picked up speed she would not be able to stand. She pictured herself being blown over the icefields like a tent or a sleeping bag, tumbling over and over until she was tipped over the cliff and into the icy sea.

The idea of the plane was so strong in her mind that she nearly willed it into existence. The plane blaring through the sky, vermilion, ecstatic.

But even as she thought it, she knew he was gone, due east, to Midas. There he will land and someone will notice she is not with him. She is logged on the roster, Adelaide base Ops know she went out as his co-pilot. Midas will radio to Adelaide to say, something's happened.

But what if he tells them she is dead, that there has been an accident, the body unrecoverable? Would they believe him? Would they come to look for her anyway? The burn of the sun disappears under a skein of thin cloud. She is already thirsty. Unless she finds a manfood box and a Primus with meths, she will not eat, she will not be able to melt snow. She will have to eat snow, but this does not satisfy the body roasted under a summer polar sun, cooling its insides even as it dehydrates from insufficient liquid. She remembered this particular irony from one of her field-training sessions: people die of dehydration in the Antarctic, because although surrounded by the greatest mass of fresh water in the world, it is in the wrong form. The human mouth cannot melt enough ice on its own to quench its thirst.

She jolted awake, fully clothed, into the blare of perpetual day.

I am very cold. Then, another hasty thought, too quick, on the back of an accelerating heartbeat: *mustn't sleep*. All her training told her that she must sleep only when protected by goose down, by the heat of a Tilley Lamp.

She went outside the weather haven and looked out to sea. Loose pack. Ice pans. Glare ice. A steep descent toward open water. She would run to the edge, and throw herself off. How else to avoid slowly freezing or starving? Even if an emperor penguin did wander across her field of vision, she would have nothing to kill it with.

She had been reading *South*, by Shackleton, that past winter, just before Alexander's accident. She read how the old explorers were sickened by an unrelenting diet of penguin and seal-meat, its rubbery, fish-stew taste. How small fissures in the ice yawed like chasms, how they lived in a perpetual terror of crevasses. Shackleton's men were so tired of waking in their tents, alarm surfacing through them as the ice shifts beneath them. They were stranded on ice floes in the Weddell Sea, not far from her weather haven. They might never see England again. Trapped on the ice, watching their ice island become smaller and smaller, they watched as killer whales circled, mistaking them for seals, the shriek and gurn of their voices. For two of the men, the experience erodes their sanity, their trust in their God, which after all might be the same thing. Although strangely this disintegration was a slow process, taking many months to happen, and the men held it together until nearly the end, only becoming insane on the eve of their rescue.

She can see them on the horizon, just behind the curtain of sea-smoke that rises from the ocean and billows out over the ice plateau. Figures bundled in grey, marching through snow. Are they soldiers, or refugees? No, now they are playing a game of soccer, they rush toward each other, hug, rush away.

The visions evaporate with the sea-smoke.

She listens for the voice. But the voice is not there, or it has nothing to say.

Rummaging around the camp she finds the ice-coring chamber is empty of anything that might keep her alive, such as food or a radio. Although she does find an old report, fuel, boxes of machinery and drilling fluids. She looked up: the sun was mistaken, square, a tile plastered against the sky. The air hurt her lungs. Sweat had dried now, and created a layer of subtle chill on her skin. She shivered and went to try to find a shovel.

Firn, ablation. Basal shear stress. Alexander is looking at scars, at foliations, the convex direction of flow. Narrow tensional cracks which have closed or been filled with snow or refrozen meltwater, cracks into which water has percolated and frozen.

Fourteen thousand miles away in Devon, as far away as it is possible to be on this planet, Alexander is at work in the spare room of his mother's house.

Glaciers formed by the merging of two or more tributaries often have a separate system of arcs corresponding to each tributary with longitudinal folaition near the boundaries between them.

Ice never lies. It is older than us, better than us, with its intersections of honesty, its shards of hard truth. Ice exists only to build more of itself, and to preserve the record. There is no melt in the crystal desert, no possibility of erasure. The bodies of the dead explorers may never be found, but they are still there, trapped in the ice.

His virtual ice is less treacherous than the real thing. He discovered that he did not need to live on the ice in order to believe in it. He did not mind theorising without data. His was a theoretical field, after all; he built his own horizontal distances and velocities. He built the ice sheets of the past and the future, with no thought for the land they covered, which would one day be unburdened from its glacial slumber, into spring.

His needs are equally simple. He needs to be unconfined. He needs no one to have a piece of him. He is interested in other people only in inverse relationship to the extent to which they are interested in him: a simple equation, with perfect symmetry. What he can keep for himself, what he can give away. He is one of those people who will give very little, and for this reason someone or other will always want him.

It is New Year's Day and he goes for a walk on a small crescent beach near his mother's Devon home. He has already decided to return to the Antarctic in February, to finish his fieldwork. Without another two months on base he cannot complete his PhD. An uncompleted PhD means no conferences, post-docs, papers, panels, invitations to speak, no colleagues, no place in the world as a prophet of its disintegration.

It is ten degrees; England is warm now, even in winter, although within ten years the mean temperature could drop ten degrees, plunging the British Isles into its own ice age. This is if the Meridonal Overturning Current – the Gulf Stream – shifts, dislodged by cold fresh water melted from the Greenland Ice Cap. He has seen the models, they mostly agree on this scenario.

For now, he will enjoy this perpetual spring which has replaced their winter. The diluted spring light, the English Channel. The Antarctic feels very far away, now. He has no idea of the drama which is playing out there, for Nara, as he sinks his bare feet into the cold sand on a beach fourteen thousand miles away. He can almost not believe in the Antarctic's existence, as if it is a shape which has been hastily sketched on the globe, an experiment in balancing the symmetry of the planet. Even though he has lived through a winter there – or part of a winter, his mind still skates over the accident – still it is not quite real.

She saw the plane before she heard it, coming at her through an unbroken veil of ice crystals. The sun dimmed and flared in the sky. The lace of ice, dry as dust, filled the air. The sun shone through it, rigid silver pearls of polar sun. She wanted to touch them. She took her hand out of her glove, fingering them. They settled upon her skin, where they melted. Slowly, as if from a long way away, the sensation came to her: her fingertips stung. In another few seconds they would freeze. She put her hand back inside the glove.

Then he is coming toward her and she wants to put her hand out, again: Stop! You're not real! Go away! Then his arms are around her, her cheek thrust into a boiler suit. A cascade of words, all the same: *I'm so sorry, sorry, sorry.*

She sat down, or collapsed. She got back up again; she was reluctant to stop moving. As long as she kept moving and was under the heat of the sun, her core temperature would stay high enough. She ran in a circle. Her throat was parched. She stopped, and sat down again. The snow was coarse and grainy, it smothered her footsteps. The wind was not wind, but a thousand tiny fiery quartz spears.

The knot in her gut spelled an old word, something to do with sin, with memory. With a vanishing. Light, but within it a black pit, the stone of an olive. Her mind was a curling black bone of treason. She was alone, finally, caught in this bright albedo snare. She saw no aliens, no wolves. Only this rigid God's country spread all around her, its vacant glinting squalor.

Luke – he must be real! – was still saying *sorry, sorry, sorry.*

A thin curtain of snow crystals blew up all around her. Refracted through the sun they turned blue, and suddenly she saw the sheets of ice all around her as blue, fields and fields of throbbing turquoise, indigo, cerulean: Bluefields.

4

It happens on the sea ice, only twenty kilometres from base. Luke is flying very low, at the lowest threshold of the altimeter, 100 feet, to fix a landing track. They strafe the icefields so that a smoky curtain of ice crystals is blown in their wake.

Nara looks out the window, her face turned away. For the first time since she arrived in the Antarctic, she does not want to see the ice beneath her. She shirks her co-pilot duty, which is to watch out for bird strikes and icebergs.

He is tired and he does not see the nearly invisible silhouette of the iceberg. The plane's skiwheel snags on its top; it is a pinnacle berg, those triangular lumps of weathered ice that look like spinnaker sails.

Of the actual impact, Luke will remember nothing at all, nor of the moment that preceded it, nor the time immediately after. His memory will be erased. Later, he will report to the authorities that the aircraft was destabilised by the berg strike, although very slightly. If he hadn't been coming in to land he would have had the time and room to correct the plane's tilt.

The left wing dips, toward the ice. He corrects it quickly – he is an excellent pilot, no one has better reflexes or judgement – thinking for a moment that it would be all right, but gravity tugs at it again. If he'd had just a little more altitude, he would have recovered the situation. Nara puts her hand out on the console, and this is the last thing he will remember of her, a right hand reaching out toward the altimeter, to steady herself. It is New Year's Day, 2013.

*

They came for them in the RIBs. It took them two hours to reach the plane, portaging over unstable ice, looking for leads between ice pans. The ice was shifting, blowing in, then blowing out on the Bellingshausen tide. They came for them even though there was no certainty they would all get back; later this is what would impress Luke most, because he knew that in the Antarctic, such missions were not mounted lightly. A few years before a Norwegian man who survived a Twin Otter crash not far from base with only a broken leg was left to freeze to death, because the sea ice was too unstable to rescue him. There was no point in endangering many lives just to save one.

The plane was largely intact. A week later the Navy ship would arrive to salvage the body, winching it up from the ice. Its undercarriage was smashed, but otherwise, not a scratch. Luke had been right in his feeling that no matter what happened, he would always be able to get the plane down, in some form. It would not end in disarray.

He was knocked unconscious by the jolt, but he was only out for ten minutes, he estimated. However long it was, when he came to, Nara was gone.

The Southern Ocean constructed itself piecemeal over 120 million years. Only 38 million years ago the Drake passage appeared, revealing its island archipelago arcing up toward the southern tip of Tierra del Fuego, the land of fire. The proto-ice sheets of the Antarctic also date from this event. In the early Pliocene, 3 to 4 million years ago, the Antarctic circumpolar current that Nara and Alexander helped study on their journey into the Antarctic by ship that summer stabilised its flow and has not changed much until this day.

The cold current it spawned fanned cold water out to the world's oceans – the Indian, the South Atlantic, the southern Pacific – causing the earth's temperature to plummet. That the early Pliocene was also the date of the onset of the most recent planetary glacial epoch was no accident, Alexander knew; the birth of the Antarctic was in part responsible for the last global freeze.

There is nowhere on earth like the Antarctic, with its consuming vortex, a static frozen whirlpool moored at the bottom of the planet, its weight so heavy that it drags down the magnetic field of the earth, so that the planet is not spherical at all, but pear-shaped. A fulcrum, the coldest place on the planet, far colder than the Arctic. In the Antarctic there is only ice, which makes more ice, and it goes on forever. It is a sinuous, remote, abstract reality. To live there, you have to accept this – that it is not a place, not really part of the world. It is like living in the deep ocean, or on the moon. But also, there is something else, some element of a trick involved. The Antarctic is a hoax, a visual puzzle. It never happened, it does not exist.

PART VIII

Iceblink

1

'So what do you do, at work?' Helen asked.

'I make policy.'

She smiled. 'I know that, but how do you make policy? How does it actually work?'

David drew a breath. 'Well, it's all a bit mysterious. I spend a lot of time consulting with ministers on – oh, science, resource exploration, territorial claims, military matters, foreign policy. Then we work with lawyers to draft legislation, and go to conferences, and consult with other Antarctic Treaty member states. And then,' he said, shifting in his seat, 'I do a whole lot of very secret stuff I can't tell you about, or they would shoot me.'

The place has become so familiar to Helen and David, by then, with the low buzz of the squash dispenser and fizz of water boiling in the tea urn, the cans of Nido powdered milk stacked below. On the walls the Antarctic photo gallery: pilots, skidoos, elephant seals. The dog-eared climbing magazines, ten-year-old *National Geographics*. All this had not changed since Nara's year on base.

They talked more now; in their captivity a new complicity had sprung up between them, more cautious than what they had shared on the ship, yet at least now David spoke with her without those boards nailed across his voice, which simultaneously issued a challenge and refused her entry.

'What about the future?' she asked.

'Oh, that. We spend vast amounts of money on the future. Consultants, presentations by scientists – the NASA guys, they're the best – and future scenario modelling. They're by far the most amusing, the scenario people. They show us everything from dystopia to utopia, the whole gamut laid out on the table. They talk about the Icarus scenario, where we all fly too close to the sun, we want everything, we aim too high for a perfect sustainable society, and we fall, scorched by our own ideals. Or the Lame Duck scenario, where resource poverty cripples growth, and the political momentum that's driven the democratic process atrophies, slowly, over the decades. There's another scenario, but I can't remember what it's called, the To Hell in a Hand-Basket scenario, probably.' He laughed. 'But how much this changes anything, I don't know – all these futures, floating in front of us like ogres – but we have to choose, that's the problem. We have to choose now, how we want the planet to be, in the future, because there is no way back.'

He paused. 'My brother is one of them, in fact.'

'What does he do?'

'He's an economist by training, but these days he tells the future.'

'How can he do that?'

'Don't ask me. All I know is that these days banks, governments, the corporate world, they all go to visit Ben and his crystal ball.'

When had he seen Ben last? David realised he couldn't remember. They must have had lunch, sometime around – could it really have been Christmas? He had a vague memory of a tree blinking on and off in the corner, one of those lavishly decorated trees, in what used to be called a Gentleman's Club. *Ben looks so young* – this is what David kept thinking, over and over, during their conversation that day. He was only thirty-six. Although there was something about his face, his physique, that suggested he might age in giant leaps, the sort of age acceleration seen in presidents and prime ministers made suddenly old by the stress of running the world.

'Ben took the right route,' he said it absently, so that Helen barely heard him.

'To what?'

'To power, I suppose. PPE at Brasenose, an early career internship with the FCO, then the Treasury, then industry. Next up, government.' David rapped the table, hard, with his fingers, startling Helen. 'I took the back door, as it turned out. I studied history and science. I wanted to be a scientist. But I suppose I knew from the beginning that I didn't have the stamina, the dedication, for research science. But I never really fitted in at the FCO – Ben did – and they just didn't know what to do with me. So they gave me the Polar Regions. Well, I earned it, actually. My name helped, of course.'

'And how do you want the future to be?' she asked.

'A version of this, I suppose.' David swept his eyes around the dining room. 'Little Antarctic bases, recycling their own rubbish, treating their own sewage, desalinating encroaching floodwaters, producing their own entertainment. Victorian pantomimes, burlesques, vaudevilles.' He laughed. 'This is how we should all be living.'

'Don't you miss anything from the outside world?'

'Only friends. Anonymity. Restaurants. I want to go into a restaurant and order something from the menu, something I want, instead of queueing up at the cafeteria like I'm back in university, or in the Army. I miss swimming. Heat. Being able to walk outside with only a shirt on. Not having to wear socks. Travel.'

'I only ever wanted to live in cities,' she said. 'I wanted that anonymity, the choice they give you. We can go to this play, or this concert, or this restaurant. The strange thing, we never do. Near the end of our marriage Eric and I never went out. We were always working.'

Eric would prepare his classes, she would go to her job on

a daily newspaper, and at night they would sit at separate computers and catch up on their emails. When they ate dinner together the television would be on; they would watch the news, and exchange views about what they saw happening in the world, their alarm growing in concert. Day after day they had seen each other only this way, and in bed – to sleep. For a long time, bed had been only about sleep.

'Do you love your brother?' she asked.

He looked away. 'I feel pride, and envy. Mixed together.' He looked back at her. 'Do you think that's love?' He meant, *Is that the answer you were looking for?*

The drinks machine switched on, its buzz filling the silence.

They sat back in their respective chairs and allowed their eyes to roam the dining room, the photographs now so familiar: planes landing against a watermelon sunset, Orcas probing the surface with their lapidary heads, skidoos pulling Nansen sledges across a featureless plain of white.

Night gathered outside the window. Helen knew that in some obscure way she would be the Antarctic's prisoner forever now, that a cold fire had been lit inside her. To keep it stoked she would either have to find a way to return, or run the risk of an eternal homesickness by extinguishing it forever.

There is the dead, and the living, and what between them? Dusk. A collusion. That is why, in this duskless place, life seems unreal. There are no ghosts. So we haunt ourselves, having no one else to do the haunting for us.

Nara wrote in fragments, mostly. Many of them make little sense: *I hear it now. The voice. It says:* Moss hours. Our confessions.

But it is clear she thought she was reading the planet, as if it were writing its diaries or memoirs, and had simply arrived at the last chapter. Too exhausted to write on its own, now, it required an amanuensis – a translator, a scribe. Why had it chosen her? She was at the end of the earth, alone and grappling with an impossible love. The Antarctic winter had driven many strong-minded men insane, and why should a young woman biologist not succumb to the hallucinations of the most total winter on earth? She has been abandoned – that much she understood. She needed a voice to fill the silence.

Now, Helen wonders: is it possible she was telling the truth? It was a radical thought, but perhaps it has a voice, and was trying to communicate, in its distress, and it found a willing receptor tuned by anguish to its frequency.

At night in her pitroom, Helen tries to tune herself into its voice, but she can only hear the hiss of snow, the hollow ringing wind, a sound like no other on earth. Black with emptiness, and also something else, if Helen allows herself to be fanciful: despite its ferocity, a quiet kind of sorrow. A longing.

The Wintering file stops on the night before the Berkner trip. Nara must have been in a rush, Helen decides: all she had had time to write was 'tomorrow – Berkner trip with Luke. Leave base at 0800, refuel at Bluefields, then Berkner.'

The old maps of the Antarctic show endless archipelagoes of islands, ice caps draped across their vacant names: Lassiter, Wilkins, Sweeny, Charcot – all men, all long departed. Men of the desert, of the hollow places, glass, crystals, following a parallel code through time. They were famous, they had charted the world Helen occupies now, and that was about it. They moved across this transparent world where there is no lightning, customs, music, where water has never flowed, except as ice.

Nara had confided to her diary that she had reached a dead end with men. Why then, Helen wonders, did she volunteer to go to a place so suffused with men, their presence, their exploits, their pasts and deaths? These men had marched across the polar ice caps in pure summer, the sun pounding them from above. *Hel-lo there*, she could imagine them saying, in their sharp Edwardian diction, as if swords were being driven through their words. They had been here, in this ghostless chalice of the world, a hundred years ago.

For the first time in her life, in the Antarctic Helen feels a true kinship with men, in particular with the old explorers, also long dead, and also something more mysterious: it is if she can feel the remnants of forgotten life, a life she has lived, that definitely existed, but which she cannot remember. All that is left is the residual impression of having been given a formal gift: of passion for cold, for this frozen world, its flaxen, diligent light.

In her office, the same one Helen occupies now, did Nara ever have such thoughts? There, beside Helen, although separated from time, Nara plays with the plastic bull from the wine bottle, the last one she shared with Luke before his departure, turning it over and over in her hands so much she will wear a groove in it. Objects you keep, without knowing why.

2

On a night not long before Luke flew out at the beginning of the Antarctic winter of 2016, Helen took a walk to the aircraft hangar. She did not have her mini-disc recorder with her. She had no hopes of encountering Luke, or if she did, of speaking to him.

She pulled the hangar door open and stepped inside. There in the half-light sat the large interncontinental plane. It gleamed, a deep satisfying red in the semi-darkness. She walked around it, running her hands along the fuselage, passing her fingers over the penguins-and-propellers emblem, feeling its rivets, its seams. It was surprisingly delicate, this machine which could land on an ice runway with wheels, which could fly five hours through the air, back to the real world.

'Thinking about stowing away?'

She started. Luke emerged from the fuselage. 'Didn't give you a scare, did I?'

'You did,' she said. 'I didn't think anyone was here.'

He saw her hand lingering on the fuselage. 'She's a great plane, isn't she?'

She took a step back.

'Don't go.' There was a plaintive note in his voice which surprised her.

'I'm cold.'

'I'll make you a cup of tea. Here, come round to the Portakabin.'

She sat down, amidst the dustless books. The flying manuals were still on the shelf. An atlas lay open in front of her to show the Alps. Helen had read Nara's account of the nights she had sat there with Luke, drinking Bailey's, the things they had talked about. She stepped inside with Luke, into an air of regret. She had an impression, fleeting and not entirely fanciful, that something or someone followed at her heels.

He saw her looking at the atlas. 'Planning my summer holiday,' he said. 'That's if I ever get one. I think I might be spending the rest of the winter in the Falklands. And you, you're staying here.'

'Well, as everyone keeps saying, how many people get an enforced winter in the Antarctic?'

'That's true,' he said. 'When you become a winterer, it's like joining the Special Forces. You enter into an élite.'

They sat in silence for a while. When she finally asked the question, it was on impulse, not at all premeditated.

'Did anything happen between you on that trip to Berkner? There was a mention in the report that you'd had some trouble with the aircraft there, that you'd had to take it airborne to see how it flew? You reported your position to Midas base and that Nara wasn't with you.'

For a moment, Luke was silent. 'There was nothing wrong with the plane. I just flew off.'

'Flew off?'

He looked at her, and in his eye was an open expression, without a hint of challenge.'Something just came over me. I couldn't have done anything else. It was an instinct, a reflex. I didn't know I was going to do it. Do you think it would have made any difference if I had?'

She looked at him. Luke was a thinking man, she understood, not a dumb brute. If he could do such a thing, then anyone could.

Helen suspected that our deepest natures, our real selves – if such a thing could be said to exist – have their expression in these momentary firings. She wondered if it could be true, that we were all driven by sparks toward conquest, abandonment, the many gradations between the two. These were only the same rank sparks that drove animals into hibernation, impossible migrations. Knit together, these sparks write the code to our existences.

And Luke, in that moment in the Portakabin, with the stranger in front of him who had come to write Nara's story; he also remembered those nights drinking Bailey's, looking at maps, talking about Rio de Janeiro, Senegal, the Canary Islands. For years after the accident he had been coming back to this base, to the hangar and his makeshift office, unaware he was returning as a ghost.

For every action there must be an equal and opposite reaction. Luke had read this in one of the books left behind on base by a scientist, a book about theoretical physics. Much of it was beyond him, but this basic principle made sense: that everything we do in the world carries the energy of its own riposte.

He did not know why he'd flown off without her that day at Berkner, only to turn around in the sky well short of Midas and return. Sometimes there is no *why*. This is what he would come to think, in the ensuing years. It was an instinct – curious, inexplicable. Neither in nor out of character; in any case Luke was not convinced that there was such a thing as *character*, as in a suite of things one individual would or would not do.

He would wait four years before anyone would ask him the question, before the woman journalist or historian or writer – whatever she was – would come to base and ask him why? Not why had the crash happened, the question posed by everyone else in the interim, by HQ, the Chief Pilot, the Coroner, the FCO man. But why had he left Nara at Berkner alone for four hours; not long, but long enough perhaps to provoke some sort of breakdown.

His favourite moment is when the wheels leave the ground; that precise moment when thrust and lift collude against gravity, the moment when he is uplifted. And what of the people left behind? The woman writer would ask this: he could tell she was a friend of the underdog, of the person left behind by history, of the person standing on the runway in the snow and the sudden bitter wind, watching the plane depart.

Now that he is ready to leave the Antarctic forever, he can admit it. He wanted Nara only as a secret. If they had been lovers, he might have become bored with her, then spurned her. It took three years for the thought to occur to him: might Nara have understood that would be the outcome, and knowing she could not bear it, would not go near him at all?

And his love for the ice desert, what has happened to it? The white vortex of passion he had once felt was muted to ordinary awe now: awe at its frigid glamour. You couldn't call that love.

The Antarctic, that half-invented desert. Could it exist? But he saw it, every day, passing beneath his plane. He, more than any of them, knew it was real.

The rescue team searched for Nara for ten hours, until they too were in danger of becoming trapped on the sea ice. The inquest, held the following year in the Falklands, concluded that she had very likely been concussed in the crash. On regaining consciouness she had become confused and disoriented. Nara had probably headed off in the direction of base; she knew how close they were to home. If she had been thinking straight she would have known to stay with the plane rather than take the risk of walking across twenty kilometres of disintegrating sea ice. But no one would know for certain what choices Nara made, because her body was never found.

The one who comes looking for you is the one who loves you. Only this person can rescue you from your own loss. Of all the people who pored over Nara's death – the base commander, the coroner, Nara's parents, lawyers, insurers, distant officials in distant rooms lined with green leather furniture and bound volumes of legal tomes, even David himself, looking for legalities, loopholes, exclusion clauses – only Helen would accept that Nara may have walked away over the ice not for rescue, but to embrace death. Only Helen would think about how it takes so much cold and fright to pluck a body out of the world, even one as slight as Nara's, or might be awestruck at how long she survived, and at how much she missed him, the man in the plane, only two, three kilometres from where she stood now, but there was no going back, because the ice had broken up behind her, and what had been a puzzle of pancake floes was now open water, and she was drifting on the ice, out to the Bellingshausen.

Helen would come to know that people who have not been to the Antarctic do not understand. No ships will rescue you, no helicopter will swoop low. Here there is only a violent, intimate solitude, and the white sweep of time on the horizon. This place so ravaged and Spartan and raw that it might actually be holy.

On base, during one of their late-night conversations that winter, David would tell Helen, 'I never thought about Nara's death. I never considered what she endured. It was just an accident, and incident. A story.'

As an FCO official he countersigned the Falkland Island coroner's verdict of death by misadventure. Her body was never found. No one knew how she died; whether her abandonment of the plane was deliberate, or whether she was concussed and disoriented. She may have tried to swim for it. She may have been killed by a leopard seal, or a killer whale, the nemesis of the old explorers. Or perhaps she stayed on the ice, in the hope that it would deliver her to land.

In any case, the area was vast, the tide could have taken her anywhere. Men (and until Nara they had always been men – she was the first woman to die this way in the Antarctic) lost on sea ice were almost never found, although mariners on early explorations had spoken of being haunted by men's faces looking up from the icy waters, or staring at them from within an iceberg. The body must be somewhere, the old mariners reasoned, entombed either in the icy depths, or ground through the ice sheets. But the continent rarely gave up its dead. It ate people whole. They disappeared without a trace.

As he told her all this, Helen said nothing, only looked out the window. She saw a dark night, a glacier shining silver in the moonlight. A cold place.

3

The glassy air of early morning was unzipped by flares. It was ten-thirty and still dark. To the northeast, the sky plumed with light – the glimmer of the short-lived Antarctic day.

The ship pulled away and the flares were flames of red burn igniting darkness. Water frothed where the thrusters worked, and the red was reflected in its inky silk. The metallic groan increased, and the ship turned on its haunches, spinning delicately around to face Adélie Island.

Their enforced winter had ended two weeks before, with the news of the lifting of travel restrictions. Thermometers dropped into the waters of the bay from RIBs showed a surface temperature of –1.5 degrees; the sea froze at two degrees below zero. A decision was taken, to send in the Navy icebreaker, because the supply ship, the *Astrolabe*, was only ice-strenghtened and not an icebreaker, and if the ice locked around the continent sudden and hard, as it often did in the beginning of winter, the ship would be stuck.

Satellite images showed the pack ice moving north from Pine Island Bay. For a week they had stayed tuned to the internet site which showed the icebreaker's progress, expecting to hear at any moment that the pack had drifted north, encircling the Navy ship, and they would not be going home. But one night in June a giant arrived in their midst; it heaved and hurled itself against the wharf on a suddenly powerful swell called the Bellingshausen gyre, a current that picked up speed when the ice was near.

Helen was shocked – they were all shocked – by how quickly their winter sentence had been commuted. She felt the strange dread of an unexpected imminent release. She realised that in facing an Antarctic winter she had been committed to time in a way that was new for her. Not unlike facing the pregnancy she had never had, nine months in the Antarctic would be a time to be faced down, a task. Now an empty space yawed in front of her.

They watched the ship arrive. The winterers, those who were committed to stay in any case, watched it for a while, then straggled off. Helen and the thirty-two other people who had been detained in the Antarctic stayed on the rocky outcrop, rivetted despite the wind and the cold, watching the ship pick its way among the icebergs, as if its progress depended on their gaze.

Helen had put herself down for the mooring team and she left the monument to walk down to the wharf. She stood behind three men, a rope in her hands, anchoring the slack end as the men hurled the rope onto the bow. The bar on the satellite tower swung round and round. She heard the creaking as the swell tossed it against the wharf. She watched it rise and sink, rise and sink.

There was a figure beside her, dressed in an orange boiler suit. In the darkness it took her a moment to recognise David.

'It doesn't look real, does it?' he said.

That night they all went aboard the ship for a party in the bar. The shock of strangers, after having been with the same fifty-six people for nearly five months, was immense. They were eager for news of the outside world. Everything was normal in the Falklands, the Navy sailors assured them. *Or as normal as it gets, in the Falklands*, someone said. Then laughter, and the sound of forty men laughing in the same space entered her head like an explosion.

Suddenly their gear was on the ship, their cabins assigned,

and she had no time to think, barely time even to return her library books, which she did at the last minute, only two hours before shore leave expired.

She went to see Gerry, the base commander, to return the books.

'That's quite a reading pile you've got there,' he said, eyeing the covers. *The Return of the Native*, *The Death of Ivan Ilych*, *The Magic Mountain*.

'I was going to take them with me,' she said. 'But then I figured you could use them.'

He took the books. She was about to say goodbye when he spoke.

'You know, I've been thinking about what happened that year. I wasn't on base that summer, I spent it out in the field in a couple of tents down in the Dry Valleys. But the next year I came back and I noticed that no one would speak about it. Reports were filed, but I don't know...people are superstitious. They don't like to talk about accidents or death here. They're too much of a possibility, even now.' His gaze drifted to her pile of books. 'That novel *The Magic Mountain*, it's about people shut away in a sanatorium, isn't it? They stay there because they're sick.'

'Yes.'

'It's just what we're doing here, isn't it? The world is sick, and we're staying here because it's safe.'

'You're staying here because you signed a contract.'

He shook his head. 'I thought you would all be here, through the winter. Now that you're all leaving, I don't know why I'm staying here.'

'The world's not safe, Gerry,' she said. 'Think of that. We're going back to a terrible situation. People are dying.'

'But it's the real world, isn't it?' Gerry looked unhappy, confused, but also elated.

He said, 'I hope you found what you were looking for here.' He pointed to the clock. 'You'd better go, the ship's due to sail in the morning. I'm surprised they even let you off. Navy, you know, do things by the book and all that stuff.'

'Goodbye,' she said. 'And good luck.'

'Good luck yourself, out there in the cruel world.'

Leaving the Antarctic was like leaving nowhere else on earth. The winterers stood on the wharf, holding flares to keep the darknesss at bay. The leavers lined up on the deck of a ship, sailing north, into daylight, into life. Two tribes, both joined in a fraternity of loneliness. For a while, as the ship pulled away, only a few metres of water separated them and they shouted and called and gestured to each other.

But then the ship seemed to wrench itself free, and shift gear. They pulled away quickly now, turned around, and sailed out of the bay. Helen had heard it said that in the Antarctic, the departure of the ship at the beginning of winter was never a mere leave-taking, but the closing of a door called winter. Only time would prise it open.

Once clear of the sheltered peninsula waters, the seas worsened. The Navy ship had a peculiar grinding motion; like a fairground ride, it pitched, crashed, then turned around on its haunches – the ship's crew called it 'corkscrewing'. The crew told Helen the ship was technically too small for the seas of the Drake Passage, where rogue waves were on the increase. These were waves the height of ten-storey buildings. Earlier in the season a rogue wave smashed the bridge windows out of a giant cruiseliner, and it had to be towed into port in Punta Arenas.

For the first two days everyone was seasick, apart from

Helen and the crew. She wandered the ghost ship, bumping into the Bosu'n, or the chief engineer.

'Why aren't you in your cabin throwing up?' the engineer asked.

'I'm trying my best, but it looks like I don't get seasick.'

'We'll put you to work, then.'

Of course – she remembered she had joined the Army. She'd better find a boiler suit that fit.

The following day David appeared. He looked wan. 'I guess you found your sealegs.'

'I didn't need to look for them in the first place.' In fact she'd been out on the back deck that morning, helping the Bosu'n secure cargo containers which had shifted during the night in heavy seas. When she'd finished that she'd taken an inventory of the food in the freezer for the purser. 'A hard worker,' the crew had said, with approval, and offered her extra helpings of hot custard with dessert that night.

Later they sat alone in the mess, a bottle of wine between them, which he was not quite well enough to drink.

'Ships are lonely places, don't you think?'

David nodded. 'I've often thought that.'

'I like you more when you agree with me. I try not to, of course.'

He smiled, an open, honest smile, in which she could see the shadow of his relief.

The journey back is mostly in darkness. On their trip into the Antarctic nearly seven months before, they had run past the edge of night into a perpetual daylight. Now, in June, there is only a day-long dusky light. Some people never appear from their bunks. The Navy doctor makes cabin visits, accompanied by a saline drip. Slowly, Helen and David are joined by one or two seasickness survivors. But by then they are used to having the ship to themselves, it has become *their* ship.

All night they talk, or sit on the bridge together, watching as snow is driven against the windows, marvelling at how it looks like fireworks, lit from underneath by the ship's powerful searchlights. Growlers scrape against the hull, the seas mount and slacken.

Helen tells David what she has learned in the Antarctic about the rules of vision. There are twenty-four basic geometric shapes. The easiest shapes for the human eye to perceive are those that are closed, such as circles and squares. The more basic the shape, the easier it is to perceive, she tells him; we see circles first then squares, then rectangles. We need to look at complicated shapes longer. The brain assembles these shapes into patterns, and compares them with patterns it has seen before; mostly these are stored in long-term memory. If you have grown up with trees, then the mind wanders across the white plain, looking for them.

In the Antarctic, during a whiteout, the human eye sees a visual field without any shapes or contours. Visible light is distributed perfectly evenly. Caught in this field of vision, the human starts to lose balance and coordination almost immediately. Quickly – within fifteen minutes – blindness, although temporary, follows.

In this white blindness the hallucinations begin. The brain begins to fabricate something to see: shapes, rectangles, circles, trees, a horizon – anything will do. Then vertigo arrives. Then, the only thing to do is close your eyes and imagine yourself upright in this white diffuse maelstrom of directionless light.

Outside the panoramic windows on the bridge a hostile sea roils into being – mountains of steel water, horizontal snow. Cape petrels dart on updrafts, hunting for krill in the wake. David spends hours looking out at the sea, which is too stern to be beautiful, but yet it is.

He wonders if everyone has an obstacle in their lives, so immovable and permanent, even after it has been dislodged. For Helen, it is the death of her husband – or not quite his death, but how he died, under what circumstances. For his great-grandfather, it was those days on Elephant Island. He wonders if you could call these obstacles destiny.

Kate cannot have children. His particular branch of his great-grandfather's survival genes stop with him. Not that this is the reason for his distress, for the mounting grind within his heart, so painful that sometimes he fears he will have a heart attack.

He practices saying it to himself, out loud: *I might have to leave you*. Then, *I will leave you*. Thank God for the Antarctic, for its dangerous seas and even more dangerous interior. He thinks, no one who has not been here can understand its bizarre allure. *I am leaving you.* Blue, white, blue, white. Unlit rows and rows of the ice desert. Chunks, loaves gone wrong. A white current. Cloud. The moon sweeping the icefield, a silver glaze. The mistakes he has made, errors of judgement and the heart. All those talks he has attended, and conferences, and meetings, on the future and destiny of the polar regions at the Royal Society, the Geographical Society. Long, learned faces in the audience, he cannot imagine any of these people laughing, shouting, clapping, hugging each other, having sex. All his life, he has been fascinated by cold, and there has been so little warmth. He wants to *live*, before it is too late. This is all he wants.

In the narrow cabin bed Helen runs her hands through David's hair.

To the south, near the Pine Island glacier, the ice is fastening. Soon its scrawl will interlock, and rebuff the sun once more.

There are so many kinds of ice that exist in the world: ice clouds, ice vapour. Icebergs, ice mountains, ice plateaus. Then the sea ice: ice floes, pack ice, pancake ice, grease ice, undersea ice, rotten ice, ice ridges, ice hummocks. An ice planet, in the process of melting. What will it be like, to live in a world without ice? The white warp gone, the mirror gone. The earth and its hot oceans, dense with methane. The conversation between the ice and the sun is both an acknowledgement, and a rebuff. But soon the conversation may be over.

4

In a good ice year, the sea ice freezes to the thickness of a man's torso. Sealed in this winter cauldron live killer whales, seals, the giant sea-sponges and starfish Nara studied that year on base. Not only could these creatures survive in the near-frozen water of the Antarctic, they flourished. But the water was warming rapidly, and the animals were dying.

On the horizon she sees the strain of night and fire. Cities burning, far away on desert shores, torched by Romans, or some dead army. A dream within a dream.

Where the cold river of wind meets warmer seas, snowspouts – miniature ice tornadoes, also called Ice Devils – and sea fog, also known as sea-smoke, form. A haze hangs on the rim of her senses.

She is puzzled, wary, cold. The wind has died in the place where the wind is born. A bluish silence billows in and out of the ice, borne on this frozen wind.

Night snags on day. Shadows increase. The pillage of light by darkness.

Nara drifts among bergs, rolling and floating like stricken ships. She could climb aboard them, if she chose. Weddell seals eye her, unalarmed by her presence. In their eyes is moist indifference. They want only to swim, eat fish, loll on ice floes, soak up the solar burn of the polar sun.

The wind slams into her body, curves it into a small pine like those stunted bonsai shrubs called Diddle-dee that she and Alexander had seen on their walks in the Falkland Islands. On the horizon a glimmer of persimmon light vanishes into a dark water sky.

Nara thinks, if I can never touch flesh again, never hear

the heartbeat of another human, then please let me go. She talks to this thing which has her life in the palm of her hand, addressing it in capital letters: You, It. She wonders, who are You? A will is imprisoning her there, on the ice. It is a mysterious force. A black wall, shimmering in the whiteness: magic. Alexander has the same quality, now, when she thinks of him. He is an amulet, a statue. He transports himself through time, he barely needs to move across space. Like a moving target on a radar screen, she cannot track his every moment, only his trajectory.

The body endures longer than she expects. The first immersion is a lurching shock. Her heart rocks sideways in her chest. She breathes in desperate gulps, her brain suddenly starved of the oxygen that has deserted it in order to try to warm the extremities. She can't move her limbs; she is a diver, a strong swimmer, but her arms are made of lead suddenly, and they sink.

Her life has been the same as any other: years of striving punctuated by fleeting moments of exhilaration, of enlightenment. Fear has hung heavier over her life than most, just like the mantle of Antarctic clouds which drop so low that the sky is only a sliver of light on the horizon, trapped between cloud and sea.

It is more than a year since she has been warm. Still, some part of her does not want to let go.

The sea ice congeals in giant pancakes; it bunches into ridges where the plates of ice have driven against each other, much the same as when continental plates grind mountain chains into being when they collide. Above her, in this empty quadrant of sky at the bottom of the planet seen by only a chosen few, are nebulae and supernovae, with their bursts of strange red flare. The stars are cold, the space between them dark caesuras.

Not six months before, she and Alexander had spun

underneath the stars on the first clear night in weeks after a bout of winter storms. On that night Alexander recited the names of the Southern Ocean stars, still unfamiliar to both of them, their spook names: *Centaurus*, *Musca*, *Carina*, *Pleiades*. *Orion*, *Betelgeuse*, *Aldebaran*. He pointed out the Southern Cross, how Venus and Mars sit low on the horizon, almost tipping over its dark seam, the reversed planets hurtling through an abandoned sky.

Her eye fixed on Pleiades, also called the Seven Sisters. At that extreme southerly latitude the constellation flickered on the horizon like strobe lights. It might have been Alexander who told her the baleful story behind its name: there were seven sisters who all committed suicide for sorrow at the death of their father, Atlas. The seventh star was named for Merope, who shined dully because in life she shamed herself by having an affair with a mortal.

Nara was alone. For the whole of the following day her ice floe drifted toward Adélie Island. It thinned, melted by the heat of her body until it was only a sagging meltpool beneath her; unstable and wallowing, like a child sitting in a deflating bouncy castle.

Cold starts at the perimeter of the body and travels inward. Nara knows when she is chilled to the core because her lungs hurt. A small pain at first, it expands and turns a yellow hue, threaded with black branches of agony. Each of the polyps on her lungs is slowly freezing.

It occurs to her that it would be quicker to die in the water. The immersion shock speeds up her heartbeat until it groans under the pressure of cold.

Beside her, Alexander spun. He was tall, quite dark-skinned, for an Englishman. His skin had an unusual hue – burnished, like wood. Even then, months after they first met, she still stared and stared at it, as if she had never seen skin before. There was an Asiatic tinge to his eyes, the shape of mussel shells.

Satellites streaked across the sky, spewing bolts of greenish light. If a satellite were to have fixed its lens on them, what would it have spied? Two people in the dark of the Antarctic winter, necks craned. They must be friends, or lovers; why else would they be alone, spinning round and round in the night, two of the only one hundred people left on the Antarctic peninsula, an area the size of France and England combined.

Was it possible to be traumatised by joy? The shock of it rippled through her: to have discovered joy, only to be immediately cut off from it…Nara was only beginning to understand that love could be something entirely different from the exalted force most people take it for, the romance and beauty in which she herself always believed, but rather a dark masquerade, a stalker, moving from her future backwards, silently, toward her.

Beyond the iceblink she sees black open water, a grind of shadow. St Augustine wrote, *Whatever has flown away is past, now. Whatever remains is future.*

Like everyone who sets out on a journey, she had hoped she would arrive unscathed. What could she do to make another man exactly like Alexander, this time a version which would love her? She wishes she had never seen him.

Even now her office on base and her cabin on the *Astrolabe* are saturated with her thoughts of Alexander. Dreams, fevers, meetings real and imagined, turnarounds, ruptures in the fabric of fate and time. Luck.

One star, or is it a nebulae? – it is dark, elusive. Nara watches it flicker on and off, sees the shadowy vortex its intermittent extinguishing leaves in the sky. 'I don't like that star,' she says, more to herself than anyone.

For some years after her death Luke flies above the haze, this swirl of frontal passages, of lapse rates, the transfer of heat and moisture from the ocean to the air as the interior ice is pushed outward.

Season after season he will fly, drawn again and again to the frozen continent on the pull of its cold voltage. The light on the horizon, that prowling, infinite light. He flies into this valley of whiteness and returns with presentations, slideshows like the one he gave on the Midas III rescue the winter Helen was trapped on base, deploying the capable language of the Antarctic: *traverse*, *expedition*, *sastrugi*, *katabatics*.

Everything else is an unnecessary disturbance. Only this place matters. It is real, but so unreal. *What am I going to say to this young woman?* That was his thought, when he found her beside him in his cockpit on the way to the Ellsworths. This place they had come to was the least likely theatre for love on the planet. The unmistakeable bright ringing of its name, like a bell: the sound of Utopia, for a world beyond this world – Antarctica – a name as arid with endeavour as the desert which it describes.

In flying to and from the Antarctic there is always a Point of No Return. It is not a fixed place on land or in the air but a wandering axis, calculated on the basis of fuel, wind and knottage, weight carried and the weather forecast. For years he has always known when there was no turning back.

The doctors told him he'd had it for years. A mole, unnoticed on the back of his leg. By the time they caught it, it had spread. His PNR was passed, but he had not called it, radioing the comms manager on base as he habitually did, or even known it was there. He was told that his skin cancer was a result of all those years flying so close to the polar sun, absorbing its dazzling wattage of radiation.

But what a life!

He flies through days abandoned by night. A slim, pale moon, far above, stale in the sky. Migrating between the darkless polar summers, underneath dissolving stars.

Helen cannot sleep. Everything about David is unfamiliar. He sleeps fitfully, drawing in air in gasps, snorts. He sounds as if he is fending off an attack. She wonders if she should wake him.

She listens to the reassuring grind of the engines. They are making good time now, eleven or twelve knots. Outside her portal window is a winter light, watery and dissolute. By tomorrow they will be in the Falklands. They will return to the real world, to shops and money and newspaper stories of death and of melt. Bangladesh is battered by successive cyclones, its delta flooded. Greenlandic women are giving birth only to daughters because of environmental pollution that warps the genes which assign gender. Crops in sub-Saharan Africa have failed for the fifth year running. Fortress Europe's boats and helicopters patrol the oceans, forcing refugee boats back to the coasts of Tunisia, Senegal, Cape Verde.

David's body offers small suprises which stun her. He is boyish in his limbs, his ankles are thin and graceful, so unusual for a man, his skin is taut. Apart from her own husband, she has never slept with a married man. She can feel the ownership of his body, the stamp on it. This lean body is on loan to her, for how long? She is unaccustomed to having a body beside her. The warmth is reassuring. She listens to his breath, his heartbeat. It seems to be keeping time with the ship's rhythm, the plough, followed by a sigh as the ship mounts a wave, then a slide down the trough, a smash, and the cycle begins again.

There will be a surprise.

The crystal river woman lays down the cards. 'There will be a man, yes, but he will be married. He must be resolute.'

For Helen, she lays down the Queen of Hel. 'The woman who is in charge of her life,' she says. 'But what kind of life? A life white and cold with silence. Its meaning is loneliness.'

Helen watches as one by one, the cards cancel her hopes. If she had gone to see the crystal river woman before Eric's death, how would she have coped with the knowledge of what was to come? If Nara had known, before she set off to the Antarctic, what would happen to her, would she have gone? The future is a trap, she thinks. That is why we are not supposed to know it. And also, if we do know the future, how to carry the burden of this knowledge?

Nara came to the Antarctic with hope, Helen will realise in the coming northern hemisphere summer, as she sits in the flat she and Eric once shared, reading and re-reading the file called Wintering. The entry for Nara's first day on base is giddy with shock at leaving the ship, with the stony glamour of her new environment, her eyes blinking, her heart astounded by the thrill of everything that has happened to her on her journey: *Yes, it is cold*, she writes. *But so light.*

Fennoscandia

Finland, Sweden, Norway. A two-page spread in the atlas lies open on the desk to show a glacial, watery landmass so like the province where Luke had grown up and which he had told Nara about: bog, gneiss, schist, clouds of summer blackflies, studded with moose and wolves.

Alexander walked in the door. He had gone outside to make a phone call which Nara presumed he did not want her to overhear. Immediately the prowling presence of a life-flooded creature soaked the room.

'I'm mapping Fennoscandia in the LGM. Here, I'll show you.' He clicked the mouse and his computer screen dissolved into a landmass – the dips and troughs, drumlins, the moraine, waterlogged interior.

'We can have some chocolate.' He rummaged in his desk, the same long fingers which had picked her backpack off her shoulders in the Falklands so that he could carry it, searching inside an ordinary desk drawer.

The city is limp and dull, trapped in a heatwave, the third of the summer so far. Nara reads an article in the newspaper about what happens to the human body in temperatures over 38.5 degrees. As it turns out, it boils. Proteins in cells congeal, as when you poach an egg – stringy formations, clumps of albumen, form. Water evaporates from the blood, and salts are lost. Nara reads that the heatwave is set to kill many more abandoned elderly people in anonymous apartments on the outskirts of Paris, of London.

In England temperatures of twenty degrees in late October are now routine. By April summer has arrived. In between, a shallow dip into a mild winter. It has not snowed in seven years. Many trees keep their leaves through the winter now; by spring they are yellowed and frayed; new, pale green leaves form a mottled patchwork with these old remnants. Some birds no longer migrate, and squirrels are dying en masse from a kind of nervous collapse; their nervous systems, programmed for hibernation, have been unravelled by wakefulness.

Nara has just emerged from a winter of the kind that now existed in very few places on earth. She had longed for heat, but now that she is back it feels unnatural; her back burns in a way it never did before, her legs sweat. An inner thermometer has shifted and she is no longer comfortable in temperate climates.

On that day she sits on a dank commuter train out of Paddington, electrical storms brewing to the west. She has to pass through the security cordon before boarding the train: metal detector, explosives-sniffing dogs, hand-searches, identity-card check, iris scans.

The new rule, she learns, is that people arrive an hour before the train is supposed to depart. Hygiene checks are obligatory now. This means passing their hands under scanners emitting violet light; when she was a teenager and went to nightclubs she had done this, to check that she had paid and was stamped in. Now the scanner routine is accompanied by disinfectant gel which must be rubbed on hands, between fingers, a cool astringent sensation in so much heat. Someone in the queue behind her says, *I remember when you only had to do this to go into an intensive care unit. Now we have to rub gel on our hands to get into a bloody train.*

Everyone around her seems angry, nervous. Gone are the resigned exhausted hordes of public transport. Stewards dressed in yellow vests flank the entrances to platforms, where ticket barriers used to stand. They are checking identity cards against tickets, even though identity cards have to be scanned to buy rail tickets online. Each time there is an attack, a new step is added in the security regime. Airport-style electronic scanners must be passed through; they scan for liquid explosives, traces of explosives and plastics. Laptop computers had to be surrendered for manual checks. Once on the train no one reads; rather everyone looks vigilant, on the lookout for invisible threats, illness, explosions, deliberate contaminations.

She has been out of the world for a year and a half and in her absence the world has changed. Still, she gets used to it surprisingly quickly, this and the barrage of other new regulations. Humans are too adaptable, she considers, they just go with the flow. What would it take, for them all to take to the streets, to demand change? She is back in the Real World. Luke's emails were sometimes called *News from the real world*. But she finds she is visiting a foreign country. The Britain she left is not the one she has returned to.

The station advanced on them, and suddenly they had arrived; trains were so silent now, hermetically sealed canisters. You couldn't hear the wind, or the tracks.

She got out and breathed the fresher air. She was there out of curiosity, really. She wondered if time had immunised her to him. She had not considered what she would feel if she found it hadn't. She wanted to look at Alexander clinically now. He was an obstacle in her life, something she had to get beyond in order to get somewhere else.

In his office Alexander closes the Fennoscandia page and they go for a walk by the river, where it begins to rain. She wears a small, light dress, the lightest material she could find.

She is walking with him beside the river, and everything is normal and as it used to be. They walk along the Thames with its leafy elm trees, a blue summer evening. She has missed all this, she realises: trees, evening, herons and ducks floating on water that does not freeze.

They come to a standstill on a bridge to watch the river traffic. Canal boats putter by. Sailboats sit with their sails furled, like giant white storks resting.

He tells her he is slow, emotionally. A bit tortoise-like. It takes him a while to feel, a while to figure things out. He tells her it amazes him, how long it takes to come to any understanding about his feelings, and meanwhile time is passing, faster and faster. Time is elastic and does not want to be known. He tells her that when the raindrops come thick and fat and widely interspersed it is because they are negotiating ice crystals in the clouds. He tells her he didn't love her. Doesn't love her.

She looks at Alexander's intense, resolute gaze as he says this. He is awkward; not embarrassed, but slow, as he says, feeling his way. She realises he may have tried to love her, for a while, because of what she did, but gratitude and effort have killed it. She will be lucky if he does not end hating her. Men do not want heroic women (if that is what she is). They do not want peculiar, fascinating characters as lovers. He would never, ever, choose her. This is what she learned in the Antarctic, where everyone makes do with the people around them, where the most unlikely couples form, simply because they are both marooned at the end of the earth, and there is no one else. Nara would have consented to be a convenience for him, because she loved him. But if he did not choose her there, he would never have her.

They are standing on a bridge overlooking the Thames and he is telling her about rowing, how the skull is like a blade in the water, and very unstable. You have to practice rowing with both arms, he says, and she notices a raw patch on his elbow. Ever since she met him, he always has some scar, some slight blemish on his skin. They healed badly down South: for some reason the aridity impedes the scarring process. This time the scar on his elbow, also a scratch across his chest. Might it be some woman's fingernail? There are not so many ways to get scratched across your chest.

He asks, 'Do you think you will ever go back?'

Nara replies that she hopes to return to the Antarctic one day, although she is not sure.

In the future she will go to conferences where people will avoid her, subtly. She is tarnished by rumour. She does not yet know how rumour gets embellished, malformed, stretched until it is something greater than it ever was: heroism, rescue, a polar medal, mental illness, breakdown in the dead of winter, left stranded, a tribunal, her word against that of a pilot of twelve years' Antarctic experience. A real mess. The biggest mess, in fact, in years. Officially, she would be given a medal. Unofficially she would be barred from the programme. Not openly, of course, but in the form of funding applications denied, research contracts not renewed, abstracts for submission to conferences mysteriously not accepted. Until she did the only thing she could do: shifted to working in the Arctic and in sub-tropical waters.

She tells him about the conferences she has been to or will soon attend in San Francisco, Vancouver, Lisbon, always ocean cities, fittingly for these acronym-named oceanography summits called CRYONWED and ADELIE, one of a large science army dedicated to charting a disaster: ecosystem collapse, oceanic dead zones which last for months on end, volatile wind patterns, plankton blooming and dying equally mysteriously, siphoning all oxygen from the water. Nothing survives these vacuums; the crabs first, then fish, then the seabirds, then higher predators, whales, sharks.

It is July now, and she does not know where the time has

gone. She left the Antarctic on the ship at the end of the season in early April, then came straight back on the RAF flight from the Falklands. Other winterers planned thawing-out holidays in South America. But she rushed back to a country which many on base feared.

A heron swoops low over the water, grazing the surface of the canal with the tips of his wings. Alexander has something of the heron's grace, she thinks, the way he folds his leg beneath him as he stands, his weight thrown on one hip, an origami figure of vigilant angles.

Alexander does not ask, what really happened to you? He does not ask, what went so badly wrong for you; was all that despair just because I couldn't love you, is all that distress really necessary? Alexander doesn't want to talk about it, she supposes, because he would not want to give her the impression she is in any way important to him. He is not intrigued by her being a figure around whom controversies swirl. Nara knows she does not fit the description of a woman disgraced, she has none of that tribe's corroded glamour. And anyway, he is not interested in other people's damage.

She couldn't bear to be that far away from him. She couldn't bear not to be able to touch his body. She is jealous of him and she is frightened of the power of her rage. Jealous of his barbecues, his grad schools, his dinners out with people every night this week, of which he makes sure to tell her she is only one. He does not suggest they have dinner that night.

She leaves him to walk through the rain, which she knows now is avoiding ice crystals in the sky. To the west, an electrical storm gathers. She boards a train after a similar but less rigorous security regime and she does not think, cannot think, for the entire half an hour journey into London, the sky a scorched orange. Thinking might unleash some dangerous, possibly lethal, substance.

July 26th, 2013. The day was almost over. Neither of them had referred to the anniversary. She wondered if he was even aware, if he paid attention to things which marked the lives of lesser mortals, such as dates on calendars.

They had made it through the most difficult chapter of winter. On the 22nd of July the sun came back. It had gone away so profoundly, but it came back, and it was like the return of some living yet prehistoric creature. Days of twilight lit by a sudden aurora. Faint at first, then fiery. Soon those viscous days which began and ended in darkness would be over. Soon the hungry, sideways glances would be no more.

Sometimes she liked the storms, the sheer viciousness of them. She liked looking out from the entrance of the sledge store to the accommodaton block, twenty yards away, yet not being able to see it. The wind tore past the door like a ghoul. She liked being battered by the elements. The hounding coziness, the strange confidence it produced, that they could take all this, mentally. That they could be so stricken with winter and still function. That they could take care of themselves. This was the greatest pleasure: the self-sufficiency, the pride they felt in being able to withstand the punishment. And the relief to find that winter still existed. To feel its power, when it was weakening in so much of the world.

She looks up to find a child, very young, staring at her from the aisle of the empty carriage. The child has a bruiser's face, already very male, a square forehead, small eyes. On his cheek is a large patch of skin rubbed raw – some injury, she guesses, a burn, or eczema perhaps. Where has he come from? Where are his parents? She is almost alone in the carriage; it is nearly midnight. The child stares at her with those strange depthless eyes of very young children, scanning her, not unlike the iris machines with their flitting laser beams which blind her with her own retina's reflection, those dark veining trees, long after she has passed through. The child bursts into a sudden reckless smile, then runs away.

Outside, glass buildings have begun to appear on either side of the high suicide barrier. They are nearing Ladbroke Grove. Soon she will be on the Tube, alone, heading to her flat, where she will spend countless similar nights. They stretch in front of her like a dank chaperone.

She had wanted nothing from Alexander but that primal satisfaction, feral, warlike. This is what her experience of sleeping with him had been: not kind, but ferocious. She loved him, not who he was in everyday life, necessarily, but who he was sexually. This makes no sense, she has never before known lust and it took her many months to recognise it. She is in love with him and to live without him has been like being in another dimension, beyond human life, a frozen dimension, but without the purity and splendour of the Antarctic. She has no name for that place.

The train arrives. The nocturnal stragglers pour off, and melt into the night.

'What's that you're writing?' David puts his hand on my shoulder.

'Another future, a possible one.' I don't say, had the crystal river flowed in another direction. We no longer talk about that. I no longer go to see the woman with the Norse myth cards. I no longer want to know the future. I've learned the future is far more slippery than we think. And there is another danger: once we know the future, we feel it owes us to turn out as we have been told it will. And when it doesn't, the sense of betrayal feels more like insanity.

'I don't know why this happens,' the crystal river woman

said, when I told her that the cards had been wrong about one thing. 'Sometimes it misreads the shapes, usually in small ways. But sometimes it gets it very wrong.' Like Nara did in her diary, the crystal river woman calls it *It* – not *them*, or *God*, or even *the cards*. In any case, the cards are a means of communication with this It. The entity knows all the future, and all the past – everyone's, for all time, because as the crystal river woman says, the future has already happened on some level we are unfamiliar with, and possibly unable to conceive. Through the cards, it transmits its message to us. 'I am only the translator,' she says.

David left his wife because she had never been to the Arctic or the Antarctic, and had no reason or interest to go there. This is what he says, now, that he can never again live with anyone who has not known The Ice. We were trapped there together. Everyone will think we were lovers there, but that happened later, on the ship, because for some reason we needed to be released from the ice before we could love each other. The thrilling loneliness we felt there, which threatened to strangle us and instead gave us a new life. And here we are: a new life in a different world.

The book I will write about Nara's death will have an alternative ending, just as if the crystal river had shifted and taken a different path. *No one is allowed to know the path not taken.* This is another thing the crystal river woman said to me. She was quoting the book, *The Lion, the Witch and the Wardrobe*, in which a young girl enters an alternative world through the portal of a wardrobe. In this other world, it has been winter for a hundred years. Everything is frozen, because of the spell of an evil ice queen.

In life we may not be able to know the path not taken, but in books we can. We may not be able to excavate the fleeting moment and the truth it holds locked in its crystal embrace, but we can know what would have happened, what might have, what should have – if only the destiny-givers that day of the plane crash had been more lax, or kind, or less vigilant.

This other future is only marginally less real than the one that actually happened. In this future, Nara will return from the Antarctic to her concrete university. Soon it will be autumn and she will teach Earth Sciences courses with titles such as 'Oceans Past and Present'. Each year in late September she will walk into a crowded lecture theatre and face students who get younger and younger each year until they look to her like children.

The symposia, colloquia, conferences and seminars where Alexander might be present she will avoid, just as she will avoid knowing where he is teaching, whether he is married or has a family or which country he is in, even if the polar research community is small and such evasions are not easily maintained.

The avoiding will become automatic for her, a mere consideration, although the pain on which it is built will curiously not drain away over the years, but will remain as fresh and raw as the day Luke flew him out from base, or the day she went to see him on the anniversary of his rescue. Grief is curious, she will come to understand. It operates by the same laws as love: when taken away it does not diminish or decay, but remains intact, an empty statute to its former gleam.

Nara will never let go of the conviction that she and Alexander are linked, and not in any ordinary way. Their survival is somehow bound up with each other – but it is her survival that is linked to his, and not the other way around. That was why she had saved him. As long as Alexander was in the world, she would be alive. She would have a chance.

The planet would continue changing, and each year her

students' research proposals would be increasingly driven by the cataloguing of extinctions, taking the measure of the loss. As the years passed and meadow grass colonised the tip of a warming Antarctic peninsula – she found it hard to imagine, although she had seen the photographs of long prairie grass scythed by the summer katabatic gusts, carpeting valleys that had only recently been choked with ice – the entire ecosystem would change and the losers would be the endangered Ross seals, the giant squid, both which would be declared officially extinct within thirty years. The blooms of coldwater krill, those life-sustaining organisms on which the entire Antarctic fed, would shrivel. For most of the planet's history extinctions had had their own reasons, Nara instructed her students, they had been programmed into the species net, the food web, the set of mutual obligations that linked predator with prey: all the laws and rules which humans had so wantonly broken. Now we are causing the extinctions, and the balance can never be restored.

As the years pass she will think less and less of Berkner Island, of what happened there. She never went to counselling, or to therapy. She kept the polar medal she had received for saving Alexander with her always, even when she travelled. She slept with it beside her bed.

Even though Nara is convinced she will never return to the white continent, each year as the northern hemisphere autumn rolls round again, she will think of it. At any given point on the calendar she knows what is happening because every Antarctic season is the same: there is a method, a pattern, a way of doing things which has been tried and tested over decades. There will be advances in technology, yes, a reorientation of the scientific focus, a new aircraft, perhaps, once every thirty years a new ship will be commissioned, but otherwise each year is identical.

It begins with the Antarctic Conference in September, held at a gloomy Cambridge college. The conference brings together hundreds of recruits, new and old, summerers and winterers, for workshops on IT, seminars on fair play, breakaway groups for those on long scientific ship cruises or people wintering on the more temperate islands of the South Atlantic. Meals will be taken in the cafeteria, and just as in the Antarctic itself, she will find herself sitting next to anyone – a meteorologist, a paleo-geologist, or the Foreign Office representative for the polar regions. On the last night an evening ceilidh in the Great Hall will bring all these strangers together, as will those nights in the subterranean bar, future intimates ranged round the pool table. They are all embarking on the biggest adventure of their lives. They all think something wonderful is about to happen to them.

Then October and the journey South, flying via the Ministry of Defence flight to the Falklands or LAN-Chile via Madrid. Then waiting-room days in Stanley, Land Rovers rattling down the streets, a plague of Union Jacks, ever the outpost with its one grocery store and two hotels. These days offer the last chance for a year or more to drink in pubs, to get drunk with strangers. Trips to see the penguin colony at Volunteer Point, group walks to Gypsy Cove, the pilgrimage to the Stanley lighthouse, the same one Nara made with Alexander under the glimmer of southern Atlantic stars. Suddenly there is no 'I', there is only 'we'. We ate dinner, we boarded the ship, and they begin to understand the pleasures of not having to face experience alone.

Then the journey to the continent, on the ship or on the Dash-7 or the model which will replace it, when the plane has clocked up its maximum allowed hours, even if it will prove difficult to find a better version than that Antarctic air tractor, the slow, reliable plane grinding through the icy skies.

By December they will be encountering their first icebergs just south of Elephant Island. A cocktail party, birthday drinks, or the Master's birthday perhaps; there will be some occasion while on board. The Navy or the supply vessels will come on side, and the newcomers will experience the fraternity of the Antarctic in all its bonhomie. They will understand that human relationships in the Antarctic are not like anywhere else; a warmth and cameraderie thrums between the firmest strangers or political foes, merely for having encountered each other at the end of the earth.

They may or may not be stopped in ice.

Alexander comes out of the bathroom that night, naked, and she has to hold her breath, to draw all the oxygen she can into her. The suddenness and intensity of their intimacy has shocked them both.

He begins to get dressed. 'Don't take this the wrong way, but I don't want to be seen coming out of your cabin in the morning.'

She wonders how he thinks she should take it. She wants to remind him that there is no morning, or evening anymore. They have run out of night and into a three-month-long day, they will not see the sun set until February.

She says, 'That's very logical of you.' She cannot say, *Please don't go*.

He comes out of the bathroom naked and she stops breathing. This is all that happens. Night is gone, and suddenly there are many suns and moons in the room with her.

She watches him get dressed. He puts on his father's ring, his father's necklace. He had taken these off, very ceremoniously, in order to make love. He struggles into his dress shoes, a pair of brogues. Dinner on the ship is formal. Every evening they all put on their finest clothes.

There is a bloodstain on the sheet underneath her, as if

she were a virgin. It has been some time since a man has made her bleed.

The tungsten light of iceblink floods the cabin. He is standing, fully dressed, before her. She sits on the bunk, a sheet drawn around her, more in self-protection than in propriety.

'Well,' he says, 'goodnight.'

She turns her face to the window and sees the field of pack ice, the seals which loll on its floes, the silver eye of the midnight sun revolving, the darting shadow of a skua. The ship is still and silent then, as the ice fastens all around them.

Short Glossary of Antarctic Terms

Albedo	the extent to which an object (in the polar regions, ice) reflects light from the sun
Avtur	aviation turbine fuel specially treated to withstand low temperatures
Blank down	to tie down (usually aircraft) to the ice using ropes and ice screws
Col	a pass between two mountain peaks, literally 'neck', from the French
CTD	in oceanography, an instrument used to measure conductivity, temperature and depth of the water column
Field	away from base; being 'in the field' means living in a tent; 'deep field' refers to living and working in a very remote area
Field assistants	mountaineers charged with helping to look after scientists
Frazil ice	cinder-like accumulations of ice on seawater
Gash	cleaning and housekeeping duties of the day on Antarctic ships and bases; a Navy term
Gator	a utility vehicle designed for off-road and rough terrain used to transport people and goods around Antarctic bases

HF/VHF	High Frequency radio
Hummock	a mound or hillock of pressure ice
Iceblink	a white light seen on the horizon, especially on the underside of low clouds, due to reflection from a field of ice
Ice flowers	tufts of frost or rime resembling flowers that form on surface ice around salt crystals
Iridium phone	satellite phone
Katabatic wind	a wind that carries high density air from a higher elevation down a slope under the force of gravity; most commonly found in Antarctica and Greenland
Manfood	as distinct from dogfood in the days when dogs were used in the Antarctic; the term is still used; wooden boxes that contain ten days' supply of dried and tinned food for two people
Melon hut	an oblong-shaped fibreglass hut used for field operations
Met	the meteorologist; weather forecasters deployed by the UK Met Office to base in the summer
Nunatak	an isolated hill or mountain of bare rock rising above the surrounding ice sheet
P-bag	Personal Bag containing a sleeping bag, sleeping mat and sheepskin, for use in the field

Pitroom bunk bed accommodation

PNR Point of No Return – the point at which there is no longer enough fuel for the aircraft to return to its point of origin; PNR means the airplane is committed to land at its destination

RIB Rigid Inflatable Boat

Sastrugi wavelike ridges of hard snow formed on a level surface by the wind

Sit Rep Situation Report, a weekly briefing given by the base commander on base matters